# Praise for *The Sacred Flame*

"*The Sacred Flame* is a sweeping saga of love and redemption. I couldn't stop reading. The book kept me up after midnight when I wanted to go to bed three hours ago."

Fran Stewart, author of the Biscuit McKee Mysteries
and the ScotShop Mysteries

"The languid, poetic flow of the story, the description of its characters, their dress, their emotional state, the state of the manipulation and abuse of power and plain old envy are handled with a great touch. The end scenes, especially that of the heroine, were just raw!"

Aarti Nayar, author of *Eggshells of the Soul*

"Littlestone has created a luscious journey through ancient Rome, replete with pleasure and sacrifice. She has brought characters to life out of marble and shown us their surprising realism. For what can be more real than love and the relentless quest to have it, damn the consequences. Such is the drama of this exquisite tale, told with sensual, transportive language. Such is this story of love that entices and eludes yet calls the soul regardless—no matter how innocent and unprepared—leaving us utterly haunted."

Suzanne Baker Hogan, Spiritual Writer and creator of TwinFlameHelp.com

"Ancient Rome comes to life in this engaging story. The author's research into this time period comes through in her beautiful descriptions and adds to the authentic feel of the characters. I love Littlestone's lyrical writing and her ability to immerse the reader in a different world."

Barbara J Hopkinson, Grief Mentor and author of *A Butterfly's Journey*

"This fascinating story takes you on a journey that is calm and soothing then passionate and dangerous. I felt deeply for Livia's troubled quest for love. We all want love. We all want to be loved. But are we all willing to follow where our hearts lead us? I love her courage, her bravery, the fact that she took risks and stood up for what she believed. I will definitely be reading Ms. Littlestone's next book."

Maureen Roe, Self-Expression Coach and Ageless Grace Educator

"I absolutely loved this book! Littlestone's historical information, ancient yet modern characters, and insightful commentary stirred my imagination. Brava!"

Bonnie Salamon, Autumn's Fire, S-aging Well Life Coach
and Life Cycle Celebrant

"With captivating characters who pay homage to Roman mythology, along with vivid imagery, Nanette has spun an intriguing, at times haunting tale of love, tradition, duty and sacrifice. Beautifully crafted!"

Terry Crump, PhD, Crump Wellness Services,
licensed clinical psychologist and board certified hypnotherapist

"Nothing pulls me in more than a story from a bygone era about love and loss. *The Sacred Flame* is exactly that. I've read a number of novels about ancient Rome, but none from this time period, and I knew nothing about Vestal Virgins. Nanette Littlestone's poetic writing style and research immersed me in this setting. She did such a good job that I could see the buildings, taste the food, feel the elements. And the drama! I won't spoil the ending, but suffice it to say it will have you turning the pages—quickly."

Rebecca Kirson, Your Sacred Truth,
Akashic Record Practitioner and Transformational Coach

"*The Sacred Flame* is beautifully written. Lovely and tragic. I read it in two days on vacation and I can't remember the last time I enjoyed a book so much. I could not sleep after finishing it, thinking about the fact life used to be like that (and sometimes still is for some people)."

Sheri Bagwell, Health and Wellness Coach, the Pain Eraser

"Captivating characters and story line. I love the history but more the HERstory."

Corinna Murray, veterinarian and IPEC Certified Professional Coach

"*The Sacred Flame* is a tragic story of forbidden love. Nanette has a masterful ability to weave historical detail with entertaining storytelling. Her tasteful love scenes lend an air of class to the 'romance.' She is a skillful wordsmith taking you on a journey to the past. *The Sacred Flame* is a beautiful read."

Michelle Mechem, Keller Williams Realty

"From the smoldering, glowing ruby ring on the front cover to the feel of the smooth paper inside, you will be seduced by the picturesque, detailed narrative of *The Sacred Flame*. It is more than a beautifully-guided tour of living in Rome at 216 BC. The texture, sensory smells, and visuals of the complex people and the world of their beguiling empire, their lifestyle and beliefs, their loves and fears, hopes, and dreams entice you to the thrill of reading page after page. You will be seduced and welcome the journey."

Melinda Musser, Pure Romance Sales Consultant

# THE
# SACRED
# FLAME

# THE
# SACRED
# FLAME

A Novel

Nanette Littlestone

WORDS OF PASSION • ATLANTA

THE SACRED FLAME

Published by Words of Passion, Atlanta, GA 30097.

First Edition 2015
Second Edition 2021

Editorial: Nanette Littlestone
Cover: Yocla Designs
Interior Design: Peter Hildebrandt

Library of Congress Control Number: 2021901779

ISBN: 978-1-7364640-1-4 (paperback)
ISBN: 978-1-7364640-2-1 (e-book)

To Peter

You are truly my rock

# Chapter I

*Rome, 216 BC*
*The year of the consulship of Gaius Terentius Varro*
*and Lucius Aemilius Paullus II*

I t could not come soon enough. The end to the world Livia had known since she was six. An end that would begin the life she had always dreamed. Five more months of servitude. Just a short time until that new beginning.

The house on the Aventine hill swelled with noise and laughter. She stalled in the *vestibulum*, its long narrow entranceway greeting visitors with a mosaic of black points on white tile. Guests edged by while she watched in a gripping unease. The High Priestess should have brought Valeria, the sharp-witted Vestal at home among company.

Horatia grasped Livia's elbow. "Come along, my dear."

1

A plain dove in her *stola* of white wool, Livia joined the purple-striped togas and women's gowns of waxy yellow, marigold, red-orange, sky blue, sea blue, and luxury scarlet that filled the atrium. Despite the chill of the April night, she felt overly warm. Livia longed to leave this gathering of distinguished titles and put-on airs. People she did not know or care to know. The air wrapped her in sticky wetness, sheathed her in stifling heat until she could not move, could not think, could not breathe. And she gasped, a loud sucking gasp that echoed through the room. Mortified, she pressed her back against the tiled wall to feel the cold.

To gain composure. Composure she should always show.

In her thirty years as a Vestal, Livia still had not found the inner peace to carry her through these public gatherings. Only near the sea did she experience that calm, or with Kaeso. She closed her eyes for a moment and thought of him, her dearest friend and companion, the man she would finally marry in September at the end of her service.

The smell of honey teased her nostrils. Nearby a couple lounged on a soft couch, feeding each other small pastries. The man kissed lingering crumbs from the woman's lips, grazed his fingers down her arm. Their physical affection mesmerized Livia, yet there was no need to be so vulgar.

She turned from the spectacle and bumped a slave carrying a tray of fruit and cheese. "Your pardon, Priestess," he apologized, his gaze lowered, before he moved on. Livia lifted the edges of the *palla* that covered her hair, hoping for circulation, and inhaled fetid air sticky with perspiration, as sticky as her gown and *tunica* beneath. How she wished for a cup of water to quench her thirst, but there was only wine and bitter ale. Be calm, she told herself. The evening would soon end. She would pay her regards to her host, wherever he might be, find Horatia, and excuse herself.

A large black Laconian hound bounded her way, screeched to a halt, and sniffed her crotch. Laughing for the first time that night, Livia pushed away his nose, then stooped to pet him.

"Achilles!"

The voice belonged to a man of casual grace who strode toward her as if he belonged there. The yellow tips of his hair sparked a sense of familiarity though she had never seen him before.

The dog licked her cheek, her jaw, across her lips. She laughed again and wiped her mouth with the edge of her *palla*. The fur was soft beneath her fingers, its silky thickness reminding her of a cashmere yarn she had once felt as a child.

"Achilles, sit." The dog barked, then danced around the man with obvious joy. "Forgive him. He has no manners."

The intensity of the man's gaze surprised her. Did she know him? "There is nothing to forgive. Receiving love is always a pleasure." She swept her fingers once more through the thick fur. When she tried to rise, his hand circled her arm and held her in place. With his other hand, he stroked a thin curved line just below her wrist.

"I once kissed that mark."

The memory brought heat to her cheeks. Gaius. The child cupid with golden curls and wide blue eyes. She had not thought of him in years and could not remember his full name. Now his sunlit hair and eyes of the sea made him a living Apollo.

He bent to kiss her wrist once more and she pulled back. "Remove your hand. Have you forgotten I am a Vestal?"

"I forget nothing." Yet he still clung to her arm. People were staring.

"Please," she said, and his fingers trailed across her skin in a slow release.

She stood, her face hot with embarrassment.

"You let me kiss you that other time," he said.

Achilles whined, threading his way through the legs of his master.

Livia forced herself to meet Gaius's gaze. The child's eyes had deepened, matured. Much had happened to change him from a boy to a man. She wished he had remained the sweet boy she once knew. "You were just a child then. And quite charming."

"Have I lost my charm?"

She did not care for the way her skin prickled. Their acquaintance must end here. "Yes," she said, firmly, decisively. "But not your arrogance."

"Gentlemen, ladies," a strong voice boomed. Heads turned toward a man standing on a raised platform. The purple stripe of his toga denoted senatorial status. Her host, Livia surmised.

"Tonight we honor our equestrians and celebrate Rome's victories. Through their efforts the republic remains strong against the conquering forces of the world. To the Equites." He raised his drink in salute. "And now, with the help of the High Priestess, we pray for continued blessings and safety." He extended his hand to Horatia.

The High Priestess lifted her hands in benediction, closed her eyes, and crashed to the floor. Those nearest to her jumped back and dropped their drinks. Wine pooled as other guests pressed around the body. "Step back, everyone. Let her breathe," the senator said.

Livia pushed her way through and knelt by the High Priestess, clasping Horatia's hands. "Is she alright?" one woman asked. "She looks so white," said another.

Livia's heart pounded. "Horatia, can you speak?" The priestess's hand was cold and limp. Blue veins stood out against pale skin. Skin that just moments before had pulsed with vitality. Fear burned in Livia's chest. "Please, someone get a physician."

"Livia," Horatia breathed, the voice barely a whisper.

Livia pressed her cheek to the hand of her leader, her mentor, her confidant. "I am here."

"I had hoped . . ." She gasped for air and feebly squeezed Livia's hand. "I thought I would have . . ." Eyelids fluttered and those deep brown eyes that had led Livia through many trials stared directly at her. "Trust you," she said then closed her eyes. The strength left her hand.

"You cannot do this to me," Livia muttered, then pressed her lips together, ashamed of her behavior.

Gaius scooped up Horatia as if she were a child. He whispered to a servant who nodded and left the room immediately.

Despite her earlier sentiments, the warmth and compassion in his gaze brought tears to Livia's eyes. "Please," she told him. And with that plea she remembered. Gaius Postumius Albus. The stuffy name did no justice to the sensitivity she had just witnessed.

"She will be spared no expense," he said. "My house is open to you at all times."

When he carried off the prostrate woman, Livia wrapped her arms around herself. *His* house. It was obvious now. Only the host would be so forgiving of an animal's intrusion.

She shivered in the still heat as people resumed their normal flow of chatter. If Horatia were unable to serve, Livia would become High Priestess. Her service would not end this year; there would be no marriage to Kaeso.

What had she done to anger the Goddess?

# Chapter II

Only one priestess returned that evening to the *Atrium Vestae*, the sanctuary Livia had known all her Vestal life. Until now. This night peace eluded her. The house wept in quiet misery, as if it sensed Horatia's absence. As if somehow Livia was at fault.

With the full moon directly overhead, Livia entered the Temple of Vesta and took her place before the fire pit. She would watch for several hours until Valeria relieved her and Patricia after that.

Foreboding filled her when she stood before the sacred flame. As Vesta ruled the hearth at home, so did she bless the temple, the heart and hearth of Rome, the symbol of security linked to the Vestals' obedience. Innocents they were when they were chosen and innocents they would remain until the end of service. While the flame existed, Rome remained safe. But if it died, Vesta had withdrawn her protection. A Vestal had acted wrongly. And must be punished. Harsh rods and blood and screams filled Livia's mind until she pushed away the gruesome pictures. Years and years had passed without wrongdoing. No one was in danger now. She must focus on purer thoughts.

The flame burned hot and bright, yellow and orange and blue leaping before her eyes, hypnotizing her with flickering tongues. Smoke drifted upward to the apex of the rounded temple and the vent at the top of the ceiling. The floors gleamed from the purification rites, scrubbed daily with water from the sacred spring at Camenae. How well she remembered her body aching from the chore. Tonight she wished herself young again, that she might have those simple tasks and not the complications of maturity.

She settled on the faded rug her mother had once used and bowed her head. "Bless us, Vesta. We send you our prayers and devotion this night and all nights. Keep your faithful servants and Rome safe from harm. Speed the healing of our High Priestess, Horatia. Bring her back to us free from illness." She clenched her fingers, hoping the tight contact would instill more fervor in her words. But the Goddess was not listening. Images of Gaius, Achilles, and Horatia scrolled through Livia's mind.

*Be well, Horatia.* She gazed into the fire, into the heat. *Be well.*

This time of meditation usually relaxed her, but tonight her body pulsed with restlessness. Her birthday in September would mark thirty years of service. More than enough, her soul cried out, wanting freedom from her bonds, the luxury of serving no one but herself. She wanted love, a marriage, a family. To live in peace beyond the boundaries of the city, beyond the reaches of Rome's eternal grasp.

How did Horatia suffer her position? Had she never wished for that freedom?

Minutes rolled into hours. Valeria would come soon. This day meant new decisions, changes to a well-ordered schedule.

With Horatia indisposed, Livia must assume the High Priestess duties. She must relinquish the privilege of guarding the flame, which meant that Antonia, the youngest, would need to assume that duty. An afternoon time, Livia thought, would be easiest. Or perhaps early morning. Poor child to be thrust into such responsibility. But it could not be helped.

All of them would make concessions. Concessions. Changes. These she did not welcome. Her time was nearly done. She had served Rome well and faithfully. She had no desire to lead, no craving for power. A simple life was all she asked.

Her throat burned with hopelessness. She was ready for the comfort of her bed, a few hours of forgetfulness before she faced the new day.

"Here you are," Horatia said. "I was afraid we had forgotten you." She lowered herself slowly next to Livia. "My joints protest more and more these days. Thank the Goddess you are taking over my duties."

Surprise washed through Livia's body, then terror. She blinked but the apparition remained.

Horatia smiled with great warmth. "There is sadness in your eyes."

"You are . . ." *Unwell*, Livia wanted to say. But the Horatia sitting beside her appeared vibrant and strong.

The High Priestess massaged her knees. "I am sorry to bring this hardship upon you."

Hardship? Livia's throat tightened with resentment. How long had Horatia been ill? "How long have you known?"

"Devotion guides us in many ways," Horatia continued as if she did not hear the question. "We must always be prepared for new directions. Even now a change in temperament blows softly in the night wind and courses through the ranks of leaders. Where

9

it will settle, I do not know. But you will always be protected. As long as you serve Rome, no one shall harm you."

Resentment turned to disgust. "I have served for thirty years. This was not my choice. I did not bargain for this." Was there no end to Livia's obligation to the mighty republic? Her future splintered like broken glass and a jagged shard sliced her being. But her gown showed no sign of her torment.

Horatia vanished. "No," Livia cried, her fingers reaching. "I will not do this. Horatia, come back."

But there was no one.

"You will not do what, Livia? Whom are you talking to?"

She turned slowly, her face composed. "Antonia. You should not be up. Why are you awake?"

The ten-year-old Vestal ran to Livia and gave her a hug. "I could not sleep. The house feels . . . different. Is something wrong?"

Livia patted the floor. "Sit with me." Antonia curled next to her where Horatia had appeared. But Antonia was no apparition; here was flesh and bone. The warmth of the girl's body soothed the tightness in Livia's muscles. "Horatia is ill. She is staying with Gaius." She had not meant to be so informal. "The host of the celebration tonight. Until she is well." The simplest thing to say for now. "Will you pray with me for her recovery?"

Antonia nodded and bowed her head. Long blond curls covered her face. "Vesta, grant us your blessing for Horatia. Give her strength and make her well. We need her here at home with us." She raised her head. "Will Vesta hear my prayer?"

"I am sure she will." Livia kissed Antonia's head. "And I am sure Horatia will hear it too. Now to bed with you, dear child. You need your sleep. Tomorrow will be your first day to watch the fire and you must be well rested."

Antonia's broad smile warmed Livia's heart. "My first time." She fairly wriggled. "I will be ever so awake. I will not take my eyes from the flame for one second."

Livia opened her eyes to the morning light. In the few hours of sleep after her shift no alarms had sounded; there was no further disaster. She stretched with a new ease. A rosy glow of sunlight radiated soft warmth around her face. *Thank you, Vesta, for the small miracles you perform.*

Antonia skipped into the bedroom with a plate of fresh bread and spring water. She set the food on the nearby table, then hopped up on the bed and hugged Livia with gusto. "It is a beautiful morning, Livia. Come outside. The sun waits for you."

"Sweet Antonia." Livia caressed the girl's face, then kissed the top of her head. "I have many things to attend to today. As do you."

Antonia scampered off the bed, her gown riding up to show bare legs. Livia smiled at the girl's eagerness until she remembered the hallucination. Panic set in.

"Antonia, you must say nothing about last night. I talked to no one but you."

The girl paused at the door. "I am as silent as the water through the water clock. Horatia told me so."

Horatia told her. Did Antonia know Horatia's secrets? "I have your promise?"

Antonia placed her hands together in prayer. "My word is my truth." She flashed a grin before she ran from the room.

Such a darling girl. And as trustworthy as they come.

# Chapter III

How dare Gaius fawn over a Vestal. In public, no less. As if his own wife was of no consequence. Did he think no one would notice? That people would not talk? His brain was addled with too much wine. Or self-importance.

Justina wound her way through the *peristylium*, past cypress and acanthus, letting her hands graze over the roses, narcissus, gladioli, seeking solace in their simple beauty. But tonight the satiny petals failed to soothe her. She would not stand for such behavior.

Since his return from the ambush at Lake Trasemine he had given her barely a greeting, much less any continued conversation. He would rather engage his horse, so he said, a barb that had burrowed into her calm façade with an acid sting.

The cool night air did not touch the heat of her body. Her anger simmered in her stomach and her chest, seeped through her organs with malicious intent. She wanted to take his head in her hands and snap his neck. That would end her troubles. No, that was too quick. Let him suffer while she gouged out his eyes or plunged a dagger in his heart and watched him bleed. She would praise the gods when he was dead.

*Peace, Justina.* But peace did not come quickly. She tried to calm herself with pretty thoughts. Her last birthday. A cluster of well-gowned women and stately men. Senators, an architect, a writer from Greece who read from his latest work of poetry. A woman played the lyre while her guests nibbled on delicacies prepared by a gifted cook. And Gaius, her dear husband, gave her a pair of white doves for the fountain. The birds touched her so much she had actually cried.

Damn him! Lately all he gave her was disdain. Indifference. She must woo him back. Show him the tender care worthy of a wife. The sudden bile in her throat made it difficult to swallow, but she swallowed it and her self-importance. Time had served her well. She would not go back to her former life. She would never go back. Gaius was hers and hers alone.

She strode down the corridor toward her bedroom. A moan sounded, followed by deep coughing.

Was it too much to ask for quiet? Justina clutched the doorway, soft flesh grinding against hard stone. Her skin was pale, too pale. If she did not care for her body, she would look like the poor priestess in the nearby bed, whiter than the fine linen on which she lay. Wrinkled. Shriveled. A barely breathing corpse.

A servant stopped in front of the room and steadied a heap of fresh towels. Justina breathed in lavender. "What are you doing?" she demanded.

The servant bowed. "They are for the High Priestess, madam. To soothe her pains."

"What of my pains?" Justina yelled. When the servant cowered she snatched a towel and shooed the bumbling fool into the room. Continuing down the hall to her own chamber, she pressed the towel against her forehead, then the back of her neck, then dropped it on the floor.

She sat at the small table lined with bottles of perfume for her skin. Mementos of her husband's past affection. These he afforded her. These he gave her freely. She was pampered and cosseted, had only to speak her demands to have them satisfied. Why was this not enough?

Dipping a finger into the perfume, she dabbed behind her ears, then stroked slowly down her throat. Another dip and this time she lingered between her breasts, letting the heat of her body warm the scent, mingle with it. Her breasts were firm, beautifully rounded. Once he had worshipped her body, adored her curves, the sheen of her skin. Treasured the fall of glossy hair. Once he had loved her as no man had ever loved her. They had talked of ambition, of the future of Rome and his place in it. She had inspired him, and he inspired her. Her husband.

She slipped her gown off her shoulders and caressed her flesh. She was beautiful still. Somehow she must make him notice. Make him remember.

"Do you forget we have a guest?" Gaius glanced at her, his gaze unreadable.

"She can go back to the temple where she is more welcome."

"She is here now. And while she is in my house you will treat her with kindness and caring."

"Your house? This is my house, given to me by my father. Mine to do with as I please." Her father gave her nothing, had nothing to give, but Gaius was none the wiser. He knew only that the house came as part of her dowry.

"What is yours is mine, Justina. Believe what you wish, but Roman law protects the husband. Or have you forgotten that as well?"

Her anger burned. She had not forgotten. Watching him, she stroked her breasts, yet there was nothing in his eyes. No flicker of desire. He must have a lover. There was no question that he favored other women. But she had no idea how many. Publius had told her to take a lover to make Gaius jealous but she knew it would do no such thing. And she could not bring herself to be intimate with another man. She wanted the safety of her husband.

"Make love to me, Gaius."

He simply stared for a moment. "It is late, Justina. I am tired. Good evening."

"Wait." She threw herself against him, rubbed her breasts on his tunic while her hands slid down his arms to his hips. Her mouth found his neck, his ear, the soft spot beneath his collarbone. But he made no move, said nothing.

"I used to please you, Gaius. You used to hunger for me like a wild stallion does a mare in heat. Where is your desire?"

He held her away, his fingers digging into her arms. "Save your wiles for another man, Justina. I assume there are those who still find you attractive."

She spit in his face. When he released his hold, she slapped him. The imprint of her hand on his cheek glared.

"I wanted you once," he said. "But even that is gone. I have really loved only one woman. And I will love her until I die."

He bowed to her, yet another insult. "Cover yourself, wife. You would not want the servants to see such unadorned beauty." Then he left without a sound.

Justina seethed and ripped the gown that failed to serve her. Then in a screech of agony she swept her perfume bottles to the floor and felt her heart shatter as the glass hit the tile.

# Chapter IV

Pristine rows of vines stretched before her. Livia smelled the musty ripeness, imagined future grapes glowing in the light like amethysts. In the fall they would harvest the fat clusters and stamp them into juice. For now she let the sun's meager warmth wash over her skin and chase away the earlier April chills. She was allowing unforeseen events to assume importance. Her duties, simple though they may be, required a clear head and pure heart. One could not serve the Goddess well without those.

Nonetheless, she could not shake her disquiet.

Around the stakes coiled greedy tendrils, their tiny shoots green, giving, tender, yet sturdy. She brushed her hand over these bits of new growth, the promise of richness yet to come. The vines cared not for man's emotions or worries, whether he was well fed or hungry, or how much money he earned. They simply followed nature's plan. She would do well to do the same.

Here in the fertile hills of Tusculum her property flourished. Nearby new holes were dug, new rows plowed. The furrows were straight and even. Tidy. The way her life used to be.

Kaeso waved from across the field. "Livia."

His joy traveled straight to her heart. For the few moments it took him to cross to her, she stood quietly, basked in his love, and wished the feeling could last.

"I hoped to see you soon and here you are." He hugged her tightly.

She turned to the *lictor curiatus* standing a short distance away, his eyes hooded from the sun. Their relationship spanned many years, almost since the beginning of her second decade as a Vestal. Displeasure showed in the tightness of Titus's lips, but he said nothing. She trusted him to protect her, and he trusted her to stay out of harm. What freedoms she enjoyed here on her property, away from the city—the hand holding, the quick kisses—would not be allowed in Rome. Not in public. How fortunate she was to have a forgiving bodyguard. Not all *lictors* were so . . . tolerant.

"Come," Kaeso said. "Let me show you the new vines. We are planting them eight feet apart this time to help invigorate the soil."

She held back. "There is news. I have much to tell you."

Kaeso stared into her eyes, then kissed her forehead. "It can wait." With that, he pulled on her hand as would an eager child. Even though her thoughts warred, her body yielded. There was time enough to speak of disappointment later.

He stopped in front of a row of newly trained vines. Elm trees supported the stalks which slanted like the sloping roofs of Roman houses. "See how the branches are guided to the south to catch the sunlight?"

"And to protect them from the northern winds," she added. "I remember."

Farther down the row a man stood and turned. "Livia," he called. "Greetings, fair lady. The day becomes more sweet because of you."

"So have your words, Manius. The vineyard looks wonderful."

A burly man with an armful of baskets pushed Manius from behind and sent him sprawling in the dirt. "It is my doing," Marcus said. "Manius sours the grapes with his flowery spouting."

Livia laughed. "I am sure the vines love you both."

Manius picked himself up and barreled into Marcus. "You oaf."

Baskets flew and spun and rolled in the soil. Marcus fell and smeared the bottom of Livia's *stola* with a rich brown. "You idiot," he yelled.

Kaeso led Livia from the fracas. "It is a wonder we grow anything at all. Let us leave the children to their play."

They walked in the vineyard for hours, exploring like adventurers, counting the new leaves, measuring the distance between the supports. She helped with the pruning and trenching and leaf-plucking, traveling up and down the rows until dirt found its way into every crease of the wool and her back felt permanently bent. And even then her labor filled her with exhilaration. This is the life she would live after the priesthood, after Rome released her from her obligations. Here she would relax and grow happy with the man she loved at her side, their stomachs full with the wine from their own land, their minds content to dream of sunny days and starry nights.

That time would come, she told herself. She had but to wait for it.

Afterward, she changed her clothing. Rarely did she gaze at her body, but she did so now in a bronze wall mirror as she removed her soiled gown. Without the many folds of the *stola*, she was slender with only moderate curvings of breast and buttock. Too slender, in her opinion, to incite the fancy of most males. Except Kaeso. Her closest playmate when she was just a toddler. He seemed pleased with her.

Would he still be pleased after her news?

"Livia?" Kaeso's voice boomed through the house.

She dressed, staring at her reflection, wishing she could leave this role behind, wishing she could magically become someone else.

She joined him at a table by the hearth and sipped pomegranate juice while Titus stood nearby. There was nothing but peace. Slow, even breaths, a sultry evening, the warmth of a dear friend by her side. She twined her fingers with his and released a deep sigh. In these moments she could almost forget all her worries.

"Dearest Livia. What a fortunate man I am to have you for my wife. Daily I count my blessings and give thanks to the gods. But I do regret that you changed your clothing." He grinned. "You look divine in brown."

She thought of the men grappling on the ground, heedless of their clothing, their vanity, mindful only of pleasure. She had played like that as a child, but those days had passed. She would have to clean the cloth with a brisk rubbing of salt and water. "I am sorry. I—"

"I tease, my love. But I anticipate the days when we are truly united—"

She stopped him with her fingers to his lips. The sweet peace fled and her worries rushed back. "There is . . ." Her hand fell to her side as she looked on in agony. She could not crush his hope. He had waited so long. They had both waited so long.

He raised her hand and gently kissed her fingertips. "What is it, Livia? What has you so distraught?"

Be swift with truth, Horatia once told her. The more you prolong the misery, the more difficult it is on the receiver. But she was not Horatia. She had not the experience or the courage to look Kaeso in the eye. So she gazed into the fire. "Horatia is ill. She collapsed last night at the celebration for the equestrians."

Kaeso squeezed Livia's hand. The pressure, usually comforting, seemed to make her task more unbearable. "I am sorry for you, Livia. And for the High Priestess. I know how much you love her, how much you look up to her. I am sure she will recover. Give her time and all will be well."

"No. You do not understand." Fear brought tears. "She said she trusts me."

"Of course she trusts you. You two have been together more than twenty years."

Livia shook her head. Why was he so dense? "Something is wrong. Horribly wrong. She would not have used those words if . . . if . . ." Her lip quivered and she could do nothing to stop it. "I think she is dying."

She felt Titus's disapproval while Kaeso stroked her hand. Could she not just stay with him, here, now? Just let this moment supersede all others? How lovely it would be to resign her Vestal duties and let someone else take charge.

He stopped his stroking and moved away. "If the High Priestess is dying, then the Pontifex Maximus will appoint someone to assume her position."

Livia nodded.

Kaeso held her gaze as the silence stretched and thinned until it was a tight thread that bound them both. "You," he finally said.

21

Tears ran down her cheeks and she dashed them away with her hands. "What can I do? I see no alternative. I am the oldest remaining Vestal. I am the one Horatia has trained to carry on in her stead. But I always thought that training was merely for emergencies. Brief illnesses. Short journeys. A death in the family." She wiped her eyes again. "Never did I imagine something like this."

She rose and stood in front of the fire. The heat burned her ankles but could not stop the ice forming in her chest.

"I want nothing more than to leave the temple and marry you, Kaeso. You must know that."

He leaned back his head and closed his eyes. The sigh from his throat cut at her. She knelt before him and took his hands. "Kaeso." He looked at her with love, with warmth, but the spark had left his eyes. "Talk to me, please. Tell me what you feel. What you think."

"There is nothing to say, Livia. I cannot change what has happened."

She sank to the floor. "I am afraid for us."

"I love you as I have always loved you," he said. "And I will wait for you as I have always waited. For now, that must be enough." He pulled her to her feet. "Go back to the temple, Livia. Straighten your affairs. If you are to be High Priestess, there is nothing we can do but wait."

"I am tired of waiting. All my life I have waited."

"Then you have much experience. A few more years will pass quickly."

"How many years, Kaeso? What if Rome can find no replacement? Will I die a virgin?" The slip flamed her cheeks. She meant to say Vestal. Kaeso was not to blame for her predicament. Indeed, he had honored and respected her throughout her service, stood by her steadfastly, with no visible regret. She often wondered if he harbored some remorse inside, if he wished to put aside his promise and make other arrangements. He could find many a willing woman to marry, to bear children, to ease the loneliness of age.

"Have patience, Livia. I trust the gods to find a way for us."

"Why are you so patient, Kaeso? You could choose—"

"We make choices every moment."

His simple words gently berated her. "Then choose more wisely. Find a woman who will make you happy."

"You make me happy, Livia. Where the heart loves, there must we obey."

She shivered then, as if the gods knew of her reluctance. "I would counsel you not to listen to your heart but to use your mind and your sharp wit for your betterment."

"And I would counsel you, dear Livia, to leave me to my course."

Steadfast, determined Kaeso. Her friend, her companion. She would care for him with her whole heart. And if she did not love him with the passion of Venus, surely tenderness and warmth would fill the void and carry them to the end of their years. Long years together, just as her mother and father lived.

"When it is time, we will marry," he said. He laid a hand upon her cheek. "Do not grieve for me. It is my destiny to be with you and I embrace it willingly."

Compassion burned her eyes. "You have more courage than any man I know."

"That, my dearest friend, is a lie."

But she knew it to be true. And it haunted her every moment.

# Chapter V

L ivia's feelings felt as fickle as the sun's rays, now warm and golden, a moment later cool and skittish under cloud cover. To disguise her unease she browsed the marketplace with Titus close at hand.

Spices were heaped in mounds of color. Fresh bread beckoned with its yeasty aroma. Tight rows of fish gleamed belly side up. But the food only reminded her of the recent celebration and Horatia's collapse.

A merchant thrust a honeyed tart at her lips and her stomach turned in revulsion. She hurried away and drifted through the stalls of fabric, stopping to finger a woolen shawl almost transparent in its fine weaving.

"If it will lift your sadness, I will buy it for you."

Recognition tightened her hand on the cloth even as her eyes looked up. Gaius. Pleasure warred with wariness. He was standing at the edge of the canopy, his face half in sun, half in shadow. The light gilded his hair and brought out faint crease lines by his eyes. Blue eyes that did not leave her face. The shawl slid from her hand. "I do not need your gifts."

Titus clenched his fists in warning but made no move. Livia shook her head.

"I seek only to comfort," Gaius said.

How could he console her when even Kaeso could not? Gaius had not the power to reverse time or Horatia's illness. "The only comfort I wish is the news of Horatia's recovery. How is she this morning? Is she improved?"

"She is resting. I have no other news."

"But surely the physician must know . . ." She was pushing for answers that did not exist. Healing was a mysterious art and even the most gifted of physicians needed time to diagnose and offer a remedy. She must be patient. "I am grateful for your hospitality. Thank you for your concern." She moved on, her gaze averted.

Gaius followed, stepping around the *lictor*'s bulk. "Achilles was like an eager puppy when he saw you. He has been forlorn since you left. I think he misses you."

The thought of the dog's playful antics and soft fur brought a smile. She wandered past the fabrics into an open square filled with crates and baskets of fresh fruit and vegetables. Bunches of purplish beets and creamy turnips. Bright red radishes as large as a baby's fist. Mounds of red and green apples that glistened with morning dew. Juicy slices teased her nose. Despite her unease, her stomach rumbled with hunger.

"Did you come for food this morning?" she asked. "Surely a household such as yours would send servants in your place."

"I come for a bribe."

Her startled eyes met his.

"The Praetor Urbanus worries about the amount of grain for the army," he continued. "Tomorrow I meet with a potential supplier. It is always wise to come bearing gifts."

An envoy. She tried to remember the Praetor Urbanus and could not. Politics was not one of her strengths. "Why would the praetor send *you?*"

"He is my father," Gaius said with finality. Then he changed the subject. "Such a tragedy last night. What will happen if the High Priestess cannot serve?"

Livia's momentary lightness fled. She pulled her *palla* close about her shoulders as if the light cloth could protect her. "I had no knowledge of any weakness." Her anger at Horatia's guardedness crept back. "And now I am to take her place until she recovers or until . . ." she shuddered, "until someone else can be found."

"Is it not an honor to serve Rome? Many women would gladly fill your position."

"Married women who are bored with their lives?"

A faint smile played upon Gaius's lips. She must guard her tongue around him. Words slipped too easily from her mind to her mouth without thought.

"Is being a Vestal boring?" he asked. "My wife wants an accurate report."

His wife, the proud hostess who wove through the throng of guests, her head tilted in private conversation. A beautiful woman, at least ten years younger. Livia felt old in comparison.

"A Vestal serves the goddess," she said, "and in doing so, serves Rome as well. There are numerous duties, responsibilities to the public and the dictator. Anything a Vestal does must be done well, with the whole heart, and in keeping with the principles that guide all of us."

"A speech worthy of a senator, though you hardly answered the question."

"Did I not?" The repartee amused her, intrigued her. Allowed her mind to relax. She turned to the vendor who polished apples on a towel. "How are you this day?"

"As wonderful as ever, Priestess." He gave an exaggerated bow. "Seeing you makes my morning complete." He took a hefty bite of green apple.

A young boy snuck between shoulder-high crates and snatched a handful of slices.

"Here, now. You," the merchant yelled. The boy raised his head, eyes wide, and made to escape, but the man's hand was quick and sure. He grabbed the neck of the boy's tunic and dragged the child out into the open. "Are you stealing from me? I beat thieves." He brandished a stout cane.

Dark ringlets framed large brown eyes and a dirty face. The hem of his tunic was frayed, seams ripped along his ribcage. His feet were bare and crusted with black. And black rimmed the fingernails, as if he had been digging in the dirt. His body was lanky, but well formed. Livia guessed his age at ten years, perhaps twelve. He stuffed the slices in his mouth as fast as he could.

"Away with you now," the vendor said. He cuffed the boy on the head and pushed him toward the open street.

The boy lingered and looked longingly at a just-polished row of apples. "Give me one." His hand inched forward.

The merchant raised the cane over his head. "Leave us, before I beat you."

"Beat him now," Gaius said, "so he will remember you and tell his friends to stay away."

Livia could take no more. "Let him be. He is hungry. Is he to be punished for the circumstances that landed him in poverty?"

The boy turned his large eyes upon her and grinned.

"You are too trusting," Gaius said.

"What is life without trust?" Horatia often chided her for her innocence, Davina for her gullibility. But she believed in people, in their innate kindness. The poor souls of this world wanted only a chance to prove themselves. For as long as she was able she would give them that chance.

"You cannot trust everyone," Gaius said. "Trust is earned with good deeds, with respect. What thing of worth has this urchin done?"

"How can he perform good deeds if no one will give him the opportunity?" She turned to the boy. "What is your name?"

He rubbed his neck where the vendor had gripped him. "Sextus."

"The Temple of Vesta needs a messenger. Will you serve us?"

"Priestess," Titus interrupted, "the temple needs no—"

Livia put a finger to her lips.

"What do I get?" Sextus asked.

"Miserable wretch," the merchant said. "All he cares about is himself."

Livia sshhed the vendor. "You will get food, and a bath, and clean clothing. Will that suffice?"

The child's eyes brightened. "All right. What do I have to do?"

"Give Sextus three apples if you please," she smiled at the merchant. "The temple will pay for them." She looked into the boy's eyes and gently pushed the curls off his forehead. Such soft hair. Such fine features. "One apple is for you. Take the others to the temple as an offering to Vesta. Ask for Antonia. Tell her she is to take you to the baths. Then report back to the temple when you are clean."

She patted his head and rose. Sextus did not move.

"What are you waiting for?" she asked.

His eyes clouded, then his arms circled her body in an awkward hug and he mumbled, "Thank you." He was gone before she could think.

"What an adorable child," she said.

"What a monster," the vendor stated.

Gaius plucked an apple slice from the plate and popped it in his mouth. "I think you have created a disaster."

The merchant returned his attention to Livia. "How may I serve you, Priestess?"

"Two baskets of your best fruit delivered to the temple."

"With pleasure." He reached into a small hole and pulled out a small bag. "I do not forget."

Livia opened the drawstring and breathed in the honeyed aroma of dried figs. She thanked him warmly, already contemplating a quiet moment with a cool drink and her special gift.

"One of the benefits of being a Vestal?" Gaius asked.

"One of the many." When Gaius chuckled she blushed. "What of your wife? I saw her briefly at the celebration, but she does not seem the type of woman who would seek service in the temple. She must be used to much more excitement."

Something in his eyes shifted, dimmed. "Justina cares only for my position and her status. All else means nothing."

Justina. Was she as just as her name implied? "I am sorry for your misfortune."

"Misfortune. What a polite word." He held her gaze quietly. "You would not use that word if you had ever been in love."

Her heart gave one solid thud before it settled. All she had ever wanted was the kind of love her parents shared. A quiet love. A constant love. A love that gave and comforted and embraced without restraint. The love she hoped she would have with Kaeso. But what could a Vestal know of such things? Thirty years of service to Rome with little reward. There was no time for the pursuit of one's dreams, no space in which to allow them. Fantasy did not serve a civilization intent on ruling others. "I have no time for love."

Gaius gave a great laugh. "Love surrounds you, Priestess. Your temple. Your ceremonies. All that you do. Every act of service to the Goddess, to Rome, is an act of love. Do you disagree?"

She had expected him to speak of men and women, the great poetry of Rome or Greece, the story of Ariadne and Dionysus. Not her tasks. Livia thought of the *mola salsa* to be prepared for the Vestalia, the hours of grinding to combine salt with spelt in perfect proportions. The tired muscles and sore knees. Fingers that throbbed from rolling. All that dedication and commitment. Were they acts of love? She remembered when she was Antonia's age, the first time she was allowed to grind the grains. Her hands were clumsy. The roller skittered over the coarse salt and bumped against the edge of the dish. Time and again Caelia had patiently corrected the movements. Through all of her efforts, Livia remembered the excitement of the task, the joy of finally seeing a fine powder. She remembered the beat of her heart, the flush in her face, and Caelia's warm hug. Yes, there was love. Lately, though, love seemed to be as inconstant as a jealous god. "Love is where you choose to see it."

"Where do you choose, Priestess?"

She swallowed the wash of sadness that tightened her throat. "Wherever I can," she said lightly. Emotions with Kaeso were something she was used to, but not with a man she barely knew. "Did you become a sea captain as you planned? I imagine you have stories of amazing adventures."

"Adventures, yes. But no, I am not a sea captain, although my heart still lies with the sea. I am a leader of the equestrians. A centurion."

The hard lines of his body were gained in battle, then, astride a horse, sword in hand. In all of her daydreams, she never pictured warriors in combat. Hers was a peaceful mind, an ordered mind, leant to meditation and prayer. Blood, lust, death seemed far away, and she kept them there. Now they started to creep closer.

"Then the celebration was in your honor."

"Mine, and others." There was no bravado in his answer, merely a statement.

Uncertain of a reply, she chose to end the conversation. "I must return to the temple."

"Of course. The High Priestess asks for you."

She nodded. She should have called upon Horatia right after morning prayers, but stepping foot into the place where her mentor had collapsed required more daring than she possessed. Even more time had passed because Gaius made her skittish, and she worried that Horatia must feel forsaken. "I will come before the evening meal."

She clutched her bag of figs as she left the marketplace with Titus and found comfort in its weight and smell.

"Until this evening," Gaius called.

# Chapter VI

This time Livia had no excuse.

Twenty-nine years had passed without her presence at the Fordicidia. Horatia, the eldest Vestal, had presided over the festival, the celebration of Tellus, goddess of the earth, marriage, fertility.

Fertility consecrated by sacrifice.

Livia knelt by the altar in her room, hands tight in breathless prayer. Since Horatia's illness, Livia had counted the days and worried. Mornings passed into evenings and each day her fear blossomed. She could not attend. She would not attend. She would publicly humiliate herself. Someone else must go in her place.

Yet there was no one else. Roman law decreed the eldest Vestal must collect the ashes.

This year she had no excuse.

The third day after the Ides of April arrived, the morning clear and cold. A beautiful day to revere the earth, to give thanks for the crops to come, the cattle to multiply. Livia prayed once more before the hearth and blessed Vesta, herself, and the other Vestals. A miracle might happen. She believed in the possibility of miracles. Tellus might appear and lead the ceremony. Or Neptune might flood the land and make it impossible to perform the rites. Or Jupiter might strike the altar. Any number of opportunities arose. One would be enough.

At midday the summons came. "It is time," Valeria announced.

She did not ask if Livia was ready, if there was anything she could do to help. She stood with that blank, steely stare of judgment, waiting to find fault. Once again Livia wondered why the animosity between them. Was it real or did she simply imagine it?

"You did not share our morning meal," Valeria said.

Again, the criticism. "I was not hungry."

"You need your strength."

Livia needed support, understanding. Not a lecture. And not a full stomach that might revolt.

"I am fine. I will eat afterwards."

They left the *Atrium Vestae* and gathered with the Pontifices at the Temple of Tellus on the Esquiline Hill. Thirty sacrifices took place three days ago from each of the *Curiae*, the oldest meeting places of the city. Livia understood the need to placate the gods, the superstitions that formed the basis for the many ceremonies of Roman culture, many that began with the founders of Rome. King Numa initiated this very festival. But did they have to kill animals? All life was precious. Could they not pretend with statues?

The altar fire burned high. Smoke wafted into the heavens to appease the goddess. Livia looked out over the gathering crowd. Eyes turned toward her, anticipating, expecting. Words of blessing. Words of promise.

She glanced down, at her feet, at something solid, familiar. She mouthed a prayer to Vesta, her benefactor. *Give me virtue, give me the strength to perform my duties.* This was not a feminine ritual. Women did not celebrate with blood. Male energy caused this. The warrior in man gloried in death and killing. She should pray to Mars to stop the slaughter. And to Ceres, gentle Ceres who favored plants and flowers, who nourished the earth with seedlings. Stop the sacrifices. Celebrate with things that grow.

The crowd grew louder.

Her lips moved again in silence. No one would change the rituals. Rome thrived on sacrifice. Five hundred years of ceremony would not alter today. No, she must bear it somehow. *O Goddess, give me strength. I implore you. Let me not betray my sisters. Or Horatia. She believes in me. Let me believe in myself.*

The Pontifices marched forward with a cart heaped high.

Livia's stomach lurched. She pressed her hand to her mouth, breathed deeply, and focused on the blue sky.

The crowd cheered, then quieted for her words of blessing. Valeria stood by, her face wreathed in joy and anticipation.

Livia raised her hands.

"Blessed is this third day after the Ides of April. We gather here to praise Tellus, goddess of fertility. Blessed is the pregnant cow, fruitful with calf. Blessed is the teeming earth, pregnant with seed. We offer up these calves torn from their mother's wombs," she paused while her stomach pitched and bile rose in her throat. *Not now,* she prayed. *I can do this.* "The entrails that we lay upon the smoking hearth. As we burn the dead calves in the fire, so let their ashes purge the people on this special day."

Her arms dropped and her body shivered. She had yet to see an unborn calf but she could imagine it. Too well. Saliva gathered in her mouth, a certain sign of impropriety. She turned away, gulping air to settle her organs.

She did not watch the priests bring the bodies to the altar. She did not see them heap straw and blood. She fought her own battle.

"Livia," Valeria said with a forceful nudge to her shoulder. "Look."

And Livia looked. Right at a fetus coated in blood and mucus. More vivid than her worst imaginings. The still form seemed to chastise her. *You did this to me. You ripped me from my mother. You killed me for your pleasure.*

She looked up into Valeria's gloating smile and her stomach voiced its protest. She vomited on Valeria's feet, on the altar, in front of the priests and thousands of Romans. Wretched, she wiped her mouth with shaking hands. "Forgive me," she said, her voice weak with misery.

Valeria's eyes gleamed as bright as the sun and as cold as the River Styx.

Three days later, on the 21st of April, Rome celebrated in tandem. This day Romulus began to build the city. It was also the day of the Parilia, a festival that honored Pales, the guardian of shepherds.

Shamed by her previous disgrace, Livia remained at the *Atrium Vestae*. She gladly appointed Valeria to carry the blood of the October horse to the public purification.

The prior year the High Priestess blended blood, the ashes of the calves, and shells of beans, and burned the mixture. Livia did not watch the mixing; blood made her queasy no matter the source. But she stood in good faith and sprinkled the people with water in praise of Pales.

That evening she imagined the ceremony, washing her hands in spring water, drinking milk flavored with must. She imagined the shepherds cleaning the stables with laurel branches and sprinkling them with water, then purifying them with a fire of sulphur, rosemary, fir, and incense. But the part she would miss, the part she loved, was the bonfire and music. The cheerful sounds of flutes and cymbals. And the food. The open air feast.

The night air scraped Livia with its cold bite, a sharp reminder of her Vestal failure. She sat in the *peristylium* amid white iris and yellow roses. She loved spring with its advent of new growth, the promise of life. But tonight her life felt doomed.

Antonia walked towards her with cup in hand. "I brought you some milk and honey. You always say it makes you feel better." She set it on the table and rubbed her arms. "It is cold tonight. We should be standing by the bonfire. Then we would be warm."

Livia put her arm around Antonia's shoulders. "Sweet Antonia. Always so thoughtful. Do you know how precious you are to me?"

Antonia giggled and burrowed into Livia's embrace. "I am sorry for what happened at the Fordicidia. Valeria should have known better than to—"

"Shhh," Livia said. "The less we talk of it the better."

"Then tell me about Rome. And her birthday."

Livia pulled Antonia's chair closer. Why did some have the gift of making people more comfortable when others could only irritate? Antonia and Valeria were both Vestals, yet complete opposites. Livia would be so content to send Valeria somewhere else where she could put that aggression to good use.

Antonia laid her head on Livia's shoulder. "Livia," she yawned. "Tell me about Rome."

"In the beginning," Livia began, "there were two brothers. Twins. Their names were Romulus and Remus. Mars, the god of war, was their father, and Rhea Silvia, a Vestal Virgin, was their mother. But Rhea Silvia was the daughter of King Numitor. And her children posed a threat to the throne. Numitor's brother decided to kill the children, so he put them in a basket and threw them into the Tiber.

"That might have been the end of the story, but the boys did not drown. A shepherd named Faustulus found them and took them home. He gave them to his wife, Acca Larentia. Some people believe they were raised by a she-wolf, but—"

Antonia's soft snore interrupted Livia's storytelling. She shifted in the chair and gathered the girl close. The night was not a total loss. The weight of the child's body lifted Livia's pain, eased her tension. She wished she could spend all of her days like this.

But Valeria was a permanent member of the sisterhood. And Livia the High Priestess. Her life was filled with chores, some welcome, others loathsome. The welcome ones she performed with pleasure and gratitude. Teaching the younger Vestals was an honor. A great reward. It was the repulsive ones she feared.

If she disgraced herself again would Rome ever let her go?

# Chapter VII

Livia settled the basket of food on her arm. Titus grumbled with each step, protesting that they should have ridden in a *carpentum*. The horse-drawn carriage was much faster than travel on foot. But Livia welcomed the exercise. She had hoped the journey up the Esquiline hill would free her mind of thoughts of Horatia. Instead, it only tired her body.

This was a test. The gods frequently placed obstacles in the paths of mortals to determine their worthiness before showering them with great rewards. If the gods were content, the people would move on with little difficulty and eventually achieve a happy outcome. But if the gods were angry, a house might burn, a business collapse, a person suffer injury or even death. Countries would go to war. Republics would be overthrown. While the intellectual part of her understood that legends were exaggerated stories, the emotional part of her believed in the old tales. Still, she would find a way. Horatia's illness would not break Livia. The gods would not win this battle.

She left Titus at the door with more grumbles. Before the servant could announce her, a voice called, "Come in, Livia. I have been expecting you."

Even after years of close friendship, Davina's sensory powers were still amazing. "I bring fresh bread and fruit," Livia said as she walked through the atrium.

"I could smell the apples from the hall. And rosemary. My favorite. Bless you." She waved an arm in welcome.

Livia removed her sandals and stood quietly, breathing in and out in the measured rhythm she had used so often for relaxation. After the long walk, her bare feet savored the coolness of the tiled floor. But she could not relax. Irritated with herself, she took her usual seat on the large saffron pillow near the loom where the older woman worked diligently on a pattern. The shuttle moved back and forth in a hushed cadence broken only by the light tapping of Davina's right foot.

Chestnut hair tipped with gray hung in loose coils down her host's back, a style of marked rebellion. Livia had never asked Davina's age, though rumor said she had surpassed her fiftieth year and their friendship spanned over twenty. No lines marred the clear face. There were no darkened spots of age on her hands. And the eyes that saw, yet did not see, remained clear.

Livia inhaled the subtle vanilla scent from the white candles that lined the mantel above the fireplace. It was empty now, used for storage for the many skeins of wool Davina needed for her artistry. Rose, blush, soft pink tumbled over scarlet, crimson, and mulberry. In another bowl lay the colors of the sea. By Davina's feet were five shades of green. So many to keep track of. Too many.

If Livia sat here in quiet repose the world would come aright. How you choose to view the world has everything to do with the results you see, so Horatia had taught the Vestals. The Goddess wanted the best for all of her devotees. Livia had put aside her personal desires and learned to focus on the rituals and ceremonies of the temple. She obeyed the principles of the priesthood, the laws of Rome. Up until the other evening that practice had seemed to work.

Why had she not seen Horatia's illness? Why had Horatia kept it from her? She picked up a ball of yarn and wound the end around her finger, again and again, as if the fiber could absorb her anguish.

"How are you today, Livia?"

"All is well." The yarn tightened around her finger and the flesh turned purple.

Davina uttered a quiet "hmm" and continued with her work. At the bottom of the weaving, dark greens twined and Livia envisioned the beginnings of a grassy meadow. Farther up the greens paled, a play of light upon the grass. Livia pictured herself beneath a canopy of branches, passing the time in a dreamy state of perfect joy while around her birds chirped and butterflies flitted from flower to flower. When she was young she wanted to be an artist. One who made exquisite mosaics. She practiced laying out designs with the pebbles she scratched out of the dirt around her house. Had she been born a boy, she would have studied with a master, and introduced more blue into the designs.

Davina held out her hand. "Will you pass me the crimson yarn?"

Livia rummaged in the basket and handed over a ball of red.

Davina fingered the yarn and gave it back. "This is scarlet. I need the darker red."

Livia found a slightly darker color and made the exchange. "I can barely tell them apart. How do you know which is which?"

"Each fiber has a certain feel, each dye its own scent. When the new yarns come in I hold them in my hands and get accustomed to them. They have their own peculiarities, their own properties, just as your hair is specific to your head and unlike any other. The yarns are my children. A mother knows her children."

"Teach me about the different wools, Davina. I want to know all you know."

Davina's laugh was rich and throaty. "Livia, sweet Livia. I love you dearly, but you are too gullible. A blind woman must cloak herself in mystery and so I spin my stories to keep people beguiled. But you did not come here today to learn about my yarns. Will you speak to me of your troubles?"

"I do not want to disturb you. Please, continue. I will sit quietly."

"If you were disturbing me, I would say so. Tell me what bothers you."

Livia did not answer. Discussion would bring up suppressed emotions and she would not give in to them.

"You came to me for help," Davina said. "How can I help?"

She *had* come for help. Davina was correct. But it was much easier to listen to gossip then unburden herself. How did Horatia handle her worries? In all the years Livia had served as a Vestal, the High Priestess had to deal with new residents, changes in the political temperature, food shortages, the constant cloud of war. Yet through it all Horatia remained stable, placid, generous. How did she retain that grace? The daily routine wore at Livia. There were days when she silently pleaded for release. Nights when only the Goddess witnessed her tears. And as the morning broke she would beg Vesta for forgiveness.

Marriage to Kaeso gave her hope. Counting the days until the end of her term focused her thoughts on the future, not on the present. Looking forward was her salvation. She dreamed of easy days with the sun on her face and the wind in her hair, walking amidst the rows of grapevines as the fruit grew fat and juicy and ready to press. She dreamed of witty conversation with the man she loved, good food, rich wine, and waking up whenever she pleased. Oh, the joy of answering to no one but herself. Yes, this is what she would think about.

"I am fine."

"You most assuredly are not."

"How can you know my mood?"

Davina's smile exuded kindness and wisdom. "My ears have sight, dear friend. I know your walk, your breathing, the little sounds you make. Today your footsteps are heavy, slow. The footsteps of an old woman. Your breathing is irregular. And you sigh. These are not the sounds of a woman of peace."

"Your ears see too much." But the rebuke was only half-serious. This was Livia's sanctuary away from the temple, a place where she could unburden her soul, if she chose.

Davina set her hands loosely in her lap and hummed a soft melody. Her eyes, though unfocused, gazed into Livia's heart. *Be not afraid,* they said. Livia took in a deep breath and let it out slowly. Then another. "I am . . . worried." There. The confession released some of her tension.

"The High Priestess may not recover. It is natural to worry." Davina held up her hand. "Do not be so surprised. I have ears, do I not? Gossip travels quickly."

"What else do you know?"

"I heard about the Fordicidia."

Livia grimaced. The less said about that unfortunate debacle the better.

"And I know of a golden-haired man who captured your attention," Davina continued.

Livia could not suppress the quick intake of breath.

"So the rumors are true then?" the weaver asked.

"Rumors. What rumors?"

"People talk, as you well know. Someone said he paid you more attention than befits your station. Another said you two conversed like lovers. And another—"

"They are mistaken." Livia squeezed the ball of yarn, wound her fingers through the strands.

"Remember your vow of chastity and the penalty—"

"I am well aware of my vow, Davina. He is simply an acquaintance. An old acquaintance. Someone I knew when I was younger. We met again just the other night. There is nothing between us." Her chest tightened at the omission of their encounter at the marketplace. She shifted her position to ease the discomfort as her thoughts took her to stories of Minucia, Aemilia, and Licinia, Vestals of history who were found guilty of being unchaste.

Davina tilted her head, as if she saw someone in the background. She stayed that way for several moments then her body slumped. When she gazed again at Livia, the light in her face had winked out. "Be warned, my friend. Something dire is at work. I cannot tell the cause, but I feel he is not a man to trust."

Sextus wandered the city until early afternoon when the baths were open to men. He discovered a half-buried bronze piece on the Via Appia, just outside the Circus, and another off the Vicus Tuscus. Good finds he added to his collection near the warehouses on the Tiber. With the money his aunt was paying him, soon he would have enough to be a soldier.

After midday he made his way to the Temple of Vesta. Antonia was as pretty as his mother. All he remembered of his mother was her light hair, as soft as fur, and a wide smile. He didn't know the color of her eyes or if she sang to him as he fell asleep. But she was beautiful, and he loved her. When this girl smiled at him, he had that same warm feeling.

Sextus held out two apples. "The lady at the marketplace told me to come here and give you these."

"What lady?" Antonia asked as she took the fruit. "Why are they for me?"

Stupid. He had not asked the woman's name. "She had dark hair. And green eyes." The girl stared at him, waiting. She might be younger than his twelve years, but she already had the patience of an adult. Then he remembered. "The men called her Priestess." She gave him no reaction. "Never mind." He reached out to snatch the apples and she covered them with her arm.

"Your hair curls," she said. "Mine does too." She fingered one of the blond coils by her face that escaped her *palla*. "But you are covered in dirt. Do you not bathe?"

A bath. That was it. "She said the apples were for the temple and you were to take me to the baths." He grinned, proud of his memory.

"Then we will do what Livia says."

Livia. He would not forget again.

Antonia gazed at him as if she were trying to see inside. "What is your name?" she asked.

"Sextus."

"Did the Goddess send you to Livia?"

"What goddess?"

"Vesta."

How stupid could she be? "No, of course not."

"How old are you?"

"Twelve."

"I am ten. Where do you live?"

"In a big house on the Esquiline hill," he made up. Her even stare told him she doubted his words.

"What does your father do?"

"He is a soldier." Another lie. "Do you always ask so many questions?"

"Livia says I am the most inquisitive person she knows. I am interested in everything."

"Well, I have a bath to take and we are wasting time."

Even after his rudeness, she smiled at him. "Wait here." Antonia ran up the steps with the apples and disappeared.

Sextus perched at the bottom of one of the marble columns and waited. White stone columns surrounded the temple, like the houses on the Esquiline Hill. Places where wealthy people lived. Antonia—he liked her name—wore simple clothing, but sometimes people with money spent it on other things.

Run a few errands, get free food. Clean clothes. He was ready for a new tunic.

His mother used to tell him he would make something of himself. A messenger for a temple was a start. Fine for now, but he had bigger ambitions.

Antonia skipped down the steps, followed by a *lictor*. The same one from the market. The man scowled and raised both hands as if he would clobber Sextus.

"Come with me," the girl said. "After your bath we go to visit Gratiana on the Esquiline Hill. She is teaching me about herbal medicines and how to make infusions. Do you know—"

"I will go to the baths, but not the healer."

"There is nothing to fear. You do not have to try anything. Some of the mixtures taste horrible," she made a face, "but others are very good."

"I am not scared of a woman. I have things to do."

"But I want you to go with me."

The *lictor* harrumphed and Sextus ignored him. Antonia's eyes held such expectation. A glow of trust surrounded him, held him. He gave in, for now. The agreement was to go to the baths. After that he would find an excuse.

He was better off on his own. Relationships were complicated, and the feeling he had with her could definitely lead to trouble.

# Chapter VIII

Despite the privileges accorded the Vestals, Horatia's chamber was plain. The bed, the rugs, the furniture were simply crafted, comfortable without extravagance. So like the woman who had presided, not with false airs but an easy humility and grace.

Livia packed a small chest with Horatia's brush and comb, clean garments, a potpourri of aromatic herbs to soothe the nerves. She thought of bringing sweets or fruit but discarded the idea. The physician would have the High Priestess on a strict regimen and would not appreciate Livia's interference.

Disquiet whispered through the room. Livia was intruding, invading her mentor's privacy. No one entered this space without permission. She had been here a handful of times and only for counseling or benediction. The warm hand on her head, the soft words of comfort, and Horatia's patience were things Livia easily recalled. She had tried that patience often.

The Pontifex Maximus had brought Livia to the Temple of Vesta just after her sixth birthday. Her father proclaimed the honor her service would bring the family, what a privilege it was for her to dedicate her life to the Goddess, and thus to Rome. Her mother spoke softly of duty and responsibility, two words that meant little to Livia. She longed for the sea, to cast her fate upon the wide expanse and let it take her where it might. She was a water child, with wings of light, ready to fly high above the sea as Icarus had journeyed toward the sun. That she was a girl made no difference. She would travel beyond the boundaries of Rome, farther than the great civilizations of Greece and Egypt. She would go to the ends of the Earth. And after that she would marry Kaeso and live the rest of her days in the same sweet love shared by her parents.

But her dreams had died that day. There would be no sailing upon the great, wide sea. No journey around the world. Duty anchored her to the temple and the sacred flame. Responsibility structured her daily routine, serving the Goddess and the people of Rome. She learned to hide her feelings inside, to shelter her fantasies in the whorls of her imagination. She became a devoted servant of the Goddess as she performed the many rituals and blessings, but there remained a piece of her that could not be chained. A portion of her soul that cried out for the happy childhood she once enjoyed.

Livia stared blankly, remembering her shaky beginnings in the temple, the first time she was called upon to guard the flame. It raged in the sacred pit, a fiery beast ready to pounce. She was mesmerized and afraid, afraid the flame would go out and she would die and there was nothing she could do.

Somehow she had survived.

Now it was her duty to visit Horatia, no matter her feelings about the High Priestess's illness or the possible succession that weighed heavily on her conscience. In truth, Livia could not use Gaius as an excuse after their meeting at the marketplace. He did not seem nearly as arrogant as the previous evening when his fingers had tightened uncomfortably around her wrist. What then would create this anxious feeling that crawled beneath her skin? Was it being in the company of his wife?

"Livia."

*I have tarried too long.* She picked up the chest with Horatia's belongings and hurried out.

"The Pontifex Maximus waits for you," Valeria said.

Pain fluttered at Livia's temples. If she had not wasted time in idle memories . . . She left the chest outside her own room and met the priest in the atrium.

"You are looking well, Priestess." The usual stern countenance softened as he gazed upon her. "I am sorry for Horatia's illness."

"Thank you for your concern." Livia noted the droop of his eyelids, the sag around his mouth. His weariness lightened her distress. Whatever trials she faced, he faced them as well. She waited for him to speak.

"You have done well for yourself, Livia. The Vestals speak highly of you. The temple runs smoothly."

"Horatia . . . the High Priestess runs the temple, not I."

"You are too modest. I have spoken with her. She trusts you implicitly."

There it was again. Trust. "What did she say? When will she return? The temple needs her loving hand. And we . . . we miss her."

"The gods direct us as they will. Where they command, there we must go." He took Livia's hand. "You have been a faithful servant all these years."

"Yes, I have." He was going to say something horrible.

"Over twenty-nine years. You are almost at the end of your service."

Livia nodded, wishing he would release her hand. She wanted to turn from him. Flee.

"Sometimes we are required to make a sacrifice. For the good of the people. For the good of our country."

The good of the country. Quintus Fabius Maximus had done little to ensure Rome's good. She had hoped the new dictator's experience and age would revolutionize Rome and bring peace. Instead, he resorted to massive sacrifices to win the favor of the gods.

Livia had already sacrificed twenty-nine years of her life. Had that pleased the gods? What more could the Pontifex Maximus want of her? But she already knew the answer. She had known the answer the moment Valeria spoke his name.

"The High Priestess needs more time. Her recovery is slow, but even. The physician believes she will be fully restored in a matter of months. In the meantime, you will — "

A dull roar filled her ears and drowned out his words. Months. Not years as she had feared. Months. O blessed Goddess.

"Dear Livia," he said, "I hope those are not tears of sadness."

She wiped her cheeks, surprised to find them wet, and shook her head. "Tears of relief. We all want the High Priestess well. And back with us." Her smile was wide. "Thank you for the good news."

"I only do my duty. You are the High Priestess for the interim until Horatia returns. So Rome decrees. If any should question you, this document proves your position." He placed the scroll in her hands and bid her good day.

The seal of Rome leapt out at her with claws of power but this time she was not intimidated. This time Rome had served her well.

Preceded by her *lictor*, Livia held Horatia's belongings close to her body as she crossed the Forum Romanum and wound through the city blocks to the house of Gaius on the Aventine Hill. Joy swelled her heart until she feared everyone would see it balloon under her *stola*. But no one gaped or gawked at her and soon she eased her grip on the chest and slowed her pace to enjoy the last of the day's warmth. The streets seemed cleaner, less dusty than usual. The air smelled fresher. Two patricians, linked arm in arm in heated conversation, passed by in togas that sparkled. Perhaps she was a little giddy with happiness.

By the time she reached her destination her heart was beating faster. Trepidation sent an alarming shiver across the back of her neck. As the door opened, her smile wobbled. A servant asked her to wait in the atrium. On the walls, smiling cupids lazed in dreamy splendor. Beneath her feet, a mosaic depicted a she-wolf with twin babies. Romulus and Remus. A short distance away stood the *impluvium*, the small pool. She gazed into the center, her eyes drawn to the calming blue. For a moment she was sitting at the edge of the sea, toes digging into the sand while frothy waves licked at her feet.

"Greetings, Priestess."

Gaius. Her anxiety vanished before his friendly gaze, a twitch of his lips that spoke of playfulness. She felt a lightness bubble up inside, no doubt due to the recent good news. "Please, call me Livia." She smiled and wondered at her boldness.

"Then so I shall. Livia."

There was pleasure in his eyes. How easily he was pleased.

"Have you come with gifts?" he asked.

She had almost forgotten the chest. "They are simple things, for Horatia . . . the High Priestess."

"Would you care for wine?" he asked. "Some food, perhaps? We have dates, nuts, even those figs you love."

She did not like to be teased, had never understood the need for sarcasm or those who flaunted it as easily as their morning prayers. Just then the servant appeared with a tray of food and she saw the figs, small morsels of seeded sweetness. No teasing, just a gesture of thoughtfulness. One that touched her heart.

As much as she loved figs, she had no appetite. "May I see the High Priestess? I . . . I wish to know how she is."

"Of course. You must have been quite worried about her health. About the temple. I know how it is to lose a friend. And one in command."

She wondered whom he had lost. What made him think Horatia was a friend and not just her superior? Livia restrained further questions and followed Gaius to the guest room. The small chamber allowed just enough space for one person to navigate around the bed. A side table held potions and herbs, towels, and a pitcher of water. Horatia rested, her body still but for the rise and fall of her chest.

Livia set down Horatia's belongings and perched on the edge of the bed, gratified by the softness of the mattress. A soft breeze drifted through the room. She smoothed back a few strands of hair on Horatia's forehead that had escaped the coil at the back of her neck. "Is she any better?" Livia asked softly without turning. "The Pontifex Maximus came to me today. He said she is recovering." Tears welled unexpectedly. How much she depended on Horatia. How great would be this task ahead.

Gaius touched her shoulder briefly, giving warmth, support. "She is better, yes. The physician says her heart is weak. Strained from wear. Some childhood condition that has worsened with age. The responsibility, the concerns of her office, these take a toll on her."

Livia gently stroked Horatia's face. She had known the High Priestess most of her service. Lived with her, learned from her, obeyed her, and come to love her. All those years Horatia had been strong for the Vestals. The decisions she had made, burdens she had carried. She deserved rest now. Selfish was all that Livia could think about herself. How selfish she had been to want to cast off her obligations. This was her life. This was her duty.

"Take as much time as you need," Gaius said. "I will wait for you in the garden."

His footsteps echoed softly. Livia took Horatia's hand and felt a light squeeze. The High Priestess's eyes opened.

"There is still some life in this old body." A feeble smile spread across her lips.

Livia rubbed the hand that had often soothed her own fears. "If I am not old, you cannot be old."

"My heart tells me otherwise."

"Horatia." What could she say that would not add more pressure? She was here to give relief, not burden an ailing patient.

"All will be well, Livia. No one else could serve the Goddess with more strength."

*What about patience, compassion, understanding? Where will I find those?* "I am afraid I do not have your grace, your ease with people."

"They come with practice." The squeeze this time was fainter. "Just obey."

"The Pontifex Maximus says this is only for a few months. Then you will resume your duties."

The High Priestess's breath rattled in her chest. She coughed and closed her eyes.

Livia bit her lip. Then things would be back to normal.

Gaius lounged at a table shaded by cypress trees. The food he had presented earlier lay untouched. Livia watched him for several seconds. He seemed to blend with his surroundings, as if he were a statue. Then he turned toward her and she saw the understanding in his eyes. Understanding she should have given the High Priestess. She breathed deeply to steady herself and sat next to him. From now on she would do as Horatia suggested—just obey. "Will the High Priestess stay here? It must be an inconvenience for you to watch over her." Livia tried to dispel thoughts of an earlier time when her own body needed care. Had she stayed elsewhere, her heart would not carry such haunting memories.

"The High Priestess is welcome as long as is needed," he said, "but I was informed that she will rest in Campania, at her sister's villa in Capua. The countryside is beautiful, rich pastures, and above all, peace. Family is certainly a better choice. The love of a sister will do much to improve her health."

Family. Torn from hers as a child, Livia barely remembered her childhood at home, her mother's touch. Horatia had become her substitute mother. And for the second time, Livia was losing that connection.

"I see that you worry for her," he said. "And your responsibilities. But perhaps this is a blessing. The god Janus shows us both sides of his face for a reason. One sees the end of something, the other the beginning."

Was this a new beginning? If so, she must keep faith. She must stay strong. "The Vestals owe you a deep debt of gratitude for your care."

"It is my honor. Our honor. We could do no less. Livia, you owe us nothing." He touched her cheek, the softest graze of her skin, and her lips trembled. "I still remember when my family cared—"

She rose quickly. Where was her *lictor*? "Thank you again for your hospitality. It means more to the Vestals than you know." She could not meet his eyes. "I hope you will keep us informed about her recovery."

Then she fled, hurrying through the hall to the atrium where Titus waited, swinging open the front door before a servant could escort her out. She was rude, inexcusably rude, but Gaius made her feel things she did not want to feel.

Dusk surrounded the city with a cloak of indigo as Livia walked the familiar path towards the temple. She paused at a fountain to catch her breath, to calm her thoughts, the erratic beat of her heart. She was no young girl to get excited by a pleasing face but a woman, near the end of her child-bearing years. A mature woman with a man who loved her and cherished her and waited to marry her.

Livia sat down hard on the stone lip and trailed her hand in the water. Titus waited nearby. She could still feel Gaius's touch on her cheek, still hear the throb of her heart.

Why did she not feel these things with Kaeso?

# Chapter IX

The hot water of the *caldarium* opened Gaius's pores and relaxed his mind. Things had seemed simpler on the battlefield. No women there to warp his thoughts, no female shapes to feed his fantasies. Just straightforward maneuvers. His squadron had a specific number of men and horses. He knew how they marched, how they fought, their strengths and their weaknesses. His strategies were solid, unquestioned.

He lowered his hand into the water and drew it out slowly, in and out several times, fascinated by how the angle of his arm appeared to change. How much of life was an illusion, how much real? Perhaps he should let go of his need for Livia. Each time he saw her, the arrow of love pierced deeper. And she gave no indication he meant anything to her.

A broad hand clapped him on the shoulder then Lucius slid into the pool. "There he is, playing with the water again."

"Be careful," Servius said. "You could have an accident." He fell on Gaius from above and pushed him under.

They came up sputtering. Water streamed down Gaius's face, into his eyes. "Thank you, kind friends. Let me return the favor." He grabbed Servius by the neck and wrestled him below the surface. Lucius punched Gaius in the gut. Soon, all three men were behaving like children, gasping for breath as the heat of the water and steamy air forced them to give up their antics.

Gaius escaped to the *frigidarium* where he plunged into the icy pool. Shivering, he watched his friends linger at the edge. Servius dipped in his right foot and drew back in distaste.

"There are times when a man must brave the cold for the sake of victory," Gaius said with a signal to Lucius.

Lucius pushed their comrade into the pool and jumped in after him. It took only seconds for all three to exit and gather in the warmth of the *unctorium* where they lounged on couches, awaiting massage. Gaius stretched out face down on a towel. Thirty laps in the outdoor pool had produced the warm muscle ache required to keep his body in shape. Now he could relax. Were it not for his friends, he would have closed his eyes and drifted off.

A trained slave produced a curved, metal strigil and proceeded to scrape Gaius's body with a firm motion that started at the top of his shoulders and worked down. The skin along his arms reddened as the blade drew out the dirt and restored the flow of energy.

Servius stood and raised his arms overhead then twisted and held various positions.

His wide chest and muscled arms and legs reminded Gaius of the figures of athletes on Greek urns. "Showing off again?"

Servius grinned and struck a pose which accented his biceps and thighs.

"Quintus Fabius is calling up the army," Gaius said. Despite the soothing warmth of the massage, he felt his body tighten as haunting visions of the bloodshed at Lake Trasemine filled his mind. He had no desire for more killing. Now was the season for gentler pursuits.

"We have tried different strategies against Hannibal," Lucius said. "How does our new dictator propose to save Rome this time?"

Gaius grunted at the heavy pressure on his ribs. "I hear he wants to weaken our enemy. A little at a time."

"We could cut off one appendage for every Roman killed at Lake Trasemine," Servius added.

Gaius laughed at the same time the slave scraped his inner thigh. The curved metal nicked his testicle. "Away from me," he roared. "You dare wound me before I can lie with . . ." He stopped, painfully aware he had said too much. "Give me that." He grabbed the instrument.

The slave backed away, eyes downcast. Gaius sat up and looked for blood. Thankfully, there was none.

"Castration here," Servius called out. "Free of charge."

Gaius glared at his friend and proceeded to scrape his own body. He did his best to keep his face neutral, his eyes on the blade. He could feel his comrade's gaze, imagine the narrowing eyes and brooding look. Friendly Servius, the good-natured soul who tried to fix everyone's problems, who would worry at this until all was resolved.

"So, Gaius," his friend began, "I had to remind myself you are married, and Justina has certainly had good use of your manly parts. A loving wife would not care if her husband were wounded . . . there," he pointed with a tilt of his head. "But another woman might. Someone new." He looked at Lucius who shrugged.

Gaius stopped with the strigil in midair. "There is no one. Were you drinking before you came here?" Did his friends spy on him? Had someone seen him with Livia? He recalled kissing her wrist at the celebration in full view of several people and the casual conversation with her at the marketplace with the merchant. Why had he not been more careful? An image of her came to mind, the prized memory he carried with him always. Just a boy then, he had chased his puppy through the house and wandered into the room where she was resting. The puppy had leaped from his arms onto the bed and licked her face. The face of a goddess.

"Look at him," Servius said. "He is like a young girl with her first love. Who is she? Do we know her?"

"There is no one." He cursed himself for his wandering thoughts. It would do no good to parade his feelings before his friends. Livia must be kept above reproach.

"Lucius, help me here," Servius said. He advanced on Gaius with meaty hands spread wide. "We will wring his neck until he talks."

Lucius doubled with laughter while Gaius covered his face in mock fear. "I have nothing to say. I swear." The false bravado accentuated his fear of discovery.

Servius circled Gaius's neck and squeezed gently, grinning all the while.

"All right. No more of this torture." He waited for Servius to sit down. "You do not know her." He beckoned to the slave to oil his body. As the massage commenced on his neck and shoulders, he continued. "She is young, but not too young."

"Then she is pleasing?"

"She is not so old that she is unpleasant and not so young that she is inexperienced. Her father arranges a marriage for her with a much older man, but she has . . . needs. She seems to appreciate my experience." He spread his hands wide, as if to say he had tried to resist, but he was only human.

"By the gods, how fortunate you are. And you not so old yourself." Servius gave Gaius a friendly slap on the arm that knocked Gaius sideways. "What is her name?"

Gaius fumbled for something agreeable. "Serena. Her name is Serena."

Servius nodded. "Tell me, Gaius, how do you do it?"

Relieved that his friends seemed to go along with the story, Gaius smiled. "I pray for good fortune, gentlemen. I simply pray." He bowed his head then, gave into the strong fingers that rubbed his back, and prayed that good fortune would indeed favor him on his quest.

"The evening meal awaits," Lucius said. "My wife is anxious for my return." Gaius raised his head in time to see him elbow Servius.

Servius rose from the bench and twisted his neck right, then left. Loud pops echoed through the room. "If we go to war, Serena will not have you for much longer. Make love while you can."

Lucius pushed him towards the exit. "You oaf." He paused to whisper in Gaius's ear. "Servius means well, but his tongue is loose. And slaves have ears. Be wary, my friend."

The gray stone around the entrance to the weaver's house was worn smooth. Sextus stood with his eyes closed, face tilted to catch the mid-day sun. This messenger job was a good thing. He had sold his new tunic for a whole *as*, trading up from 8 bronze pieces to 12, and he managed to weasel out of going to the healer's house with Antonia. A pretend stomachache after his bath did the trick, although she almost dragged him to the healer for a cure.

Thank Jupiter he was a good liar, plus he was scared of strange concoctions. Next time, if there was a next time, he would need a better plan.

He pressed his hands against the stone to feel its warmth. They came away with grime, which he wiped on his tunic. The message from Livia sounded in his head. He had memorized her hair, almost black, the slim nose, her eyes the light green of his mother's favorite shawl.

He had hidden just inside the temple while she talked to the tall man. Someone of authority, he knew, from the broad purple border on his toga. They embraced then held hands. She trembled and stared at a scroll with a wax seal on it. Sextus ran down the steps before the man found him. Something was bound to happen and he would be there waiting. A short time later Livia had sent Antonia to find him and he was only too happy to deliver a message to the house of Davina. A blind lady.

A servant opened the door, told Sextus to wait, then returned and ushered him inside. At the entrance he felt a whisper, someone asking who was there. But he saw no one. He moved forward and again felt the presence.

"Come in. You are welcome."

The woman's voice was gentle, soothing.

He found the lady around the next corner, sitting in front of some vertical contraption with colored threads. While he watched, she pushed a long string back and forth between the threads, time and again, and shades of blue mixed and swelled and rose and fell until he could feel the sea come in and go out. Amazed, he moved closer, closer, until he was standing next to her, touching the colors, the tight weave of stitches.

"Do you feel the different textures?" she asked.

He nodded, forgetting that she had no sight. But it seemed to make no difference. She guided his fingers to the row just completed. "This yarn, smooth and fine, is silk. As precious as sapphires and rubies. This one," his fingers touched a bumpy yarn, "is from the sheep of Pollentia. The unevenness gives it more texture. And this one is the hair of goats. Slightly thicker than the silk but not as soft."

It was silly for a man to be fascinated with this, but he could not help himself. She drew the long string through the threads again and he wanted to try. "Can I . . . can I push the string through?"

Her laugh was light and comforting, not at all condescending. She let him take the wooden handle. "Give it a strong push," she said. But his hand was clumsy and it stuck halfway across the row.

Sextus stamped his foot. "Stupid."

"Proficiency requires patience and practice." She completed the row and then another to return the handle to the right side. "Try again."

Sextus pressed his lips together in concentration. This time he focused on the end of the row and let go. The handle flew easily through the threads into Davina's waiting hand. "I did it." Enthusiasm bubbled in his throat, emerged in a wide smile.

"You did." She took up the work again. "You could become a weaver. Would you like me to teach you?"

Someone would find out. And laugh at him. "Weaving is for women. I have more important things to do."

Davina hummed a lilting melody and continued her work without response.

Sextus examined the baskets of yarn, touching the different hues and textures. He took two balls of silk, no larger than the inside of his palm, one the red of wine, the other yellow as the sun, and hid them behind his back. She would not know he had taken them and if they were really worth as much as she had said, he would be rich.

Then he remembered the reason he had come. "Livia sent you a message."

"Read it to me."

Sextus snorted. "It is in my head. She said to tell you she is the High Priestess now. For as long as it takes."

Davina stopped her work. "Are those her exact words? Did she say any more?"

Questions. Why did adults always ask questions? He was no mongrel from the streets without a brain. He was smart, crafty. He played back the memory. Livia stood in front of him, bending forward to lower herself to his level. Adults did that with children as if being the same height made them equals. She had made him repeat the message several times. *I am the High Priestess now. So Rome decrees. Until Horatia recovers.* He liked his version better.

"Those were her words."

"Then I give thanks. Tell Livia I have received them."

He squeezed the stolen balls and began to edge sideways out of the room. "Good day, then." He had just reached the doorway when her soft voice called out.

"You only hide from yourself, Sextus."

The words crashed into him. Stumbling, he reached out blindly for support and dropped the yarn. Strands of red and yellow crisscrossed on the floor as the balls rolled. She knew his name when he had not told her. Days had passed since he met Livia at the marketplace and news traveled quickly in the city. Perhaps the blind lady had heard about him.

He snatched up the silk and wadded the strands, forced his hands to stop shaking. She was staring at him with a sad smile, the same sort of smile on his mother's face before she died.

Sextus glared at her. "You do not know me. I hide from no one."

"You are correct. I do not know you. But God knows all."

"Which god? I pray to Jupiter and Mars," and Pluto, the god of wealth, he added to himself. "They protect me."

"There is only one god, the god of Abraham and Isaac."

"You are wrong. There are many gods. I know because . . ." He faltered under her quiet gaze. He believed there were many gods because everyone believed. But he had never seen a god, never felt the presence of one. Did he truly know? His ignorance made him angry. "There are many gods," he declared and smirked when she bowed her head.

He turned to leave and again her voice stopped him. "Take the purple silk. It is worth four times the ones you have."

She was facing her work, building the picture. For several moments he stared at the movement of her fingers, the tilt of her head. The melody she hummed wove around his brain. Across the room the purple silk twinkled like an expensive jewel. Four times the worth of the red or yellow. He itched to take it. Started to reach for it, even though his hands were full.

Then he heard her words inside his head. *God knows all.*

He escaped without it.

# Chapter X

Sextus cursed himself the moment he left the weaver's house. The silk balls burned his hands, as if the sun collected in the threads and created fire. Several times he stopped to examine his palms, certain he would find angry red marks.

He wanted the purple. He should have taken it. She told him to. When had he become such a coward? First with Antonia and then this. But he knew why. Davina had put a spell on him.

*God knows all.* The words branded his mind. What did the blind woman mean? Who was this one god? All Romans knew there were many gods. Jupiter, Juno, Neptune, Apollo, Mars, and, of course, Vesta, his new mistress. He prayed to Mars each morning for the courage to fight—the streets were full of beggars and thieves, ready to relieve people of their money—and to Jupiter at night to protect him while he slept. To Pluto he said a special prayer that riches might come his way often.

Below the Aventine Hill, near the warehouses on the Tiber, stood a tiny altar to Clementia, goddess of mercy. The chipped nose and missing fingers from the right hand made her look sad. No one seemed to pay her attention. The same lone silver piece gleamed dully at the bottom of the shallow bowl at her feet. There were no extra coins to add to his collection. The street was empty now, so he reached into the hollow area at the back of the statue and pulled out the wadded cloth, creased with dirt, musty from age. The jeweled comb caught the sunlight and cast a rainbow against his arm. He had found it in a garden on the Esquiline Hill. It would have looked beautiful in his mother's hair, the yellow stones bright against her braids. He squinted at the sting of tears. Soon he would find a buyer.

One day he would fulfill his dream and be a soldier. A mighty warrior to fight against the barbarians. But before that he would change his name. Add a nomen and cognomen that people would respect. He had never known his father, and he refused to go by the same name as his aunt. A good plebeian name that originally belonged to the patricians would work. He had thought of the Julius Caesars and Cornelius Scipios but they were too well known. No one would believe he came from those lines. He needed something less pompous. Maybe Cassius Varus or Junius Pennus.

He was tired of being without a name. Slaves had only one name and he was better than that. On his next birthday, when he turned thirteen, he would decide.

Footsteps sounded on the pavement. Sextus kneeled before the statue, his hands raised in prayer. After several moments the footsteps receded. "Praise Jupiter," he whispered, and stashed the balls of silk in the bag.

When he reached the Temple of Vesta he sank down on the upper step, more out of breath than usual. He was not himself and it had started when Livia hired him as a messenger. Sextus had to find a way to rid himself of the spell. Perhaps Antonia knew of a medicine he could take. He slapped his leg. Yes, he would tell her some evil woman had cursed him and that was the reason for his strange behavior.

There were 750 paces from the front steps of the Temple of Vesta to the spring at Camenae at the foot of the Caelian Hill. Or so Livia had heard. Counting the paces was absurd, but it would serve as a mental distraction. She had been serious too long, ever since the celebration for the equestrians. Today she would find her joy.

She set off with her vase to fetch water before the other Vestals were awake. No other Vestals accompanied her, nor did Titus. This one time by herself would not matter. She was alone, and she reveled in the freedom, the quiet, to better concentrate on her task.

How difficult could it be? After all, any child could count to one hundred, and then it was just a matter of increasing those hundreds until she reached her goal.

Legionary paces, she reminded herself as she began her morning walk along the Via Sacra. She had seen the long strides of Roman soldiers and knew her steps did not compare. Still, it was something for her to focus on rather than her last encounter with Gaius, the color of the panels in his house, the mosaics on the floor. The offer of figs. How he and his wife were caring for Horatia.

She could not get them out of her mind.

So she challenged herself with this simple exercise. She was a Vestal, pledged to the Goddess and to Rome. She was the High Priestess now, the *Vestalis Maxima*, no matter how temporary the office. Responsibility came first so she must set an example for the other Vestals. She did not have the luxury to spend in daydreams about a man, however handsome and charming . . . a married man who could be nothing other than an acquaintance.

The count began easily enough. A light breeze, with a hint of warmth, blew the wisps of hair that curled around her ears. The days had begun to lengthen. The month of May was just around the corner. Soon summer would come to the city, lush and full.

She resumed the count at forty-two, her thoughts already straying. As she followed the edge of the Palatine Hill she recalled sitting on Horatia's bed and Gaius's touch on her shoulder, the warmth of his hand. His support. Understanding. Exactly what she needed to ease her fears about Horatia's illness.

A block later she remembered to count and arbitrarily picked up with sixty. Then along the Vicus Longus she lost count again. A reprimand to focus and she was on track. Then she remembered the garden and Gaius's hand on her cheek, the softness of his fingers, the blueness of his gaze that held her eyes.

She lost count again. She stopped to breathe in the morning air, to fill her mind and soul with the harmony of nature, and gave up her pursuit. Her mind was as fickle as the changing breeze and much too easily influenced by the memories of someone she needed to forget. The story of 750 paces would remain unchallenged. Perhaps another day she would try again.

The grove was deserted, peaceful in the early morning. Each day she had dutifully come to the spring and collected water in the *futile* without it touching the ground, ensuring the sacredness of the water and the act. But today she breathed in the stillness and felt herself relax. No one was there to see her, and, she rationalized, she had not yet collected the water, so Livia set the wide-mouthed, narrow-bottomed *futile* on a flat rock beside the spring, slipped off her shoes, and eased her feet into the water.

Her skin prickled from the sudden cold and shivers ran up her calves, yet the exhilaration sparked a smile. Abandoning herself to the moment, she closed her eyes, leaned back on her hands, and imagined the Vestals dancing naked in the spring, laughing, splashing. Long hair dipped into the silvery liquid and came up dripping. Trickles streamed between breasts and over thighs. In her mind she launched a spray at Patricia's face. Patricia countered with a vessel full of water over Livia's head. As the daydream wove on, Livia kicked her feet and laughed.

"I would swear that is a wicked smile on your lips."

Livia gasped and clutched at her naked body to shield herself from view, only to realize she was fully clothed. Her shock at being disturbed was secondary to the source of the disturbance.

Gaius stood several paces from her, balanced easily on two jutting stones. "I seem to have startled you," he said. "Again. Are you easily startled?"

She sat up and forced herself to relax. Her feet continued to dangle in the spring. A small bit of impropriety which she decided not to mention. "You seem to take pleasure in surprising me."

His smile was wide and teasing. "I do."

"Why are you here?"

"I have waited each morning these past few days, hoping to speak with you."

He had waited for her? Why did he not send a message to the temple? She would have come at once on an important matter. "This is not a place for men to gather. The spring is sacred, consecrated for the followers of Vesta."

"Yet Numa Pompilius consorted with Egeria in this very grove."

"He was the king—"

"The second king of Rome."

"Yes, the second king of Rome. A king, not just a man."

"And I am just a man."

She let the silence emphasize her point. "And Egeria was—"

"A nymph who gave him the foundation for Rome's religious tradition."

She wanted to argue against him being there, but his knowledge delighted her, and she fell easily into the discussion. "And after Numa's death . . ." She expected him to interrupt. When he did not, she continued. "After his death it is said she was transformed into the spring."

Gaius dipped his hand into the water, let the droplets run down his fingers. "Some say that Egeria is the goddess Diana. They believe she is the one who presides over the spring that flows from the roots of the sacred oak at Lake Nemi."

"Egeria and Diana? A nymph a goddess?" She gazed at the flow of water, how it gushed at the mouth of the cavern and tumbled over and around the many rocks, then slowed to a sleepy crawl in the shallow pool before winding onward. The spring was sacred to her because she had been taught so, not because she had ever felt its magic. Armed with this new knowledge, the water took on a brighter sparkle. "Egeria, Diana, Artemis to the Greeks. I have heard many stories of how the gods and goddesses take different forms. My nurse often told me about Zeus and Leda, how he came to her as a swan. I thought swans were the most beautiful birds and how wonderful that a swan would love a woman. I did not understand that Zeus loved her . . . that he made love to her . . ." Livia blushed.

"The gods are indeed fortunate to have the capacity to love mortals."

Someday she would experience that love, an unfit subject for their discussion. "You should not be here. It is forbidden for a Vestal to be alone with a man. If I were found with you, the punishment is . . ." Her breathing clogged. Her arms tingled as if they were numb, as if she were already suffocating.

"Rome would never harm its Vestals. You are too important to our well-being. All of that is to keep you obedient. A perceived threat is just as frightening as a real one."

A perceived threat. Was it just imaginary? She had believed for almost thirty years and he was telling her those beliefs were false. "What of the Vestal Tarpeia who was accused of treason?"

"Was she found guilty?"

"She proved her innocence by carrying water from the Tiber in a sieve."

"Exactly my point. How could anyone carry water in a sieve? They are legends, Livia, just as Romulus and Remus were suckled by a she-wolf. You know as well as I that is impossible."

As much as Livia loved animals and heroes, his argument had logic. Reason. He was, after all, a military commander, steeped in practicality. But thirty years of habit did not dissolve in an instant. "No matter your fine words, it is the law. And one I must obey."

"The law is only as good as those who defend it. But let us talk of other matters."

She could not dally here with him. "The other Vestals will be coming soon."

"Antonia, Oppia, Patricia, Valeria," he counted off on his fingers. "And, of course, you. And the High Priestess."

"You know all their names?" she asked, then answered her own question. "Of course. The Vestals are public servants. Anyone might know who we are." She brought her feet out of the water onto the rock that they might dry in the sun.

"There is much of public record if you take the time to inquire."

She gave him a sly look. "Then you are aware that I am High Priestess?"

"For the time being. Until Horatia recovers."

"Until she recovers," Livia echoed, praying that the time would be short.

"How long will that be?" he asked.

"You do not know? Surely it is a matter of public record."

"I gave up my divining powers on my tenth birthday." They both laughed. "If everything were known," he continued, "life would be quite dull." He sank down on the grass beside her. "Tell me, High Priestess, what will you do?"

"I will continue with my duties as a High Priestess should. There are many things . . ." She had begun the morning with a focus on her task, to take her mind off her other thoughts. Now she was loath to interrupt the conversation and begin her day.

"When your duties end, then what? Do you have plans?"

"My plans were destroyed by unforeseen events." The anger lingered, though it was quieter now. Her plans were not destroyed, merely delayed. She must not resist so much. This was her fate now. "Forgive me. That was too harsh. When I am no longer a Vestal I will marry and live happily on my property. So I pray. One never knows how the gods will choose to move us through life."

"Move us?"

"Sometimes I picture people as pieces on a game board that gods move at will through obstacles or along a pleasant path. For their amusement, of course."

Gaius ran his fingers through the grass, then began to plait several strands into a tight, even braid. "And we, the people, I mean, have no recourse?"

"Only to deal with our troubles as they come." She watched in fascination as he wove in stems of clover. "Where did you learn to do that?"

He looked down at his work, unaware of his creation. "Oh." He restored the grass with quick swipes of his hands. "While we wait for battle some men practice maneuvers on horseback, some with weapons; others draw diagrams for attack. A leader is meant to instill courage in his men, to inspire them with great words. I seem to borrow more and more of my speeches from those who came before me."

She found nothing wrong with that. History was meant to inspire and teach. How much easier it was to use the stirring words of someone else than to fumble for your own. She expected to do just that in the days to come. "Not all who lead are great speakers."

"And not all who speak well are great leaders. Nevertheless, they expect it of me. I was sitting on a hillside one day, thinking of battles we had lost, the waste of death . . ." She felt his sigh more than heard it. "When I looked down I had braided the grass blades as a woman does her hair." He cleared his throat. "The weaving stills my mind . . . it settles me . . . my thoughts seem to flow more easily."

His honesty moved her, the effortless way he shared his thoughts. How easy he was to talk to. "I remember when you first told me of the sea. You wanted to go around the world. When I think of the water I am at peace. I can feel myself floating, weightless, as if I had wings to hold me aloft. Other times I seem to be a single drop, alone, yet part of the whole. The gods are with me then, lifting me up to the heavens to be with them. I wish we could travel upon the water, go explore the world." She put her arms around her knees. "Lately, it feels as if the gates of hell are swinging open. The gods seem to be inventing obstacles for me to hurdle."

He took her hand in his. "Come with me, Livia."

His touch was alive, unsettling. "What do you mean?"

"Come with me. Away from Rome. To the sea. This time we will explore." He caressed the back of her hand with his lips.

Her hand tingled. Nerves prickled, shivered. She drew her hand from his grasp and stood. The sea was her fantasy, a place of dreams; it was not the real world. She could not leave Rome. Her life was here. Duty awaited. "The Vestals will be here soon. Please, you must leave."

He rose slowly, his eyes never leaving her face. "I care for you, Livia. Is it so difficult to imagine that someone could be interested in you?"

Rome needed her for protection. Vesta used her for service. Her parents had traded her for prestige. What interest could Gaius have?

# Chapter XI

Beneath the table in Pomponia's *peristylium*, Justina's leg swung in wide arcs. May's gentle warmth settled over the garden, enough to welcome the sun on her skin. They sat side by side, a plate of fresh fruit drizzled with honey within reach. Juice ran down Pomponia's plump hand as she bit into a slice of peach.

Justina batted a fly that swarmed the fruit and tried to curb her restlessness. It would be so much easier if Gaius would behave, or some circumstance would force him to do so. With magical powers she could conjure a spell to make him beg for her favors. Sighing, she realized her only path was action.

"I so needed this break," Pomponia announced. "Praise Juno you came when you did. Without your company I would still be entangled in my sadly neglected weaving." She slurped the wetness from her hand and grabbed another slice of peach. "You *will* be here for the dinner tomorrow."

"Mmm." Had her life become just a series of entertainments, one more tedious than the next? She wanted more. "He does not want me."

Pomponia closed her eyes and leaned her head back. The fly crawled over her fingertips. "Who?"

Justina shifted her position and purposely bumped her toes against the table leg. The contact helped to release the jittery feeling. "Gaius."

"You disappoint me. I thought you had some juicy tidbit to share."

"How dull of me. I beg your forgiveness." A gust of wind ruffled the oleander leaves and blew across her hair. She patted the flyaway strands back into place.

Pomponia laughed. "Use your acting on someone else, my friend. You know I feel for you, but how long can you ache for a man who cares nothing for you? Heal your heart, Justina. Take a lover. It will do wonders for you." When she reached for more peach her flabby arm jiggled.

"I can see the wonders it has done for you."

A frown pinched her friend's forehead. "Be kind, or I will send you home to sulk alone." She wiped her chin then touched Justina's hand. "I know someone for you. Handsome, muscular, his skin is bronzed and smooth. I remember how you dislike hairy men. And he is young. You know what that means."

"Gaius is young enough."

Pomponia glared.

"The young ones have nothing to say," Justina said. "I would rather have a man with brains than one who can last all night."

"Of course. I forgot how happy Gaius makes you."

Justina gave the table leg a resounding thwack. "Now who is being unkind?"

"I only tell you what you already know is true. Take matters into your own hands. You are still beautiful, my friend. Men want you. I see the way they look at you when we are in public. If you gave any one of them the slightest sign . . ." She sighed. "The one I mentioned is called Eros."

Justina snorted. "Truly?"

"Truly." She patted Justina's hand then leaned back again to relax.

"How original." She chewed a peach slice slowly, meticulously, while the glimmers of a smile began to form.

From across the square, Justina clutched the *palla* against her face so only her eyes and forehead showed. The coarse slave cloth she had secretly borrowed from her house servant irritated her skin. But the disguise proved necessary. She did not want recognition.

She crossed to the Temple of Vesta, her legs stiff with tension. Once subterfuge had been an eager ally. Since marriage her skills had rusted.

The temple door stood ajar. She rapped with her free hand and stepped inside. Darkness swamped her vision, increased her discomfort. *Be still!* she commanded silently, standing rigid until her nerves calmed.

"Hello," she called quietly. When no one anwered, she walked around the room. Polished marble lined the inner walls, a continuous line of smooth stone slightly lighter in color than the floor where foot traffic had worn the stone to a dull gray.

A blaze of fire drew her near the center. The flame of Vesta, she assumed. She had expected a great roaring bonfire. Instead the sacred flame reached chest high, contained in a circular stone pit not much different from the hearth in her home.

This was the great flame that gave Rome its power? She covered her mouth to still her laughter. The whole space was ridiculous. Not at all like the sanctuary for Juno, a fitting place for a priestess. This one was too small, and round. Proper temples had straight lines. She would not have her husband associated with something so pathetic. And what could six women possibly do here? If she had her way, she would throw the Vestals in front of stampeding horses, or at the very least, loose them among drunken men for leisurely rape. Her Gaius would not be so eager then. If he truly loved Livia he would want to be the first. Justina thought back to her wedding night, the careful plans she had laid to make sure she appeared unschooled and innocent. The success of that evening made her smile. Her husband was none the wiser.

What had happened to their relationship? Why did he stray now?

Footsteps neared and a voice called out. "May I help you?"

Late twenties, Justina guessed of the woman who stood with her hands at her waist. Long past the bloom of adolescence yet the telltale lines around the eyes or mouth were difficult to detect. Serenity radiated from her being, a characteristic Justina would never possess.

"I have come . . ." Justina coughed to ease her throat. "I wish to speak with the High Priestess Livia."

The Vestal's eyes narrowed for a moment but the voice was calm and polite. "The High Priestess is unavailable. If you wish to leave your name—"

"No." The word came out harsher than she intended. Even though she had practiced before now, determined to be pleasing and assured, the ruse was getting the best of her. But that something in the Vestal's eyes might be used to her advantage.

"My apologies." She bowed her head a moment then resumed her speech. "It is a private matter. . ." She trailed off on purpose, hoping to draw out another facet of the Vestal's personality.

"Anything you might say to the High Priestess you may say to me. I am more than capable of handling any matters that involve the Temple." The eyes flashed with an arrogant glimmer of assumed importance.

Ah, Justina breathed. Ambition. The perfect ally. Someone she could use to further her plan. "In truth," she began, "the High Priestess is the reason I have come. I fear there is a problem."

"There are many problems where the High Priestess is concerned."

Dissension. Glad for the *palla* that hid her smile, Justina continued. "My husband," she said and looked around as if she were nervous. "Can I trust you?"

The Vestal's lips curved for an instant. "Of course."

"This is a matter of great importance. It requires the utmost discretion."

"Secrecy is prized above all within the temple."

Justina nodded, not at all fooled by the woman's words. Gossip and women twined like heated lovers. She lowered her *palla*. "The High Priestess goes where she is not wanted. I need a pair of eyes to watch her movements."

"I see many things that others do not."

The Vestal seemed to glow with purpose. A purpose, Justina surmised, that grated on her sister priestesses but would serve Justina quite well. "Then I may count on your observation?"

The woman nodded.

"When may I meet with the High Priestess?" Justina asked.

"Come tomorrow at midday. To the *Atrium Vestae*. She will see you there."

"And whom do I have to thank for this meeting?"

"I am Valeria."

Outside the temple, glee bubbled at the back of Justina's mouth, tickling her palate like fine wine from Pompeii. No matter that she had not seen Livia today. A seed was planted. She had executed her plan and done it well. She may not be a centurion like her husband, but she would pit her strategy against his any day. Her visit with the High Priestess and Valeria's secret scrutiny would stop further temptation before it grew into anything serious.

There was also the matter of the lover Pomponia had mentioned. Eros. Naming a child after a god was as ridiculous as the pitiful size of the temple she had just left. She tried to imagine herself with this bronzed man, limbs intertwined, flesh heated and straining. Revulsion raced along her skin and left a sourness in her mouth. Why did it seem so distasteful? Other women took lovers. Her husband certainly had his fill. And she badly wanted to teach Gaius a lesson.

Justina raised her head high and held the palla tight. Some things in life were simply unpleasant. But she would do it. And do it well.

Yes, today was a splendid beginning. She thought ahead to her visit with the High Priestess. A few calculated remarks and all would be as she wanted. Gaius would come back, as cowed as a beaten dog.

The High Priestess was no match for her. No match at all.

# Chapter XII

J ustina sat on the couch, then stood by the chair, then perched again on the couch, and finally stood by the small window which looked out on an alley. Dark now, she saw nothing but the glimmer of pale light from the moon.

Would he never come? She began to pace the small bedroom in Pomponia's house. Here she had privacy, something she could never have at home. Perhaps later she would bring Eros to her own house and let Gaius find them together. Show her husband she could play the game as well.

The momentary satisfaction fled and her fingers pressed against the window ledge. The pouch of silver coins lay next to her, payment for this tryst. Looking at the bag she knew this was a mistake. A huge mistake. No matter what Pomponia said or people thought. Justina could craft her outward appearance with style and cunning, but tonight her nerves were telling her no. Eros could go back to his friends and his tavern or wherever he wasted his time. She had no need of him.

"You are younger than I imagined."

She whirled to face the speaker, impressed with the deepness of his voice. Eros stood at the opening to the room, just as Pomponia described. Dark hair waved back from his forehead and around his ears. His eyes seemed golden in the lamp light. He was taller than Gaius, more muscled, his features pleasing in symmetry, with his tunic falling to his knees. So he was not a plebeian but of good family. She had hoped he would be poor, to discard him more easily.

He stepped forward and extended a bright pink arum lily. She took it silently, stroked it once, and let it fall to the floor. She would not be swayed with gifts.

A servant appeared with wine and goblets and departed. Eros filled one and handed it to her. He took none for himself. "You do not drink?" she asked.

"I have no need of wine. Your beauty fills me."

She laughed, a nervous titter. Was he an educated man or did he merely mimic pretty phrases? "Please. Save the flowery speech for some other woman who can bask in your admiration."

"I speak the truth, Justina. You are beautiful."

She saw it in his eyes, the frank regard, the glimmer of delight. And seeing it, she felt the stirrings of arousal. Then anger that Gaius did not look at her that way. "What good is beauty if it does not serve you? If it gets you nothing in return?" Ashamed of her outburst, she turned away. He had nothing to do with her marriage, the pain in her heart. If she could not control her words she should go.

"I apologize if I have upset you."

Justina gulped wine to steady herself. "It was nothing you said." She chewed on her lip and forced herself to relax. She was in control. Any moment she could choose to leave.

"Shall we sit?" he asked and motioned at the couch.

"I prefer where I am." Being close to his body, breathing in the odor of his skin, no, she was not ready for that. What regimen did he follow to prepare himself for wealthy women? Then she wondered if he slept only with the affluent or if he paraded his wares for anyone.

He stretched out on the couch, legs crossed, his head propped up on pillows as if he were settling in for a nap. Light danced on his skin, sculpting curves of strength and solidity. Against her will, she was drawn to him. Still, she made no move.

"Pomponia speaks highly of you," he said.

Justina gritted her teeth. She wished her friend had not spoken at all. "How did you get the name Eros?" A rude question, but she had no desire to discuss herself.

He grinned, white enamel against dark skin. "What would you like to call me?"

"Your real name."

He held out his hand, waited for her. At last she took it and let him pull her down. She sat erect, uncomfortably so, by his thighs.

"My parents died in a fire when I was just an infant," he said. "My nurse raised me on her own. Ever since I was a little boy I have loved women, all kinds of women. And women seem to love me. So she called me Eros. It was just a joke, but people liked the name." He took the goblet from her hand and sipped her wine. "But you do not like it."

She could see him as a little boy, tiny arms and legs, eyes wide with wonder. Curious and bold, as children often are. But he was a man now. "It is unnatural. For a woman to name a child after

87

a god, it is just . . . ridiculous." And unwise. The god might take offense. Yet as she gazed into his eyes, took in the beauty of him, her argument began to lose its power. "Not to mention that the name brings to mind many qualities, the first . . . the one most people think . . ." He was staring at her, the way Gaius used to stare at her when they were first married.

He brushed the hair above her ear with a finger. "The first quality?"

Her hand trembled. Thank goodness there was little wine left. The next time he touched her she would make sure to feel nothing.

He rose and refilled her goblet. "What is your pleasure, Justina? Do you like art, science, politics? I am versed in all three. Or we could talk more about Eros." He stood completely at ease and gave her a knowing look.

She threw the wine in his face. Strictly an impulsive move and one she did not regret. The shock on his face pleased her. Then he laughed as the wine dripped onto his tunic.

"Thank you. I love new experiences." He wiped his face with his arm. "Now," he pulled her to her feet and took the goblet from her. "Tell me what I did to deserve that."

She was treating him like a boor and he had done nothing wrong. "I do not know." But she did. She hated being out of control and he was too calm, maddeningly calm. She moved out of his grasp. "Is there nothing I can do that will make you angry?"

"I will be sorry if you leave." Neither his stance nor his expression matched his words.

She toyed with the idea of leaving, but that would be too easy. She would gain nothing that way. No bait to dangle in front of her husband and no knowledge that she had conquered her fear. "Then I will stay."

His smile lit up his face. She felt it was the first genuine emotion she had seen from him. For some reason it touched her. "So," she began, searching for a conversation topic. She would not discuss his counterpart and, unlike her companion, she knew little of science and politics. "Tell me what you know of art."

He reached for her hand, pulling her closer. "Are you interested in mosaics? Pottery? What of the statues of the gods? Or the paintings in the dictator's home?"

"You know about all of those?"

He traced the line of her cheek, her eyebrow, trailed his fingers down her arm. "Whatever pleases you."

Amazed at his wealth of knowledge, she almost skipped over his words. "What do you mean *whatever pleases me?*"

"Pleasing you is my duty. Anything you want." He stroked her hands and kissed her fingers. His actions seemed unconscious; he had been seducing women his whole life.

He was offering exactly what she wanted. She should leap into his arms. Instead, her past taunted her with memories. She was using him exactly as others had used her.

"Why do you hesitate? Does my touch not please you?" he asked. "Most women are easily moved by me."

That arrogance again. Irritation rose. She would not degrade herself like this. "I am not most women. This is a mistake. I am sorry to have wasted your time." When she turned to leave, Eros grabbed her by the shoulders, fingers digging into her skin.

"Take your hands off me," Justina snarled. "I will have you whipped for touching me like that."

He lightened his grip but his tawny eyes held hers. "I am not your slave. You are paying for me. Or did you forget?"

She tried to relax, to simply stand while he looked at her. He was beautiful. When had she lost her interest in beautiful men?

"Justina." His voice was gentle. "Please stay. You seemed ill at ease. I thought to distract you with conversation. To seduce you with gentle touches. But you are well aware of what happens between a man and woman." One hand caressed the back of her neck, the other pressed her close.

Her body reacted as it once had with her husband. But he was not her husband. She pushed at his chest. "No, I cannot."

His hands kept her in place. "I have never forced a woman. And I will not now."

Torn, she asked the question that burned in her mind. Its answer would decide her. "How old are you?" She had never been with a younger man and, despite Pomponia's recommendation, she would not start now.

Another flash of white teeth. "Old enough. I was eleven the first time I lay with a woman. Now kiss me and say you do not want me."

The challenge seduced her, she told herself. Not his voice or the tingle of her skin that seemed to breathe on its own. Not the heat between them. She touched her lips to his, a brief meeting of flesh.

"That was not a real kiss." Before she could say another word, his mouth came down on hers and crushed her resistance. And beneath his prowess she tasted a need buried deep inside.

When he lifted his head, she had decided. She would live with this as she had lived with the other agonies of her life. She was doing this for her marriage. For her husband.

"Yes."

# Chapter XIII

Wonder, curiosity, and worry absorbed Livia's mind. How could she advise another person? There must be someone else the lady could see. Counseling was an area where Horatia excelled. Livia had no practice, at least not with the public. Teaching the younger Vestals their roles as priestesses, their functions as servants to Rome, occurred as a natural element of growing older. There was no manual to guide her; she merely passed along what she had learned. Yet the woman had specifically asked for the High Priestess. Not Horatia, but Livia.

If she was to offer guidance, then so be it. Vesta would be with her. And Livia would add some small touches to the meeting room to dispel her anxiety. She pulled two chairs together at one end and set out candles. A small bowl of water to wash the hands and fresh towels. A pitcher of spring water and a tray of fruit.

Everything was ready for the visitor.

Valeria showed the woman into the room. She stood slightly shorter than Livia with a quiet demeanor. Her *stola* was plain, without the decorated border often associated with nobility. The *palla*, usually draped over the head, covered most of her face. She could be any of the million people that inhabited Rome. Why come here?

"Please," Livia said, "be seated."

The woman nodded and moved gracefully to her seat. One hand continued to hold the *palla* in place. The woman's skin was smooth and unlined, the nails clean and trimmed.

Livia sat, uncertain what to do. "There are refreshments, if you like."

"Thank you, no."

For the first time Livia realized how much she counted on facial expressions to aid her with conversation. A smile, the light of interest in the eyes, these little cues relaxed her. Facing this cloaked woman put her at a disadvantage.

The silence drew tight until Livia found her fingers clutching her *stola* for support. Horatia trusted her to carry on. She placed her hands on her lap and breathed in and out, summoning the Goddess.

"May I know your name? Valeria did not inform me, and it is easier, I find, to talk when a relationship is established."

"Please, no names. I am afraid that . . . that he will find out." Her voice sounded weak. Perhaps it was just the cloth covering her mouth.

The secrecy baffled Livia. But the Goddess had brought this woman here for help. "How may I help you?" Livia poured two cups of water and sipped her own. The cool liquid helped maintain her calm.

"I . . . I did not know where else to go. All this time and I have had no one to talk to." She paused and turned her head. Her foot tapped a quick rhythm on the floor.

The poor woman must be nervous talking to a complete stranger. Livia touched her hand, jumped at the woman's sudden jerk, then pressed her hand down gently again. It felt good to comfort, nurture. She could see how Horatia would come to enjoy this act of giving. "Please do not feel embarrassed. The Goddess understands the plight of women. Through her we become strong and selfless."

"Selfless," the stranger said. Bitterness seeped through her voice. "I have tried to be a good wife. Always I put my husband first." Her fist clenched under Livia's hand. Light glinted in her eyes and turned the soft brown to hard ebony. "The choicest meat, the finest wine. We have little but I give him the best of everything."

Livia wondered how that could not be enough.

"And still," her guest continued, "still he . . ."

"Yes?" Livia did her best to give support, courage.

The *palla* lowered barely an inch, just enough to witness the angry red mark beneath the woman's eye. She turned away again, drawing the cloth so her entire face was covered.

Livia started to withdraw her hand in revulsion, but the woman's fingers grabbed and tightened. Stilling the automatic recoil, Livia relaxed her hand. There was no excuse for domestic abuse, but she was not in the position to judge. The gods gave mortals their fate to bear, but no woman deserved that kind of life.

The visitor wiped her eyes. The hint of tears went straight to Livia's heart. There must be something she could say, some words of wisdom that would alleviate this woman's pain and help her chart a new course.

"Have you . . ." the stranger coughed. "Have you ever been in love?" she asked. Her nails dug into Livia's flesh.

The pain this woman must suffer. Livia gently withdrew her hand and rubbed it. Love. That magic she had dreamed of all her life. Like the heroines in the stories of her youth, she longed for love. And as a Vestal she knew little of it. Images of Kaeso winged through her mind, followed by the memory of Gaius's touch. She had thought love was a steady caring that burned through the years, like the deep affection between her parents. Then what was this unsettling feeling with Gaius? And what kind of love allowed a husband to hit his wife?

"I . . . the Vestals . . ." Her cheeks felt warm.

"Your face is red," the woman said. "Are you unwell?" She stared for a moment then focused on smoothing the cloth over her knees. "You must forgive me. I am too blunt and had no right to ask. The Vestals are such gracious servants of Rome and I have certainly overstepped the boundaries of—"

"You have every right to ask. Anything." Livia forced herself to cast aside her wayward thoughts. "You came to me for help. If you cannot speak your deepest feelings, then I am not providing the proper environment."

Even with the *palla* in place, Livia felt her guest smile.

"You are so kind." The woman stroked each finger of her hand, each knuckle as if she were remembering the hardships of her life. "My husband is a good man. Twenty years we have lived together, raised our children, prospered, and sometimes faced defeat. But he never gives up. We never give up. It is just lately . . ."

Such devotion. Livia's heart warmed to think of a relationship that had crossed so many obstacles and continued to survive.

" . . . I fear he is not attracted to me. He seems to have lost interest."

Dear Goddess. Livia wished she could cover her face.

"What am I to do?" the woman asked. "I miss him. The closeness. The companionship. You must know how I can get him back."

The pleading in those eyes. Livia understood the torment, the need for someone to fulfill that ache within. As she searched for an answer, she was not sure whether she asked for herself, or her guest, or both.

The words came from her soul. "Let us pray." She took the woman's hand once more and ignored the vibrations from the foot tapping. "Dearest Vesta. Goddess of the hearth and home. You see before you a woman in need of wisdom. Give her the strength to honor her loved ones. Give her the courage to honor herself. Help her to know what lies within her heart and to speak that truth in a way that serves and heals her. Through the divinity you grant us each and every day, we reach out to you."

Livia bowed her head in the silence that followed the prayer. Peace settled deep within her. Divine energy rippled through her, bathing her cells, her body, her mind with the power of the Goddess. When she raised her head, she knew victory.

"Go to your husband. Say to him, 'I love you. I have loved you all these years. And I will continue to love you until I die. But I am not less than you. From this day forward we are equals.'"

Her guest straightened, breathed deeply. All nervousness seemed to have fled. "Thank you, High Priestess. Those words. Oh, such beautiful words. I knew you could help me. The wisdom of Vesta never fails." She kneeled and kissed Livia's hands then rose without the *palla* in place. Her face glowed with health and vitality. And a vague familiarity. But this time the smile was neither pure nor gracious. "Look at me, Livia. Remember this face. I am the wife of the man you seduce. Your innocent ways do not deceive me. Stay away from Gaius. Stay away from my husband, or you will wish you were never born."

She was gone before Livia could react.

Her husband. Gaius.

A painful flutter started in Livia's stomach, then radiated outward. Dear Goddess, what had she done? The flutter turned to a ceaseless thrum that made her dizzy.

Livia drained the cup of water. Cool liquid flowed down her throat and she called upon her training to still her nerves, to quiet her dread. She wanted to bask in the spirit of the Goddess, the radiance that had filled her when she went within and opened herself to Vesta. She believed in the words she had spoken, known them to be true. But she had given those words to Gaius's wife. Justina. A woman who had come to the *Atrium Vestae* in dishonesty.

*Oh, Vesta*, Livia prayed, *why did you not protect me?*

# Chapter XIV

L ivia woke before the sunrise, anxious about the new day. If her counseling yesterday were any indication of ability, she would forego all future sessions. The middle of her forehead twinged when she remembered Justina's spiteful words.

She was braiding her hair when Valeria knocked at the open door. "Come in," Livia said, wondering if the Vestal brought gloom or joy.

Valeria entered the room and bowed.

Only yesterday they seemed like equals. Now Livia wore the robes of power. She doubted she would get used to it. "Shall we go to the market this morning?" she asked, injecting a positive tone to offset her edginess. "I have a craving for something sweet. Perhaps some apples with honey and fresh cream." She could already taste the spicy concoction.

"You have been summoned." Valeria held out a sealed note. Her hand quivered.

"Who . . ."

Valeria shook her head. Livia broke open the message.

*Your presence is requested by the Consul Gaius Terentius Varro.*

Why was the Pontifex Maximus not here? He was the one who governed the Vestals. Fear blocked Livia's breathing. She placed her hand over her heart and felt nothing.

"The guard waits outside. There is a carriage for you."

A carriage? The Consul met with the Senate in the *Curia*, just a short way from the temple. She could walk there. With a rush, her breathing began again. The uneasiness remained.

Valeria gnawed her bottom lip and rubbed her fingers.

Serene Valeria. Worry did not sit well with her. "I go to see the Consul," Livia said. "I will be back shortly."

"The Consul? What have you . . ." She stopped, as if remembering she was no longer questioning an equal.

Livia touched Valeria's hand. A gentle touch, as from a mother to a child, as much to soothe herself as the other. "I am sure it is nothing." Her lie trembled in her throat and shriveled the inside of her mouth.

The horse-drawn *carpentum* felt pretentious, as if she were hiding from someone, or something. She preferred to walk whenever possible but this time she had no say in the matter. When the Consul summoned, you obeyed. Horatia rode in carriages from time to time and seemed none the worse for it.

The wheels clattered down the roads, the rhythmic sound accentuating Livia's nervousness. What could he want with her? Valeria was right to ask, though a subordinate did not interrogate her superior. Still, the question remained. What had she done? The temple was clean, the sacred flame burned bright. Every morning and evening the Vestals prayed to the Goddess for harmony and goodwill throughout Rome. Livia blessed the Vestals before bed and burned sage for mental clarity to help her with her role as High Priestess.

For the moment, Rome was at peace. Talk of war continued and the people wanted retribution for the last slaughter at Lake Trasemine. But there was no word of movement. She wondered how Gaius felt. When they last spoke he seemed reluctant to fight. Did anyone really enjoy bloodshed? No, what a ridiculous thought. People did not want to harm each other. They fought because of stubbornness and pride and misplaced ideas of ownership.

"We are here, High Priestess."

The guard opened the carriage door and helped Livia to alight. She faced a house with the doorway in a shaded entrance. The guard stood behind her. Had she been alone, she would have surveyed the premises for a sense of location. But there was no time for that.

A servant led her through the atrium to a small chamber with two chairs, a table, a platter of grapes, two glasses of wine. Tapestries hung on the walls, barely visible in the pervading darkness. Livia's skin chilled as she stood and waited. Minutes passed and her legs grew heavy with fatigue, but she could not sit without invitation.

To pass the time she studied one of the tapestries. Soldiers clashed with drawn swords. Horses struggled on a slippery slope. Blood dripped from ghoulish wounds. Livia thought of the tapestries made by Davina's skilled fingers, colors of the sun and sky melded in warmth and hope, a tribute to the spirit. Not the despair of battle that she faced now.

"High Priestess."

She turned toward the voice and bowed. "Consul." When she raised her head, revulsion raced through her body. It was Publius Postumius Albus. "You!"

"So you do recognize me. I had hoped you would." He sprawled in the chair and hooked one leg over the side.

Memories flooded her mind, crawled beneath her skin like an angry insect. She wanted to run from his sight but her legs refused to move. Twenty years had passed since she had last seen Gaius's father. "You are not the Consul."

"He was unavoidably detained."

She would not let his rudeness upset her. Not this time. She shifted her weight to ease the discomfort in her legs and called upon the Goddess for patience and courage. Horatia would be calm throughout this, and strong. Yet Horatia did not have a history with this offensive man.

Publius waved his hand. "Oh, please, have a seat. Women faint so easily these days."

Livia sat and asked in a guarded tone, "Why have you called me here?"

He appraised her, as if she were an animal for sale. Gray tipped the ends of his hair, once almost as black as hers. Deep furrows creased the sides of his mouth and a fan of wrinkles swooped upwards from the dark eyes that slowly perused her body, lingering at her breasts and the joining of her thighs. She pressed her legs together as if she could ward off his imaginary fingers. She thought of Gaius and wondered how such a golden god could come from a man like this.

"There will be no more talk of equality for women."

She gasped in surprise. Equality? How had he known? She had only mentioned such a thing yesterday, when she counseled . . . Justina. Gaius's wife. She must have talked to Publius. Was the woman's confidence just a façade? Was she really so meek that she needed a champion? "Women deserve equality. There is nothing wrong with that."

Publius drained his wine. "Everything is wrong with it. Women have never been equals and never shall be. Females are meant to satisfy men," his eyes gleamed with an arrogant light, "to raise children, and to build a proper home. That is all."

"How can that be all? Women are intelligent. They have strength and courage and wisdom. A woman could govern Rome just as easily as a man." She drew in a breath, invigorated by her passion. "And do it better."

"Meddling women. This is exactly why Tarquin the Elder established chastity for the Vestals. Four hundred years ago they were getting in the way of the ruling class. I see nothing has changed." He slammed his goblet on the table. "You will do as I order. This is not open to debate."

On her own, she might have cowered. But Vesta herself had given Livia those words. Ones that had felt so right, so powerful. To deny them would be to deny her very foundation. She rose to her feet. "I obey the Goddess."

Publius's fist smashed the grapes into pulp. Juice spattered Livia's *stola*. "You obey Rome!" He licked fruit residue off his hand and circled the table until he loomed over her. His breath reeked of wine and something stale. "I have missed you, Livia. All this time and never a word from you." His fingers stroked her cheek. "You may leave now. But be warned. Rome will not be so lenient next time." He flicked his fingers at her in dismissal.

Livia hurried outside before Publius could witness her tears. She was the High Priestess. She commanded respect. Why then did she feel like an ordinary servant? Years ago she had hated Publius for his ability to humiliate people. She had done her best to submerge her memories, her feelings, but this meeting resurrected them.

Gaius came down the walkway as she stepped into the carriage.

"Livia. Why are you at my father's house?"

She could not speak.

"What has he done to you?"

She shook her head.

"Has he hurt you?" Gaius demanded.

Tear-stained eyes met his then she turned her head. She simply wanted privacy. The carriage moved away.

"He will not get away with this," he called after her.

"Publius! By the gods, I . . . Where are you?"Gaius shouted as he barged into his father's house, pushed aside the servant, and stormed down the corridor. He found his father in the small room used for private meetings. "If you hurt her, I will—"

"Gaius. How nice of you to visit me."

"She was crying. What have you done to her?"

"Sit down. Have some wine." Publius offered the untouched cup.

Gaius nearly swatted the cup out of his father's hand. Instead, he gripped the back of the chair.

"Who are we discussing?" Publius asked.

"Livia. She is everything to me." He had not meant to say that. His father's eyes pierced him with the steady gaze that used to make him squirm. Even now Gaius felt the edge in that stare.

"You have a wife. Save your feelings for her."

"You know that Justina and I . . . I have no feelings for her."

"Then you are a fool. She is exactly the woman you need."

"Need? What do you mean by that?"

"Sit down, Gaius. You make me nervous."

No one made Publius nervous. It was just a ploy to bring him down to his father's level. "I prefer to stand."

"As you wish." He sighed. "Justina cares for you."

"She only cares for my money. My position." The one his father had bought for him.

"One you seem to care little about." Publius let the barb sink in while he sipped his wine. "She wants you to succeed. There are worse things in life than a woman who appreciates power."

Gaius said nothing.

"You used to find her irresistible," Publius said.

"I was infatuated with her beauty." And her skills. "I have loved only one woman."

"Do you think I am blind to what goes on around me? Do you think I did not see the attraction between you two? I still remember her visit to our house. My six-year-old son lapping at the heels of a woman ten years older. You were pitiful."

"I was in love."

Publius continued as if he had not heard. "She would have made an excellent wife. Sweet, considerate, submissive. But she is a Vestal. You cannot have her."

"I already have." The bald-faced lie soothed Gaius's temper.

"I am not so easily provoked."

"I merely state the facts."

"You would not dare such a forbidden thing."

"I would. But I did not come here to discuss my love for—"

"Love means nothing. A man is only remembered for his accomplishments."

"You are wrong. Just because you never loved Mother—"

"I loved your mother in the beginning." For a moment Publius lost his focus, seemed to look inward. A smile touched his lips and the stern face warmed, youthened. Then he grimaced. "By the time I was your age I had two sons. They took precedence."

"Only one son mattered. My brother."

"And he was taken from me." Publius threw his cup across the room. Wine ran in crimson currents down the wall.

Gaius tensed against the old pain. "I feel his loss too."

The empty eyes that gazed back belonged to a stranger. "Your brother died in my arms. You will never know how that feels."

The old wound festered again. Gaius drew in a deep breath. "Enough. I came to ask your permission to resign my post."

Publius slumped in his chair. "What are you talking about?"

"I am tired of war. I have no desire to command the troops any longer. Let someone else take my place."

"It is not your decision."

How many times had he cowed before the man that had dictated his every move for twenty-six years? This time would be different. "It is *my* life. I will do what I want with it."

Publius sneered. "And what will that be?"

The answer was simple. Perfect. He would spend it with Livia. But his father would want something more logical. Gaius had always dreamed of the ocean. He could hear the roar of the waves, feel the rise and fall of the deck beneath his feet. Taste the salt on his lips. "I will go to sea. I have always wanted to sail. The water is in my blood."

"The only thing in your blood is stupidity. You will command your troops until I give you leave to do otherwise. Now get out of my sight." Publius waved a hand in dismissal, as if his son were under his command.

A small muscle below Gaius's chin began to pulse. "I know how you look at me. I see you hoping for a glimpse of my brother. But I am your son too, *Father*. When will you accept me for what I am?"

With a roar, Publius lurched to his feet and crashed against the table. Grapes and wine tumbled to the floor in a purple mess. A large vein on his temple sprang to life with grotesque twitches as if it would leap off his face. He gave his son a mighty shove. "Get out!"

# Chapter XV

Pain shrieked through Livia's head. She massaged her temples to alleviate the throbbing, but the pressure only made it worse. She longed to throw dishes in the kitchen, to watch the pottery break into shards, to hear them smash against the floor. But a High Priestess did not indulge in tantrums. Instead, she tugged at the bed linens, pulling and pulling until the sheets and coverlet were a tumbled mess upon the carpet. Then she stamped on them, over and over, seeing Publius's face beneath her foot as the fine cloth flattened and wadded and stained from the dust on her sandals. And finally, she slumped to the floor, fingers pressing into her head in a vain attempt to isolate the pain and pluck it out.

If she sat completely still with her eyes closed, the ache was manageable. Snatches of conversation flitted through her mind. Women who used headaches as an excuse to avoid sex. Why she would think of that now she had no idea. Nothing could be as bad as this awful pulsing that filled her mind with a hollow drumbeat, on and on, its rhythm so constant that she wanted to shut out everything around her and just dissolve into oblivion.

She needed to see to the lessons, make sure the flame was being watched, speak to Patricia about marketing.

Her mind drifted again to sex. The physical act between man and woman that had existed since the beginning of civilization. Perhaps even before. What was it like? Did it indeed bring pleasure? Livia envied the girls who were made brides in their teenage years when romance ran strong and true. How wonderful to fall in love with a handsome boy, to wed, to bear children. To round out your days with a happy family and the constant support of a devoted husband.

A dagger of pain plunged between her eyes. She let out a muffled moan and prayed for release. Minutes passed until the agony dulled enough to let her mind wander anew. Kaeso. Her friend, her trusted companion, the man she would soon marry. She had let her obligations come between them. The day of her last visit rose in her memory, the revelry, the childish teasing. Their closeness. How she missed that. How she missed him. Yet even as she tried to concentrate on those moments her mind conjured the image of another.

Gaius's concern for her, his determination to make things right, flowed within, as steady as the gush of water at the sacred spring. Livia turned her face into her pillow, breathed in the calm of lavender. These were the musings of a troubled soul, not worthy of a Vestal. She moistened her finger with saliva and rubbed it behind her ear to rid herself of these unwanted thoughts.

"Leave me," she whispered. "I cannot think of you now."

A banging in the distance disturbed the quiet. The door to her room opened. "Your pardon, High Priestess," Valeria said. "A visitor awaits."

"I am ill. Surely you can see to her needs in my absence." She did not mean her words to be so harsh.

There was a pause. "It is a man."

Livia opened her eyes. Valeria stood with her head bowed, patiently waiting. The perfect model of submission. Publius would never have chastised Valeria. "Send him away."

Valeria maintained her pose. "He is in the atrium." Her thumbs brushed against each other once. "Antonia is with him."

Livia sat up and swayed, her head heavy, her body sluggish. Few came to the *Atrium Vestae* uninvited. A man . . . And to leave him with a young girl . . .

Valeria raised her eyes. In that single glance Livia knew. She swept out of the room, shaking off the dizziness that threatened to engulf her.

Antonia's voice drifted through the corridor, talking easily of herbs and potions, her latest fixation. She was describing the methods to produce tinctures and extracts. They made a charming picture, two blond heads next to each other on a simple bench beside the *impluvium*.

"Thank you, Antonia," Livia said, her smile forced, her eyes on the child. "You may go now."

Antonia shook the man's hand, gave Livia a great hug, and flitted away.

At last, Livia faced her visitor. She was too fragile now. He should not see her like this. And she should not be alone with him. "You are not welcome here."

"You were in tears when I saw you." Gaius cupped her cheek, gazed into her eyes. "I had to make sure you were alright."

Livia stepped back from his touch. "As you can see, I am fine. Now please go."

"Come away with me."

How easily he made demands. "I have duties to perform. People count on me." The last was strictly an excuse. The temple would run quite well without her. For a time.

"If not today, then tomorrow. Just for a day, Livia. Even a High Priestess can spare one day." He stepped forward and held her wrist, stroking just below her thumb.

She did her best to disregard his touch and focus on his words. One day. One day to escape her responsibilities. Then she remembered Kaeso, another who had suffered because of her position. "I must see a . . ." There was no need to elaborate. Her personal life was her own. "Someone is expecting me." She had ignored him too long.

Gaius smiled. "Visit your friend this afternoon. Or when you return. One day will make no difference."

Why did her heart melt when he smiled? Such a silly thing. Her mother had said the same about her father.

Gaius held her hand, stroked her fingers. "I will send a carriage for you tomorrow. I have somewhere special to take you."

"No, I cannot." But her protest was half-hearted and he was already taking his leave. As he disappeared down the hall she knew she should have been firm. Gaius did not command her life. Yet she could not ignore how his visit sparked a gladness within her.

Her headache faded. Contentment bloomed slowly in her heart that afternoon. She would visit Kaeso after her return, as Gaius suggested. For now she reflected on her daily chores and let the excitement of anticipation drown out her previous anxiety. Publius belonged in the past and there he would stay. One chance encounter with him would not ruin her life or even one morning of her existence. He was neither the dictator nor the consul. He had no power over her.

She was the *Vestalis Maxima*. The one chosen by Rome to lead the Vestals. No one could tell her what to do.

The glow of importance infused her being. She caught herself smiling at odd moments, laughing at the simplest remarks during the evening meal. Finally, Antonia asked, "Is it Gaius that makes you laugh so? Will he come back tomorrow?"

The innocent words dampened her glee. How easy it was to think she was above reproach, to assume no one noticed or remembered her activities. She must be more aware. With a gentle voice, she answered, "You are so kind, Antonia, to make him welcome here. But, no, he will not be back. He has his own home to attend to." And a wife. "It is time to retire."

"We must have a story first," Antonia said.

Livia nodded. "We must."

While Valeria guarded the sacred flame, Patricia cleared the food and dishes and young Oppia swept the floor. Then the Vestals settled on pillows in the meeting room. Antonia nestled in Livia's lap. A spider clambered across the pillow and up onto the girl's hand. She smiled in delight. "Will you tell the tale of Arachne?" she asked.

Livia watched the tiny creature. Was this a sign? "Many years ago," she began, "there was a young girl in Greece named Arachne. She was beautiful, with hair of gold and eyes as blue as the sea." Like the man who had visited her today. "What Arachne loved best was to spin and weave. She used flax and wool and silk and she made tapestries so fine that people came from all over to see them. And Arachne claimed her tapestries were the best in all the world."

"You know someone who weaves beautiful pictures," Antonia said.

"Yes, Davina is very gifted."

"Is she as gifted as Arachne?" Oppia asked.

"That is not for me to say. One day a woman asked Arachne who had taught her to weave. The young girl said no one; she had learned it on her own. Then the woman said maybe it was Minerva, the patron goddess of weaving. The girl scoffed at the idea. How could Minerva teach her such a skill? No one could spin or weave as she could, and she would show Minerva a thing or two."

"In Greece, Minerva is called Athena, is she not?" Oppia asked.

"Yes, she is."

"If the gods were in Greece first, why do we call them by different names?"

Livia had asked the same herself as a child. "Once Greece was the highest civilization and the gods had Greek names. Then Rome became the ruler and the gods were given Roman names." The simple answer seemed to satisfy Oppia, but Livia often wondered what would happen if Rome were ever conquered.

"Go on, Livia," Antonia said.

"The goddess appeared as an old woman and warned Arachne about offending the gods. But Arachne did not change her words. Then Minerva revealed her true form and stood tall and stern, with eyes of gray that were sharp and bright. She challenged Arachne to a contest. They would each weave and Jupiter would judge. If Arachne won, then Minerva would weave no more. But if Minerva won, then Arachne would never weave again. Arachne agreed.

"Minerva began. She took sunbeams and summer clouds and the blue of the sky and the green of the fields and she wove pictures of the history of the gods, and all who looked at her tapestry were taken with its beauty and wonder.

"Then Arachne took her finest silk and wove a web so light and fine that it floated on the air. In it she portrayed the gods and their infidelities. Even though she showed no respect for the gods, her work was brilliant. Flawless.

"In anger, Minerva destroyed Arachne's work and her loom. And in the goddess's rage, she turned Arachne into a spider. A disgusting creature, but one with the skill to weave."

"They are not disgusting," Antonia said. "They are wonderful." She nudged the spider onto her other hand. "Poor Arachne. As much as I admire spiders, I would much rather stay a human. Sorry, little one," she said.

"Exactly," Livia said. "The gods can be vengeful. Let none of us forget that."

The Vestals gathered in a circle for their evening prayer. With heads bowed, they asked for Vesta's blessing for continued peace and goodwill.

Livia kissed Antonia's forehead. "To bed, now." She watched the Vestals rise and depart for their chambers.

The spider paused on the pillow where it seemed to study Livia before moving on. She had learned her lesson. No more of her petty boasts, silent or otherwise, that could lead the way to danger. She would weave her web with caution.

# Chapter XVI

The small confines of Livia's chamber were inadequate for pacing. There was barely room for two strides before she ran into the bed or the narrow cupboard where she stored her clothes. She bristled with anxiety but there was nowhere to go. With a groan, she separated her hair into the required six sections and began plaiting them. Almost thirty years of living in accordance with the rules of Rome and she still felt that rebellious spark. Gaius had said just one day. Freedom to be as she wished, to do as she wished. What a glorious notion. She longed to take advantage of that rich promise. Yet the lesson of Arachne weighed on her. She coiled the braids around her head and settled her *palla* over them. She would meet Gaius as planned. It would be rude not to. But there would be no outing.

The carriage ride to Ostia relaxed her. A *lictor* drove. Not Titus, who had been called for other duty, but someone to watch over her. All was well. Livia leaned her head against the seat back and closed her eyes. Sunlight splashed over her lids and warmed her face. She could be a young wife traveling to meet her husband. They would celebrate their love and pledge themselves to each other for all time in a secluded place away from the public. The romantic notion swirled in her mind and filled her with yearning for the day when she would finally settle into married life. There was still the possibility of children. She was old for that, she knew. With age came complications. But the monthly reminder kept her hope alive.

Her fingers gripped the edge of the seat while she looked out across wide grassy fields. Today was not a day for dreams. These meetings with Gaius must come to an end. She was pledged to Kaeso, her childhood companion. The man who would move heaven and earth to make her happy. Why then did Gaius fill her thoughts? She had spent more time lately with him than the man she planned to marry. Tension inched along her neck and shoulders as the carriage came to a stop.

In all the hours pondering this meeting she had never imagined Gaius on horseback. He sat erect, his simple tunic grazing his thighs, skin and muscle and strength exuding from his quiet pose. Like a beautiful marble statue come to life. And the horse. Black did not describe the color. It was more an extension of darkness, a flowing of night that intercepted the light of day.

Warmth flickered in her chest and lit her cheeks.

"Good morning," he said. The horse shook his head and stamped his front hoof. "Livia, meet Apollyon."

The Greek word for destroyer. "I can see why you would name him that. He is enormous."

"He is a war horse," Gaius said, as if that clarified everything.

She nodded, hesitant to end the illusion. Perhaps they could spend a few minutes in idle conversation before she must return. "It is a beautiful day."

"A perfect day for what I have in mind." Gaius slid from the horse's back and tied Apollyon to the *carpentum*. The *lictor* alighted, accepted payment, and walked away toward the city.

Where was the man going? What was happening?

"Are you ready for an adventure?" Gaius asked.

It sounded like the perfect antidote to yesterday's worries. But . . . "Every day is an adventure of life. One moment full of fear," she shivered at her choice, "the next full of gladness. It was a joy to ride out here, to . . . meet your horse. But I must return. The temple awaits."

"The temple will still be there this evening."

"I am needed now."

"Yes, here."

"Gaius, the *Vestalis Maxima* does not have time to dally."

"You have no choice, Livia. You made a promise."

She had not, unless by her silence. Truthfully, she was curious about the adventure. What did he have in mind? She would never know unless she accompanied him.

The temple could wait. Valeria was extremely capable. All the Vestals were.

"I will go with you. But only for a short time."

He grinned. His obvious joy embraced her, softened her resistance.

Gaius took the reins and the carriage rolled out. The road took them to the seaport of Ostia and beyond. Fields flattened and turned to marshy areas then sandy expanses. The smell of salt wafted on the breeze. They turned south down the coast for several miles. In the distance sunlight glittered on the water.

Gaius stopped the *carpentum* in a covered area and helped Livia out. "Your adventure," he said with a broad wave of his arm.

The sea pulled at her with invisible strings, lifting her, breathing with her. She was here, at the place she had dreamed of. But there was no ship. "When do we sail?"

"There will be no sailing today." He untied Apollyon and took Livia's hand. Their palms kissed, warmed. She had often held hands with Kaeso and enjoyed the connection. She squeezed Gaius's fingers and smiled in delight when he squeezed back.

Together they walked towards the water. "I have something better."

She was rocking, rocking, in a rhythm as timeless as the flow of the tide. Above, the endless sky stretched to the horizon, warm and clear without a cloud in sight. Power surged between her legs and she closed her eyes, lifting her hands into the air in complete surrender. Nothing could have prepared her for this feeling, this utter wonder, this bliss as sea spray drenched her face and hair. For this moment she had no cares. She simply soared.

They slowed to a trot, then a walk along the shore. Each step heightened her awareness of the man behind her. The smell of leather and male and salty air wrapped Livia in a fine mist.

The horse's muscles bunched and shifted. She touched the ripples along Apollyon's shoulder as her body swayed with the movement. Carrying two people seemed to be no strain for the animal. Indeed, she could stay like this all day, on top of the world with the wind blowing across her hair and face. Her *palla* lay draped around her neck. Her *stola* gathered about her legs, exposing her calves to the air. A scandalous exhibition of skin. But there was no one to see her, no one to pass judgment. She had tried sitting sideways on the saddle, a more ladylike position, and started to slide off with the first few steps. After some convincing from Gaius, she sat astride, embarrassed at first, until success made her admit he was right.

His hand rested warm upon her arm. "I am glad you are here with me."

She wanted to say the same, to tell him how his touch steadied her, how the solidness of his body comforted her, how she wanted to lean back into the security of his arms. But the words would not come. There was something more about him, something she did not have with Kaeso. The excitement he made her feel worried her. To calm her concern she focused on the water. "Will you sail someday?" she asked. "Will you realize your dream?"

His arms tightened around her. Apollyon's body tensed, as did her own. A strange wanting rippled through her. "I spoke to my father about that yesterday. I asked him for permission to resign my command. He refused."

Pain flickered at the memory of his father. But it could not hold court with the brilliance of sun and water.

Gaius dismounted and held onto the reins. Water licked at his ankles, splashed across his sandals. "No more dark thoughts. This is a day of pleasure." As Apollyon continued along the beach, Gaius ran his fingers down Livia's leg, tickling her. Her leg jerked in response then she wished he would graze her skin again. "When did you first fall in love with the sea?" he asked.

"When I was a little girl. My father held my hand while I stood on the sand and the waves splashed over me. I saw a face in the water. A beautiful woman, kind, with eyes that sparkled. I wanted to follow her but my father held onto me."

"You saw a Nereid?"

"Perhaps. My father does not believe in sea nymphs, but she was real to me. I envied her freedom."

"You are my Nereid." He stroked her leg. "Someday we will be free to sail. Would you sail with me, Livia?"

He was speaking only of make-believe but how she would love to leave this life and live on the water. If she shaded her eyes she could just make out a flash of white far on the horizon. A ship, she imagined, bound for India to buy pepper or ginger. What luxury to travel across the water, friend to all creatures of the sea, with the sun to warm you by day and the stars to guide you at night. What a wonderful fantasy. "Yes, I would sail with you."

"Then we shall. In the meantime . . ." He slapped Apollyon on the rump and the horse broke into a canter. Livia screamed in surprise. "Hold on," he yelled.

Thrown forward, she snatched at the horse's mane, fingers tangled in the long hairs that flowed against gleaming ebony. The shore streamed by while she prayed not to fall off the monstrous animal. After long moments her body adjusted to the horse's gait, an easy back and forth rocking just as before when she rode with Gaius. She did not need him to lean against. She was safe on her own. The breeze blew across her face. The sun warmed her back. Water splashed her ankles and still she rode on in dreamy wonder, her legs hugging the horse's body while she gained the nerve to let go with one hand, then the other.

She was free. Free to swim like a sea nymph. Free to fly like a bird.

A sharp whistle slowed the horse then another command reversed his direction toward Gaius. Livia breathed heavily, exhilarated by the ride and the primal energy of horse and water. She hugged herself while her eyes watered with joy.

Gaius patted Apollyon's neck and gently rubbed the horse's nose. "A special reward tonight for you, my friend."

"You could have killed me," Livia said, half teasing. "I could have fallen off and been trampled."

Gaius smiled up at her. "Never. Apollyon is always careful." He helped her slide off, holding her against his chest until her feet touched the ground.

Her pulse jumped. They remained that way for a moment before he released her and took her hand. "Are you settling into your routine as High Priestess?"

The sand caressed her arches, squished between her toes. She had missed the sea's tranquility, the way it somehow eased the uneven spaces within her and allowed her to breathe deeply, evenly. But that evenness was punctuated with erratic pauses. "I doubt I will ever settle in. I fear I worry too much about things I cannot change."

"Then let us be content with what we have."

Contentment. Lately it seemed to run away from her. She had been raised to accept her life, to abide by the wishes of Rome. To always serve the Goddess. Vestals before her had endured with grace and pride and gone on to live in peace and happiness.

Only a short time spanned the bridge between servitude and her own freedom. She looked at the man at her side then out at the sea, the place which had brought her this small piece of satisfaction. When she was married . . . Guilt hissed at her with its forked tongue and a shiver started deep inside. How could she enjoy this day so much with another man? A married man?

Gaius turned her to face him. "Livia, will you have me? I have dreamed of you for so long. We are meant to be together. Will you have me as your own?" Before she could answer he put his fingers to her lips. Then he kissed her. Not on the cheek as Kaeso did, but mouth on mouth as husband to wife. His lips were soft, warm, with a hint of salt and some unknown flavor. The kiss lingered, unhurried, until the heavy weight around her heart relaxed and she leaned against him, safe, secure, at peace.

Afterwards they walked back to the carriage and he drove her to the *Atrium Vestae*. If he said goodbye she did not notice. If they were to meet again she did not know. Somehow she walked up the stairs and inside.

# Chapter XVII

She would think of him, Gaius was certain of that. The joy on Livia's face when she came toward him after her ride matched the way he felt about her. If her feelings for him were not yet as strong, they would grow. He had dreamed of her for twenty years. He could afford a little more patience. But soon they would be together.

The diplomacy of trade intrigued him. He enjoyed the repartee, the give and take, so different from the direct orders of military life. With wealthy merchants he could engage in intelligent conversation, dine on savory food and wine, relax amid luxurious surroundings. But he was glad to be back in Rome, home again. Near Livia.

He strode into his house, welcoming the cool respite from the summer sun. In his excitement to finally spend time with Livia, he had forgotten her fair skin and the cruelty of the heat. He would have to be more careful in the future.

All was quiet. Strange that the servants did not make their usual noisy patter cleaning rooms or preparing food for the evening meal. His wife might be any number of places. They kept no schedule of each other, and as long as Justina fulfilled her role at the occasional dinner and public gathering, he neither cared nor wanted to know how she whiled away the hours. Sometimes he wondered about her. About them. If he had been less swayed by her beauty and his father's demands, how would his life have turned out? Did she really want him? Or did she only crave power, as Publius said. Surely, if power were her ambition, she could have found someone more worthy. Someone with whom her charms would last.

He poured wine to quench his thirst and remembered a time early on when he had just returned from battle, weary and aching. He wanted to sleep for weeks without interruption, but first he had met with Justina and presented a gift. A perfume bottle in shades of green—her favorite color. A small token he hoped she would like. She had cradled the glass in her hands, delicately stroking its smooth curves, her eyes shining with childish delight. Her obvious joy warmed his heart. She then led him to bed, undressed him, bathed his body and covered him with clean linens, and lay down beside him while she stroked his head and whispered how much she loved her gift.

Never in all that time, Gaius recalled, had she said she loved *him*.

He finished his wine and walked down the corridor to the room he thought of as his library. Scrolls on strategy collided with maps and drawings of past battles. Gaius headed for a small cabinet in the far corner where he kept special belongings. He retrieved a leather pouch and extracted a gold ring set with a large ruby. After his latest negotiations with Hiero II in Syracuse, the grain supplier pressed it into his hand. "A little something for you or your wife," he said. "To inspire courage or protect you from danger." Then he leaned close. "It also works wonders in the bedroom." Gaius had smiled graciously and pocketed the ring but it would not be for his wife. No, he would give the ring to the one he truly loved. Holding it in his hand, he felt her, as if Livia were standing beside him. He had waited for the right moment to give it to her. Now was the time.

Laughter broke the silence. Then voices drifted down the hall. Gaius replaced the ring in the pouch and followed the sound. At the door to Justina's room he stopped. On the bed a man and woman lay face to face, naked bodies tangled. Justina. And a stranger.

A man younger than she.

Fury raised him up and smashed him like the grapes on his father's table. Even though Gaius had told himself Justina could live as she liked, the proof of her affair revolted him. She dared to bring another man into their house?

He watched while she caressed the jaw of this stranger and felt a callus grow over his heart. "Forgive me for interrupting," Gaius said. "I thought no one was home."

The man jerked and pulled on the sheets to cover them but Justina stayed his hand. She smiled at Gaius and turned to fully expose her body. "Hello, husband. I did not expect you back so soon." She plucked a date from a nearby platter and bit into it slowly, eyeing Gaius with her play of lips and teeth. "Will you join us? As you can see, we have wine and fruit."

Her partner looked from her to Gaius with a helpless gaze. "I must go, Justina."

She kept him trapped with her leg over his and her hand about his wrist. "There is no need, Eros. Is there, husband?"

"No," he agreed. There was no need for there was no love. Had there ever been love? "Excuse me. I will leave you two alone."

Without any argument, Justina had given him what he needed, an excuse to be free of her, to spend his time with Livia. Why then did he feel such pain?

He left the room, the house which moments before had felt peaceful, and walked into the street. He had no destination in mind, other than being far away from the poison he had once called his wife.

Justina stretched in the sated aftermath of sex. The sheets were still warm, still redolent with the earthy smell of their bodies. She passed her hand over the imprint of her lover. *Lover.* The word rolled in her mind in tantalizing deliciousness. As much as she had feared compromising herself for an affair, the sex bolstered her confidence which had lagged from Gaius's negligence. Eros had called out her name when he climaxed, this young man with the body of a god and a philosopher's wit. "Justina" echoed in the room and whispered down the hall. He was so sweet, wanting so much to please her. Unlike her husband. How many men still cared about pleasing their wives? She could not even count a handful.

She slid her toes across silken softness and recalled the look on Gaius's face. Oh, the luscious satisfaction of revenge. She had not seen such anger in years. Gaius, the diplomat, the leader of men, the stoic who treated her with no emotion. Well, Justina smiled, he could still be moved. Let him see who had the power.

Pomponia was right after all. A lover was good for a woman's well-being. Bringing Eros to the house had been risky, a move Justina worried over for hours. It was a measure of her resolve, and in the end a good one. Yet she would not have foreseen the glorious consequences.

Her body felt well-used and honored. The attention he paid every inch of skin, every fold, with soft caresses then rough desire, as if he could not hold his passion but was forced to empty it into a sacred vessel to be offered to the gods. Even Gaius had not shown her such devotion. If she were a reader of souls, she would say that Eros had pledged his to her. It was a pity she would eventually cast him off.

She reached for more wine and knocked over the cup. Deep red licked the white linen, devouring the pristine cloth. Irritated, Justina pushed away the sheet and left the room, padding naked down the hall, the floor cool against her bare feet. Fingers trailed along the walls, grazing over bumps and rough nubs too small to notice. She stopped at Gaius's study, a room she rarely entered. The maps and drawings held no interest but something drew her in, as if an invisible hand pulled her along. Excitement shivered across her breasts and for a moment she touched her flesh, briefly caressing herself. Then she moved inside, the mustiness of parchment harsh after the heady taste of lovemaking.

There was nothing to catch her eye, no baubles, no glints of bright color. Uninspired, she sank into Gaius's chair and spread her hands out on his desk over a map of Lake Trasemine. The battle was horrible, she knew, though she had dismissed any talk of the details. She traced the curves around the lake, her mind calling up his words from last year: *Leave it alone, Justina. You do not want to know.* She had never asked again.

Her hands gripped the chair arms. It was hard not to get caught up in fear when the city constantly talked of Hannibal. Was Rome in danger? What did Livia think of battle? Such a fragile woman was clearly unsuited for a soldier's life. What was Gaius thinking? She pounded the desk and turned her body.

Her glance landed on a small, brown pouch. Inside it, she discovered jewelry. A stone of dark red that seemed to pulse with life. A vibrant red like blood against her skin. She slipped the ring on her finger, the clasp of metal cool, stimulating. All this time she thought he was neglecting her and he was just waiting for the right time to present his gift. She preferred green, but the workmanship was exquisite, the gem obviously costly. A gift she would savor. With regret, she put the ring back in the pouch and returned to her room.

The anger in his eyes when he saw her with Eros made perfect sense now. If Gaius did not care, there would be no emotion. But to have such rage meant he wanted her. Her plan was working beautifully.

There was much to think about. The perfect dinner to woo her husband back, a massage with scented oils to showcase her body. Thank the gods she was still young. Beauty had its advantages. She would forgive Gaius for lusting after another. People made mistakes. She had made one with Eros, but all was in the past and they would start anew.

Justina rubbed her lips, dry from the heavy kissing of her assignation. She must remember to anoint them with a soothing balm. It was a woman's duty to prepare herself, to keep the illusion of youth as long as possible. She doubted the Vestals paid such attention to their bodies, and it was there she would triumph. She knew Gaius's likes and dislikes, his favorite positions, what excited him. She knew how to use her body to bring him pleasure. Mistaken were the men who thought women were weak. Women had the power to control a man's desire, to bring children into the world . . . She stopped and cradled her abdomen, gently held the barren center that would never know life, the emptiness that was the hunger and violence of her own childhood. No, she was better off without that burden.

There was still one responsibility. She had ignored him of late and it was time to check on him, to make sure he was following her instructions.

# Chapter XVIII

Gaius sat on a hard stool in the tavern's shadows. The lower classes crowded the bar, leaning against the counter in various poses of drunkenness. The bartender sloshed wine and men elbowed and shoved each other and yelled over the constant din. It was possible his own servants frequented this establishment.

He pulled the hood of his robe down to cover his face, watching the scene. Rage pounded him like the waves upon the sand, casting him high then pummeling him with brute force. Had Justina taken a lover quietly he would not feel this shame, but to cuckold him . . . How dare she wound him this way? Word would spread throughout the city. He would be laughed at, pitied. He would not allow that from his friends, and especially not from strangers.

He slammed his mug on the table, forgetting his desire to be unobserved. A nearby group of men glowered at the intrusion then went back to their gossip.

"Only five *denarii* to sway the vote," one man said. "Not much backbone for a Senator. I would have demanded at least three times that much."

"And bedded his wife," another said.

The others roared and clapped the speaker on the back.

Gaius squeezed his cup. One sip when he first sat down had convinced him not to take another. The crude wine burned his throat. How the peasants drank this swill he did not know.

The din increased then voices chanted "Eros, Eros." In the dim light the man seemed to be part specter as he moved through the shadows, his skin casting an eerie glow then seeming to disappear. Several men gathered round him and pushed him to the front of the bar.

"Wine for the conqueror," one said.

Others gave him forceful slams on the back and shoulders. Eros grinned and slammed them back in kind. Their cups were raised.

"A toast to the greatest cock in all of Rome."

"Here, here."

Blood heated Gaius's face. His fingers tightened on his cup. It would be so satisfying to just hurl his knife and kill the bastard outright. But his own life would follow.

"Tell us about her," one friend said, his arm about Eros's shoulders. The leer on his face showed great anticipation.

"Spare us no details," said another.

Gaius gulped his wine. The sear blistered his throat and helped propel him across the floor. He took care to move in a slow hobble like a cripple until he faced the group of men. The reek of sweat and sour wine engulfed him. He forced back a gag.

"You are Eros?" he asked and bounced a bag of coins in his palm. The jingle brought all the men to attention.

"I am," Eros said with an easy smile. The young man was easily half a palm taller and well-muscled.

"I have heard of your . . . skill," Gaius said, the hood still covering the upper part of his face.

The men cheered then the smallest of the group said, "I am just as good if not better."

A voluptuous female toting two cups of wine pushed her breasts at Gaius. "I am worth more than the whole lot of them."

"Away with you, woman," Eros said. "I am bargaining." He gave her a deep kiss and smacked her bottom.

Gaius ignored the boasts. "A word with you," he said to Eros.

"Speak," Eros said with a gulp of wine. "I am all ears."

"Outside. In private."

"Stay," one demanded. "We want to hear."

Eros elbowed the man in the ribs. "Later, Decimus." He set down his cup and turned to Gaius. "Lead on, my friend."

They stopped outside beneath the torch light. Shadows from the flickering flames danced on the crude tavern wall. Gaius turned so the light revealed Eros's face and kept his own hidden.

"How much do you charge?" he asked.

"That depends on the service. Is the woman young or old?"

"Why does it matter?" Gaius slowly reached behind his back to grasp the hilt of the knife secured in his belt.

"Women are like rosebuds, each to be slowly opened one petal at a time."

Gaius nearly snorted at the unexpected poetry. He wondered if Eros was all talk or if his prowess was indeed deserved.

"Different maturities require different tactics," the man continued.

"She is young," Gaius said, playing out the imagined script. "But not a virgin."

"Virgins are tiresome. I much prefer a woman with knowledge and resources."

Gaius could take no more. He whipped the knife forward and down as he circled Eros's neck with his arm and pulled him close, trapping one of the man's arms. They were torso to torso, almost mouth to mouth, separated only by the blade which threatened to nick the younger man's testicles. "If you move I will cut you." Gaius heard the quick intake of breath, watched the man nod.

"I know about your women, Eros. Women who pay you well to give them pleasure when their husbands cannot perform. Married women whom you ply with poetry and caresses. Do you satisfy them, Eros?" He nudged the knife forward and Eros jerked. He tried to shove Gaius aside but Gaius had strength and a weapon.

"I told you not to move."

Eros nodded again, his eyes wide with fear, his breathing shallow. "Please," he said. "Tell me what you want."

"Leave Justina alone."

"Justina? How do you—"

Gaius threw his head back to dislodge the hood. The light shone on his face. "She is my wife."

Eros sagged and stumbled against the wall. Gaius's knife slipped. When he brought it up to the light it was slick with blood. Eros held his crotch but there was no gush that stained his tunic, merely a spatter of drops. "*She* was the one who asked for me," the young man said, looking Gaius in the eye. "She wanted to make you jealous."

Gaius wiped his knife on his tunic. "Remember this face. And leave my wife alone. If I see you near her again I will kill you." He tossed the bag of coins at Eros and was about to walk away but the rage rose up again.

He must be getting soft. When he was Eros's age he would have killed for revenge. At the last second he slammed his fist into the man's nose. The gush of blood was thoroughly satisfying.

# Chapter XIX

June brought summer warmth to Rome. And a sense of peace. No one hounded Livia for misbehaving. Nor was her outing with Gaius a subject for conversation. It was as if the scene with Publius had been a dream.

For three days Livia helped to purify the temple in readiness for the Vestalia. Floors were scrubbed, the walls washed, the hearth swept. Engaged in repetitive motion, the kiss floated in her mind, bright and promising. She found herself lost in the heady feeling of that day and did her best to put those thoughts aside and concentrate on the tasks at hand.

Last month Antonia ground the spelt for the *mola salsa*, back and forth with steady pressure, never complaining when her face reddened from her efforts, or she banged her fingers with the rolling pin, or her back ached from the constant bending.

"Rest, Antonia," Livia said. "You are tired."

"Not until it is finished."

The child continued in silence, with more patience than Livia showed all the times the task had fallen to her. At last the grain was smooth and even and fine as powder.

The morning of the solstice Antonia prepared the sacred cake with ground spelt, salt, and water carried from the sacred spring. Her fingers shaped and pressed the mixture into small loaves before baking. When the loaves had cooled, Livia demonstrated how to cut them into slices and wrap them in a cloth. Each step of the process she pressed her lips together to quiet her criticisms, not to interfere. Learning, she knew, came from experience.

At last they sat at the kitchen table with cups of water and a reward of sticky nuts. Dried meal coated the ends of Antonia's fingers and dotted her forehead. Livia's heart swelled with the pride of a grateful teacher for a gifted student. She should love all the Vestals equally, but Antonia was special, like a bright blue stone among grey pebbles.

"They are perfect, Antonia. No one has ever made *mola salsa* so well."

Antonia smiled in delight and wiped her forehead with her arm. Little bits of meal dropped on her portion of sticky nuts. "Do you mean that? It is such hard work. Harder than all the scrubbing and washing. Or bringing water from the spring. Someday I will think of an easier way."

Livia kissed Antonia's cheek. "Such a dreamer you are. I hope you *will* be the one to ease our tasks. But until then we can be thankful we do not do this every day."

"Just every other one," Antonia teased.

They both laughed.

"And when you are older," Livia said, "you will teach a young Vestal just as I taught you."

Antonia grasped Livia's arm. "Will you be here then?"

The gesture both warmed and pained Livia. Unknowns towered as high as the statues of the gods in the Forum Romanum. The plans for her future had washed down the Tiber.

Who knew when she would marry? If she would marry. She wanted a simple answer. Two months from now. Three months. But she did not know who held the solution. Was it the Pontifex Maximus? Rome? The gods?

She placed her hand atop Antonia's, savored the warmth of the child's skin, the comfort there. "I will be married and living in the country. And you will come to visit."

"Yes. Of course." She paused. "I will miss you, Livia. When I am older and you are no longer here, I will miss you the most."

The longing in her eyes squeezed Livia's heart. "I will miss you the most too." She blinked away the threat of tears. "Go change, now. The women will be here soon. We must be ready."

The noonday sun rose high in the sky when Livia opened the doors to the temple and welcomed in the first breath of summer. With the fresh air came the women of Rome. They left their shoes outside and entered barefoot, carrying offerings to Vesta, food baked on their own hearths.

Livia greeted each person with a genuine smile and a slice of *mola salsa*. "Vesta thanks you for coming and gives you blessings."

For these nine days Rome honored its very heart, the essence of the Vestals, the reason for their sacrifice of thirty years of service. The smiles on the women's faces filled Livia with contentment and joy. This festival she loved.

Nine days Livia lived in peace. Each night she prayed for Horatia's recovery. Each day women flowed in and out of the temple in a stream of benevolence. Perhaps they did not revere Vesta as Livia did, but they left the temple with a sense of love and brought that love back to their own hearths.

On the last day of the Vestalia, the Ides of June, the city celebrated with a holiday. While the other Vestals cared for the temple and the visitors, Livia and her *lictor* took a short walk through the shops of the Forum Romanum, where she breathed in the perfume of the flower garlands and loaves of fresh bread that hung from the stalls. She made sure to give thanks to the merchants who supplied the grain and the daily bread for the Vestals.

When she was five years old, she had darted from stall to stall, tearing off chunks of bread and gobbling them as fast as she could. When her parents threatened to punish her, she hid behind a donkey and waited until they worried she was lost. Then she mysteriously appeared and ran into their arms. They spoke sternly to her, but they forgave her.

With that memory in mind, Livia approached a donkey bedecked with garlands and stroked its velvet ears. "I know you are not the same donkey who befriended me years ago," she whispered, "but I love you just the same." She fed him an apple, childishly happy at the nuzzle of soft lips on her hand.

She returned to the temple for the last of its visitors. "Blessings upon you," she said to the woman who stood at the door, her face covered by a *palla*. The woman said nothing as she entered and left her offering by the sacred fire. She lingered there for long moments with no movement.

It is almost over, Livia thought. We have done well. Rome is in high spirits and Vesta is pleased. We have all done well.

The woman reversed her steps and stopped in front of Livia.

"Thank you for coming," Livia said.

The *palla* came down and Livia stepped back aghast.

"Do not thank me," Justina said. "I want nothing to do with you. Stay away from my husband. This is my last warning."

# Chapter XX

Sextus planned to surprise Antonia with flowers, just a little something to show he appreciated her kindness. Women liked that, he knew, from listening to men talk at the taverns. You always wanted to give a woman some kind of gift and then she would be nice to you. His mother would smile and hug him when he brought her a stray coin or picked a flower for her, and then she would give him the tender slices of chicken breast or the first piece of bread right from the oven. She always saved the best for him.

Three white roses bunched together in his hands like tiny, fluffy clouds. Antonia loved white. She had told him white was fresh and pure, just like the wings of the goddess Nike. Or Cupid.

Gods with wings. What a silly notion. Everyday life was enough to fill his mind.

There was no one about on the Vicus Patricius where the healer lived, no one to see him wait in the bushes for her. He had not stolen anything since the incident with the yarn, but people were wary of young boys standing around, especially in nice neighborhoods on the Viminal hill. He glanced up the street where the medicine woman lived. "Come out now," he whispered, willing Antonia to appear.

He turned back to the rosebush and circled the stem of another perfect flower. Were three enough? Should he give her another?

"You there," a voice called.

Sextus snatched back his hand and turned.

Two men followed his movement and walked toward him. "What are you doing here?" asked the one with dark hair.

Sextus edged away from the bush, sized up the men, and dropped the flowers. He sprinted down the street but the man was faster. Fingers closed on the neck of his tunic and yanked. His feet flew out from under him as a loud rip tore the material. He landed in a sprawl against the legs of the stranger.

"I think we have us a thief, Gnaeus," the dark-haired man said. He hauled Sextus to his feet.

"I would say so," the other agreed.

"I am not," Sextus argued, trying to strike his captor.

"Do you suppose there is a reward for him?"

"For this wretch?" Gnaeus asked. "Hardly. Throw him in the river and be done with him."

Sextus wriggled in vain against the man's strength. "I stole nothing. I was only giving flowers—"

"Flowers that you picked from a bush?" Gnaeus demanded.

"No one will miss them. There are plenty of other roses."

For that Sextus received a cuff on the head that made his ear hurt. The man dug into Sextus's arm. "Come along, boy."

A woman approached the group, her head and most of her face covered by her *palla*. "Servius, you are late," she called. "Excuse me, gentlemen. I have been looking for this boy."

Who was this woman? And who was Servius?

"We were just taking him in for punishment," the man said. "He was stealing roses."

Sextus lashed out with his foot but missed his captor's leg. "I was not." The roses lay trampled on the street. He cared nothing about the lie but he wished he had come earlier to avoid all this mess.

She grasped the boy's chin and tipped it up to look in his eyes. "Did you explain that you were picking flowers for me?" She turned to the men. "I do apologize. I told him to hurry, that I would be back soon." Her slender hand ruffled the boy's hair. "Come along, now."

The man released his grip on Sextus. "We beg your pardon." He stared at the woman for several moments. The look in his eye reminded Sextus of bullies who had beat him when he was small. Then both men nodded and continued down the street.

The woman uncovered her head.

"Aunt—"

"Hush," she commanded.

"Why are you covered up?" Sextus rubbed his arm. "Thank the gods you were here. I almost got thrown in—"

"You stupid child. How many times have I told you to stay away from here? Do you hear anything I say?"

"But I was just—"

"Picking roses for your little girlfriend?" She sneered. "You cannot even keep your hands off of other people's property. No wonder you will never amount to anything."

She was wrong. He would be something. He would be a great soldier and show them all. "How did you know I was here?" She stood so close to him that he felt the breath hiss out between her teeth.

"I have eyes and ears. You are supposed to watch Livia."

"I saw them together," he blurted.

"Who?"

"Gaius and Livia." The sharp intake of her breath made him glad of his news. "They were in a carriage going towards Ostia."

"Ostia." She gazed over his head into the air. "What could he want in Ostia? There is nothing but ships and water. No woman would want to go there." Taking Sextus by the shoulders, she demanded, "Did you follow them?"

"N-no. They would have seen me." She showed no emotion, no reaction. Then he remembered an important piece. "Livia was crying the day before. She went out somewhere and she came back crying."

The woman's eyes lit with a heartless gleam. Her fingers pinched his flesh before she released him and patted his cheek. "Go back to the temple, Sextus."

She had no right to treat him like an imbecile. "I want more money."

She stood completely still for several moments then she slapped his face hard. "Go do what I am paying you to do." She placed her hands on her hips. "Go. What are you waiting for?"

He took a step backwards, still wanting the flowers. The glare on her face made him stumble and fall. He scraped his hands. His cheek still stung. Nothing had gone right and now his aunt was mad.

Justina seethed as she watched Sextus hurry away. Insolent brat. Trying to be more clever than she. Where was his sense of loyalty?

Did he think the gods would shower money on him because he wished it? Without her he would be dead or starving, living on scraps of garbage collected from the refuse of fancy dinners, his body scarred from whippings, his hair ridden with lice.

Memories assaulted her, paralyzed her legs. She groped for the nearby wall and leaned against it while she remembered the man who had visited her father.

She was only twelve. Shy, but not afraid to speak her mind. Someday she would be rich and beautiful and marry a man of importance. A senator perhaps. Someone who had power. She respected power.

She was playing in the streets with other children, kicking a leather ball, when her father called her inside. A man was there. A stranger with a barrel chest and fat hands who smelled of sweat and the sour wine her father drank. Her father introduced her and the man grabbed her arm, pulled her onto his lap. He put his hand between her legs and then slipped his other hand under her tunic and rubbed her breasts while her father looked on with a greedy smile. She squirmed and tried to kick the stranger but he pinched her nipple hard enough to make her cry.

"What a ripe one she is," he said. Then they haggled over money. Before the stranger left he said, "Make sure she cleans up."

Justina willed the image away and bent her head, forcing deep breaths into her lungs. What had happened in the past could hurt her no longer. She was a married woman now, a mature woman, with beauty and prestige and that power she so desired. Her plan was in motion and she would take the necessary steps to see it through. Gaius would come back.

Her legs trembled as she pushed off from the wall and stepped upon the crushed roses. Sextus had a soft heart, like his mother. She, too, had loved roses, filled her room with them whenever a spare coin came her way until the sweet smell drowned out the stench of poverty. "Promise me, Justina," she had said with the death rattle in her throat. "Promise me you will take care of him."

Justina stooped to touch the fallen petals, smooth as her sister's shining hair. Then she ripped the flowers into shreds and watched the slivers of hope fall to the ground. There was no room for pretty wishes in her life. Strength came from doing. She would care for Sextus, but on her own terms, and only for as long as he behaved.

She continued up the Viminal Hill, winding slowly along the line of osier trees whose long hanging branches gave partial shade to the houses. Plebeian houses. *She* lived on the Aventine, among the senators and statesmen of Rome, the wealthy and the powerful. She belonged among those people, not in the hovels of her birth. That was her rightful place.

The sound of laughter floated through the open door of the healer's house. Did the woman care nothing for her safety? Vandals would strike if Justina left her own house unattended and the gods would cry tears of mirth at her stupidity.

"Gratiana," Justina called. She removed the *palla* from her head and folded the cloth. There was no need for disguise here. "Gratiana," she called again from the atrium.

"In the *tablinum*."

Justina made her way to the small office at the end of the atrium. An array of greens and browns covered the table. Dried fern fronds, a powdery mound that looked remarkably like face powder, something curled and feathery, spiny needles. Justina recognized only a handful of the plants. Paging through a thick text were the healer and a young girl of nine or ten years whose head was covered with a *palla*.

"Welcome." Gratiana waved her in. "Antonia and I were just reading about thyme. Did you know that sleeping on a sprig of thyme can cure melancholy? Perhaps," she grinned, "we can sprinkle it in everyone's wine and create a city of happy people." Justina gave a half smile. Other things occupied her mind. She nodded at the young girl and took a seat in the corner of the room.

"Antonia is learning the medicinal uses for herbs," Gratiana said with a fond caress to the girl's cheek. "If all my pupils were so bright, the city would have no need of my services."

Justina wished the girl would leave. Since when was a child more important than a woman? But Gratiana seemed to be in no hurry. "Do you wish to become a doctor?" Justina asked.

Antonia beamed. "I love plants. I want to learn all about them so I can help the Vestals when someone is sick, and when I am older I can help heal people who are ill. Like Gratiana."

Justina gripped her chair. "The Vestals?"

"Antonia is the youngest Vestal," Gratiana said.

"Sweet child," Justina murmured. So this was the girl that Sextus fancied. Questions swirled in Justina's head. How much had he told her? Did she talk to Livia?

Antonia packed a small bag with a coil of green. "Vesta gives you her blessings," she said to Gratiana. "I must go now. You have company."

"Oh, please," Justina said, "pay me no mind. I am in no hurry at all."

They looked at her then resumed their talk. Justina sat back and listened, alert to anything she could use to move her plan along. The girl shared a house with Livia; she must know something. Women did not congregate in close quarters without revealing their thoughts.

After a while Antonia asked, "Is there an herb for lovesickness?"

Justina pretended to yawn while paying strict attention to the conversation.

"Who do you know that is in love?" the healer asked.

"It is a secret. I promised not to tell."

Gratiana squeezed Antonia's hand. "Then we must adhere to that person's wishes." She searched through scrolls of papyrus. "Is this for a young person or an adult?"

"An adult. A woman."

"Is she the one in love or is it the man?"

Antonia frowned and twisted a stray curl around her finger. "Both. I am sure of it. They love each other but they are staying apart and it would be so much better if they were together." She leaned close to Gratiana. "He has the most beautiful blue eyes. And his hair is gold, like the sun."

Justina was right. This was about her husband.

"I have many remedies," Gratiana said. "We shall find something for both people."

Justina snorted before she could stop herself but no one seemed to notice. Rubbish, all of it. Love potions were for dreamers and people who could afford to waste their money. No good had ever come from augurs or incantations. Better to spend the money on fine clothing and perfumes, something tangible that would impress the beholder.

She tired of waiting for the session to end. "Antonia, would you carry a message to the High Priestess?"

The child jerked and turned to her. "How did you know it was Livia?"

Justina's serene face gave nothing away, especially not the satisfaction of Antonia's confirmation. "Forgive me, child, but I have no idea what you mean. Who is Livia?"

Confusion filled the girl's eyes. She clutched the bag of herbs and hugged Gratiana. "Be well," she said and ran from the room. Gratiana lifted her heavy locks from her neck and let the chestnut strands trickle from her hold. "I wonder what that was all about?"

Justina shrugged and took Antonia's seat. The lovers would have to wait. It was time for her own concerns. "I need your help."

"Of course. A sleeping draught? A cream for your beautiful skin?"

She shook her head, impatient now. "I need something to calm my stomach. I have felt ill this past week."

The healer studied Justina's eyes, her face, her hands, her feet. "Are your courses regular?"

"Certainly." Her cycles followed the ebb and flow of the tides as they had done since the beginning. Only now did it occur to her that her monthly flow was late.

Gratiana continued to look deep into Justina's eyes with an intensity that vexed Justina. Finally, the healer said, "Are you with child?"

Justina almost slapped the woman's mouth. "I do not care for your impertinence. Can you help me or not?"

Gratiana's face hardened like a mineral facial mask before she left the room. When she returned she held a vial filled with a dark brown mixture. "Were you not pregnant I would give you seeds of silphium to prevent a child. But it is too late for that. This is birthwort, to induce birth if you are already with child."

Justina's face heated with indignation. She slapped the remedy from the healer's hands and the vial broke on the ground. Liquid spread across the tile in a muddy river. "You are wrong. I know exactly what I do and I will find someone else to help me."

Gratiana faced her with a bitter smile. "Take your business elsewhere, if you must. But I am never wrong."

# Chapter XXI

Fields of wildflowers grew near the Forum Romanum. Sextus picked purple, white, and yellow clusters for Antonia to match the brightness of her eyes. He even stopped at his secret cache and took a piece of the silk yarn to wind around the stems. It made the flowers look more expensive. And Antonia would not know it was stolen.

Anger toward his aunt burned in his chest the whole way back to the Temple of Vesta. She was wrong about him; he would be a great soldier. The best soldier there ever was. Stronger than her husband and faster with a sword. He recalled Gaius on his huge black gelding, the demon horse that was faster than one of Jupiter's lightning bolts. Sextus was a little scared of horses. He had seen one kick a man in the head and after that single blow the man fell over in a great heap. Dead. But Sextus would be careful. He would have a great horse, silver like the wind that blew through the hills on a cold winter night. And he would feed him apples and brush his coat until it blinded everyone who saw it.

Some soldiers borrowed horses when they could not afford to buy their own. But he would be rich and have his own horse.

The thrill of that stilled some of the anger.

The temple was quiet when he arrived. Many minutes passed after his knock and he ventured inside, silent as the mouse that stole bits of bread from him at night. The flame roared high near the middle of the room. Mesmerized by its power, he crept closer, closer, until its heat lapped at his face.

"Out!" Valeria glided toward him, her features calm but full of purpose. She took him by the shoulders and pushed him toward the door. "You are not welcome here."

He twisted away from her grasp. "Where is Antonia? I am waiting for her."

"Do your waiting outside." She guided him firmly to the entrance.

He grabbed at the door to stop himself. "Tell her I am here."

"She is busy. Now go."

"Tell her I am here," he shouted as she forced him through.

The door closed behind him and he realized he had dropped the flowers inside. Would Valeria give them to Antonia or toss them away?

Forlorn, he perched by the column. He had nothing else to do and he wanted a friend to talk to. He would wait.

He leaned against the marble and closed his eyes.

A nudge on his shoulder woke him and a soft voice said, "Thank you for the flowers." Antonia sat nearby on the top step. "Why did you wish to see me?"

"I missed you," he blurted. Curse his aunt, he was getting tired of all this sitting around and waiting, having to be at her call whenever she wanted. The few extra coins she was paying him did not win his loyalty. If she cared about him, well . . . Sextus doubted that would ever happen. In the meantime, Antonia was his only true friend. "I wanted to bring you roses," he began then felt embarrassed.

"Roses are my favorite flowers."

"I know. They were white."

"White," she sighed. "Like Cupid's wings."

Now he felt bad that he had mentioned them.

"Thank you for thinking of me," she said.

He stared in complete confusion. "Why would you thank me for not giving you something?"

"But you wanted to, and that makes me happy."

He still did not understand, but her smile was enough.

She rested her chin on her hands and her smile faded. "I am afraid for Livia."

He would rather talk about Antonia. But he was trying to be nice. "Has Livia done something wrong?"

"I cannot talk about it," she said.

Her hair was thick like sheep's wool. And probably soft. He wanted to touch it. "You can tell me anything."

"It is private. If she finds out I told you I will get in trouble."

"I promise not to tell anyone."

She was silent for a long while. The sun warmed his back and a light breeze ruffled his hair. It did not matter if she talked or not because she was next to him and he wanted to stay like this. He wondered if he dared to kiss her. He imagined her lips would be warm and sweet as honey. But Vestals were not to be touched, even though he wanted to, and she would probably laugh at him if he tried.

When she spoke he felt a great sigh go through her. "I think it hurts her to be in love. I know they love each other because I see it in her eyes when she thinks of him and I saw it in his eyes when he mentioned her. Grownups are funny that way. They think no one knows what they feel. But everyone can see it. If they would only stop pretending, it would be so much easier."

Sextus did his best not to move. He knew who Antonia meant. He had seen it too, just a brief glimpse when Gaius and Livia passed by him on their way to Ostia. It was as if they wore a cloak of love around them. "Does Livia know that you know?"

Antonia sat up. "I have not said anything. But I want to. She is so happy when she thinks no one is looking. I wish she would be happy all the time. Is it wrong to be in love? When I am older I want to be in love all the time."

He snickered. "Love is for fools. Everyone knows that."

She rounded on him with a glare. "Do not say that."

"Why not?" He did not mean to upset her, but it was the truth. "Besides, Gaius is married and my aunt needs him to . . ."

"Who is your aunt?"

He had said too much. But the way his aunt treated him left him with a taste for revenge. "My aunt's name is Justina. She is Gaius's wife."

"I met someone named Justina the other day. She came to visit Gratiana while I was learning about herbal medicines. She is beautiful but not as beautiful as Livia." She stared at him with wide eyes. "She is your aunt?"

"It does not matter. What matters is they cannot be together."

"Who?"

"Livia and Gaius. The ones you were talking about."

"But they love each other. They have to be together. He cannot love Justina if he loves Livia." She crossed her arms with a defiant glare. "Gaius must give up Justina and marry Livia. That is the right thing to do."

Sextus laughed. "It will never happen." He thought of his aunt's stubbornness, the way she acted better than everyone. She would never accept being second place. "She is doing what she can to keep them apart."

"What do you mean?"

"I take messages . . . when Livia sends me . . . oh, never mind."

Antonia pushed at him. "Tell me. What do you do?"

He tried to ignore the feel of her hand and shook his head. "Never mind. Just sit with me. I like talking to you."

"Tell me, Sextus. What is your aunt doing?"

My aunt, he thought as his hatred blazed. It was all her fault. If she were nice to him, he would keep quiet. "She pays me to spy on Livia. I follow her around and tell my aunt what she is doing. Whenever Livia is with Gaius, Justina knows."

Antonia turned away and hugged herself. "I trusted you," she whispered.

He wanted her to look at him again. "You can still trust me," he said. "I would never hurt you."

She shook her head. "I thought you were my friend. You said I can tell you anything, but then you tell your aunt. I shared secrets with you. Why did you lie to me?"

The pain in his stomach told him he did it because he was tired of being poor. But he could have stayed on his own, alone, the way he used to be. The problem was that he liked her. Little in this world made him feel good except Antonia. He wished he could take back everything he had said.

"Why, Sextus?"

He shrugged. There was nothing he could say to make it better.

"I must go." She clambered to her feet.

He grabbed her hand. "No, wait. When will I see you again?"

She pulled away from him. "Do not touch me. I must go. I have to tell Livia what is happening."

"No. You cannot tell her. Everything will be . . ." It would all be ruined. He would have no job, no money, no excuse to see Antonia. Without the money he would barely stay alive and wonder if he would make it to his next meal.

"They are in love," she said. "It is the right thing to do."

"The right thing?" he scoffed. "There is no right thing. People do what they need to get by. There is no happy future for Livia and Gaius. What can she hope for except to be his whore?"

Antonia slapped his face. She staggered back, her eyes wet and bright, her lower lip red where her teeth dug in. "You are hateful." She stared at Sextus with such agony he felt he would shrivel into nothing. Then she ran from him, into the shelter of the temple.

"Antonia, wait," he called out after her too late.

All this talk about love and happiness. Were they even real? Sextus knew little of the joys of life. His mother was the only person he had ever loved and she died. The gods only gave people small bits of pleasure, like this time with Antonia, before they snatched it away. People who thought they were happy were fooling themselves.

He touched his cheek where she had slapped him. The heat was fading but he would remember the sting and the anger in her eyes. It was the first time he had hurt her. He vowed never to do that again.

# Chapter XXII

One kiss. Gaius had kissed her once at the beach and Livia had relived it more times than she could count. Why could she not keep her mind on her duties?

The Vestals had watchful eyes, especially Antonia. Livia knew the other women meant no harm, but gossip spread easily, even within these sacred walls. And Antonia was just a child. A sweet girl, lovely and innocent, with a heart too big for her tender age. All she wanted was to set everything aright but she had already seen Livia and Gaius together. The Goddess only knew what the girl was thinking. If Antonia spread word about them or talked to Sextus . . . He was the likely suspect for a young girl's troubles. If there were somewhere Livia could send him, somewhere away from the city center until things calmed down.

She wrote to Kaeso and sat wreathed in guilt as she penned the words. He was her dearest friend with no news from her for far too long. He would be busy tending his vines and caring for her property. She said a quick prayer to the Goddess to thank her for watching over him and keeping him well. Then her hand paused as she wondered if he still thought of her. Perhaps he had found someone else. There was no marriage contract between them, merely an understanding. Either party could break it if it was so desired, though in all her years as a Vestal neither one had given any indication of wanting to do so.

"Livia, Livia," she muttered, hearing her mother's voice in her own words. She was letting her imagination fly on the wings of eagles. Now was the time to be grounded and present. She finished her letter, signed her name, and sealed it.

When she emerged from the temple Sextus was strolling towards her, his eyes cast down, as if he was deep in thought. His legs seemed longer and his tunic strained at the shoulders. How quickly boys grew. Well, he would need those long legs for this journey.

"Sextus," she called and waved her hand.

He looked up and slowly climbed the steps.

"I have a message for you take to Kaeso Acilius Severus, my good friend. It is a long trip so you will spend the night. And if he has need of you, you may stay there a few days."

He pulled at his tunic and wiped his nose on his arm. "I will need money."

There was no joy, no excitement in his eyes. Instead, she felt resistance. "Are you feeling well? If you are unwell, I can send someone else."

Sextus snatched the letter from her hand. "I feel fine. Where am I to go?"

Livia breathed a sigh of relief. "To Tusculum. The countryside is beautiful this time of year. The vines are rich with clusters of grapes, readying themselves for their final bounty. Kaeso makes wine. Perhaps he will show you how."

"I know how wine is made."

His eyes flashed with self-importance and Livia smiled. Of course. In his own eyes he was almost a man. She would do well to remember.

She nodded and handed him a pouch filled with bread and fruit and sweet nuts. "Here is food for the journey. Follow the Via Latina out of the city and continue southeast. And money for your trouble." She pressed a coin into his hand. "Thank you, Sextus. This is important. I am glad I have someone so trustworthy to help me."

The boy rewarded her with a smile that did not reach his eyes. In a quick flash of legs and swirling tunic, he was off.

*Goddess, see him safely on his journey.* When his boyish frame turned a corner, Livia returned to the temple. She knew Kaeso would understand her absence and see to his visitor. He might even enjoy the company of a young mind. Still, her guilt had not lessened. Why did he not berate her for her shortcomings? She could picture his kind eyes, his unflagging patience, and she wanted to throttle him as she imagined any other man wanting to throttle her.

Edgy, she stepped behind a tapestry to the small niche in the wall that held the symbols of the power of Rome. From there she lifted the *ancile*, the ancient shield of the god Mars that fell from heaven upon Numa Pompilius. Livia ran her fingers across its surface, weighing the relic in her hands. Horatia had told her of the special connection, the mysterious tingling that transmitted from the metal to her fingers and throughout her body. But Livia felt nothing. She had hoped over time to feel the sacred energy. Yet here she was in her last months of service and still there was no bond. Perhaps if she stilled her mind, grounded herself as

159

Horatia had taught her. She let the outer world fade into gray, a soft nothingness, until there was no sound. Moments of silence passed. And still she felt no energy at all.

The shield was small, just the span of two of her hands. She grasped it in her left hand and pretended to wield a sword in her right. How would a man protect himself with such an item? A sword or javelin or arrow could easily strike a fatal blow. If Gaius carried such a shield, he could be wounded seriously, fatally. The pang of worry caught at her heart. Why must she have two men who occupied her mind? How could she choose between them when she feared she loved them both? Must she choose between them?

With these heavy thoughts she returned the *ancile* to its niche. Try as she might she was floundering and each step seemed to mire her deeper in the mud of confusion. Where was her sign from heaven? When would Vesta show her the way? *Please, Goddess,* she prayed, *bring Horatia back to us. Give me leave to be as I was. I cannot bear this weight upon my shoulders.*

"Livia."

Valeria moved with the grace of the majestic swans that glided on Lake Bracciano. Livia sensed her distaste before another word was spoken. "Yes, Valeria. What is it?"

"You have received a package." She held out a small cream box tied with a satin ribbon.

"Thank you," Livia said and started to walk away.

"It is wrong."

She could not help the sigh of impatience. Why did Valeria disapprove of her? "It is a gift. All gifts are welcome. How can an offering be wrong?"

"This is not an offering." The Vestal's lips tightened to a harsh, thin line that drew in her cheeks and added unflattering years to her appearance.

Livia subdued the next sigh. She would play this game with Valeria and hopefully win back her ally. "Shall I return it? I would not want your disapproval. If the gift is uncalled for, then I will not welcome it."

Valeria shook her head, her lips still pursed. She exhaled heavily through her nose, a little snort like the ones Apollyon gave after his run on the beach. Livia did her best not to laugh. "It is too late," Valeria said. "The damage is done." She turned her back on Livia and left.

Damage? What damage?

Livia hurried to her room with as much dignity as she could and closed the door quietly. Then she jumped onto the bed like a young girl and tore at the ribbon. Before she lifted the lid of the box she knew who had sent it. Eagerness rippled through her chest and spread in a warm glow to her stomach. On a bed of creamy satin lay a gold band that encompassed a magnificent red stone. The note said:

> *Red as the rose that blooms in spring*
> *Red as the stone of this ruby ring*
> *Red are the lips of my true love. So sing*
> *to me of happiness.*

There was no signature, not even an initial. But there was no need. Rubies were known to promote wisdom and prosperity, a thoughtful gift from a teacher to a student. But they were also known to elicit passion and allow the wearer to experience all forms of love. Only Gaius would make such a personal gesture.

Valeria was right. The gift was altogether wrong. Nevertheless, Livia slipped the ring on her finger and marveled at how the gem sparkled and caught the light. She longed to wear it, to show it off, but Vestals were forbidden jewelry. Servants of the Goddess must show proper decorum at all times. One day, very soon, she would take the rules of proper decorum and cast them to the four winds. When she was free of her service she would wear jewelry in her hair, on her fingers, around her neck. She had even heard that in some cultures women wore rings on their toes. She wriggled her toes then fell back on the bed and laughed a delicious laugh. Oh, the sumptuous joys of freedom.

In the meantime, she hung the ring around her neck, under her robe, on a thin chain that Kaeso gave her on her last birthday. A promise for the future when they were wed. It was forged by an artisan from the Orient, so he said, complete with intricate links and ancient good luck charms. She shrugged aside the flare of uneasiness—she *would* see Kaeso, soon—and pressed the ring against her skin. It was warm, as warm as Gaius's hand on hers, his lips on her mouth.

She could not wait to see him again. She must send her thanks. Oh, why had she dispatched Sextus? She needed the boy now. Clearly someone else would have to go.

There was no one in the hall to see her so she scurried to find Antonia, her gown flapping about her legs in her haste. The child sat on a stool in the kitchen, eating a mixture of stewed dates, nuts, and honey, her mouth sticky and glistening from the sweets. Livia halted at the doorway and summoned her "adult" bearing.

"Antonia, will you deliver a message for me?"

The girl nodded vigorously and crammed the last bite in her mouth. "I am ready."

"Have Titus escort you to the house of Gaius, I mean Gaius Postumius Albus, on the Aventine Hill. Speak to him and none other. Tell him his gift is beautiful and that I will wear it close to my heart."

Antonia smiled with glee and wrapped her arms around Livia's waist. "I am so happy, Livia. I knew my prayers would be answered. Gaius will be so glad."

"Do you not like Kaeso?"

"I do like him, Livia. He is nice to you and to all of us. But Gaius makes you light up. You are different with him."

Different. Yes, she was different with Gaius. How perceptive of Antonia to notice. Livia gripped the girl's shoulders lightly. "You must tell no one about this. If Gaius is not at home, do not wait. Say nothing to the servant or . . ." She thought of the disaster that might arise if Justina were there. It may be better if she did nothing at all.

"I promise to tell no one but Gaius," Antonia said, her eyes glowing with joy. Watching that happiness, Livia surrendered again to impulse.

"Go then," she decreed. "And hurry."

Antonia gave Livia one more hug. "I love you, Livia. Everything is as it is meant to be. Sextus is wrong. Nothing bad will come of this." She ran from the room, her feet tiny patters on the marble floor.

Those words echoed in Livia's head and heart and a shiver coursed through her body.

# Chapter XXIII

Where was the ring?

Justina had willed her face and actions to remain soft, sympathetic. She played the part of the good wife, the caring wife, calling pleasantly to Gaius when he came home, waiting on him with graceful movements and sweet endearments. But Gaius paid no notice. He barely lingered in the house, always having appointments and friends to meet that took him away from her. Did he really go to meet with friends? Or was he with *her*?

If he had bought the ring to show his love, he should have given it to Justina by now. How long would she have to wait?

She pressed her hand to her abdomen, molding her flesh, probing as if she could see beneath the layers of fat and muscle. Could Gratiana have been right? Never in her life had she been cursed with children. For years she had taken precautions—

vinegar when she was young and poor, then pastes of ground dates and acacia bark or pomegranate pulp and ginger. Even when Gaius had wanted an heir she refused to comply, all the while telling him a woeful story of infertility.

Justina thought back to those three nights in the winter when Gaius had taken her away to relax, just the two of them in a small house in Herculaneum, drunk on fine wine and sweetmeats and huddled before the fire while a storm raged outside. Three continuous days and nights of lovemaking when she was extremely fertile without any pastes or juice to stop conception. And nothing happened. After that she was convinced Gaius was sterile.

Still, she was a cautious woman. A prepared woman. She always used her special paste of acacia bark with Eros. Every time.

Gratiana was wrong.

She sat at the table decorated with a host of new perfume bottles and tapped her foot. Where was the ring? Seconds passed until she was sure that no servants lingered in the hall. When all was quiet she made her way into Gaius's study. The scrolls were neatly stacked, the maps rolled, the books shelved. There was no pouch to be seen. Damn those tidy servants. If she started pawing through Gaius's belongings, he would know and the surprise would be spoiled.

Perhaps he had taken it to be wrapped in beautiful cloth. He knew her penchant for vibrant colors and sensuous materials. Yes, that must be it. Visions of scarlet and gold bloomed in her mind. And the ring would be nestled on rich fabric of the same color in a beautiful box she could keep on her table. Gaius would see to her satisfaction. He had always done so well in that regard in the past.

Then Justina realized how long it had been since Gaius had done anything to satisfy her. Her only fulfillment now came in the arms of Eros. If he were not so young she might contemplate a long-term affair with him, as Pomponia had suggested. But she was not ready to trust someone else. Relationships were altogether too taxing, too full of promises and hurt. Her head already reeled from Gaius's duplicity. And her heart . . .

Damn him! Where was the stupid ring?

# Chapter XXIV

There were hills and valleys as far as Sextus could see. One area of green disappeared into the next. He stood at the entrance to the property and sank down on his heels to rest. The journey had taken far longer than he imagined. Almost the whole day. He wished he had not slept an hour away after lunch, but the warm sun on his back soothed him like his mother's gentle fingers.

He reached into the pouch for another bite of honeyed nuts and realized there was nothing left. He threw off the pouch in disgust, let it lie there in the dirt and stamped on it for good measure. He was almost a man, with a man's appetite. Not some little boy. The few pieces of fruit and bread had been consumed in one sitting. The sweets only made him want more. He hoped this man Acilius Severus would feed him.

The path to the villa curved gently up a slope. When he reached the top he looked out over the nearby hills of neat rows of green and purple. Grapevines, he guessed. He had lied to Livia. He had no idea how wine was made. He had never seen a vine before. If he was nice, maybe the man would show him around, let him taste some of the wine.

A grunt startled him and someone grabbed his shoulders. Hard. "Who are you? What do you want?"

The man was large and burly with hands that could easily squash a boy's head. A simple tunic stained with dirt and dark red floated about meaty thighs. Sextus tried to wriggle away but the man held fast. "Let me go. I belong here."

"I have never seen you before. Now I ask you once more, what do you want?" Even the dark beard held traces of red. Had the man been fighting or drinking?

"I have a message for Acilius Severus." But the note was in the pouch he left on the ground at the bottom of the hill.

The man switched one hand to grip the back of Sextus's tunic and held out the other. "Let me see it."

"No. You are not the one I came for." He could not imagine Livia with this brute. She was too nice and this man had a temper, the kind that usually resulted in bruised eyes and smashed noses.

A sneer showed two rows of large teeth that chomped together like a mad horse about to bite. "How do you know?"

Sextus kicked the man's knee and the man let out a yell. "Livia's friend would not treat me like this."

A tall, slender man emerged from the house and strode towards them. His face seemed kind and thoughtful, not at all like the man who kept him captive.

"What is all the commotion, Marcus?" He came to a stop in front of Sextus and looked at him with soft brown eyes. "Who is our visitor?"

Marcus twisted the material in his hand, yanking Sextus closer in a stranglehold. "He says he has a message for you."

"I do," Sextus swore. "For Acilius Severus. From Livia."

"Call me Kaeso," the slender man said. "Let the poor boy breathe, Marcus. He means no harm."

The sudden release on his tunic pitched Sextus against Kaeso. The man gently steadied him and stepped back to give him room. "Now what is your name?"

"Sextus."

"And where is this message?" he asked.

"I left it in the pouch, down the hill," he pointed.

"Liar," Marcus roared. "Thief. Do not trust him, Kaeso."

Sextus backed away from the mad man, afraid that the next time Marcus touched him would be his last. "I swear. It is the truth."

Kaeso patted Sextus's shoulder, the way a friend would. "I believe you. Marcus will not hurt you. He is merely protecting our property." He nodded at Marcus then led Sextus away. "Come. You look like you could use some food and drink. There are refreshments in the house."

A short time later Sextus dug in to a hearty meal of eggs and cheese and fresh bread. He ate with noisy gulps as fast as he could before someone took it away.

"Easy, boy," Kaeso said with that friendly pat on his arm. "Take your time. There is more if you wish." He talked about the vines and their new growth, the temperature, the soil.

Sextus looked up with cheese dangling from his mouth. He slurped it in, taking a moment to taste the flavor, to let it sit in his mouth before he swallowed. "Is there really more? I can eat everything here and then some?"

Kaeso smiled and left the room. Sextus wolfed down another hunk of bread and cheese and helped himself to more eggs. He was halfway through when Kaeso returned and set down a large tray of olives, grapes the size of walnuts, apples, and another loaf of bread, fresh from the oven.

Marcus arrived with the dusty pouch and the note from Livia. Kaeso broke the seal and read quietly for several minutes. Then he put the note aside. "Livia tells me you are to spend the night. I will take you back to the city in the morning."

Sextus stared at the tray, unable to take his eyes off the bread. It called to him, saying his name with each puff of steam.

"How is she?" his host asked.

Sextus tore his gaze from the bread to look at Kaeso. Beneath the man's pleasant smile was something else, as if he were holding himself back. But from what? Why were adults so complicated? They should say what they mean. "She spends time with Gaius, not you. If she is to marry you then why did she not come here instead of me?" He stretched his arm toward the fresh loaf, hesitant, then drew it back.

"What else did she say about Gaius?"

His voice was calm, too calm for a man whose woman was drifting away. Where was his anger? He should be shouting, pounding the table, though Sextus felt relieved to sit in the peaceful quiet. The question slipped away from him. All he could think of was bread.

"Does she mention me?" Kaeso asked. "Does she talk about us?"

The smell overwhelmed Sextus and without answering he tore at the spongy dough, stuffing his mouth until his cheeks puffed out. Then he choked and coughed up a disgusting gluey glob.

Shame pricked his eyes and he pushed away from the table, pretending to be full. "I am tired now. Where can I sleep?"

The joy had left Kaeso's face. "I will show you your room." As they walked away from the table, his host said, "The food will be there if you get hungry later."

Sextus nodded even though he knew that was not so. Kaeso was just putting on a show. People said things to be polite that they did not mean. Like the room. He would really sleep in a barn or under an overhang, somewhere out of the way.

The room was clean with a narrow bed, a chair and table, a basket with towels, and a bowl of flowers. A basin and pitcher of water stood on the table for washing. Was Kaeso expecting someone rich?

"I trust this is adequate," Kaeso said. "Is there anything you need before you retire?"

Sextus gaped. "This is for me?"

"We do not have many guests. I apologize about the size of the bed. If it is too small, I can—"

"No, it . . . it is fine."

"Well, then, I will say goodnight."

Sextus nodded, watched Kaeso walk away, then slowly circled the room. He leaped onto the bed and sank down on the soft mattress. A bed. A whole bed just to himself with sheets and a coverlet. He rubbed his fingers across the material.

Was this a dream? Had he died and gone to the Fields of Elysium?

He stretched out and his stomach made a satisfied gurgle. He could still taste the freshly baked bread. Maybe Kaeso was telling the truth. Maybe he would leave the food out. As Sextus closed his eyes he decided that someday he would live in a house just like this with a bedroom for himself. A large room with a bed twice this size. And rooms for guests.

He woke in darkness. Confused, Sextus reached out and rammed his fist into cool tile. He nursed his bruised knuckles then lowered his hand and felt smooth material. It was not a dream. He really was lying on a bed in a room in a house.

His stomach gurgled again, this time with hunger. Quietly he tiptoed down the hall and found his way to the dinner table. Strange shapes covered the surface, shapes that became more familiar as he got closer. The food was still there. Sextus tore into the bread, cold with a hardened crust, but still full of flavor. He followed it with bites of cheese and tart olives and a sweet cluster of grapes. Satisfied for the moment, he went outside to explore.

A half moon gave enough light to make out a building close to the house. Sextus wandered through the opening into a space filled with jugs. Some of them rose higher than his head. He had seen containers of wine like these in the taverns in the city, but never so many stacked so neatly. He ran his fingers over one of the handles expecting dust and grime, but they were so clean he could feel each groove in the ceramic body. With this much wine, Kaeso must be a wealthy man. No wonder Livia wanted to marry him. But if she was to marry Kaeso, then why was she spending so much time with Gaius?

His head ached from thinking about grownups. Sextus sank down on the ground next to the jugs and felt something wet against his leg. The ground was sticky and his finger smelled of grapes. With a little more exploring, he discovered a broken jug. The neck had been destroyed but the base was still in one piece. Curiosity got the better of him and he found a cup nearby. It was not his fault the jug was broken. But since it was, why not have a taste?

The first sip was sour. More sour than usual. Kaeso was not much of a winemaker. Did he forget to add the honey? Even the cheap wine in the taverns was better than this. Sextus took another drink, quickly. If he gulped it, it tasted better. Soon his cup was empty and he got another. After the second cup he lost his balance and fell against another jug, broke it, and swore. It felt as if he was sitting in a marsh. Then his eyes drooped and a short time later he dropped off to sleep.

The chirp of birdsong crept into Sextus's brain. Then he heard that beefy man from yesterday bellow, "You insolent lout." When he opened his eyes to greet the morning, the thing that greeted him was Marcus's hand. A mighty wallop across the face stung his eye and jammed his nose so hard it bled. Thick drops of red splattered his tunic while he looked on in complete surprise. The hand started to swing again but Sextus was awake now. He threw himself out of the way.

"What did I do?" he yelled as he looked for a way around Marcus.

"As if you did not know." Marcus lunged for the boy and missed. "How much wine did you think you could drink before someone noticed?"

Sextus backed farther out of the way, ready to dive between the man's legs to escape if needed. "You can have your wine. It tastes like horse piss."

The man's face turned almost as purple as the wine. In those seconds of anger, Sextus feinted right, watched Marcus reach in that direction, then he ran to the left, out of the building, and smack into Kaeso.

"Easy, my friend." Kaeso held Sextus's shoulders in a firm grip. "What seems to be the trouble?"

"He is a thief," Marcus shouted. His face had lost its purple color but the anger in the eyes remained. "He was drinking our wine."

"The jug was broken. I just helped myself to a little bit." Sextus wiped his nose and came away with a bloody hand.

Marcus glared. "He called it horse piss."

"Well, it tastes like it." Sextus tried to edge away but Kaeso's hand held him firmly in place.

"You see the disrespect he gives us," Marcus said, "after all you did for him last night?"

"That is enough, Marcus. I will take care of this. Perhaps you can find a clean tunic for Sextus."

Marcus grumbled his way back to the house.

Kaeso urged Sextus into the storage room and handed him a cloth. "Tell me what happened."

The morning light showed several jugs leaning at different angles at the back of the stacks. One of the necks was broken and wine had spilled on the ground. A pile of ceramic pieces lay nearby.

Sextus blotted his nose, wishing Marcus had hit him somewhere it would not bleed. "I sat down on the ground there," he pointed to the spot, "and felt something wet so I looked around and found the broken jug. It was like that already, I swear it. I wanted to taste some of the wine so I . . . I . . . ." Kaeso was staring at him intently and Sextus got nervous. He decided not to mention breaking the second jug. "It was just a taste. You cannot punish me for that."

"No one is going to punish you," Kaeso said.

"Did someone try to steal your wine?" Sextus asked.

"An animal probably wandered through here." Kaeso leaned over the broken jug and dipped a cup into the liquid then brought it to his lips. He spat it out and wiped his mouth. "Horse piss, eh?"

Was Kaeso agreeing with him or testing him? "Um, well, it was pretty sour."

The man's smile made his eyes twinkle. "Probably the worst wine I have ever tasted. Definitely not one of my better samples." Sextus grinned.

Kaeso put his arm around Sextus. "Marcus lost his son recently, about your age. I suspect you remind him of his boy. Give him time, Sextus. He will come around." He squeezed Sextus's shoulders. "In the meantime, let me introduce you to our grapes. The good-tasting varieties."

They walked through the fields where Kaeso showed Sextus how the vines were planted. There were clusters of Aminea and Nomentana grapes, the best wine grapes in all of Rome. Sextus said the names over and over to himself to impress Kaeso with his memory.

"Do you always have so many am . . . am . . ." He could not remember the fancy word for the jugs. "The jugs."

"Amphorae."

"Amphorae," Sextus repeated. Another word to add to his vocabulary. A soldier needed to know many words.

"It depends on the harvest. We have had good harvests the last few years."

"Will you show me how the wine is made? Livia said you might." Sextus rubbed his nose again and more blood appeared on his finger.

"Leave your nose alone. If you keep bothering it, it will not heal. Are you interested in winemaking?"

Sextus shrugged his shoulders to hide his eagerness. "I suppose."

"Then I will show you."

Kaeso took him back to the storage room, to the opposite side, and demonstrated how the crushed grapes were pressed between beams of wood. The juice was collected in a basin. "The grapes are pressed several times," he said, "and stored in a large earthenware jar so the juice can ferment."

"What happens when it ferments?"

"The yeast and sugar in the grapes turn the juice into alcohol. Afterward we separate the juice from the skins and seeds and store the wine in the amphorae. Before we serve it we mix in honey or herbs and spices for flavor."

Sextus nodded. "That sounds easy."

"It is a man's work," a gruff voice said.

Marcus stood at the opening to the shelter. Kaeso placed his hand on Sextus's shoulder. "I must make ready for our trip to Rome. You are welcome here anytime to learn more about winemaking." With a squeeze, he left Sextus alone with Marcus.

The man blocked the opening like a huge granite boulder. Just looking at him made Sextus's nose and cheek throb. Having to face this man was his punishment for hurting Antonia. The boy sucked in his breath and prayed. *Please, Apollo, if you get me out of this I promise I will never lie again.*

Some outer force propelled him forward until he was standing directly in front of the large man. For several seconds no one spoke. Sextus's knees started to buckle and he had an overwhelming urge to just fall to the ground and give up. But he was not a quitter. Then words popped out of his mouth. "I know about your son."

Marcus clenched his fists and that meanness came back into his eyes. Sextus's body shook and he wished he could take back what he said. But his mouth seemed to be out of his control. More words came out. "Kaeso told me. He said I remind you of him."

Marcus took a powerful step forward and raised his fists. "You are nothing like my son. He was a good boy, and kind. You are nothing like him."

"I am sorry," Sextus blurted as he raised his arms to shield his head. "I know what it feels like to lose someone." He could see his mother's sweet face as she took her last breath. "I am sorry." He closed his eyes and cringed.

The air was crushed out of him by Marcus's squeeze. Sextus gasped and fought to breathe but the pain lasted only for a moment. Then the big man howled in agony and wept, his arms still making a vice. "Numerius," the man whimpered over and over while his tears fell on Sextus's skin.

Now Sextus was scared and embarrassed but he could not ask the man to stop crying, especially when the man was practically squeezing him to death. After several moments he patted Marcus on the back. "It will be alright," he said. "You will see. It will be alright."

Marcus pulled back and wiped his eyes with his arm. "You will say nothing of this. Nothing." He raised his fist in warning.

Sextus shook his head quickly. "Nothing. It never happened."

"Get back to the house. Kaeso is waiting."

Sextus sprinted past the hulking man, out into the safety of the vines. His heart pounded and his head ached. What had come over him? What strange thing had possessed him to speak those words, to comfort a strange man who had wanted to kill him? He sank down onto the earth, pulling his legs into his chest. Life had been simpler before this spying business with Justina. Then he only worried about finding food and avoiding people who could harm him. These days he had to think about his aunt and Gaius and Livia and Antonia, and now there was Kaeso. A good man with a nice house and lots of food. And unmarried. Everything a person could need. Why would Livia want Gaius instead of Kaeso?

He thought again of Antonia. He had never meant to hurt her. He swore it to the heavens. She was his life now, the only good thing that had come his way since his mother's death. Without her . . .

Sextus straightened and gulped in fresh air. Already the terror of his exchange with Marcus was fading. He had survived once again, no thanks to the gods. They should have struck Marcus dead on the spot. No, it was his bravery that got him through the ordeal.

The blue sky overhead, the vines ripening in the fields, the sun shining on his shoulders, all promised a good day. If he had not yet decided to be a soldier he would consider winemaking. First, though, he would definitely get rid of Marcus.

# Chapter XXV

Livia personally fed Sextus after his return from Tusculum and hovered about him until he pushed her away and sought out Antonia's company. Then she browsed through the basket of goods Kaeso had sent to the Vestals—clusters of fat grapes, homemade bread, jars of honey, and two bottles of wine. Such a thoughtful man. Such a gracious man. Tiny needles pricked her skin as she thought of him and the message she must relay.

She paced outside the temple, quick steps back and forth, struggling against her trepidation as she waited for Kaeso. It would be easier not to say anything, to simply let life move on. But that would be the coward's way. A High Priestess must be strong. And she would be meeting Gaius shortly. A special rendezvous, he had told her in a message given to Antonia. A happy dizziness trapped Livia's breath for a moment. Then she saw Kaeso walk down the the wide pathway of the Forum Romanum. She gripped her arms to instill that elusive strength she so needed.

He looked as she remembered, though with a few more lines about the eyes and a deeper crease around his mouth. His eyes still twinkled, the soft brown shining like the rich silk in Davina's tapestries. Hurrying down the stairs, she flung her arms around him in greeting. There was no one about to see them, no one but Titus to frown on her lack of modesty. "Kaeso, my friend. How good it is to see you. I am remiss in my visits." The touch of him momentarily eased her fears. With him she was comfortable; she had always felt that way.

He gave her a warm hug and a quick kiss on the cheek. "Careful, Livia. One might think you have missed me."

"High Priestess, you fool," she teased. "But I have." It was true. Despite her reasons for staying away, his presence cheered her immensely. "Now tell me, how are you? How is the vineyard? Are the grapes healthy this season? Will there be a good crop?"

They strolled along the well-worn Via Sacra past the *Regia* which housed the Pontifex Maximus, past the booths that held the silversmiths on the north side and the butchers and money lenders on the south. Titus preceded her with an air of importance. Once again Livia wished she were free to dispense with his protection.

In the distance rose the Temple of Concord at the foot of the Capitoline Hill. Kaeso discussed the grapes, the vines, the quality of the soil, and all other matters pertaining to the health of the crop. He ended with the sad news about Marcus's son.

"Forgive me for not keeping in touch," Livia said quietly. "I will dispatch a note immediately."

Kaeso nodded. "Thank you for sending Sextus. I enjoyed showing him the vines and how the grapes are pressed. It brought me back to my own childhood when my father taught me."

"Beneath the soiled clothes I detect a willing mind. He could use a good teacher."

"He is welcome anytime. An interesting boy, that one. Smart and full of courage, but so guarded. He is not one to trust another lightly."

Livia nodded. "I know little about him, but I fear he did not know much love growing up. Or security."

"Or sustenance." Kaeso laughed. "You should have seen the way he gobbled the food before him. It disappeared in seconds." There was silence for a few strides. "Well, despite his interest in grapes and winemaking I think he has his heart set on being a soldier."

Soldiers. Instruments of death and destruction. Her heart beat a wild rhythm as she thought of Gaius riding off to war. He could be gone for weeks, perhaps injured, or even killed. She hugged herself as a sudden chill enveloped her.

"Livia, are you all right?"

"Mmm." She rubbed her arms and increased her pace while they walked. It felt wrong now, this casual conversation, wrong to lead Kaeso astray. Did he know that she had changed? He must understand that feelings were impermanent, malleable. She should tell him about her newfound love, but she did not know how to begin.

At last he said, "I have missed your visits. Everyone misses you. Even the grapes long for your presence. I wish you had come instead of Sextus."

She hugged herself harder against the inevitable.

"Will you visit soon?" he asked.

She shook her head. It was easier not to speak.

"Surely the other Vestals will give you leave. I promise great entertainment and a lavish feast," he tempted with a broad smile. "You may even bring Sextus again if you wish."

"He is more than welcome to go, but I . . ."

"What is it? Is there some reason to prevent you?"

She stopped and faced him, her body trembling with anxiety. "I cannot see you, Kaeso."

"Is it Horatia? I had hoped she was recovering."

Livia pressed her lips together to curb her impatience. She was not a child to simply blurt her news. She was an adult and must feel her way slowly and with care. "It is not Horatia. Something has changed."

"I am confused. What do you mean?"

"I have changed." She tried to relax but every muscle in her body seemed tight. "I do not love you the way I once did."

Kaeso chuckled. "And I no longer love you as I did. Is that all that bothers you?" He reached to touch her arm briefly but dropped his hand. The public wove around them in a constant flow. They moved off the common path to stand in a narrow walkway between buildings.

"Livia, everyone changes with age. We are no longer children but mature adults. Love grows and deepens over time. I am not a love struck boy but a man who desires a mate."

"I cannot be your mate." Hurt flared in his eyes. She flinched but she did not back down from her words.

"What has happened, Livia?"

"I am so sorry. I did not ask for this."

"Tell me it is not Gaius. Tell me it is someone worthy of you."

She gaped at him, astounded that he would know, unable to say anything in her defense that would not further wound him.

"How you once loved me does not matter now," he said. "Have you no feelings for me at all?"

"Of course I have feelings for you, Kaeso. You are my friend, the dearest of friends. I have always cared for you and always will."

"Then stay with me, Livia. Give up Gaius."

"You cannot ask me that."

"He will hurt you."

"You only say that because you are hurt. If I could take away your pain I would gladly do so. But Gaius . . . Gaius is not to blame. He has awakened me. His love has . . . he has breathed life into me." She stroked the chain around her neck and a glint of silver flashed.

"What is that you wear?"

She adjusted her clothing, touched the chain briefly again. "It is nothing."

"Is that the necklace I gave you? Vestals are forbidden jewelry. When did you start wearing it?"

"Only a short time ago. Really, it is nothing. I only wear it . . ." She could not tell him why.

"What? What are you hiding?"

She dropped her hand, embarrassed by his scrutiny. "It is nothing," she declared.

"Three times now you have said those words. Yet your eyes state something else. The Livia I knew was honorable and truthful."

"If you would stop badgering me I would not have to . . ." She stopped, exasperated with his questions. "Here." She pulled out the chain with the ring and held it up. The sun glinted on the gold and the ruby sparkled. "Are you satisfied now?"

Kaeso scowled. "You dare to wear such sacrilege?"

"You gave me this necklace. It is not sacrilege. Neither is Gaius's ring. They are tokens of love."

Kaeso shook his head. "Love? He does not love you. I have seen men like him. To him, you are the most precious of all things, like the sacred flame is to Rome. He cannot have you therefore he craves you. But once he possesses you his need will die and he will cast you aside."

"No, you are wrong."

"Livia, please. Use your head, not your heart. He is married. What can he offer you?"

"You told me once 'Where the heart loves, there must we obey.' I am sorry, Kaeso. But my heart chooses him."

"You will regret this."

She kept her silence.

His fists clenched, his shoulders tightened in a rigid line. "This is not like you. Why are you choosing to oppose me now? To challenge *us*?"

Her temper rose like a willful creature full of self-importance. "I am tired of forbidden things. Do you know how wearisome that is? Jewelry, marriage, children, all these are prohibited. All around me Rome proclaims its freedoms yet what are mine? My life is not my own. I cannot choose how I dress. I cannot even choose whom I . . . whom I love. Daily I pray for the welfare of Rome, but does Rome pray for me? I am sick of it. Sick of it."

"Livia, I implore you. Put Gaius out of your life. You belong with me. I have waited for you all these years. Do they mean nothing to you?"

"Oh, Kaeso." Her heart ached for his pain. "There is someone else for you."

"You are the one for me."

"No, I . . . I love another."

"Then forgive my meddling." He bowed his head then and his shoulders curved as if he had broken beneath a huge weight. "I have intruded where I do not belong. I wish you every happiness."

Tears gathered in her eyes but she could not change her feelings. "And I you," she said as he turned and walked away. "You will always be my friend, Kaeso," she called after him, as if she could soothe the pain she had caused. "Always."

The memory of his face haunted her, his cheeks sunken hollows where before the flesh was firm and smooth, the lines around his eyes as deep as furrows of newly tilled soil. How well she knew what it was like to hunger for someone, but she could not go against her own desires. She had tried to do as he wished. She had willed herself to forget Gaius. Being face to face with Kaeso now, hearing his voice, served only to reinforce her choice. She clutched the ring again and stood firm.

Titus stood impassively, without expression or comment. But she knew he had watched everything, judged everything. She had made her choice. The right choice. But she feared she had lost Kaeso forever.

# Chapter XXVI

The talk with Kaeso pricked Livia's joy with deep darts of regret. As she neared the spring at Camenae where she would meet Gaius, she thought about postponing their outing. Her doleful mood would spoil his plans and she had already ruined one person's day. Another time would do just as well.

She was alone now and first at the spring. In the twilight the water sounded more powerful, as if Neptune had opened an underground gate and let the natural stream gush forth. She remembered their last meeting here when she had dipped her toes in the water and daydreamed of being naked. If Gaius had not surprised her she might have steeped her entire body in the spring. She had defied the Vestal rules and come unattended that time. Tonight she did the same. How far would her boldness carry her?

She raised her arms over her head and closed her eyes, enjoying the currents of air that tickled her skin on this soft July night.

Where would Gaius take her this time?

"You look like a goddess calling upon her inner power," said a familiar voice.

"Gaius." How wonderful he looked seated on his warhorse, as casual and at ease as the time at the beach. Even though they were meeting on Vestal ground, Livia felt out of place. Nervous, she fussed with her *palla*, smoothing the cloth over her arms.

"Are you ready?" he asked. The evening sky was threaded with tufts of pink.

"It is almost dark," she said. "Where are we going?"

"Nowhere and everywhere."

She could not ride with him in public. They were in the city, not at a deserted beach. "Someone will see us like this."

"It is dark. No one will notice."

"No one will notice a golden-haired god astride a war horse?" Goddess, the words that came out of her mouth these days.

"If they do notice, all they will see are shapes." Before she could protest Gaius helped her up. He put his arm around her and settled her against his chest then draped a dark cloak over them both. "We are shadows passing in the night. Do not worry."

She leaned back, their bodies meeting and shifting. As the horse broke into a canter, she nestled her head against the warmth of Gaius's neck. For a while she rocked in easy comfort, soothed by his touch.

"There is no better feeling than this," she said.

Gaius kissed the top of her head and stroked her arm. Her daily worries seemed to fade. Lulled by the horse's steady pace she could even forget about Kaeso. Her mind was becoming blank. And in that blankness was peace.

Darkness blanketed the surrounding hills. Apollyon picked his way along an unknown path guided by the pressure of Gaius's knees. No words were spoken.

Ghostly columns rose into the sky as they made their way back to the Palatine Hill and passed familiar temples—first Apollo Sosianus then Castor and Pollux, the twin sons of Zeus and Leda. The small Temple of Vesta lay hidden amid the jumble of half-formed squares and rectangles. The few times she ventured out at night had been with an escort in a carriage, her thoughts on the gathering or performance ahead of her. Now she had the luxury to absorb the sights. From this perspective the buildings seemed larger and more forbidding.

They continued by the Capitoline Hill and the temples of Jupiter, Juno, and Minerva, then on into empty fields. She listened to the soft clop of the horse's hooves, the whirr of crickets, the sudden scurry of an animal through the grass.

Gaius drew her closer and she felt his chest rise and fall, the firmness of his arm around her waist, the warm breath in her ear. Despite her earlier relaxation, she tensed, and trembled, part in desire, part in fear.

Maybe Kaeso and Davina were right. Why had she let him take her away from her surroundings? From what she knew? These clandestine meetings must stop. Valeria, whose eyes saw all, would suspect, and suspicion would lead to mistrust, an evil that would wreak havoc for all those concerned. Livia must protect the Vestals. It was her duty, her life. Horatia would never have let her emotions interfere with her responsibility to others. To Rome.

But she was not Horatia. She could not put aside her thoughts so easily, or her feelings. She wanted him, this man who held her, who brought adventure and delight to her banal existence. She wanted him and she could not find that wrong.

Apollyon came to a stop at the top of a hill overlooking the city. Faint pricks of light glimmered in the black from the curve of houses below. Overhead the stars gleamed like the ruby in the ring around her neck. Moments passed as they sat, alone, in peace.

She finally dared to break the quiet. "Where are we?"

"The Esquiline Hill. Not far from the house of a friend."

Wealthy citizens lived on the top of the hill. People of power, ambition. Who did Gaius know? How had they become friends?

They began their descent, skirting the edges of a large garden. Narrow cypress trees rose in the moonlight. The horse's hooves crunched on a gravel path then rang faintly on wide stones that stretched to a distant entrance. Torches blazed on either side of an archway twice Livia's height and the walls loomed high into the night sky.

"Who owns this palace?"

"An equestrian friend turned politician. He is away on business and granted us the use of his house."

A shudder ran down her back, as if someone had brushed against her. She leaned forward to shake it off. "I feel I am trespassing."

Gaius kissed her head. "He is an old friend and specifically bade us welcome." He dismounted and helped Livia down. "Come. I have something to show you that you have never seen."

She took Gaius's hand and walked through the arch. Apollyon nickered behind them then she heard the sound of his hooves on the stone walkway. "He knows how to take care of himself," Gaius said, pulling her along. "He will be here when we are ready to leave."

He led her through the atrium, down a long corridor of empty rooms, and out into a small garden that smelled of mint and thyme and the sweetness of roses. A tiled path lit by small torches wove in circles through fragrant bushes and up a short flight of steps.

At the top Livia stopped abruptly. Before her lay a tiled pool, dark and deep and large enough to hold at least four rooms. Wisps rose off the water and melted into the air. There were two couches on either side of the pool and a number of wide-backed chairs and small tables. On the closest table a fat candle illuminated a pitcher and two goblets and a tray of fruit and pastry.

Had Bacchus called here and left his sweetmeats for their pleasure? What hedonism was this? She longed to sink into the water, to wallow for just a moment in the luxury of such an enormous pool. But it would not be fitting for a Vestal.

Gaius kissed her hand. "Sit, eat, have some wine. The night is ours, Livia. Whatever pleases you pleases me."

The air caressed her skin with hundreds of tiny kisses, each one warming her flesh, drawing her in with heated breaths. She sank onto the couch and reached for the pastry. The *placenta* was warm, its dough soft and sticky with honey. Gaius tore off a piece and lifted it to her lips. Layers of cheese and honey and the taste of bay leaves mixed in her mouth with the crunchy crust. A deep hum of satisfaction sounded in her throat.

Gaius poured her wine then leaned close and kissed the edge of her mouth. "As sweet as anything I have ever tasted."

Her skin tingled where he touched her and she hugged herself to dissipate her embarrassment. She should not let him take such liberties. But the air felt so good and the water looked so appealing and the food was heavenly. "I love *placenta*. We make it only for special occasions, and I never seem to get but a few bites." She took another piece and sighed with contentment. "I swear I could eat the whole thing."

"As much as you like," he said. "And when this one is finished, I will send for another."

"But who will you send? There is no one here."

"Tomorrow, then." He took her hand and kissed her fingers, nibbling crumbs off the ends. "I like to see you happy."

"You make me happy." She gave a nervous smile, conscious of her boldness. She was usually more restrained, more proper, yet with him she rode on horseback and had clandestine rendezvous. What she would give to always be so free. Her smile broadened.

"Were I an artist I would paint you just like this with the candle glow on your face and a smile that lights up your beauty." He held her hand in his, stroking her fingers one by one. "You are beautiful, you know."

His touch sent tingles up her arm. She pulled her hand free, slowly, and sipped her wine. "You must thank your friend for this lovely setting. I feel so . . ."

"So . . .?"

Livia spread her arms wide as if she could embrace the cornucopia of taste and touch. "All of this. I have no words for this bounty of sensations."

"And I thought you were a wise and educated woman."

She slapped his arm in play. "I see your game. First you ply me with sweets then you insult my intelligence. That will get you nowhere."

He hung his head in pretend shame. "I beg your forgiveness, lady. Tell me how I may atone."

"Never let this end," Livia teased but she meant it with all her heart.

"I give you my promise."

Though he smiled she felt his sincerity. Not for the first time she wondered what it would be like to be with him, to give herself totally to a man. And once she had given herself, how would she feel afterwards? Would it be the glorious beginning of a blissful love, or would she feel regret, dishonor, humiliation?

Despite the warm night air, a terrible shiver wracked her body.

Gaius took her hand. "Are you cold? Do you need a shawl?"

She shook her head. "No, I . . . I . . ." How could she express herself?

"What is it, Livia?" He kissed her hand. "Tell me."

"This night. These feelings I have. They confuse me. I have not felt this way before."

"How do you feel?" He kept her hand in his, not letting her pull away.

"Nervous, excited, as if someone else has taken control of my body. Why do these things happen when I am with you? Why is there nothing with Kaeso?"

"He is not meant for you. That is why we share this connection, these feelings."

"But he is my oldest friend."

"And I have loved you the longest."

"That cannot be. He is far older than you."

"I agree he is older in years. But he does not love you as I do. You are his friend and companion. Not his other half."

Something swirled over her like a fisherman's net, pulling her towards an unknown destination. "Do you believe in the separation of souls?" she asked.

"I did not know you are a follower of Plato."

"Maybe it is all a dream," she said, "wishing on something only the gods can attain. But I like to think a piece of us is immortal."

"And when you reincarnate, which animal will you be? A wolf? An ant? I think you would make a charming donkey." His blue eyes crinkled with laughter.

"You mock me, but beware. I will be a hawk and soar overhead, watching your every move. I will see everything." She imagined flying in the clouds, lifted by the wind high over the hills and valleys. Her pulse beat quickly as she tasted freedom. But it was just a dream. "I think if I had a choice, I would be a god. Then I could do as I choose. Do you believe in immortality?"

"I cannot reconcile Plato's theory of reincarnating as animals or insects. If we are born human, then we should stay human. But is the soul part of the body or separate from the body? That I do not know. Sometimes I feel I control my thoughts, my actions. And other times life seems to have its own direction."

He reached out to caress the curve of her cheek, let his fingers linger on her skin. Her jaw began to pulse beneath his hand. "Was it fate that we met?" he asked. "I do not know. Do you remember the day I first saw you?"

She had never forgotten. "You stole my heart. Or maybe it was your puppy."

"I fell in love that day," he said, "and I have loved you since." His eyes glowed in the dark, gazing into hers, compelling, bewitching.

She fought against the spell. "But you were just a child. What did you know of love?"

"The child grew into a man. You were beautiful then, but you were just a girl. Now," he kissed the curve of her jaw, "now you are a woman. A radiant, beguiling woman." He kissed the opposite side of her face.

The warmth of his lips, his soft voice, mesmerized her. She wanted to simply fall under his power but she was afraid to let go. "You speak of me like a Siren. I know nothing of seduction. I am simply a servant of Rome." She fiddled with her *stola*.

"Rome is out there," he waved his arm at the city below them. "Here there is simply food and drink and two people who enjoy each other's company. Think of nothing more." He lifted her chin. "Tonight there is nothing else. No one else." Then he kissed her, softly, just the warmth of his lips rubbing against hers. When he stopped she wanted more.

He leaned back and sipped his wine. "The pool is heated. Like the *caldarium*, only not quite so hot. More of a soothing warmth that loosens your muscles and relaxes your mind. Would you like to try it?"

Alone, she would have shed her clothes and gone swimming without any hesitation. Water was her ally, her benefactor. This was different than the sea, without its vastness, without its endless energy. But still she felt the call. "I would, sometime. But not now." Even though she feared the time would never come again, she could not bring herself to swim in front of him. She had been naked before no man since she was a small child.

"Then we will try it later," he said, and she wondered when *later* would be. "Have some more wine."

Tonight there were no worries. Tonight was only for pleasure. So she relaxed and drank her wine and let go.

As she grew tired she leaned against Gaius's strong body, perfectly content to be in his arms. In her comfort she closed her eyes and listened to his voice and fell asleep.

# Chapter XXVII

When Livia awoke, her cheek pressed against something hard. Where was her soft pillow? Then her cheek rose and fell with the rhythm of breathing, someone else's breathing. She sat up quietly and gazed at Gaius. Darkness bathed his face in shadow and alleviated the lines of age and concern. In the stillness he looked years younger and she recalled the child of long ago.

When they met she was sixteen, ill with a chest cold. Horatia had sent her to a local family for healing where she would be nurtured and cared for and not a distraction for the other Vestals.

Her body rested on sheets of pale blue cotton under a spread of blue swirls laced with gold threads. Like sunlight sparkling on the ocean. She ran her hand over the soft sheets once, twice, memorizing the feel of the smooth material on her skin. Her parents were wealthy but they had nothing so luxurious.

"Sleep," the *matrona* said, resting a gentle hand on Livia's forehead. The woman's rose water scent lingered as she silently left the room.

Livia coughed, a deep wracking sound that sapped her energy and made her chest ache. She wiped her mouth with a clean cloth and shifted the pillows behind her back so she could sit up. Her throat felt less scratchy now and she did not sneeze all the time. The hot herb tea must be working. She would be sure to ask for the remedy before she returned to the temple. If she were clever, she could extend her disability and wallow in this lovely pampering. She curled her toes then stretched. The covers surrounded her with warmth, caressed her body with soft hands. She closed her eyes, a little sleepy.

"Stay away from there," Livia heard. "Our guest is sleeping."

"Yes, Mother."

Livia opened her eyes to find a small boy standing by the bed. Five or six years old, she estimated. Golden hair curled on his forehead and around his ears. Bright blue eyes focused on her. Curious eyes. Strange coloring for a child whose mother had dark hair. The boy held a wriggling black puppy in his arms that leaped onto the bed and pounced on Livia's sore chest with its paws planted directly on her breast. She rolled to move the puppy's weight. A wet tongue licked her cheek and nose and mouth. She chuckled, petting the dog on its head before it burrowed under the sheet.

"Jupiter, come here," the boy commanded.

"A big name for such a little dog," Livia said.

"He will be enormous when he grows up. Just wait. Then you cannot make fun of him." He reached for the buried puppy.

"Let him stay," Livia said. She missed the dogs that lived near her parents' house. Vestals were not allowed pets. Jupiter crawled over her legs and fell between them, nosing his way with his cold, wet snout up her body until he found her chin which he started to lick. She coughed again and smiled. "I like you too."

"Who are you?" the boy asked.

"Livia." The puppy's wet tongue laved her nose and she giggled. "Is this your room?"

"No. Why are you here?"

"Horatia brought me. I have a cold."

"Who is Horatia?"

"The high priestess at the Temple of Vesta."

Jupiter bounded toward the boy who scooped him into his arms. "Are you a goddess?"

"I am a Vestal—"

"Gaius." The *matrona* entered the bedroom and took the boy by the arm. "I told you not to bother her. Forgive my son." She pushed Gaius out of the room, closing the door behind her.

The memory faded as Livia studied Gaius. Gone were the plump cheeks and smooth limbs of the little boy. Muscles delineated his legs and arms. Planes and hollows shaped his face. The curls on his forehead were shorter now, clipped in the standard military fashion. She touched his hair, tentatively at first, then she stroked the thick strands. The soft ends wrapped around her fingers as if they wanted to hold onto her. Twenty years had passed. A lifetime ago, it seemed, and here she was with him again. Was it destiny that brought them together? Were they always meant to be with one another?

This was no six-year-old child sleeping by her side. He was a man now, strong and hardened by life. A man who loved her.

Anticipation shivered down her spine. She was growing more attracted to him every day and finding it harder to focus on the daily routine. Did love distract people? She used to think love was a steady flame that warmed with its consistency. But love with Gaius, if this was love, seared her with its spark.

Uneasy, she walked to the shallow end of the pool where steps led into the water. Tongues of steam rose from the surface and disappeared.

Livia shed her clothes, unplaited her hair, and stepped in, wading until the liquid lapped at her breasts. Tonight was for pleasure, Gaius had said. She lay back and floated in a buoyant cocoon of warmth.

*Help me, Vesta,* she prayed. *Tell me what to do.*

The image that came to her was not the face of Vesta but the voluptuous form of the Greek goddess Aphrodite, naked in her splendor. Against the darkened sky, the power of her beauty surrounded her with an aura of starlight. *You are a woman,* the goddess said. *You are the mortal form of us, all that the gods desire to be. Who but you would know how to love a man?* The image vanished and Livia closed her eyes.

She knew when Gaius entered the pool. Even with her eyes shut she felt the ripples rock her body with the gentle hand of a mother lulling a baby. Completely still, panic grabbed her while she waited. When he placed a hand on her thigh, the merest of touches, she opened her eyes.

Her pulse skittered with uncertainty and wanting. She had heard women talk of the act of love—her mother and aunts, whisperings at parties, even the Vestals, each story different than the rest. There was pain some said. There was joy professed others. Satisfaction beyond compare several said with knowing smiles. But the talk had meant nothing to her. She was a Vestal, sworn to service, destined to be a virgin for many years. She wished she had paid more attention.

Gaius stroked her leg again, his hand light and slippery against her flesh. "Whiter than milk, fresher than water, softer than the finest veil. It was you that enchanted the mortals, child of Aphrodite, you the best of stars."

Child of Aphrodite. The words from the Greek poet Sappho must be a fortuitous sign. They made Livia feel as soft, as white, as beautiful as the lover in the poem.

Her breath shuddered. Tonight there were no rules dictating her actions. She was not a Vestal, she was merely a woman.

Moonlight streaked his body and gave her glimpses of sinewy muscle. His torso was broad and smooth, so different from the slenderness of Kaeso with his mat of dark hair. She spread her fingers across the tight plane of his belly and heard the soft whoosh of breath. His hand closed over hers and her pulse leaped.

"I want you, Livia. All these years I have loved you, worshipped you from afar. You are the dream I dream at night." He kissed her hand and pressed it to his chest where she felt the rapid beat of his heart that echoed her own. "Let me love you. Let me show you the beauty that exists between a man and woman. Will you give me this honor?" He pulled her to her feet so that they gazed into one another's eyes.

Water streamed from her head over her shoulders and down her breasts. She wanted to cover herself but he held her hands.

"There is no need for shyness," he said. "You are as beautiful as any goddess. And you were made for me. We were made for each other."

Her body trembled. Fear warned that she should be back at the temple, sleeping in her own bed, alone. *Stop,* it said, *before it is too late.* But something stronger awakened and her body tingled with an inner power.

It was already too late. Maybe it had always been too late. She had never wanted to be a Vestal. Others chose for her and put her on a path of service from which she had never deviated. Until now. In this instant she was given a chance to make her own choice.

A moonbeam cast her necklace in silvery light. Gaius touched the ruby then kissed the skin beneath. "You wear the ring I gave you."

"Yes." With that simple answer she felt him swell with pride.

"Livia," Gaius said, "I promise I will give you only pleasure." He cupped her face and kissed her, deeply this time, savoring her mouth as if he were drinking the finest of wines.

There was no need for him to give his pledge. She had already made her decision. This was what she was meant to do. This was where she was meant to be.

She moved against him, flesh to flesh, and twined her arms around his neck.

"Love me, Gaius. Love me as you have never loved another."

# Chapter XXVIII

How could she describe her feelings? In the aftermath of love, their bodies mingled, joined, breathed as one. A languor spread throughout Livia's limbs, pressing her down with soothing hands, comforting hands. She could not move. She did not want to move.

Contentment wreathed her with a soft sweetness that she wished she could contain in a little box by her pillow to draw upon whenever she needed her spirits lifted. Even the soreness between her legs gave her comfort.

*O dear Aphrodite,* she whispered through unmoving lips, *what I did not know, what I did not know, what I did not know. Thank you for your blessings. Thank you for this night.* Her chest rose and fell in a deep sigh and she turned her head slightly to gaze upon the man who had wrought such bliss.

With a soft touch she stroked his hair, the straight plane of his nose, his beautiful mouth and looked her fill until tears blurred her eyes. Happiness trickled down her face and into her hair. All women should know such joy.

She had never expected her body to feel so much. Other women's sly winks and smiles had done nothing to prepare her for this.

Gaius stirred beside her but did not open his eyes. Livia began to memorize the weight of him next to her, the warmth of his skin, how his leg twined over hers and pressed her into the couch. How his hand cupped her breast with familiar possessiveness.

Would he want her again? As she watched him, desire licked her skin, building slowly, steadily, until it took effort for her to stay still. She wanted him, needed to touch, to explore, to feel him deep within. Remembering how they were joined before made her blush. The exquisite tension, the unexpected release, and afterwards the blue that enveloped her, the azure blue of the ocean, an all-encompassing blue that vibrated within and spread through all her limbs with a melting warmth. She wondered if each woman had a color all her own.

Dawn woke the darkness with a rosy glow, and with it came alarm. The day was starting. She must return to the temple. What was she thinking to spend the whole night with Gaius, outdoors, on a couch, sleeping in the nude where anyone could chance upon them?

She grabbed for her clothes, stopped by Gaius's hand on her arm.

"It is early yet," he said. "Come lie beside me. I want to feel you next to me."

His eyes were tender and half-closed with sleep. How easy it would be to acquiesce, to leave her tasks to others' hands. But that was not the order of things. She was the *Vestalis Maxima*. She was the one in charge.

"I have stayed too long. The temple is already stirring."

He pulled her to him, slipping inside her, filling her, moving with a motion that caught at her with hands of silk, smooth and soft and so seductive, so wonderful, that she could only clutch at him, hold on to him, and ride it out, feeling the flame spread, warm at first, then hot, hot, until it left her liquid and breathless. Even then she did not want to move, to break the tenuous hold that bound them both. But time summoned her.

Gaius lounged while Livia pulled on her *tunica* and *stola* and wrapped her *palla* about her head and shoulders.

Why did he just lie there? "Get dressed," she cried. "I am late."

"Livia." He tugged on her hand until she sat next to him. "Something important has happened between us. Do not spoil it with worry." He kissed her lips, teasing her as if they had all the time in the world.

She pulled away. "Valeria always rises before dawn. She will notice my absence."

Gaius nibbled on her neck. "Does she go into your room?"

"She bids me good morning every day."

"You are the High Priestess." He framed her face with his hands. "It is your word that they follow. Let them know who is in charge and make them obey you. Decide what space is yours and tell her it is off limits."

"But we are family. We care for each other."

He kissed one cheek then the other, pausing to gaze into her eyes. "Your eyes bewitched me when I was a boy. Now they are even more enchanting." He kissed the tip of her nose and smiled. "Use that power with the Vestals. Even a High Priestess deserves her privacy."

With quick motions he pulled on his tunic and sandals and held out his hand. "Come, my lady. I would not want you to be late."

They rode in quiet. Even Apollyon seemed subdued, his hooves passing over pavement like a brush of air. Gaius dismounted and helped Livia down, holding her firmly in his arms.

"Tell me that all is well between us," he said.

"All is well," she said hurriedly without looking at him.

He tilted her chin up to look into her eyes. "Make me believe it."

She let herself relax for a moment. She was being unfair to him. He had done nothing but give her pleasure. Where was the woman of last night who made her own choices, who was ready to defy fate?

She pressed her lips to his. "All is well." Believing it, even for a moment, she wrapped her arms around him and felt her heart swell. "I love you," she said for the first time and knew the rightness of the words.

His arms tightened and he took her mouth in a heady kiss. At last he set her from him and leaped onto his horse. "I have always loved you. Do not forget that."

He rode away as pearls of light feathered the horizon. Livia hugged herself and entered the *Atrium Vestae*, ready to start the new day. As she tiptoed to her room she noticed the stillness. At first she thought everyone was sleeping but Valeria always rose before dawn. Patricia should be in the kitchen cutting fruit for the morning meal. Where was everyone?

She checked each bedroom, the kitchen, the atrium. Finding no one, panic spread like a bloodstain. Finally, she ran into the temple. Around the fire pit crowded the Vestals and the Pontifex Maximus who grasped Antonia by her wrists. Each one turned to stare at Livia as she slowly moved forward until she reached the pit. Her scream filled the room and clung to the walls.

The sacred flame was out.

# Chapter XXIX

Gaius had never been surer of himself than in that moment when he rode away from Livia. She was the one he had lived for, all this time, all these years since the first moment he had seen her on the bed in his house. Two souls reaching out their hands towards one another. His mother had told him that phrase when he was just a boy. If you are lucky, she said, you will find your true love. The one person who is meant for you.

All his waiting had moved towards this moment. Towards Livia. Towards their union. As the gods and goddesses had found their mates, so had the Fates blessed him with the woman to match his heart. And he would seek her out again tonight, when the stars were high overhead.

The hours stretched before him as the thought of her filled him with longing, unbearable, urgent, pain mixed with desire. How would he last until this evening? Would he ever have his fill of her? Have enough of her mouth crushed under his, his lips on the soft spot where her neck and shoulders met, the brush of her hair over his fingers?

Apollyon picked his way through the marshy fields outside the Forum Romanum. The horse's hooves left depressions in the dewy grass. Buildings shed their cloaks of gray to reveal tall columns of stone. Pigeons swooped into flight as they passed by then settled and clustered at the base of the temples.

In soft undertones Gaius repeated the words of Sappho's poem, each phrase alive with new meaning. Aphrodite had truly incarnated as Livia. Her skin so soft, so white, her body fair and firm. Their age difference held no importance. She could be thirty years his senior and he would not care. The thought of her as an old woman, the certain wrinkles on her face and body, caused him to laugh at his imagination. But the glow in his chest held fast. And while her beauty moved him as easily as a Siren's song, he knew it was not her face or form that called to him each night in his dreams, but something more intangible, something deeper.

She was meant for him.

Years had passed before he understood the meaning of the word Vestal and all it encompassed. His childhood fantasies of love and marriage were soon put aside. But he never wavered from the belief that they were destined for each other. Even his arranged marriage with Justina, the way his father sought to control him, did not deter him. A man must have some way of filling his needs until the gods saw fit to line up the stars. He had tried to treat his wife with fairness and respect. She had everything his money and position could afford, including, Gaius noted wryly, a lover. He apologized to the morning sky for his previous ill-timed meeting with Eros, the need to assuage the anger that clouded his mind. Women were not the only ones who behaved emotionally. Men had their tempers too. Some would agree he was entitled to compensation. Looking back though, it all seemed immature, especially since he had never loved his wife.

Somehow he would make amends to Justina, and her lover. Justina would make a life with Eros or find some other wealthy man through Publius's connections. And Publius would come to recognize his son's maturity and allow his choice of partner— Livia.

Gaius's gut clenched as he thought of his father. He had fought so hard for respect, taken the constant bullying, the caustic put-downs, all in an effort to achieve recognition. To earn the praise his brother was so easily given. If his brother were still alive, maybe there would be room in his father's heart for two sons.

He patted Apollyon's neck, seeking comfort in the animal's warmth. A mature man did not wallow in self-pity. Once Hannibal and his legions had been ousted and the fighting at an end, Gaius would prove himself worthy of his father's love. Surely Publius could see that an alliance with a woman who had been High Priestess secured Rome's good favor.

At last Gaius headed for home, glad that the tide of his life had finally turned in the right direction.

# Chapter XXX

Livia gazed at the line of Vestals, all standing quietly with their heads bowed. How could she have let this happen? In all of her service, and as far back as she could remember, the flame had never died. Never. A heavy shudder racked her body, the body that had betrayed her last night. *Vesta,* she prayed, *why did you not turn me away from Gaius? Why did you let me seek my pleasure and then punish me for it? I gave myself into your safekeeping.* Even as her words faded she remembered her prayer to Aphrodite, how she put Vesta aside in favor of a man who whispered honeyed words in her ear, who touched her skin with soft caresses until she could no longer think with logic.

*Never again,* she swore, even as a disloyal part of her mind wondered how long it would be before she saw him again.

She stared at the screen which hid Antonia and the Pontifex Maximus. When would the punishment begin? How long must they wait? Then she reprimanded herself for her questions. She was not the one about to be flogged. She stood, nervous, her body quivering, waiting, waiting.

The first shriek came. Then a whimper. In her mind Livia pictured the rods landing on bare skin, harsh wood against pale flesh. She knew the Pontifex would stay his strength against a child.

Antonia, dear sweet Antonia, whose childish radiance lit Livia's life with joy. Today that joy was vanquished. Because of her Antonia suffered this humiliation and pain. Tears sprang to Livia's eyes. Would that she could change the course of events, that her body could take the coming blows. But she was not the one guarding the flame.

A muffled moan, then a yell. The rods thrashed again, and again. Livia's fingers dug into her skin to prevent her own cry.

Ten strokes and the punishment ended. Livia did not bother to wipe the tears from her face. "Bring Antonia to my room with clean cloths and salve. I will see to her." She had caused this misery and she would remedy that now. She met Valeria's startled look and stood firm until the Vestal retreated.

Before Livia could leave the Pontifex Maximus pulled her aside.

"You threaten the very existence of Rome and its people with your negligence. Barbarians lurk at our borders and hope to crash through our patrols. Does your safety mean so little to you?"

Her protests would mean nothing. It was better for her to be silent.

He raised a hand as if he would hit her then dropped it. "Rome has a long memory, High Priestess. See to it this does not happen again."

When the Pontifex Maximus departed Livia commanded everyone to their rooms for prayer. There would be no discussion, no speculation.

Antonia lay upon Livia's bed without her tunic. Red welts crossed her back from her shoulders to her waist, several of them raw with specks of blood. Livia's hand wavered as she dipped the cloth into warm water and gently bathed the wounds, fighting back her tears with each flinch of Antonia's body. "Forgive me," she said softly, dabbing at the welts with infinite kindness.

"It is not your fault," Antonia said. "I am the one you should forgive. I was on watch." A sob bubbled up and escaped and Livia kissed the girl's shoulder.

"Shhhh. You are just a child. No one should have to undergo that punishment, least of all you." She pressed down on the raw welt as if she could erase her anger at the Pontifex Maximus.

"Ow! Livia, that hurts."

Livia snatched back her hand and dropped the cloth in the basin. She kissed Antonia's forehead. "No more cleaning. I promise." With a flat wooden spoon she spread thick smears of honey on the wounds and bound them with clean linen. "You may sit up now."

Antonia turned to Livia and slipped into her tunic. She wiped her eyes, still red and wet with tears. "Where were you this morning? Why were you not in your bed? Everyone was looking for you."

Guilt sliced across Livia's chest as fiercely as the rods wielded by the priest. "I, I could not sleep," she fabricated. "I went out walking to clear my head. I should have been here." *Goddess, strike me now. Kill me swiftly that I may never cause this pain again.*

Antonia grabbed Livia in a fierce hug and held on tight. At last the girl's arms relaxed. "This morning was the same as every other morning. Why did the flame go out? It never went out before. What did I do wrong?"

Livia stroked the girl's hair. "Nothing, Antonia. You did nothing wrong."

"Then why?"

What could she say? What words of comfort could she give to this child who suffered in her place? "Sometimes things happen for no reason. Only the gods know why."

"But why is the flame so important? Why does it matter if it dies?"

"The flame is a symbol. It represents the hearth of Rome. Every home has a hearth where food is prepared, where you give thanks to the Goddess for her blessings. The same is true of the city. This temple is like a home and the sacred fire is the hearth. When the fire burns then all is well and the city is safe. If the fire goes out, then Rome is in danger."

"In danger of what?"

Loss of power, security, the way of life they had always known. Things that Livia had put in jeopardy.

She kissed Antonia's cheek and smiled. "No more talk of Rome. Go rest now. Today you have only to take care of yourself."

"I love you, Livia," Antonia said. She slid slowly from the bed, her eyes narrow slits and her face pinched.

When she was gone from the room, Livia let out a muffled groan. She had commanded the other Vestals to pray, but how would *she* pray?

She knelt before the altar. "Vesta, forgive me this day for my sins against you." The face of Gaius rose up in her mind, then the memory of floating in the pool, the warm water caressing her skin, his hands on her face, her breasts, his mouth on hers. Desire streaked through her as she thought about their bodies pressed together and she doubted her prayer, her ability to pray. How could she ask for forgiveness for something she did not want to forget?

No, she must put that act behind her, burn the memories from her brain. She had sworn to live a sacred life and she must do so. The act of sex called for much greater punishment than a mere flogging. If this was the extent of her penalty, then perhaps Vesta truly watched over her.

She placed her palms together with renewed fervor. "Dearest Vesta, take from me these unwanted desires and sinful emotions. Rid me of the thoughts that lead me down dark passages. I am your daughter. I have pledged my life to you. Forgive me my sins and help me to know my place."

Hours later, the Vestals watched the Pontifex Maximus rekindle the sacred flame. Poor Antonia stood with downcast eyes, still red from crying, her body shifting from side to side to ease the discomfort of her wounds. Valeria's thin lips seemed to smirk at something private. Livia was too exhausted to worry why. She clasped and unclasped her hands, rubbing her thumbs together until they felt raw, impatient with the process. Was the slowness a sign of displeasure from Vesta? Her temper rose, climbing higher, hotter, the way she wished the kindling would light. She had prayed for forgiveness; let the misery end now. If she could relive the previous night she would have stayed in her room. Regret burned at the back of her throat with a bitter taste. But she could not undo her actions.

Valeria crossed her arms and fixed Livia with a wicked glare.

Livia turned away to stare at the pit. *Goddess, have pity. Ignite the flame!*

At last a bit of smoke appeared, then the glow of red, then a spark burst into being and the kindling caught, a smolder at first until a crowd of yellow flame licked and burned its way through the twigs.

Livia instructed Valeria to monitor the fire and gave Antonia permission to rest. In the privacy of her own room, Livia stretched out on her bed. But her mind would not be quiet. If Horatia were well, Livia would not be in this position. If Horatia were here, Livia would retire from service in a few short weeks. If Horatia were leading the Vestals, Livia would be free to pursue her desires. *Why are you not here for me?* her mind screamed.

Rebellion churned within her breast. Her palms turned clammy, her knees throbbed with pain. Relief flitted out of reach as surely as the smoke from the candles on the mantel that wafted high above her head.

The face of her lover swam before her eyes.

"Leave me alone!" she cried to the empty room.

But he did not leave her.

The dreams began that night. Sweet kisses on her mouth that moved to her neck and trailed down her arm to her fingertips. Soft kisses that barely grazed her skin. Long kisses that made her body limp. He loved her in a warm meadow with tall grasses that waved in the summer breeze, in the hot sun on pure white sand next to the endless sea. Words of devotion he spoke to her, words of longing, words of tenderness.

Each dream ended in a cloud of blue. A warm blue, a soft blue, a tender, all-encompassing blue.

When Livia woke from these dreams she ached for him.

Gaius.

His name was part of her breath. As she whispered her morning prayers to Vesta, he was there. When she brought the water from the spring at Camenae, he was there. When she stood before the sacred flame, watching, thinking, hoping, he was there. Like the food she ingested, he circulated through her system, nourished her cells, gave life to her movements.

How had she existed before his love? Now her time was spent between thoughts of him. Two beats of her heart between inhalations. Three beats to light the candles on the mantelpiece. Five beats to brush her hair before retiring for the evening.

When would she see him again? When would they lie together? Would the meeting of their bodies feel the same as the first time? How long would he desire her or would he tire of her quickly and leave her to pursue another woman, someone younger, someone with riches who could boost his rise to power? No, she would not think such thoughts. Gaius was constant in his affection. Why else would he tell her of the years of pining for her, wanting her, desiring her if he did not mean it?

But men could be heartless, cruel. She had only to examine the stories of the gods to see their deceit.

Worry needled her with quicksilver flashes, a tentative lick here, a cautious tingle there, until her mind bristled. She felt herself withdrawing from the comfort of Vesta, the security of her Vestal sisters. The temple was of no use to a woman of appetite. She must go to the source, to the one who imbued her with desire.

*Aphrodite,* she prayed, *help me with this longing. Teach me how to harness this need. Show me how to love without greed.*

A message arrived several days later from Gaius.

> *Meet me tonight. The equestrians are ordered to march. We leave Rome at dawn.*

The note fluttered in her hand as his words brought him once again to mind, as if he stood in front of her, real and demanding, his eyes bright and hot with need.

She could not see him now. She would not see him. But how could she avoid him, where could she go? If Horatia were only here to advise her, to comfort her, to soothe her untrained brain with words of wisdom.

Capua! Yes, Capua was the perfect remedy. She had yet to visit Horatia there or meet her sister, Julia. She must leave now. Before she could change her mind she summoned Valeria and gave her strict orders to watch over the Vestals while she was away.

"How long will you be gone?" Valeria asked.

The question aggravated Livia's impatience. "I will return as soon as I can."

"I see." Her frank gaze bothered Livia even more than her question.

"What is it, Valeria? What troubles you?"

"Do you trust me to run the temple in your absence?"

"I do. I would not ask you otherwise."

"Yet you seem displeased with me of late."

Livia fought against her urge to lash out at Valeria. Misgivings about her sister Vestal would serve no purpose now. The temple required someone in charge and Valeria was next in line. "I apologize for my behavior. I bear no grudges against you. Indeed, you are much better suited for the role of High Priestess than I. I trust you implicitly to guard the temple while I am absent."

Valeria smiled sweetly and bowed her head. Nothing in her gaze or composure could be suspect. Still Livia was wary. Another day she might have challenged her but there was no time now. "Let me hear no disturbing reports when I return."

"Fear not, High Priestess. All is in good hands."

Images of Antonia stayed with Sextus—the shock on her face the moment before she slapped him, the sadness in her eyes. Twisted with that horrible hurt were the beauty of her curly hair and the sweet smile she usually gave him. He would do anything for her sweet smile once more.

This time he came with an armful of white flowers from the fields in the Campus Martius. He did not know the names of them but all were wild. He had made sure not to steal someone's precious roses. Antonia would love them anyway simply because they were white.

As he neared the door to the *Atrium Vestae* his nervousness increased. What if she refused to see him? What if Valeria would not even announce him? Something was up with that woman. He saw it in the way she looked at him, as if she knew all his secrets and was just waiting for the right moment to betray him. The more he thought about it, the more she reminded him of Justina.

Sextus took a deep whiff of the flowers. The pleasing smell gave him courage and he stepped forward and knocked sharply on the door.

Valeria answered.

His heart sank but he stood fast.

"Go away," she said and started to close the door.

Sextus put all his weight on it and shoved it open. "I am here to see Antonia. These are for her." He thrust the flowers into Valeria's face, forcing her to step back.

For a moment he thought he had won. Then she snatched the flowers from him and threw them on the floor.

"You little weasel," she said, her eyes bright with a cold and hateful light. "Do you know what you did to her? She was flogged because of you."

His body trembled in horror as he remembered the sting of the rods on his own skin. Flogged? Because he had told her about Justina? "No, you are lying."

"She cried for three days," Valeria continued, "and even now she cannot bear to talk to anyone." She grabbed Sextus's shoulders and pulled him forward. "I tried to reason with her," her voice softened, "but she would not listen. I told her you did not mean to hurt her. That you are young and inexperienced in the ways of the world and only doing what you thought best." Her hand caressed his cheek as if to forgive him, then she grasped his chin and held fast. "Do you think to bend a young girl's mind?" Her breath was hot and Sextus squirmed. "Do you think a Vestal, however young, would associate with scum like you?"

He kicked her shin and cheered when she howled in pain. "You are the hateful one," he cried. "Where is Livia? She will understand. Bring Livia here."

Valeria stood tall and crossed her arms. "The High Priestess is gone. I am in charge now."

She was lying again. Livia would never leave someone else to rule over the others. "Let me see Antonia," he shouted. "She likes me and I like her." The words rushed out of him before he could stop them.

But they made no difference. The Vestal shoved him out the door and slammed it closed.

Sextus sat on the step. He wondered at his soft heart, at the change in him. Soldiers must be strong and hard. Courage and bravery were everything. Softness could get him killed. But he remembered how it felt when she smiled at him and gazed at him with trust.

He had to make things right. If that meant camping out on this doorstep for the next week, he would do it. He would gather all the flowers in the field and lay them at Antonia's feet. Anything to show how much he cared for her.

# Chapter XXXI

He rode through the night. The August air was warm and damp and seeped into his tunic, creating a wet skin that moved with him as his arms and legs urged his horse onward. Swift and nimble, his steed crossed over hill and valley, taking Gaius beyond the city, onward to Capua.

Livia, he breathed. How could the gods not want her with him? He needed her by his side, to touch her, to hold her. He remembered a warning from his Greek wet nurse to be wary of loving a mortal too much, lest the gods take away that love. But how could they be envious of the feelings he had for Livia? Certainly his nurse spoke of something else, something that was not destined.

The horse stumbled and Gaius was thrown forward. "Go easy, Apollyon," he whispered and urged the steed on. From here he gazed out over the ghostly shadows of the Servian Wall that surrounded the city and the rooftops of the nearby Caelian and Aventine Hills, home to the wealthy. The city population continued to expand as the greedy fingers of Rome pushed ever outward.

The wind rose, gusted around him, and he thought of the sea. In his youth he had dreamed of commanding a sailing vessel. Not for plunder or for domination, but to explore the mysteries of the ocean. The wide sea that stretched from Rome to Carthage, from Syracuse to Greece and Macedonia, from the western islands to the Iberian coast. He knew there were lands beyond, people and places not yet visited. Cultures to embrace, languages to twist the tongue, foods to excite the palate. Strange and exotic animals to behold, like the elephants of Hannibal's army. He had not seen the creatures, only heard stories of them. Wider than ten horses, taller than Apollo's temple, with ears the size of shields, a snout that could pick up and throw a man across a field, and feet that meant instant death. Excitement tripped through his chest, increased the pressure of his thighs. Apollyon took the encouragement and flew across the expanse like a black Pegasus winging amid the stars.

The memory of his childhood unfolded in Gaius's mind; layer after layer spread out and smoothed, until the picture lay clear and still. For years he had relived those moments, recalled them when he felt he might be losing touch with Livia. She had seemed a goddess then, with the alabaster skin of a statue and the dark hair of a sea nymph. As a boy, he knew only that she was the most beautiful woman he had ever seen. In later years he realized that Cupid had pierced his heart with the arrow of love, a love such as Aphrodite had for Adonis. He thought that he might forget Livia with Justina. Marriage was said to ease the pain of unrequited love. For a time he let himself believe it had. His dreams, though, told him otherwise. It was not his wife's brown hair or golden skin that haunted his mind at night but Livia's dark waves and ivory sheen that sped his heartbeat and woke him with aching loins.

Justina might love him, but he could not love her.

As Gaius planned his battle maneuvers, so would he design a way to be with Livia. He was mature now, seasoned, with a comfortable lifestyle. He would provide for her, care for her. She loved him. She had said so in her own words. And she trembled at his touch. Perhaps her love was not yet as deep, but it would grow in time. Like the roses in his garden.

Apollyon galloped onward to Capua, the sound of his hooves echoing Livia, Livia, Livia.

Soon Gaius would be free to be with his woman. His love. His destiny.

Swatches of iris and lilies lined the path to the villa where Horatia resided, their blue and white flowers open to the morning sun. The summer heat across Livia's shoulders did little to dispel her worry as she approached the house. If the illness lingered . . . If Horatia were to die . . . Horrible thoughts crowded Livia's mind like screaming children.

Titus waited while Livia clutched the ring around her neck for solace. Despite her prayers to Vesta, her vow to let Gaius go, she still wore his gift. It was a part of her she could not give up. But she wished he had not sent a summons. She needed to purge him from her mind and body.

An old man with a hobbled back swept the path before the villa's entrance with slow back and forth movements. Livia stopped and smiled. "I am here to see the High Priestess."

A wave of his arm motioned Livia inside. The door was open to let in light and air. Livia walked through the empty atrium until she came to the *peristylium* where a woman kneeled before manicured rows of herbs.

"Pardon me," Livia said. "I am here to visit Horatia. Where may I find her?"

The woman rose. "Welcome to our house. Have you come a long distance?"

"From Rome. I am the acting High Priestess."

"Livia. What a pleasure to meet you. I am Julia, Horatia's sister." She held Livia's hands warmly for several moments. "Forgive my familiarity. You are the High Priestess and should be addressed as such." She bowed her head.

"I would gladly give it all up for one simple day in the garden."

Julia smiled, a hesitant smile, one of disbelief. "You cannot mean that. The Vestals are the mainstay of Rome."

Livia nodded in agreement though her body screamed denial. "Our role is important. Of course. But I am High Priestess only while Horatia is ill. And I would much prefer that you call me Livia."

Julia smiled. "My sister has told us much about you. I know she will be happy that you visit. Come, sit, I will bring refreshments."

"Thank you, but I would prefer to see Horatia."

"I am afraid she is sleeping now. Visitors are allowed late afternoon."

Livia suppressed her disappointment. "May I return then?"

"Please. She will be delighted to see you." She walked to a nearby table and pulled out a chair. "Will you rest now? You must have had a long journey."

Julia returned shortly with fruit and water and freshly baked bread. To be polite, Livia took a slice of apple but she had no appetite. Horatia was resting. That could only mean she was unwell. Unwell and not recovering. And if she were not recovering . . .

"We keep to ourselves mostly," Julia said, leaning back in her chair. Sunlight sprinkled her light brown hair with streaks of copper. "It is such a nice diversion to have company. I hope you will stay awhile." She glanced to the left, then the right, then whispered. "I love my dear husband, but I miss a woman's point of view." In a normal tone she said, "Tell me of Rome. I have not seen the city since last summer. Have fashions changed? What of the theater? Is the market overrun with foreign goods? I remember the grand array of fresh foods and spices. Oh, if I had known you were coming I would have asked you to bring me some . . ." She broke off and clapped a hand to her mouth. "How presumptuous of me to chatter so. As if you had nothing better to do than see to the needs of a complete stranger."

Livia touched Julia's arm for a moment. "You are hardly a stranger. Horatia has spoken of you often. I feel as if I know you, at least in spirit. It is I who should feel ashamed for appearing without a gift." What had become of her manners? To show up unannounced, without food or wine or token of appreciation? Gaius was the cause of her forgetfulness. She must stamp him out of her consciousness.

"You have not touched your fruit," Julia said. "Is there something else to your liking? Some cheese? Nuts with honey?"

"No, thank you. This is perfect." She could not make idle chatter while her thoughts gamboled in mad confusion. "You are too kind. Forgive my restlessness. Thank you for your welcome. I will come this afternoon."

Julia rose. "It will be the highlight of Horatia's day."

Livia left the villa with its perfect gardens and pristine floors and air of well-being. Horatia could not stay there and still be ill. She must be mending. Sleep was good for the body, Livia remembered her mother saying. It restored the circulation, cleared the skin, and invigorated the mind. Horatia must be healing.

The streets of Capua bustled with market flurry. Livia wandered through the stalls, gradually allowing her mind to settle and drink in the pungent spices and fruity nectars. She should have brought her *lictor*. It was unwise to walk alone. Men might make unwanted advances. Titus had argued with her but she had made her choice and she pushed aside her disquiet.

To her right a fish vendor scaled and gutted a glistening mackerel, setting aside the intestines for the *garum* sauce. Livia turned away in revulsion and moved toward the mounds of grapes. A vendor held out a sample cup and Livia thanked him. The sweet flavor of the juicy fruit calmed her mind and turned her thoughts from unease. She had just finished the last of it when she felt a hand on her arm.

"Livia."

She looked up into blue eyes and gave a start of surprise. "Gaius." Distress flared when she glimpsed his red tunic. The red cloth of war. He had told her as much in his note and she had paid no attention. What other things had she missed?

"You are here alone, without your *lictor*?"

"Today I am an ordinary woman, not a Vestal."

"Then let us act like an ordinary couple." He took her hand familiarly, fingers laced together, and led her away from the market to a quiet spot beneath a wide umbrella tree.

The nearness of him unsettled her. She felt dizzy, as if there was no ground beneath her feet. Already her body leaned toward him, wanting his warmth, his strength, his tenderness.

He stroked her wrist. "Why did you not contact me?"

"It is for the best," she said. "I thought your troops were leaving Rome. Why are you here?"

"We are on our way. To Cannae. I could not go without seeing you."

"We cannot be together."

"We are meant to be, Livia." He touched a lock of hair that brushed her cheek and his fingers on her skin brought a stab of desire. "I have felt that since I was six years old."

"No. It is wrong. Antonia was punished because of me. Because of us."

He gripped her hands. "How was she punished? By whom?"

She pulled away and leaned against the tree. Sharp bits of bark pressed into her back, between her ribs. She concentrated on the pressure to still the thrum of her body. "The flame died that morning after I was with you. The sacred flame of Vesta. For the first time in years, more than I can remember, the Vestals were without their guardian."

Livia closed her eyes at the memory that still twisted her stomach. With this she could face Gaius and turn him away. "When I entered the temple they were gathered round the fire pit. All the Vestals. The Pontifex Maximus was there too, holding Antonia in his grasp. Sweet Antonia who had done nothing wrong. But she was punished for my crime. Flogged." Horror leant her voice power. "Flogged, Gaius. Ten strokes across her back."

Shame overcame her then and her voice dropped to a mere whisper. "There were red welts everywhere, some of them bleeding. And . . ." She looked in his face, her eyes stinging with guilt. ". . . she apologized to me. To *me*. The one who caused her pain."

Gaius's caress on Livia's cheek made her flinch. "I am not fit to run the temple. I am not fit for anything. Just leave me be." To her dismay she started to cry.

"It was an accident," he said. "Fires die all the time. It meant nothing." He held her tight against him, his breath warm in her ear, his body a pillar to lean on, to lean into. She knew he would not let her go until she relaxed so she ceased her struggle. When his hold softened she freed herself.

"No," she said, her voice mixed with anger and self-pity. For once she wanted to be just a woman in love, a woman who need watch over no one but herself. But the gods had dealt her a different hand. "We must part."

"You would send me off to war without your love?"

Why must she feel so strongly for him? Why did he have the power to tear her apart? "You have my love," she said. "But I cannot give you . . ." She could not say *myself, my body, my hand in marriage,* however much she longed to be with him. The High Priestess of the Vestals could make no such promises.

"Come with me," he said. "For now. For a short time. Before I go."

"What if I told you not to go? What if I begged you to stay home?" Desire ran thick and hot, coursing through her arms, her legs. Her heart burned for him, a life with him, a safe haven far from the reaches of Rome and her politics.

"Take me away, Gaius. Find us a ship. I will leave Rome and follow you anywhere you say. To Iberia, to Sicily, even to Carthage."

"You would live amongst our enemies?"

"They are enemies of Rome, not me. Gaius, do this for me. For us."

"How you tempt me." He pressed her hand to his cheek. "I asked you that very thing not long ago and you denied me. Now I cannot. I am commanded. The legions wait for me. Do you wish me to disobey?"

Her transgressions rose in her mind like an angry wave. She had disobeyed her teachings, disobeyed the rules, disobeyed the warnings. All of that for him. To be with him. Would he not do the same for her? "Yes," she said. "Disobey. As I have."

He bent his head and stroked her palm, little circles on the tender flesh, little circles that called to her, pulled at her. When he looked up, his eyes held a tired sadness. "I am commanded. I must go."

She stepped back. Anger seared her chest then dissolved into tight despair. She had lost him.

"Goodbye, Gaius. Do not follow me, I beg you. I must be strong. For the Vestals, for Horatia . . . for everyone." Especially herself.

She waited for him to touch her, to implore her to reconsider. She steeled herself against the heat in his eyes and knew she would step forward at any word from his lips.

He said nothing, merely looked at her with all his wanting plainly etched on his face. Then he walked away as she had asked.

"Come back to me," she called like a traitor.

He did not turn around.

Though she crumbled inside she did not go after him.

Hours passed while she meandered through the streets, barely watching where she placed her feet. Her mind was numb, her thoughts random and flitting like the flies that buzzed about the sticky remnants of food in the empty stalls.

Gaius did not love her. Not truly. If he loved her he would not have walked away. He would have taken her with him, somewhere. Persuaded her. Comforted her. Promised her. But he did not. He was commanded, he said. And she was not? Rome did not order her the way it ordered him? She had thrown herself at him, sacrificed herself. For what? For one night of passion?

She returned to the villa after her walk. Julia greeted her warmly and with smiles, but as they walked to Horatia's room, the firmness about her mouth and eyes told Livia to beware. She muttered silent prayers the last few steps and when Julia made to depart Livia almost begged her to stay. Gathering her nerves, she sank down upon the small stool by the bed and took Horatia's hand.

Horatia opened her eyes. "Livia. My dear," she said, her voice a thready copy of her usual strength.

Livia brushed a kiss across the priestess's forehead. "It is good to see you. I have missed you so. All of us have missed you." When there was no reply, she asked, "Are they taking good care of you? Do you want for anything? Just say the word and I will make sure you have it."

Horatia's eyes smiled though her mouth did not move. "I want for nothing," she said softly and this time Livia leaned forward, dismayed by her mentor's condition. In all this time, why was she not well? Had the physicians done nothing to improve her health? There were herbal tinctures, poultices, different therapies to employ. Were they feeding her fresh fruit, making her take exercise? Oh, why was she not well?

"Livia, my child, do not despair. I have lived long and seen much. You, my favorite daughter, have blossomed under my tutelage and grown into such a woman."

*A woman who is nothing compared to you.* "Do not speak so," Livia said with Horatia's hand in hers, willing the older woman to recover. "You have much life left in you."

"It is—" Horatia coughed and wheezed and Livia's heart stumbled. "It is the will of the gods. I leave the Vestals in good hands."

"No. I—"

"You cannot refuse, Livia. This is your destiny."

"But there are others. Valeria could assume the leadership."

Horatia shook her head and coughed, a deep wracking that sounded as if she would expel pieces of her lung. "You lead from your heart, my dear. Valeria has little compassion. A good leader must love her subjects. That is why I chose you for the role."

"Please, Horatia. I cannot. You must choose another."

"Livia, sweet Livia. You have much to offer. Your warmth and caring, your steadfastness. Your attention to duty. All these are important qualities." She gave a weak smile.

Horatia was wrong, terribly wrong. If the High Priestess knew what Livia had done, if she knew about Gaius . . . But it was not the time for such discussion. "If you insist," Livia relented, though she did not feel the words. The rebel inside her refused to listen. "But only until you are well."

"I am dying."

"No, you cannot. I will not allow it." She tried to smile, to make light of her words, but her fear froze her lips.

"It is my time. There is nothing to fear about death. Death is the absence of all worries and sorrows, pain and heartache. Living is what we fear."

"Horatia, please. I—"

"My sweet child. I have always loved you. Be well, my dear." She closed her eyes and seemed to sleep.

Livia kissed her mentor's forehead and left the room on leaden feet. Once, not too long ago, the days proceeded in an order as timely as the rise and fall of the sun. She had planned to leave the temple and marry Kaeso and live in peaceful simplicity. Dear

Kaeso. Where was their friendship now? Had she wounded him so deeply that he would not speak to her again? If their roles were reversed, she would have cast him aside.

Her sigh, so deep and prolonged, scared her. Where was the orderly Livia of old? If she had not taken up with Gaius, none of this would have happened.

She should have listened to Davina. She should have paid attention. The weaver told her he was not a man to trust. Only a stupid woman would not heed a warning. Yet even as Livia berated herself for her lack of judgment, an image of Gaius swam before her eyes and warmth coursed through her, a soft and delicious feeling she had never felt with Kaeso, one she had never felt with any other man. Was the issue of trust not about Gaius himself but the feeling that robbed Livia of rational thought? The feeling that took her breath, her mind, her heart?

The scenery blurred into a soft ripple on Livia's ride back to Rome and the red of Gaius's tunic flashed before her eyes like a flag of warning. Where was his commitment? His failure wormed itself into her brain. She had flaunted the rules to be with him. Why could he not do the same? Was his profession of love merely physical? She had opened her heart against her better judgment. She had let herself be charmed and seduced. She had sacrificed her virginity, and for what? O Vesta, what had she done?

The tightness in her chest made it difficult to breathe. Dear Kaeso. He came to mind so easily. The waves of brown hair that glistened in the sun like freshly turned furrows of earth. The sweet brown eyes so full of warmth and humor. The tall, lean strength of his body that worked without complaint, caring for the grapes, her grapes, her property, as if it was his own. Partners, he had said. Sharing together. Neither one superior but both equals.

If she had listened to Kaeso she could have been safe and well without this burden of guilt on her shoulders.

A sob of half-pity, half-anger rose in Livia's throat at the appalling way she had cast him aside for a man who wanted nothing more than a brief physical interlude. Kaeso was right. Perfectly practical Kaeso, her companion, her best friend, the man who knew her better than anyone. The road they had traveled from childhood until now could not be forgotten. She must work this out and tell him so.

She must ask for his forgiveness.

# Chapter XXXII

Drops of satisfaction oozed from Justina's pores as she lay on tangled sheets next to her lover. She dozed for a few delicious seconds, aware only of the heaviness of her limbs pressing down into the mattress, her cocoon of languid warmth.

"I have missed you, Justina."

She opened her eyes to Eros leaning on his elbow beside her. It took several moments for her purring mind to form witty repartee. "Are your other women proving unsatisfactory?"

Eros held her hand to his heart. "There are no other women."

"I see." His teasing always brought a smile to her lips.

He rubbed her fingers gently. "It is the truth. I am alone now, a single man who pines for the woman he loves."

She pulled her hand away. She thought she would feel a sense of power at his confession yet all she felt was disquiet. Her stomach took this moment to revolt in queasiness and she cursed the healer for planting disturbing thoughts. Turning on her side, she lay there without knowing what to say, willing her discomfort to subside.

Eros cradled her in his arms while his lips gently nuzzled her neck. "Marry me, Justina."

She flinched and drew away. "Cease your toying."

He fit himself to her again. "I love you. I want to be with you. Marry me."

"You are drunk. And stupid." And far too young.

"I am definitely drunk. And perhaps I am stupid. But I still love you. And I want you for my wife."

"I have a husband."

"He does not care for you. When did you see him last? When did he last make love to you?"

Anger grew as she silently answered the questions. She had not seen Gaius in days. If he had shown her any signs of affection she would not be in bed with her lover. Or worrying about her health. "That is none of your business."

Eros caressed her arm with warm lips. "He hurts you and I want to take away your pain. Marry me and you will know nothing but pleasure. No one can please you as I do. I will care for you always."

She laughed at his boast, though his words did carry truth. He had learned well from his many women, tricks even she had not seen. And in the few unguarded moments when she did not think of Gaius, or try to scheme against him, Eros gave her a tenderness she had never before felt. But he could not help her in the long run. "You are nobody. I cannot marry a nobody."

"I have more money than the wealthiest man in Rome."

"You lie."

"Only a little. I am extremely wealthy. Truly. I can buy you the finest of gowns, the grandest of villas."

"We are too much alike. You cannot give me what I need."

"I will give you anything your heart desires."

Desires and needs were not the same. She needed security. Position. Gaius. With the advent of war, all Rome was in uncertainty. This was not the time to throw away her hard work. "You weary me, Eros. Go away." She pushed at him.

He knelt before her, towered over her in an absurd posture. "Marry me, Justina. No man loves you as I do."

"I have already refused. I cannot marry you and I will not."

"Why? Give me one good reason."

She had given him several, yet he still persisted and he tired her with his games. "You are a whore, Eros. Simply a whore." His face paled and she was glad she had hurt him. Now he would leave her alone.

"As are you."

Justina slapped him. "I will kill you for that."

He drew his dagger from his pouch near the bed and forced it into her hand. "Do it now. Right here." He placed the tip of the knife on his chest. "One thrust and it is over. I will never bother you again."

It tempted her to be rid of him. Her scheme to make her husband jealous had accomplished nothing. Even the shock of seeing her in bed with a lover served only to widen the gap between them. Gaius could care less about her or her actions.

Her plan had backfired and it was time to change tactics. With Eros gone she could concentrate on her husband, devise another strategy that would bring him back to her.

She clasped the dagger with both hands and applied pressure. A trickle of blood ran down Eros's chest.

"Do not play with me. Kill me now."

Behind the anger in his eyes was something pleading, something intimate, a softness she struggled to find with Gaius. There were times in her past when she had longed to kill but had neither the strength nor the means. Why could Eros not be one of those men who had used her so cruelly, who had violated her without guilt or regret?

She hesitated.

"Do it!" he roared.

Her eyes smarted with tears. She dropped the dagger. The silver blade fell to the bed, smeared the white sheets with red. With her back to him she commanded, "Get out. Now!" Then she left the room, appalled at her weakness and the unaccustomed ache in her heart.

"Damn him!" she shouted to the empty hall after he departed. Then she wondered which man caused her more fury, the husband who openly ignored her or the one who seemed to love her. How could he profess his love? Love was for the innocents of life, children who were raised in comfort and security, who blissfully held onto the ideals of beauty and happiness. Love did not exist between adults. There you shared indulgences and assets; money secured the pleasures of good wine and fine clothes. But love?

Deep inside, in the hollow beneath her breastbone, lay a tender place that harbored her memories of kindness. A river rock from her father, green and flat with rounded edges, worn from the sea and warm from the sun, which he had picked from the shore along the Tiber when she was five. A ribbon from a merchant at the market, dark as the juice from fresh pomegranates, that she had worn about her wrist until it frayed from dirt and wear. The tiny kitten, black as the sky when there was no moon, handed to her by an old woman two streets over, that mewled like a baby and curled under her chin to sleep, soft and warm and gently throbbing from its throaty purrs. Those things she had cared for, even treasured. Perhaps even loved.

But a man?

Justina wandered into the kitchen where the servant had left a tray of sliced apples, grapes, soft cheeses, and sticky dates. She placed a date in her mouth and licked her fingers free of residue, then anger boiled again and she swept the fruit and tray to the floor in a messy clatter. She missed Eros already, his warm body against hers, the tender stroking of his fingers, the power to fill her with desire. She missed his mouth, his smooth skin, his words of passion and poetry that filled her ears with each stroke, each caress. And in the aftermath of their coupling, the sweet way he cradled her body, his mouth on her ear, his hand on her breast, his legs twined with hers.

Oh, yes, she missed him.

How could she raise a dagger to him when she . . . the wave of emotion that washed through her was so tender she grabbed the table for support.

Juno, help her, was this love?

This was not part of her plan. No, this certainly was not part of her plan.

# Chapter XXXIII

I t is not my fault. Some things are out of my control. I did what I could . . . Justina thought as she picked at her gown as she paced, worrying the fabric between her fingers. It is not my fault.

If Gaius would only be reasonable, she muttered, circling the floor of the atrium with sweeping strides. Despite her many visits to this house over the years, the servant had commanded her to stay put in a tone of voice he rarely used with her, and, nervous about her news, she had complied. She changed direction, walking across the mosaic of Neptune. Indeed, it helped her temper to stomp upon the god's face and body. If she could smear one god with dirt, perhaps the others who had not helped her would take heed.

At last the servant showed her to the familiar room for business. Publius sat at a table, a goblet in hand. In all the times she had met with him he had never risen to greet her or to bid her farewell. Pompous pig, she thought, though she would not say those words.

His usual sneer preceded his welcome. "I should comment on your beauty, or your gown, I suppose. Or have you done something to your hair? It looks a bit duller today." She seethed inwardly and returned his stare with perfected calm. Finally, he asked, "To what do I owe this visit, Justina?"

Her voice was honey and light. "I came to pay my respects to my beloved father-in-law. It has been much too long since I saw you last. You look well." More gray peppered his hair and the lines on his face seemed deeper. Perhaps she was not the only one who worried about Gaius. "Have you missed me?"

"As a horse misses the pestering of flies." He took a long swallow of wine and she watched the bob of his Adam's apple, wondering what it would be like to draw a blade across it and watch his blood spurt. It should have been his skin under Eros's dagger.

"I am a busy man, my dear," he continued. "A war is upon us. Or do you spend your days in frivolous talk about jewelry and clothing, with no care about the outside world?"

"All of Rome is aware of war, and I with it." Justina continued to stand. An ache began to spread through her toes and into her ankles. Another day she would have braved his temper and sat without permission, but not today. No, she needed a favor and she would have him in a good mood. "I come to talk of simpler matters. An issue close to our hearts." She wished it were a simple matter, that she could snap her fingers and Gaius would come to heel like a well-trained dog. But nothing she did caused any change in his behavior.

"Well? What is it today?"

"Gaius ignores me. Still. Even though I have taken a lover." She had nothing to feel guilty about. Gaius was in the wrong, not she.

"Your young Greek is merely a plaything. No man of any worth would worry over him."

A plaything? Nothing to worry over? Eros loved her, something she doubted Gaius had ever done, and a feeling she was growing more accustomed to every day. Collecting herself, she said, "Whatever his worth, the ploy did nothing. Gaius pays no attention to me or anything that goes on in his house."

Publius refilled his goblet and offered nothing to Justina. "I am not your guardian, nor do I care how you solve your problems." He guzzled the wine, then banged the cup on the table and smiled when she jumped. "But you will solve this. Your husband treads on treacherous ground, lusting after his little virgin. Oh, yes, I know who she is."

Justina sucked in her breath, felt its raw edges rake her throat. So Publius knew that Gaius panted after that woman, that glorified priestess, as if she were a goddess. But if so, why did he do nothing? Why not use his authority to keep Livia in check?

His gaze fixed on a spot past Justina's shoulder, staring into space for a lengthy pause. His face seemed to soften and his eyes . . . Did she see moisture? For Livia? Then he looked at Justina again, his gaze as unfeeling as before.

She forced her next words past her tight throat. "I need your help. I have tried everything." She thought of the calculated softness, the sweet endearments, taking care to dress in her finest colors and scented perfumes. All for naught. "Each time I see him I am the model of a perfect wife, yet he will not even linger long enough to talk to me, let alone feel my caresses."

Publius sat back and laced his fingers together, looking supremely self-satisfied. "Succeed or fail, Justina, do what you will. But be warned, my dear. If I take matters into my own hands, your lover will be the first victim."

"He has done nothing," she protested. "Keep your . . ." She stopped, startled by her outburst. She had taken a lover to spur Gaius into action. But these feelings for Eros, this softness that welled up in her heart surprised her. Bothered her. She could not afford to be weak when she was fighting for her way of life.

"Please," he gestured with his goblet. "Finish what you were going to say."

Her threats meant nothing to him. "Forgive me," she said with the honeyed voice she previously used. "I ask only that Eros be spared," she said sweetly. "He seeks to make me happy. That is not such a horrible thing, is it?"

"Well, well. One might think you care more for your lover than you do your husband. I did not know you were capable of such feelings. By all means, let us spare Eros. I would not want you to be unhappy."

His leer ripped at her body with sharp claws. She thought of all the times she had groveled before him, all the times he had wielded his power with a nonchalant flick of his finger, not caring how she felt or even if she had feelings. She must direct the conversation back on course. "If Livia has her way we will all be unhappy."

He remained silent.

"Have you not heard the gossip?" she asked. Thank the gods she had someone on the inside. "Our dear High Priestess is making quite a name for herself, entertaining men alone, disobeying her vows. Certainly not the type of leader one would hope for. What kind of Vestal tries to make herself more powerful than Rome?" The sudden twitch of Publius's eyebrow told her the words had effect. "Valeria would be a much better role model. Unless, of course, Livia has the support of someone in authority."

Publius ignored the bait and toyed with his cup, his face blank. "What do you know of Valeria?"

"Very little. Only that she is ambitious and seems much more willing to follow the rules."

"And Livia is not?"

"That much is obvious." Moments passed in silence before he looked at her again. "You were pretty once, Justina, but you have lost your beauty. It is no wonder Gaius strays."

She gripped her gown, her legs, for support. The sting of his words lingered. "Why will you not help me?" she cried.

"Who do you think saved you from a miserable existence on the streets? There were plenty of women to choose from, though you were quite a charming whore, I must say."

"You did that for your son, not for me."

"I gave you everything a woman could want."

You gave me nothing, she thought, her anger rising. And anger would not sway Publius. She tried once more, her voice soft. "Then why do you not help me now?"

He glowered then something in the cold stare shifted and he groaned. "When a son will not listen to his father, there is nothing left to do. It is up to you, Justina. Save him and be well."

What nonsense was this? Was his previous warning an empty threat? A man of his position had many options. He had given Gaius social standing, purchased his equestrian status, and could just as easily take it away. Publius was simply refusing to help.

She cast another barb before she departed. "Gaius is your son. It is your duty to look after him. My husband may wander, but he will come back when he loses interest in his quarry. What of your precious Livia then?"

She left the room without waiting for an answer and hurried out of the house into the open air. Only then did she lean against the wall and gasp for breath, shaken, terrified of the path ahead. She had asked for Publius's help and had been rebuffed. Why had she turned to him, the man who bargained away souls like cheap wine? Desperate or not, she should have known better than to seek his advice. If she were not careful he would throw her back into the pit she came from.

Justina's house servant stood by the entrance. The woman gazed patiently into the distance waiting for the signal to depart. Justina wished she had come alone and not succumbed to modesty.

If only Gaius were strong like his father. But he was weak. Too weak. And too easily led astray. Why could she not have a normal husband with normal desires? Why did he have to fall in love with a Vestal?

Justina pressed her hand over her heart, feeling the panicked beat beneath her palm. Something must be done. If Publius would not help her, she would take action.

She would bring down Livia and all the Vestals if she must.

Rome be damned.

# Chapter XXXIV

The *carpentum* rolled to a stop outside the *Atrium Vestae* and Livia stepped out. Exhausted. Her friend and mentor was failing. Gaius was in danger with the war. Where were the days of calm, the interludes of peace that had nurtured her through her religious service? If she could turn back time she would call up the exquisite moments with Gaius on the beach. If . . .

"Livia!" Sextus rushed forward and grabbed her with such force he knocked her back.

Titus's face was a mottled flush of purplish tan; his right eye twitched with a pulsing tic. She had never seen him so upset. "Unhand her, you ignorant child." He batted Sextus away.

Livia put out a hand to steady the boy. "You will not treat Sextus that way. He is under my care."

Titus did not apologize. "Discord brews among the people. War escalates. There is talk . . . of you."

"Livia," Sextus pulled on her arm, "I need you."

She patted his head while facing Titus. Rest, all she wanted was rest. She had castigated herself the entire trip. She did not need a scolding from her *lictor*. "You have no right to use that tone with me. I am the High Priestess of Rome. You will respect me and my position."

"You disobey the rules."

Her resentment mounted. "Enough! Leave me now."

Titus bowed his head. "I worry for your safety, High Priestess. I cannot protect you if I am not with you."

But his apology was wasted. "Do your worrying in private then. I have other matters on my mind." Titus had only mirrored the words she had told herself. The rebuke settled over her like a coarse shawl, uncomfortable and irritating. She wanted to scratch at it, to fling it off her, but she must wear it until she had resolved her problem.

"Livia." Sextus pulled again. "I waited for you. Valeria has seen the Pontifex three times. About *you*. She is evil, I know it."

"Shhh," Livia said, "there will be no such talk about the Vestals." She led him up the steps of the building and opened the door.

"But she is evil. I swear it. On Jupiter and Mars and Pluto. She said that—"

"Be calm, Sextus. I promise to hear you. Let me change my clothing and wash the dirt from my journey. Then we will sit and you will tell me everything."

"Hurry," he said, dashing past her into the atrium.

The sigh came deep and long, as if it had been buried in her chest and only now allowed release. Why did everyone demand so much?

She crossed to the bath and stripped off her gown, then slowly eased into the heated pool. Her body gave a quiet moan of pleasure. She wanted to lean her head back and close her eyes, simply drift off for a short respite, but Sextus was waiting. Something about Valeria. Her muscles tightened in response at the thought of her sister Vestal. Valeria. What had she done now? Livia tried to be respectful, patient. She wanted all the women to live in harmony. How had Horatia managed all these years?

At last she met Sextus in the atrium. The boy rushed to her, his fists clenched as if he were ready to pound something.

"Come, Sextus." She patted the bench. "Sit beside me and tell me your story."

"It is no story. I am telling the truth." He sat next to her, his face screwed in concentration, then he jumped up, unable to sit still, and moved back and forth. "It is Valeria. She is the bad one. She said Antonia was punished because of me. But Antonia did not know I was spying. She only found out—"

Livia squeezed his arm. "Spying? What do you mean?"

Sextus grabbed his hair and pulled. "I was watching her. You. I mean both of you. For my aunt. She wanted to know about you and Gaius. But you, you are the High Priestess. And Antonia, well, I like her. So I talked to her."

She had watched the young romance between him and Antonia, found joy at the goodness of Antonia's heart, the way Sextus slowly shifted from defense to openness. Antonia's kindness could heal anyone, even a lost boy from the streets. But the words spilled from him so quickly she could not process. Spies. Watching. Aunt. Why could she not connect the thoughts? Perhaps it was just his imagination. Boys liked to exaggerate things.

"I think Antonia likes me," Sextus continued. "Well, she did until she found out what I was doing. I told her it was my aunt's fault. I did it for the money, not to hurt anyone. Especially not Antonia. Or you," he added.

Money? Hurt? What was he saying? "I am sure you did not mean to hurt anyone."

"Well, I did in the beginning. When I met you at the market. You were just a nobody. Jupiter, not a nobody. I mean, of course you are somebody." He pulled at his hair again. Then he stamped his foot and grabbed her sleeve. "You have to listen to me. You have to. Valeria is evil. She said she was in charge now."

Livia took him into her arms. "It is alright, Sextus. Do not worry. Everything is alright." She combed his hair with her fingers. Over and over until she felt him relax. Until she began to relax.

"I promise not to spy anymore," he said. "I told Antonia I would stop. And I did. That day. The day you left to go see Horatia. I have not seen Justina since then. But you have to do something about Valeria."

Livia gently pushed Sextus upright. "Justina?" Sextus had seen Justina?

"My aunt."

"Justina is your aunt?"

"Yes."

Her body swayed. Her hand squeezed hard until she heard a yelp and felt something push at her. She blinked to stop the dizziness that swallowed her.

"Livia, are you alright?"

She nodded, even though she was not. "Say nothing about this to anyone."

"But what about Valeria?" he asked.

"I will handle her."

"Can I hit her just once?"

"My brave Sextus. You are the first man to fight for me." She kissed his cheek. "Go now. I will tell Antonia you asked for her." She stood and waited for Sextus to depart.

At the door he asked, "You will take care of Valeria?"

"I will," she said, her voice firm.

When he left her body sagged. Valeria. And Justina. Were the two connected? Did they conspire against her together? How did she not know this?

These evil stirrings would not have happened under Horatia's command. *O Vesta,* she prayed, *why have you allowed this? Show me how to make this right.*

Sextus clutched the red and yellow yarn he had stashed in his secret place. He was crazy to see her again, to think she could help him. Davina. The sorceress.

She would beckon him into her home with sweet words and promises, then put him under a spell. And when he was powerless, they would come for him. Arrest him. Throw him somewhere dark to rot like dead rats.

He left the grand statues and temples of the Forum Romanum and crossed the Subura, then traveled the Via Tiburtina towards the Esquiline Hill, to the weaver's house. The August afternoon heated his back and the glare from the sun hurt his eyes. After thirty minutes of walking, sweat stuck his tunic to his skin.

He was used to stealing what he wanted. Not bribing people. Would the yarns be enough?

Still soft, the silk balls seemed less bright now than the day he stole them. Was that part of Davina's spell? Taking away the shine? Taking the excitement from his thieving?

Sextus switched the yarns to his other hand and wiped his hot palm on his tunic. He should have come earlier in the day before the sun had so much power. He should have figured out a plan. He should have made Livia see the danger. But she was an adult and he was just a boy. Almost a man. But not big enough for her to pay attention.

He turned onto the Via Praenestina, his breath coming out in little puffs. Davina would not care when he arrived. If he arrived. She did not expect him. Jupiter, what if she was not there? All this trouble for nothing.

He stopped to rest, rubbed the back of his hand across his forehead and shot an angry glance at the sky. He kicked at a firethorn bush along the way.

The yarns were wet with sweat. Dull. He switched hands again to dry his palm and dropped the balls on the ground. Red and yellow rolled several feet, the colors tangled and smeared with dirt.

By Hercules! He was such an idiot.

He picked up the yarns and dusted off the dirt then held them close to his chest. For protection.

Minutes later he arrived at Davina's house. The cool air in the atrium soothed him like a welcome breeze. He stood with eyes closed, bathing in its freshness, his purpose forgotten for the moment.

"Good day, Sextus," Davina called.

His heart jumped and his body swayed. Off balance, he stretched out his arms to keep from falling and dropped the yarn. Again. This time the balls rolled into the *impluvium* where they sank to the bottom, blobs of rich color. Ruined.

He could not give them to her now.

"Sextus, come help an old woman. I need your skilled fingers."

That soft voice called to him, beckoned him. He had heard tales of the Sirens and their voices. How men gave up their will and dashed their boats to pieces on sharp rocks. He would not let her do that to him.

But he could not stop his feet.

Davina was not at her loom. She sat on the floor with a lap dog and balls of color by her knees. Green as clear as Livia's eyes. The pink of Antonia's cheeks. Purple on the hem of a Senator's toga. The dog nosed a ball of muddy brown several feet across the floor. Sextus picked it up and rubbed the strands, thick and rough and saw the dog's left eye covered in a white film. Blind. Like her owner.

"Kelila," Davina said, "these are not to play with. You have your own toys." She held out her hand, waiting.

Sextus rolled the yarn in his hands, watching her. How did she know he had the yarn? That he would give it to her?

Her hand stayed outstretched, unmoving, palm up. While her other hand scratched Kelila's ears with slow strokes, she looked at him, eyes unblinking.

Her eyes bothered him. They were clear, not the clouded eyes of old people. He knew she could not see, but the fixed gaze seemed to reach inside him, deep inside where he hid his secrets. Sextus dropped the yarn into her hand.

"Thank you." She set the ball away from the dog. "Why are you upset?"

"How can you tell?"

"I feel these things. Come, sit. Tell me what is wrong."

"I brought your yarn back. The ones I stole from you. But they fell into the pool and now I have nothing."

"You returned my yarn." Her lips curved in a smile and her eyes seemed to delve deeper, deep into his soul. "It does not matter if silk gets wet. Will you bring them to me?"

He stared at her. Who would want it wet? But he brought them to her and set the soaked balls at her feet where they lay in a puddle.

"There is a towel by the basket." She pointed to a spot nearby. "If you spread it out on the floor we can dry the yarn." She showed him how and they began to unwind the silk and stretch out the wet lengths.

"Thank you, Sextus. It takes a brave heart to do the right thing."

It was a bribe. What did bravery have to do with anything? But she seemed pleased with his gesture. And if she was pleased then she would help him.

"It is kind of you to visit me today," she said. "Do you have news of Livia?"

"Livia is in trouble," he blurted. Jupiter, he wanted to take it slowly. When would he learn to control his mouth?

Davina nodded and patted the floor next to her. "Tell me. What has happened?"

Images of people rushed through his head, all the women in his life blurring into one another. The one he loved, the one he liked, the one he hated. "It is my fault. I told Antonia that I was spying for Justina and she got mad at me. But I did it for the money. And it was before I knew her. Really knew her. How could I hurt her now? But I did. She trusted me and I let her down. And then she talked about Gaius and Livia and I said some mean things and she said I was hateful." He felt Antonia's slap again, saw the hurt in her eyes, so big, so terrible. Could she ever forgive him?

Davina's hand on his arm was warm, comforting. "She will come around. Your friend, Antonia. Give her time."

He shook off Davina's hand. He did not come for comfort. "Livia is in danger. That is why I came here. You have to help her. I told her Valeria is evil but she does not believe me. She thinks it is all a story. Tell her it is true." He gripped Davina's arm hard. "Tell her."

Kelila barked and bit him. Teeth marks on his hand that stung.

"Ouch!" He brought his hand to his mouth and sucked at the pain. "Stupid dog."

"She was protecting me, Sextus. The same way you protect the people you love."

He licked his wound once more. The sting was subsiding. "What kind of name is Kelila?"

"It is a Hebrew word that means perfect."

"How can she be perfect? She is blind in one eye."

"She is a reminder that all of God's creatures are perfect. Even a dog with one blind eye. But you came about other things. What has Valeria done that is so bad?"

"First she said Antonia was beaten because of me. Because of my spying. Then I saw Valeria come out of the *Regia*. Three times while Livia was gone. She talks with the Pontifex Maximus, I know it. She wants to take over from Livia. She wants to be High Priestess." He started to grab Davina's arm again but stopped before Kelila could bite him. Instead he growled at the dog, satisfied when she whimpered.

Davina rubbed Kelila's head and behind her ears. "Have you told Livia all this?"

"Were you not listening? I talked to her before I came here. She said she would take care of Valeria."

"Then why come to me?"

"Livia will do nothing. She trusts people. Even Valeria. How can she trust Valeria?" He knocked a ball of yarn and watched green roll across the floor. Then he grabbed a ball of purple and made to throw it but Davina stayed his arm.

"Perhaps Livia knows something she has not told you."

"Probably. Adults like to keep secrets."

She touched his shoulder. "And boys do not?"

Why did she have to remind him? Sextus leaped to his feet and walked, five strides to the opposite wall, ten strides down. "So I have secrets. So what?" The things he had done in his few short years were between him and the gods. Not that he had much choice. If he did not fight for his life, he would not be here. The fire of frustration burned in his belly. This was going nowhere.

He rounded on her and stood just inches away. "What about Livia?"

"Be calm, Sextus. Rash acts come from anger. Why are you so concerned for Livia's welfare?"

"Because I need to look out for her."

She reached out, somehow knowing exactly where, and squeezed his hand. "Beneath that rough exterior lies a sweet boy."

"Sweet is for girls. Is that all you think about? Someone needs to care for the Vestals and I am the man to do it."

"All the Vestals? Or is there one in particular?"

"No . . . not one . . . I mean . . . "

"It is Antonia you care about, is it not?"

She was twisting his words. Justina did that. "Are you going to help me or not?"

Davina placed one hand on Kelila's head. "Put your hands on mine."

Sextus eyed the dog and shuffled forward. More bites were not in his plan.

"She will not harm you. Come."

He crouched down and set his hands atop Davina's. Heat burned into his skin. But he could not snatch them back. Their flesh stuck together.

Davina began to hum, an eerie melody that pulled at him, dragged him into a place of shadows, swirls of dark gray, light gray, white. A white that made him feel empty, hollow, expanded.

Her dark eyes stared at him. "There is little hope, Sextus. We must pray that God will right this wrong."

262

Sextus wrenched his hands from hers. "No. There has to be hope." All he could see was Antonia cowering before Valeria. Evil Valeria.

"There is nothing you can do," Davina said. "I am sorry. It is out of your hands."

"Tell your god to help me. He can do it. He knows everything."

Davina shook her head. "I cannot tell God what to do."

"You lie." He kicked at the dog, which barked and snapped, but he moved out of reach. "You stupid woman. You lie just like everyone else." Sextus shoved her backwards so that she sprawled on the floor. Then he threw yarn in all directions. Greens and pinks and purples spread like tangled seaweed.

A hopeless mess. As hopeless as his plan.

Kelila ran at him with shrill yaps while Davina sat upright, her hair as snarled as the yarn on the floor. Through the twisted strands her eyes shone clear and warm, full of understanding.

"I hate you," he shouted.

He ran from the house and down the hill so fast he tripped over his feet and rolled into a firethorn bush. The tiny spikes pricked his arms and legs and marked them with red spots, as if he had been bitten by a swarm of ants.

Giving in to his temper, Sextus howled.

Women. They were all worthless.

# Chapter XXXV

Livia stood within the hallowed walls of the *Regia*, her body tense with impatience. Rarely was she summoned to the office of the Pontifex Maximus. Today he watched her with guarded eyes. There was no humorous smile to greet the sacred daughter of Rome. Today the lines around his eyes sank deeper, the edges of his mouth pulled down with grimness.

"I hear worrisome reports," he said. "You are accused of evading your duties."

Had Valeria sensed something? A spark of pain flared up the back of Livia's head like a warning. "Who accuses me?" she demanded, knowing the answer in advance.

"Valeria."

The name goaded her into outrage. "Valeria, the holy one. Always perfect, always steadfast."

"Do not mock her. She is tireless in her devotion and serves Vesta well."

"And I do not?" Where was the patience of her early years? Why could she not be a humble servant like Valeria? But she knew full well why not. A rebel lived inside her, protesting, clamoring to get out.

The Pontifex coughed and pounded the congestion in his chest. Her thoughts immediately turned to his unease. "You are ill," she said. "Antonia will bring you some honey water and warm cloths for your chest. You must apply them immediately and sip the water—"

"This is not about my health." He waved a hand to end her speech. "The temple must run smoothly. I will not have discord among the Vestals. When Horatia was High Priestess there was harmony. What has changed?"

*She is gone. The mother has left the brood and I do not know how to lead in her place.* Livia clamped her lips shut before her emotions spewed out and confirmed her lack of ability. For a moment she toyed with the idea of giving up her place of honor. How wonderful it would be to simply turn over the position of High Priestess to someone else, someone more suited to the role. But she would bring eternal shame upon herself and her family. She had been appointed by Horatia. She must complete her service.

As a small girl, Livia dwelled in awe of the Pontifex Maximus, frightened by this large man who ruled all the women in the *Atrium Vestae.* She lived in fear of punishment, expecting the lash at any moment, until the night she woke screaming after a dream where her parents had died, and the person who comforted her was not Horatia, who was away for the weekend, but the Pontifex Maximus. He held her tenderly and stroked her hair until she calmed down, then he sang her to sleep with a lullaby. From that time on they had shared a special bond.

She did not feel that bond now. His eyes were devoid of sympathy. The pain in her head grew deeper and brought a small moan. She must be more careful. She could not allow Valeria to sow seeds of distrust. "I have missed Horatia more than I can say. She is the leader among us, not I. I am a poor substitute for her wisdom. But I . . ." She paused as an incendiary idea blazed and made her stagger. There *was* a way she could continue and follow her heart. "The Vestals have served Rome as faithful citizens of a great Republic. For centuries they have sacrificed that Rome may prosper and know peace."

The priest watched her, his eyes unreadable. "As it should be. You are the heart and hearth. We depend on you."

Livia nodded, fear circling with exhilaration. She felt her courage flit like an elusive butterfly and dug her nails into her palms. *Do not fail me now.* "Many years ago, the Vestals were revered by the king and called upon to strengthen the royal line. They served the Goddess with dedication and purity, yet they were not virgins. Then Tarquin the Elder restricted their sexual activity to protect his children's bloodline. It is time to lift that restriction. Let the Vestals carry the divine energy of the Goddess. Let us be as we once were." If she could convince him to relax the ties that bound her body and mind to Rome, then would she be willing to continue service.

He rose from his chair with a gasp. "You would consort as heathens?"

"Not as heathens. As true vessels of the divine energy." Her body trembled as if she were filled with an unearthly power, a taste of the sacredness of old. Those women had been free, and free the Vestals should be again. Silently she grasped this slim chance, but it was not meant to be.

"What treason is this? Be careful, Priestess, or your words may be used against you."

Fear asserted itself and Livia bowed her head. "I meant no disrespect. This role . . . exacts too much."

"Try harder, Livia. The Vestals need you. We are in a time of uncertainty. Hannibal marches with scores of soldiers and weakens Rome with each battle. This is the time when the people turn to Vesta for comfort, for inspiration. We cannot have suspicion in the temple."

She raised her head and saw the steely flash in his eyes. Smarting from his reprimand, she said, "I will do my best."

"See that you do," he admonished. "Or else all of Rome will suffer." His gaze softened, his hand lightly grazed her arm. "I am not your enemy."

She nodded even though her soul rebelled.

"We have a new inductee. I will bring her to you later today."

Livia left the *Regia*, her ego bruised and fragile. She had not wished for the role of High Priestess, had protested greatly when it was thrust upon her. Was the Pontifex Maximus so unseeing? Did he not understand how cumbersome the position, how it grated at her very being? *Try harder, Livia* he told her, as if she were a wayward child who would not mind.

Her sandals scuffed across the tiles of the *Atrium Vestae*. Patricia bowed meekly. "We waited for you to say our morning prayers."

"Go without me," Livia snapped and stomped to her room where she slammed the door and tore off her palla. Would that she had slammed the door to the priest's office on her departure, or even told him her innermost thoughts. Oppression bore down on her, heavy and unyielding. She felt as chained as a pair of oxen to the yoke of a wagon.

"What have I done to deserve this?" she cried. But she knew there were many reasons, and they all converged in one common thread, one theme that ran through all of her conversations, whether spoken or silent, real or imaginary, the impetus that propelled her through her days and caused her feverish nights of longing. She had broken her vow. She had done the unspeakable and all because of one man.

Gaius.

That afternoon the Pontifex Maximus introduced Floria, a thin child who whimpered and trembled so violently she could barely stand. Livia took her by the hand and led her to the kitchen for a treat of sticky nuts and a cup of warm milk, two foods certain to soothe even the frailest of souls.

Floria nibbled on the nuts and sipped at the milk, tiny bird bites that reminded Livia of her own fears when she first came to the Vestals. The rite of *captio*. When the Pontifex Maximus took Livia off her father's lap and made her a Vestal. She could still feel the rawness of her throat, the ache in her chest from the tears that would not stop. "Papa," she screamed, her hands stretching to reach him. "Papa!" Yet her father did nothing.

So many years had passed, but the memories remained as solid as the ring around her neck. She, too, had cried her way through the first days, yearning for her parents, hoping they would come for her. She wanted the strength of her father's arms, the softness of her mother's hands. But her parents did not claim her and she found a haven with the Vestals.

As Floria would.

She smoothed the girl's soft brown hair. "Do you remember the words the Pontifex Maximus said to you before he brought you here?"

Still avoiding Livia's eyes, Floria shook her head and wiped her nose.

"He said 'I take you this, Amata, as a Vestal priestess, who will perform the rites, which it is right that a Vestal priestess perform on behalf of the Roman people, on the same terms as she who was a Vestal on the best terms.' When I became a Vestal he said those same words to me. Every girl who comes through these doors hears those words. Do you know what they mean?"

Floria took another sip of milk and hiccupped.

Livia fought the urge to sweep the girl into her arms. When she needed comfort, the child would ask for it. "Those words put you under the protection of the Goddess. Vesta watches over you now. As do the other Vestals. Would you like to have a sister?"

Floria raised her head and looked at Livia. Tears welled in her large eyes, sweet, warm puppy eyes. This time Livia could not resist. She stretched out her arms and the girl burrowed in. The sobs came then, large, gulping ones that swelled and echoed. And Livia murmured, "Sshh. Everything is fine. Sshh." Her own tears spilled and she wondered if things would ever change. Would she be here comforting children until she died? Or would she truly leave the temple and have the future she wanted?

The child tightened her arms and whispered, "I want my mother. Can you take me to her?"

Livia rocked the girl back and forth, her cheek pressed to the girl's hair. There was nothing kind about this, about yanking a child from its home. Nothing at all. It was cruelty. But Floria would recover. They all did.

"This is your home now, Floria." The child wailed and Livia continued rocking. "This is your home now. You have five sisters. Five of them. Valeria, Patricia, Oppia, Antonia, and me. Antonia is ten. But you must be older than that since you are so big and strong." She hoped the exaggeration would help to soothe.

Floria sat up and sniffled. Tears made tracks down her cheeks. "I am eight years old. An—" she hiccupped again. "Antonia is older."

Livia kissed the child's forehead. "Just by two years. And that is not so much. She is very nice and she will take good care of you. You will be friends before you know it."

"Will you take care of me too?"

As long as I am here, she thought. But she did not say it. Impermanence was not the proper subject for this conversation. "I will take care of you. The Vestals look out for each other." She lifted Floria from her lap and stood then called Antonia who was waiting in the hall.

"Will you show Floria to her room?"

Antonia smiled. "Floria, what a beautiful name. You have such pretty hair. I like you. I hope you like me too." Antonia held out her hand and Floria took it. And smiled for the first time.

When they left the kitchen Livia sank onto the chair and closed her eyes. Her lips trembled, her cheeks tightened with a flood of sadness.

It never got easier. Almost thirty years of service and it never got easier.

# Chapter XXXVI

Across the sandy soil the enemy gathered in the pre-dawn gray. The air on the Apulian plain already simmered with heat. In less than an hour the sun would cast its fiery glow on the waiting bloodshed.

Gaius ran his tongue over dry teeth, squeezed his cheeks for errant drops of saliva. Thirst had plagued him through the night. The Aufidus River flowed near the camp, but Hannibal's cavalry blocked the Romans' access.

He wanted to be anywhere else, wrapped in Livia's arms, sleeping in a meadow under the stars, even arguing with his father if it would take him away from Cannae. Away from this battle.

He was tired of fighting.

His fingers tightened on his sword handle, bit into the iron with years of resentment. He stood there because of Publius. Because of his father's will and stubbornness and demand for obedience.

His father had brought him here. But his father could not save him.

Hannibal was not to be trusted. Neither were the Consuls. Varro would plunge the Roman troops into war with only glory on his mind. And Paullus would have no recourse. The only one Gaius trusted was his horse, sure-footed and swift. Swift enough to carry him out of danger.

Apollo lit the sky with a ball of yellow. Hot. Searing.

Soldiers prepared for the command. Leather snapped, shields clanked. Horses huffed and stamped their hooves, tails flicking away the flies. Whispers wafted throughout the camp like a mournful dirge.

Awareness brushed Gaius's skin with a chill. He had promised himself one more fight. One last time.

The horn called the men to arms.

Row after row of Romans stepped out in full armor and filled the plain. Over eighty thousand Gaius had heard. The sheer magnitude made him dizzy, proud. Despite Hannibal's previous wins, this time Rome's greater numbers would succeed. And with the enemy anchored against the river, there would be no means of retreat.

Rome was assured a victory.

The infantry advanced in the center with the cavalry on either side. Gaius rode on the east flank, his thoughts on pressing the enemy back. Back into the river.

Hannibal's army stretched out before them. Spaniards from Iberia, painted Celts from Gaul. Carthaginians and Numidians from Africa. A long line, but thin.

They had half the number of the Roman troops. Gaius almost laughed out loud at the easy battle.

Then the sun glinted off their armor. Blinded, he threw up a hand to shield his face and yanked the reins. His horse shied.

With a nervous pat to Apollyon's neck, Gaius urged his mount forward.

*Let it be over quickly,* he prayed. *Give us victory. Get me back to Rome.*

The Africans charged. A sea of horseflesh swelled in a great tide of black. Then the Spaniards and half-naked Celts dismounted. Stunned, Gaius watched the swarm of barbarians. What kind of cavalry was this? What warrior would leave his horse?

Blood-curdling roars deafened his ears. Swords slashed. Men screamed as arms and legs were sliced and hacked. Bodies spurted blood.

He thought of Livia. Stay, she had told him. Do not go to war.

Wind clogged the air with dust and Gaius strained to see. From the back the horns blared. Advance. Advance. He shouted to his men to do the same.

He pushed closer, closer. Lines of soldiers were swallowed. Sucked into the earth and beat to a pulp.

Gaius drove forward to save the floundering men.

Horses crashed into men on foot. Soldiers reeled into stampeding horses. No one seemed to be in charge of the whirlpool of flailing bodies.

Where was Varro? Where was Paullus?

Too late Gaius realized that Hannibal had curved his line. Closing in the Roman troops. Pressing them against each other.

Gaius struggled to turn his steed, to force an opening in the crushing horde. But the soldiers pushed on. Straining. Striving.

He saw her mouth, her eyes. *Come back to me,* she called.

Someone shrieked. His calf burned. When he looked down he saw the stream of red. Then Apollyon stumbled, and Gaius pitched forward, over his horse's neck, over a writhing body, until the ground met him with a jarring thud.

Dazed, he blinked, wheezed, his back a grinding ache.

"Gaius!"

He turned toward the shout as an arrow whizzed past his face. There was no time to thank his savior. Above him a revolting blue man raised a spear. Gaius grabbed his sword and drove it into the warrior's stomach.

The man fell and rolled, his mouth a wide grimace of pain and shock.

Trembling, Gaius pushed to his feet and stared at his sword dripping with red. The life of his enemy.

"Please," the stranger gasped, his breath in sharp staccato puffs. Each heave of his chest oozed more blood from the wound.

There were no wrinkles by his eyes, no deep lines around his mouth. Just the gangly edges of youth. Barely a man.

The Celt grabbed Gaius's leg with surprising strength. Hung on, his eyes wide with fear, pleading.

"Help . . . me," he panted while Gaius watched him bleed to death.

Did he have a wife? Did he have children? Why was he fighting when he could be at home?

A ghostly chill twisted Gaius's gut, climbed through his stomach, each inch colder, draining. He could be the one lying on the ground. Dying. Would the stranger help him?

He peeled the man's fingers from his leg. Felt tears run down his cheeks.

A rough blow to the shoulder knocked him sideways.

"Lucius."

"Are you hurt?" he asked.

Gaius shook his head.

"Then move. This is no time for—"

A javelin speared his friend in the thigh. Before Gaius could help, two more Celts charged, swords drawn. Metal rang in grating harmony. Gaius slid on the slippery ground, his vision clouded by sweat.

They thrust. He parried. Still they came at him. With a great cry he buried his blade in a hairy chest.

Then a force like Jupiter's lightning split his ribs.

He tumbled into darkness, spinning, spinning. In the blackness he saw her, her hand out, reaching, reaching, almost touching.

Livia.

With a hoarse croak he collapsed.

# Chapter XXXVII

Gaius recuperated alone on an iron camp bed in a double-sized tent. There was relative quiet but for the constant movement of soldiers outside, the low voices that told him nothing yet interrupted his sleep. Tomorrow the wounded would begin the journey out of the dry, southern climes and back to Rome. Back to his love.

His father slipped into the meager light of the bedside lamp. What did the man want? Why was he not in Rome locating supplies for the army? Gaius drew in a shallow breath, wincing at the sharp pain of torn flesh and battered ribs. "Father," he acknowledged, determined to show maturity. For once let them put aside their differences.

Publius moved closer until he loomed high above. Streaks of blood stained the linen bandage across Gaius's torso. "Did you forget to draw your weapon?" The edges of his mouth turned up with humor. Or was it sarcasm?

"I had the point of my sword at this soldier's neck and he looked at me with such fear. Fear! Where was his rage? Where was his need to kill? He was barely a man. What right did I have to take his life?"

The older man dropped to his knees, his face lowered, until his breath warmed Gaius's cheek. "Promise me you will never tell another soul what you just told me. Those thoughts have no business in your head. You are a leader." He rose and patted his son's arm.

"I am no Alexander the Great. I could not keep my own squadron alive." He shifted and moaned, wishing his father would come to the point and leave him alone. "What brings you here?"

Publius stared for several moments but his eyes gave away nothing. At last he said, "Rome is in chaos. Too many men have died. Women are wailing in the street, mourning their sons and husbands and disrupting our daily life. The Senate is calling for order." He brought the palm of his hand down with a loud slap. The lamp tottered then stilled. "We must have order."

Through a haze of pain Gaius said, "We will vanquish Hannibal. He cannot defeat Rome."

Publius laid a hand on his son's shoulder, a quick, gentle touch. An unusual touch. "It is too late for you. You have done all you could. You must let others go in your stead."

Shock brought Gaius's shoulders off the cot and a fresh wave of pain through his midsection. In agony, he groaned, yet he kept his eyes on his father. "You would allow me to retire from the Equites?"

"Marcus Aemilius has already taken your place, for the time being. You are of no use to your troops as half a man. Rest and heal your body."

"What are you keeping from me?" Gaius gripped his father's arm but he had little strength to hold on. "What is all this unaccustomed kindness?"

"Can I not be kind to my son? The hero of his legion?"

The memory of the last battle flashed through Gaius's mind. Heroes saved their men from slaughter, from failure. Heroes did not stand transfixed with sympathy while comrades died around them. "I am no hero," he said with disgust, "and my men know it as well as I." He coughed up specks of blood.

Publius wiped his son's mouth with a damp cloth. "What if I told you a ship awaited you at the Port of Ostia? When you are healed."

A clean breeze swept Gaius's mind. "A ship?" The sides of the tent dissolved into blue sky and hot sun. He was standing on the deck of a great vessel, swaying in rhythm to the rocking of the ocean waves. Free and alive he embraced his good fortune with open arms.

He gripped his father's arm again. "What ship? Why?"

"I am getting old," Publius said, his focus on the spotted cloth. "Too old to argue. It is time to forget the past." He returned his gaze to Gaius. "Why should I stand in the way of my only son's pleasure?"

The words oozed from his father's mouth in an oily slide. Pretty but insubstantial. The dream began to evaporate. "Tell me the truth," Gaius said. "What has happened?"

"Why do you always fight me? Why must you always resist?"

"Because you are never content with what I do, with . . ." The words *who I am* reverberated in his head.

Publius moved away from the cot as if he could not be near his son and still say what he must. "Unrest calls for harsh measures. There have been rumors about the Vestals. Some say that the High Priestess is not fit to lead them, that she is unchaste. Some say she allowed the sacred flame to die. True or not, the Vestals are the heart of Rome, the very sanctity of our city. If something is amiss, they will be the ones to suffer."

"How will they suffer?"

"Rome will need a scapegoat. Someone will be sacrificed."

"And you will do nothing to stop this?" Gaius demanded. "You, who have the ear of the dictator?"

"Quintus Fabius listens to other counsel. I have done all I can. My power is limited."

"Then I will go to sea and take Livia with me." He remembered her plea when they last met, how she begged him to leave Rome with her.

"No!" He rounded on his son, his face lit with rage. "Can you not see they will come after you? It is because of her you are in this dilemma."

"You said the Vestals will suffer. How does that affect me?"

"Are you so naïve, Gaius? Do you not know the fate of a Vestal's lover?"

Gaius shrank back. What had his father seen? Did he know of their affair? Did others?

"You answer with silence? I suggest you ask your beautiful Vestal what will happen to you if you are caught."

Rome would not dare to lift a hand against them. This was simply bluster. "Let me take her to sea. I know she will go with me. We can leave all of this chaos behind. Then when Rome is peaceful once more we will return and—"

"You fool!" Publius stared, his face twisted with contempt and futility. "Go home, Gaius. Go back to your wife. That is your only hope." He stormed out of the tent before Gaius could retort.

That night Gaius grappled with his dreams, filled with cries of agony and pools of blood. He woke in the dark, the air hot and clinging. He longed for cool breezes and a comfortable bed, for a pause from the endless pain.

He closed his eyes and imagined swimming in the sea. The water lifted him on a gentle swell, then lowered him and washed over his body. The rise and fall of the waves rocked him in a dreamy rhythm, lulled him, relaxed his mind. His worries fell away. He was in perfect unison with life, with all that is. Only one thing was missing. And with that thought she appeared. His woman. His love. His Livia. Cradled next to him with her head upon his chest, they rocked in the heady bliss of warmth and water, secure in their love, safe from all harm.

When morning came, he ordered a soldier to deliver his decision to Publius.

Three words.

Three words that would end his father's goodwill.

*I choose Livia.*

# Chapter XXXVIII

A month had passed since Livia's last meeting with Kaeso. He was still her dearest friend. They had grown up together, something that would bind them always. But too much had happened. Horatia's illness, Valeria's scheming, the war with the Carthaginians. And above all, Gaius. Her love for him grew each day until it threatened to overwhelm her.

She knew she should spare some time for the caretaker of her property. She had meant to write him. How easily these things slipped her mind. After the market, she promised herself. In the quiet of the afternoon when the other Vestals rested and the house hummed with the melody of serenity.

Titus marched before her with solemn dignity. Neither had apologized after their last outburst, but she had requested his presence this morning in the hopes that their relationship would heal.

The Forum Holitorium bustled this morning. Freshly washed mounds of fruits and vegetables glistened in the gathering warmth. She remembered tossing wet apples with Kaeso when they were children, their arms and faces and tunics splattered with water. How fast the joys of childhood passed. She wished she could capture those moments again.

"Livia."

A tug on her *stola*, a quick hug from Antonia. The child's breath came in huffs. She must have run to the market. "Did you miss me so much you could not wait for my return?" Livia asked. Titus spoke to the young *lictor* that had accompanied Antonia and dismissed him.

"Your friend is here," Antonia said.

Livia turned her head left and right and saw no friend nearby. "What friend? Where?"

"At the *Atrium Vestae*."

A flush climbed Livia's cheeks, her heart raced, a thrill of joy warmed her body. Gaius! He was back from battle. The doubts that had warred in her mind from their last meeting vanished. If he waited for her he must be whole and healthy. Praise the gods for watching over him. She wanted to dash through the streets like a young girl, but she could not. A High Priestess conducted herself with the proper decorum. Instead, she called out for Titus, took Antonia's hand, and walked quickly.

"Bless you for coming to get me," Livia said. "I cannot wait to see him. How does he look? Is he well?"

"As well as ever."

The bud of joy blossomed. "Is he happy?" Happy to see her? she wondered. Happy to be home again?

"He was smiling when he greeted me. And he brought gifts for all of us. Fresh bread and cheese, that wonderful honey we love so much, the sweetest grapes. And pomegranates. As big as his fist and full of seeds. We broke one open when he came and . . ."

Gifts? Why would Gaius bring gifts to the Vestals? He had come to see her, not them. And food. He would not bring food. He would bring her some trinket of devotion, something to show his love.

Apprehension brought her to an abrupt stop. "Antonia, who waits for me?"

"Kaeso."

Livia squeezed Antonia's hand for comfort, security, as if the feel of the girl's flesh could ward off calamity.

Antonia continued to pull her onward. "I have decided to forgive Sextus," she announced, her face alight with the sun's radiance. "I know he did not lie to hurt me. He would not do that. He made a promise to his aunt and he had to keep it. But now he knows that was wrong and he promised not to lie again. So the next time I see him I will forgive him. I hope that is soon."

The words washed over Livia. Life was so simple through a child's eyes. Wounds rubbed raw healed over and pain abated. Friends once lost became friends renewed. Did it take a special heart, or was everyone thus equipped? Would Kaeso someday be her friend again?

He stood outside the *Atrium Vestae* with his face tilted to catch the warmth of the sun. Peace settled on his face, smoothing wrinkles and lines of worry. Could it be that he had forgiven her?

"Good morning," she said.

When he smiled, the familiar crinkle around his eyes returned. All was well. Relief erased her worry and straightened her stance. He held out a pomegranate, as large as Antonia had described. Livia accepted and took Kaeso's arm to lead him inside.

Titus cleared his throat and glared, but said nothing. Nor did he block her way. She nodded to him, a sign that she would be careful.

"I hoped a gift would ease the way," Kaeso said.

"There is no need for that among friends."

He stopped in the atrium. "Are we just friends then?"

Hesitation creased his brow, hooded his eyelids. Unease seeped silently from him like the smoke from the wood of the sacred fire. How much pain she had caused him.

She longed to erase some of that pain. "We will always be close. Nothing can come between us."

"Good, for I have much to tell you. But first, my gifts."

All that Antonia had described overfilled the basket on the bench. Fresh bread and ripe cheese; jars of honey; bunches of green and purple grapes still wet with dew; pomegranates, enormous ruby globes; and figs. Fresh figs. Ambrosia compared to the dried ones from the market in the spring. Her mouth watered. And she had treated him miserably. She must make it up to him with something special. "Such kindness, Kaeso. You are always so thoughtful."

"A simple task when the gifts are for you," he said.

"Can we eat now?" Antonia asked, fairly dancing around the basket in her eagerness.

"You can blame me," Kaeso said. "I told her we could when you returned."

"Then we shall."

They sat side by side on the bench with Antonia on the floor. They tasted and laughed, delighted in rich fragrances, relaxed in comfort and basked in the aura of friendship. Livia felt her worries fade, her fears lessen. Here was the companionship she had missed. Here was the man she had known so well. She reveled in this bliss.

"I like seeing you so happy, Livia," Antonia said.

"Yes," Kaeso agreed. "This is the Livia I know and love."

Surrounded by friends and pleasant conversation and good food, she *was* happy. The mood spoke of more gatherings to come where they could banter and laugh and finally put aside any unpleasantness.

"Antonia, would you give us some time alone?" Kaeso asked. "Livia and I need to discuss an important matter." He said it with a smile but an undercurrent of tension lingered after Antonia left.

Foreboding stole her joy. Caution tensed her body. She should not be alone with him, here, but asking another Vestal to supervise seemed ridiculous. Besides, they were old friends. "Is something wrong?"

"What happened to the Livia who is happy?"

"She is here. I am here." But she felt the misgivings beneath her words.

Kaeso cradled her hand in his. "I am worried about you."

She withdrew her hand. "There is no need."

He gazed at her so long with gentle concern that she bowed her head. "Friends do not let each other suffer alone. You were wrong to make your decision without consulting me."

She continued to look away. Why must they talk now? She had braved her fear before, that day in the Forum Romanum. There was no need to repeat the devastation they had both felt. But he did not move and his solidity began to wear at her. "Please, Kaeso. Let us not repeat our previous conversation. I grieved for you that day. Yet I hoped that time would bring forgiveness."

"There is no need to forgive. But there is a need to declare myself. I love you. And you have made the wrong choice."

Stunned by the simplicity of his statement, she stared at the face she knew so well. Kind, but firm. Steady, loyal, faithful. "I have not made the wrong choice," she said softly.

"Do you remember our pledge? We have carried that pledge in our hearts all these years. I have waited for you since we were children. I would have wed you years ago were you not a Vestal."

"My life has changed. I am the High Priestess now. Horatia is dying and I have assumed her position. Who knows when my service to Rome will end." They were excuses. Excuses to cover her confusion, to support her choices.

"But your service *will* end, Livia. There will be a time when you are free to marry. When that time comes we will settle on the property I maintain for us. As the soil is rich, so our love will be. Peace and prosperity will be ours, and children too, if we are so blessed."

Tears pricked her eyes at the thought of children. For much of her life she had carried one dream in her heart. A happy marriage like her parents and a child of her own. Kaeso had promised to make that happen. But the Fates had shown her passion with another man. Could the dream still be realized with Gaius?

She loved both men, but she yearned for only one.

"I love another, Kaeso. He is the one for me now."

"Can he offer you marriage? Can he give you children?"

Yes, her heart cried out, but her mind faltered. He loved her, that was certain. But would he divorce his wife?

"Gaius is not the man for you. Passion wears thin over time. Constancy is more important. I have loved you since we were young. I will love you when our bodies deteriorate and our minds start to fail. He cannot do that for you. He has a wife."

His plea tore at her. Tears slipped down her cheeks. Leave me, she implored, leave me alone, but she could not speak the words.

"Livia, we belong together. If he truly loves you, he will give you up."

Never. Gaius would never give her up. Her way was clear. She had already chosen.

Kaeso stood and pulled her to her feet. "I trust you, Livia. And I am a patient man. But I will not wait forever."

Her eyes blurred with tears, longing and guilt a muddy turmoil within. He drew her into his arms, held her tight, and for a moment she wished they were back in time, before the Fates had placed her at this heavy crossroads.

"Do not fail me," he said. Words that stunned her mind before his mouth took her breath. He kissed her as a man, a lover, asking and giving, hungry yet tender, his lips warm and comforting and drawing, drawing from her a response she had not guessed she possessed.

Then he released her and left the room without a backward glance.

Livia stared hopelessly after him, her fingers to her lips, her body still in the shock of light arousal. She thanked the Goddess there were no witnesses. And turning, she met the silent victory in Valeria's eyes.

# Chapter XXXIX

The *carpentum* summoned her at dusk when shadows bathed the streets and pedestrians seemed like wraiths. Livia rode in silence, fear a hard lump in her stomach that she tried to press down. But it rose and grew and by the time she alighted the lump sat heavy in her throat just waiting for the moment to emerge in a scream.

She followed the servant into the house, down the corridor, past the richly tiled walls and sculptures and prized vases, into the dreaded meeting room where Publius sat at his desk and studied a map.

"Sit down, please," he stated, his tone polite, without condescension. He pushed a goblet forward which she ignored.

"Did you misplace your usual warm welcome?" she asked, but there was no answer. Livia sat, more troubled now than before. She was used to the sharp bite of his tongue, had prepared herself for it. But this niceness. What did she do with that? Better to broach the reason than to stew in self-recriminations. "Why have you summoned me? What have I done now?"

His eyes were dark and still and penetrating. She wanted to cover herself with her hands even though she was fully clothed. Every time he looked at her she felt exposed. But there was no sneer, no cruel laughter or cutting remark. The silence deepened until he finally said, "You are in danger. You must leave the city."

"Everyone is in danger. Hannibal seeks to destroy all of Rome."

"He will succeed if we are not careful. But I was not talking of the Carthaginian scourge. I meant you, personally."

A great shiver coursed down her back. "What have I done?" she asked again, her voice thin with anxiety.

He leaned back in his chair and tapped his fingers on the wood, a steady beat that burrowed under Livia's skin. His silence infuriated her. *Say what you have to say,* she wanted to yell. But yelling would only prove that he had bested her once again. Why did the gods torture her with this man? She forced her hands to rest on her legs, palms flat upon her thighs, urging her body to relax. Seconds passed until she could take the torment no longer. "If you have nothing to say," she retorted, "I will take my leave."

The moment she rose from her chair he shouted, "Sit down." This time there was venom in his stare. "Are you so unaware of your predicament? Dare I believe you to be so naïve? Where is the intelligent woman I know and . . ."

He cut off the end of the sentence leaving Livia to wonder what he would have said. "I am caring for the Vestals the best I can, doing my utmost to see to their safety."

"And who is seeing to your safety?"

Her mouth opened but no words came out. Whatever could he mean? How was she not safe?

"Livia," he said in the exasperated tone she remembered from the Pontifex Maximus, "use your brain for once. Your antics are becoming a source of gossip. Do you think everyone is blind? Do you think no one sees you consort with my son?"

"No. No one sees. We have . . ." She choked on her breath, convulsing in loud coughs that made her eyes water. Her meetings with Gaius were private. No one could have seen them. And any time they spent together in public they kept short so as not to arouse suspicion. But Publius was telling her all their considerations were for nothing. She wiped her eyes. "It does not matter. I am sorry . . . we are sorry to upset people, but my role as a Vestal will soon be over, and then Gaius and I will marry and—"

"Marry?" Publius asked. "You and Gaius marry?" A sweep of his arm knocked the goblet and map off the table. "You act like a child."

"Why do you hate us so?" she lashed out. Try as she might, she could not control her temper around him.

Publius rubbed his face, a gesture that spoke of weariness. "You always misunderstand me, Livia." His face seemed to age, the skin to sag, his eyes to grow moist. "I only want to protect you."

"Protect me?" Was he trying to confuse her, the better to torment her? "What are you protecting me from?"

"Your belief in people. You trust too easily."

"Why should I not believe that people are inherently good? Throughout history there are those who righted wrongs, who lifted people from the squalor of their lives and gave them hope. Horatia taught us that she is blessed who gives of herself to others."

His sigh fanned her worry. "People are weak, Livia. They do whatever they can to please themselves. The sooner you grasp that, the easier life will be."

"I agree some are as you say." Certainly you are, she thought. "But not everyone. I am not. Gaius definitely is not."

"Naiveté in a child is beguiling, my dear. In a mature woman it is ridiculous."

The flush climbed up her face. Even her breasts felt hot. "Are we here, then, to trade insults?"

Instead of an answer, he reached down and placed a small leather pouch on the desk. "Here is money for you, enough to take you away from here. There is a family in the north who will care for you until you find other means. I have a carriage at your disposal. But you must leave tonight."

"Tonight?" How could she leave so quickly? And why? She must discuss her plans with Gaius. And Davina, Kaeso, even the other Vestals. She could not go without saying goodbye, without giving them good reason. "I cannot leave now. Too much is at stake. I will be more careful with Gaius. If I need to, I will stay away from him for a while."

Publius rounded the desk and pulled Livia to her feet. He shook her and seized her arms so hard she felt his fingers press into the bone. "Listen to me for once. You and I have had our disagreements, but this is no game. I fear for your life. Do you hear me? I fear for your life." At last he let her go and she wobbled on her feet.

"Then save me. Save your son." She pressed her hand to her chest to quiet her heart, to invoke the aura of Horatia who was always calm, always in control. But Horatia did not make her presence felt. Livia tried again. "You have the authority, the position. You can save us."

His eyes bored into hers, glittering pieces of dark glass that any moment would pierce her skin. Then he sank onto his desk. "My power weakens. I am growing old and others seek to replace me. Men who are hungry for fame. I no longer have the ear of those who lead us."

She could not reconcile this sunken man with the figure who had dominated her all these years. "Why are you doing this?"

"Go, Livia. Talk to Gaius if you must. He recovers at the home of Lucius Aemilius Avianus." With a wave of his hand he dismissed her.

She grasped the pouch, not at all sure what to do. "I am not a dog you can command with a wave of your hand. Why do you care? Tell me why."

He met her eyes for the briefest of moments before he looked away. "You know why."

# Chapter XL

D
o this, do that, come here, see me now. All this ordering about from the Pontifex Maximus and Publius. The commands left Livia feeling like a servant. Even seeing Gaius carried the tinge of duty rather than pleasure. And the absence of her lictor niggled her with dread. But she could not bring him with her now.

The *carpentum* rolled through the streets of Rome, up the Caelian hill to the house of Lucius where she would see Gaius again after all this time. How much had happened since they last met. Since she turned him away and wrestled with her conscience. With desire.

She escaped from Publius so quickly she had given little thought to his words. Gaius was recovering. Were his wounds critical? Would he walk again? Was he missing a limb, an eye? Was his body horribly scarred? Sweat slid between her breasts as pictures of mutilated men clouded her vision. Her stomach clenched, knotted. Aware of her position, her actions, she stifled the sounds that longed to come forth, the apprehension she wanted to vent. Horatia would never display such crude expressions. Why could she not be more like her mentor?

The driver escorted her to the house and waited by the door. Inside, the atrium welcomed her with its crosscurrents. Hot from the drive, she slipped off her sandals to stand barefoot on the tile. Then she dipped her toes into the impluvium. The refreshing coolness brought to mind the rushing waters of the spring at Camenae, the delightful conversation with Gaius. Their ease with one another. Their laughter.

Life was simpler then.

"Welcome to my home, High Priestess." A man several inches taller than Gaius wore the tunica of the Equites with the thin purple stripe. Short clipped hair framed a strong, angular face.

"You must be Lucius." She would not blush. She would not. She would act as if every woman cooled her feet in the impluvium. She bent to retrieve her sandals and decided to leave them off. The floor felt too good. Today she would enjoy it. "Thank you for looking after Gaius. I am truly grateful."

"I would do no less for my own brother. Come. He is down the hall."

She walked beside him, her thoughts on the man she was about to see.

Lucius stopped at the bedroom. "You have a visitor, my friend." To Livia he said, "Take your time, but be careful with your conversation. Too much laughter may harm the patient."

She did not see him leave. Did not hear his footsteps on the tile outside the room. She saw only Gaius stretched upon the bed. Her love. Her complement. How did she ever think she could live without him?

His fingers reached out to her. "Livia."

Just that word filled her with joy. Then pain. She had been away from him too long. The tangle of emotions confused her. How could she be happy and feel pain at the same time?

"I have missed you," he said. "Please, come closer. Sit next to me."

She pulled a chair by the bed and held his hand, felt his warmth, felt her eyes fill with tears. "I prayed for you." She kissed his fingers, over and over, pressing her lips against his skin to memorize the touch. "Are you alright? Are you . . ." She was afraid to ask the dreaded question, but she had to know. "Are you whole?"

Gaius laughed then coughed and swore. "The gods have delivered me in one piece, my love. I give thanks daily. But my chest grieves repeatedly where Jupiter's lightning struck."

"Jupiter's lightning?" She prayed to the gods, especially to Vesta, but tales of Jupiter's lightning or Neptune's trident were just stories.

"A mighty crack split me open. What else but the power of Jupiter would cause such a thing?"

She held his hand to her cheek, worried that his head had suffered in addition to the obvious wound. Then she saw the crinkle of his eyes, the glimmer of a smile.

"I worry for you," she scolded, "and you play with me. I think Lucius lied. You are in no danger at all." She pushed aside her chair and stood. "Since you have no need of me I will go where I can do some good."

He tugged on her hand. "Stay. Stay with me." He pulled her down, waited for her to sit, then drew her across him to whisper in her ear. "I have missed you, my love. Every day was an eternity without you. I thought only of you while I was in combat and longed for this time when we could be together."

Her body heated, flushed. He kissed her earlobe, nibbled at her neck and the cool floor had no effect. She had missed him. Desperately. Still, he was recovering. She must be patient. "We cannot. You are wounded. You cannot even laugh without hurting yourself."

"I will not be laughing."

"Gaius."

"Livia, you bring strength to these tired limbs. Lucius would agree if he could see me."

"Lucius is exactly the reason we cannot. We are not alone."

"We are. He promised to leave the moment we were together." He rubbed her lips lightly, slowly. Desire fanned. "There is no reason we cannot love each other," he said, "unless you do not wish to. If my wound repulses you, if you have tired of me, if you have found someone else . . ."

She put her finger to his lips and listened to her own needs. And kissed him.

"Does this mean—"

"Hush," she said, and settled beside him with great care. "Is this alright? Am I hurting you?"

He pulled her closer with a great sigh.

Her body felt like a golden-stringed lyre and Gaius the master player. Each pluck had brought forth a gentle quiver, then a trembling rush that built to a new crescendo of glorious feeling. Love. Only love could make her feel so replete. She was a goddess in her own right, as beautiful as Aphrodite, as pampered as the greatest queen.

How wonderful it would be to lie here with him like this without fear or worry. To be free of her bonds. To live the life she had always wanted. She placed her hand over her womb and imagined a child growing within.

A child of their own. To raise as husband and wife.

Children. Marriage. When would they talk of it?

Anxiety reared its viper head and writhed in her stomach. Why was it so difficult to say the words? From love to marriage was a logical progression. If Gaius knew her at all he would know she wanted that, planned on it. Her property held all the amenities they needed—a house, land, a paying crop, a good location close to the city but far enough away for peace and quiet. She imagined them strolling hand in hand after dinner, through the rows of burgeoning grapes, fat and juicy, their clusters the bright purple of full-bodied health. Standing amidst this bounty she would lean her head on his shoulder, grateful for this abundance.

*He is not for you* Kaeso whispered in her mind, but she pushed it away. Gaius was the one she loved. The one she belonged to.

Speak, Livia, she told herself. There is nothing to fear. He loves you. But the viper dug its fangs into the wall of her stomach and she whimpered.

He touched her arm. "Are you alright?"

She forced down the fear. "I am fine. It is . . . nothing." She was a coward. Even now she could say nothing.

He smoothed her hair. "I know you. You worry. But all is well. Soon you will be free of the Vestals and I will be free of my command."

She ignored his mention of her freedom. "Do you have news of your retirement? What position will you take up next?"

"I have spoken to my commander and suggested a replacement. He is not happy. We have served many years together."

Livia pressed his hand. "But he will let you go?"

"It is my decision. He cannot stand in my way."

*It is my decision.* She closed her eyes and envisioned another Livia, one without the yoke of service about her neck. A woman who stood tall and smiling, the joy of life shining in her eyes. So different from the guarded, watchful spirit that inhabited her own body. If she could throw off the bonds that imprisoned her, she would grab Gaius and run away. "And what of your father? Will he let you resign?"

"He offered me a ship."

A ship. O joyous day. Words could not express her happiness. She threw her arms around him and squeezed. He grunted in return. "My chest."

"Forgive me." She kissed his cheek, his nose, his mouth. "Gaius, a ship. We can leave the city. We can sail away, just as you wanted." This was the reason for Publius's warning. This was what he had meant. "That is why your father told me to leave."

Gaius grimaced. "Leave? What did he say?"

"It can wait. We will talk more when you are well."

"I know my father. And I know you. Tell me what he said."

"He told me to leave Rome."

"When?"

"Now. Two days ago when he summoned me. I did not understand, so I have done nothing." She remembered the violent shaking, how his fingers dug into her arms and left angry welts. Why was Gaius so upset when Publius had arranged a departure for them?

Gaius pulled her close. "If he touched you . . ."

The quick temper again, the need to protect. She loved that about him, yet it worried her. What deep well held that anger until it was time to explode? She had buried her own emotions for so long, always striving to be pleasing and calm. Such outbursts made her uncomfortable. Sometimes she wished he were more composed.

304

"It was a look he gave me. I asked him why he cared. And he said I knew why."

Gaius bolted upright, his face hard with rage. "That perverted monster. I swear I will kill—" A coughing spell racked his body and he collapsed on the bed. "I will kill him," he said weakly.

Livia lightly smoothed his hair with her fingers, over and over to calm him. What was past was past. "Sshh." She cradled him gently as she did with Antonia, and now Floria. "It is not that at all. He was concerned. He said I was in danger."

"How does he know?" Gaius demanded.

Livia shook her head.

"How does he know?" he asked again.

"It does not matter. If he has arranged for us to leave then all is settled."

"Nothing is settled. There is no ship."

"But you said he offered one to you."

His hand gripped the sheet so hard she thought he would tear the cloth. "My *father* does nothing without recompense. To take the ship I must give up you."

For a moment the world blackened, as if night had fallen early. And in that artificial night she lost something of herself. A piece of hope. A sliver of trust. Then her vision cleared and she was once again with Gaius in daylight.

His father's warning was as false as his offer. Rome had certainly suffered of late, but it would recover. As Gaius would recover from his wound. And she from the people confusing her life. If she and Gaius did not sail away, still they could live together and be happy. Rome needed a celebration to lift its spirits. A marriage. Hers.

"Marry me," she blurted and took his hands in hers. "Now. Today."

He squeezed her hand. "Livia."

305

"We need not wait. Let us pledge our love before the gods and when I am free of this title we can live together as husband and wife." The promise of those words filled her with so much joy it flowed from her eyes.

"Livia, my love." He kissed her tears and cupped her face with his hands. "Why this talk of marriage? We need no priest's words to make our vows real. What is in my heart for you will never change. I have felt this way since I was a child and I will feel this way until I die."

A chill began to build inside her. "Are you saying you will not marry me?"

He drew her close and kissed her forehead. "We are married in our hearts."

His embrace gave her no comfort. "But what of the laws of Rome? Would you not have me for your lawful wife?"

"I have a wife."

"But she does not love you." She tried to smile to lessen the severity of the mood. "Gaius," her voice pleaded, "I know it is no little thing, but divorce is not impossible." She remembered the look in Justina's eyes on the last day of the Vestalia. The day of the warning to stay away. But Livia would not stay away. She could not. She loved Gaius and he loved her. "I promise not to be so hasty. Say you will marry me next April when the gods shower husbands and wives with their love and goodwill."

There was sadness in his eyes as he stroked her cheek. Then he took her mouth in a kiss, deep and needing, searching, wanting. She clung to him and gave of herself, gave through her hands, her lips, her heart.

"Sweet Livia. How can I deny you anything? I will speak with Justina. By the time your service with the Vestals ends, the road to our future will be clear."

# Chapter XLI

She might be the spoiled wife of an equestrian with a luxurious house and slaves and the riches she deserved, but Justina's life on the streets had taught her about gossip and cruelty. Hurting people. How easy it was to do so.

Since Publius seemed unwilling to help her restore order to her home and marriage, she would take charge. Oh, yes. And when Livia had suffered, Justina would run away with Eros. The thought of his name brought a curve to her lips. She had developed a fondness for him. It shocked her still, this warm feeling, like a sumptuous dessert, that spread in her chest when she was with him. He gave her tenderness, something no man had ever given her. When she stopped fighting it, fighting him, it grew on her, slowly, cautiously, until it seemed a part of her that she had always known.

He was her life now. Not Gaius, her troublesome husband. She heard he had been injured. That he almost lost his life. She hoped he did die. She hoped Charon dumped him in the River Styx.

Justina smoothed her gown. Not too much color. The dark gray for public mourning to blend with the other women who lamented their lost husbands and brothers and sons. Today she played the role of the aggrieved wife. A woman wounded. A woman who demanded justice.

She had not thought out all the avenues of her plan, but they would align in due course. The scandal would see to that.

The walk with her servant prepared her for meeting with the Pontifex Maximus. Rehearsed lines repeated in her head. "The High Priestess has disobeyed her vows," she would tell the priest. "She is a traitor to Rome." Of course he would want specifics, specifics Justina did not have. So she would do what any good citizen would—make them up. She knew Gaius was sleeping with his little harlot. Why else would he desert his home, his wife? Once she planted the idea in the priest's head, rumor would lead to investigation and investigation would lead to an accusation. Livia would be tried and punished. Justina cared little about the form of punishment. Only that it would separate her husband from his mistress. Then they would see who had the power.

Senators gathered in clusters by the *Curia*. Outbursts burned the air with angry fervor. "We must do something," she heard. "Rome . . . out of control . . . ever since Hannibal . . . evil omens."

She quickened her pace. Rome out of control? Evil omens? The Pontifex Maximus was responsible for collecting omens, for consulting the Sibylline Books, the sacred prophecies that had ruled Rome for ages. Had he already seen Livia's crime? Did he have the answers to Justina's misery?

She bent her head to avoid recognition. Evil omens. What a perfect way to begin.

Valeria met her at the entrance to the *Regia* and showed her inside. The Vestal spoke in hushed tones to a pontiff who left to bring back the Pontifex Maximus.

Time passed too slowly for Justina. Worry poked at her hands, her arms, her legs, until her flesh felt bruised. She glared at Valeria who stood with solemn patience. Did the woman never show emotion?

Worry edged into fear. What if her plan failed? What if Livia were found innocent?

She clenched her hands to stay focused. She had not come this far to see everything fall apart. Gaius would pay for his wrongdoings.

Where was the priest? She had never liked the name Cornelius. Someone of his authority needed a name of strength. Damn the bumbling fool. Where *was* he?

At last the Pontifex Maximus arrived, huffing in the heat. Perspiration mottled his toga and beaded on his forehead, darkened the streaks of gray at his temples.

He gave Justina the briefest of nods.

"I beg your forgiveness," Valeria said. "Hear her out. She has important news."

He studied Justina, probing, making her as uncomfortable as if he had undressed her. "Come," he said.

They followed him into a small room that smelled of disease. There were countless scrolls, rolled and unrolled, some in writing strange and undecipherable. Upon the table lay knives, a curved wand, maps and pictures. Jars held pieces of organs in various stages of aging. Justina gagged and pressed her hand to her mouth to control the reflex. She knew little of augurs or the role of the Pontifex Maximus in all of it. Her life was ruled by practicality, not the whim of birds. But if Rome wanted to believe in superstition, she would bend the city's tone to suit her purpose.

The priest cleared a space on the table and sat. "Now tell me your news."

The rehearsed lines escaped her. Images of Gaius and Livia swirled together, golden hair and dark, green eyes and blue, white limbs and tanned arms, winding, fondling, kissing. Anger surged through her veins, boiling until her skin burned. Livia would pay for her actions. Her husband's sweet Vestal would pay. "Your High Priestess meddles where she is not wanted. She must be punished."

"The Vestals are sacrosanct, protected by the laws of Rome. You have no right to disparage the High Priestess."

"I have every right. It is my husband she meddles with."

"What are you saying?"

"She broke her vows. Need I say more?"

The priest grabbed her arm. "*Incestum?*"

*Incestum.* The word hovered on the air as a shadowy menace that wrapped around Justina's throat.

His hand tightened. "This is treason. What proof do you have?"

Pain shot up Justina's forearm and she wrenched away. *She is sleeping with my husband,* she wanted to yell. But she must offer it in a way that this man would believe her. And take action.

"We have proof," Valeria said. "Livia was nowhere to be seen the morning the sacred flame died."

He nodded, though he looked unconvinced. "Antonia watched the fire that morning. She was the one punished."

"Antonia is a child. She is not the one responsible. Where was Livia?" Valeria asked. "Where was the High Priestess? Why did she arrive after you gathered all the other Vestals?"

"Punishment was given and the flame reignited. Is that all?"

"She vomited at the Fordicidia. Publicly. No priestess has ever disgraced the Goddess until Livia. She cannot continue to lead us."

"That is for me to determine, not you, Valeria. You will do well to mind your position. There must be something more." He jabbed a finger at Justina. "You would not speak without knowledge of some monstrous deed." His voice deepened, judged, threatened. He seemed to grow, to tower over her. "What has she done?"

Done? Done? She would show what his Vestal had done. "She is a whore, I tell you. A whore. Your prim and proper High Priestess parades around town with my husband. At the market. At our house. In our bed. Why do you not believe me?" she shouted, infuriated with his lack of understanding. It did not matter that she exaggerated. He must do something.

His face turned the color of fresh dough, a sickening color that would haunt her from this day. With a shaking hand he grabbed for the table. "Leave me."

When Justina did nothing, he yelled. "Get out. Get out of this building. Get out before the gods wreak vengeance upon you."

Justina glanced at Valeria, saw her tremble, and ran. Away from the room of omens. Away from the building that housed the most religious man in all of Rome.

Away from the scandal that would surely follow.

# Chapter XLII

He was floating through the night on a war horse. A war horse. If the hooves touched the ground, Sextus could not tell. He clutched Apollyon's mane and bent low over the neck then gave a little whoop of pleasure that faded into the air behind him, through the streets of Rome and out of the city. He was riding southeast. To Kaeso. The last person who could help Livia.

Sextus pushed aside the guilt. He should not have stolen the horse. He had promised to be good, to be honorable. But someone had to save Livia and the Vestals.

He had watched the stables for days. At night, of course, when no one would see him sneaking in, his footsteps as silent as the moonlight. After the great Battle at Cannae the animal had been left alone. Watered and fed, but no one took him out. No one asked for him.

Sextus could wait no longer. Rome was covered in a heavy feeling as gray as the robes of the women who mourned the dead. They filled the streets with their awful wailing. Like dogs howling.

*Be a man* the voice in his head had whispered.

He was right to take the horse. Right to help a person in need.

When he first mounted the stallion, he had bounced continually, each landing a jarring contact with the spine. A rope dangled straight down from the halter, near the horse's mouth. When he tried to grab for it he started to slide. Sideways. He had no clue how to steer the animal, or control it, and in another second or two he would be on the ground. He tried for the rope again and missed. Another grab and he was hanging practically upside down with the packed dirt just inches away.

Not the view he wanted.

"Stop!" he yelled, hoping Apollyon would obey. But no such luck. Loping along, Sextus tried not to count the grooves in the road.

He yanked on the mane, on the hide, dug in his fingers. "Stop, I said. By Hercules, if you do not stop—"

The horse lurched to a halt. And Sextus slammed into the ground.

The gods had laughed at him then. Roared while he dusted himself off and stretched his aching joints. But now, now he was sailing on the swiftest ship known to man.

He laid his cheek against the stallion's neck, warm from exertion. Cool air flowed past him, whipping back the curls from his forehead. Jupiter, what a beast. When he was a soldier he would have a steed just like this. Tall, and broad, and—

Apollyon stumbled and Sextus jerked, gripping with his legs until his mount regained his balance. Sextus smiled with pride.

He knew how to ride and no one could take that away from him. Not even his aunt.

He had seen her yesterday, going into the *Regia* with Valeria. Dressed in gray like the women who mourned the dead. But she was not mourning. Gaius still lived.

Thoughts of his aunt turned his mood as dark as Apollyon's hide. Sextus focused on the way before him. Soon he would arrive. Soon he would have help. Soon Kaeso would . . . He would what? Sextus had spent so much of his energy on stealing a ride that he had no plan for his savior. No fancy speech laid out or even any idea what would happen after he arrived. Kaeso would take him in, see to food and a bed, and then . . .

Sextus hugged the horse, fear making him one with the long stretch of black that pounded across the countryside. He had no idea what would happen. And that was a definite mistake. A good soldier always thought ahead. A good soldier would not lead his men into battle without a strategy or ever let a boy anywhere near his horse.

*Stupid child. Cannot trust him. A disaster.* The words whispered in his brain. Words from adults who saw him as a beggar. A wretch. A little boy who would never amount to anything.

"I will," he shouted to the stars. "I will amount to something." He kicked Apollyon's sides, urging him on. "I swear."

He was proud to remember the way. He may not have a plan but his memory was good.

At last he arrived. Leaving Apollyon to graze, he ran to the house and yelled, "Kaeso. Kaeso." He dashed into the dark atrium, his hands before him like a blind man feeling his way. "Where are you? Wake up. Livia is in danger."

Then he bumped into someone. He was about to hug the man from relief when a lamp flickered and Sextus saw Kaeso down the hall. A hand grabbed the neck of his tunic and yanked Sextus against a meaty body. A body he could not forget.

Marcus.

This time he would defend himself. He put up his fists, ready to fight, whatever the cost. "Stay away from me," Sextus said. "I will hurt you." Marcus could tear his limbs apart but, strangely, Sextus felt no fear.

Kaeso stopped close by and the lamp cast a dim light over them. "Sextus?"

"Sextus?" Marcus echoed. "You little scoundrel." He lifted Sextus in his massive arms and squeezed. Not hard enough to damage but enough to cause an ache.

"How did you get here?" Kaeso asked.

Sextus slowly breathed, amazed to be in one piece. "I borrowed a horse. Livia needs you." He sincerely hoped they would overlook the stealing part and focus on Livia. She was the important one.

Marcus crossed his arms. "Stolen is more like it. Always the thief. I thought you knew better."

"I do. I promised not to steal anymore. This is the last time. But she is in danger. I had to come as fast as I could."

Kaeso exhaled sharply. "Then we must help her. At first light. Marcus will see to the horses and provisions." He led Sextus to the same table once spread with the best meal of his life. Kaeso sat, his elbows on the table, his body pitched forward. The lamplight caught the dark eyes full of concern. "Tell me everything you know. Leave out no details."

# Chapter XLIII

Nine *flamines* filed into the meeting room of the *Regia* for Livia's trial. Dressed in toga *praetexta* and *laena*, the woolen cloak of double thickness clasped at the throat, all the members of the Pontifical College were here to judge her. Not women who might understand the tenuous complexion of love, but men. Men of power, men of reason. These men would decide her outcome, even though love had nothing to do with reason.

She faced the row of judges from the center of the chamber. To their right stood the Vestals and Valeria, her accuser, her face the picture of purity. Opposite Livia sat the Pontifex Maximus, once a friend and supporter. Today he would allow no personal emotions to interfere. Today he was the law.

In his hands lay her fate. He once cared for her. Memories whispered of strong hands and a voice that reassured. Warmth and safety. Her parents had left her, but with him she had found a new home. Would he remember that childhood bond?

Heat lay heavy on her skin, as if she, too, wore a *laena* over her *stola*. Already the faces of the *flamines* showed beads of perspiration.

The Pontifex Maximus called the assembly to order. "We meet here this last day of August, to decide the innocence or guilt of the accused, Livia Caecilia, the High Priestess of Rome. The charge of *incestum* has been made by Justina Postumia, wife of Gaius Postumius Albus."

Justina. She would bend the truth. She was the one clinging to the image of marriage. She was the one who would not let go. A woman who refused to divorce her husband. By condemning a Vestal she dragged her husband into the mire. How would she benefit from this?

The High Priest continued. "The charge is backed by the Vestal Valeria."

Valeria allowed a small smirk before her face took on a glow of beatitude.

Livia staunched the urge to slap her. Such impulses were unwelcome and unbecoming. Whatever happened today, a High Priestess must exemplify the rigorous training that made her a leader. She straightened and projected an air of peace.

"What do you say to your accusers?" he asked.

She had broken her vows knowingly, but in doing so she had experienced the greatest gift of all. How could she be judged for being human? For being a woman? She must speak in a way that convinced her judges. It was not wrong to love a man. All women knew that, felt it in their hearts. In their souls. How could it be wrong when the gods and goddesses, the ones Rome looked to for answers, celebrated love? Love, the most beautiful of all emotions.

"I ask you again, High Priestess, what do you say to your accusers?"

Livia took a deep breath. She must set a path for the future. "I am innocent."

"So it is noted. We call for the testimony of the Vestal Valeria."

Valeria faced the panel. "I come here today to rectify a disservice. Rome is in danger. We need leaders. The scourge of Africa threatens our safety and the very heart of our city is impure."

"Rome? Impure?" asked the Flamen Martialis. "How can that be?"

Valeria stabbed her finger at Livia. "There. She is the impurity. She is the one who let the sacred flame die."

"We have discussed this," the Pontifex Maximus said. "It has been dealt with."

Valeria smiled sweetly, falsely. "Of course it has. And we have all moved on as we should. Yet for hundreds of years the flame has not gone out, not until *she* was made High Priestess."

"Why were we not aware of this?" asked the Flamen Dialis. His sharp stare picked Livia apart, as if she were a bird's liver examined for portents.

"The Vestal Antonia was on watch that day," the High Priest answered. "She was punished and the fire was rekindled. The proper actions were taken."

The Flamen Dialis fixed his gaze on the High Priest. "We are to be notified of irregularities."

Guilt bloomed like a noxious flower and wrapped Livia in its cloying scent. The cries, the welts, the blood, all these came back to torture her. It *was* her fault. Yet Horatia had told her stories of the Flamen Dialis in forbidden acts, touching black beans at the festival of the dead. Black beans that conjured the spirits of the wicked. Was a *flamen* free from blame but not a Vestal? Did justice serve only men?

Valeria's eyes gleamed with fervor. "It is *your* fault," she said to Livia. "You never wanted to lead."

"What?"

"Speak the truth, Livia." Her demeanor softened, her voice purred. "Speak the truth. We are all your friends here. You did not want the power."

"Power? No, I—"

"What kind of leader does not want power?" Valeria demanded. "Who would not seek to gather the masses? Is she another Quintus Fabius to sit idly back and watch Rome succumb to another invader?"

Livia's legs trembled. She shifted her weight but the floor moved beneath her feet. She groped for solid ground. Power? Invaders? What did Valeria mean? "Thirty years I have given Vesta as a loyal servant. I have honored the temple and my sisters. I have taught the younger Vestals in accordance with my duties. We have nothing to do with—"

"Honor, she says." Valeria spread her arms wide, embracing the room and all within. "What kind of honor allows a Vestal to betray her vows? Justina Postumia came to me three times to complain about our High Priestess. Three times she recounted details of her husband and our High Priestess in public together, behaving inappropriately. Where is the honor? We need a leader who is pure, a person who will take an active role in our affairs. Someone who will command the people's hearts. Someone who will guide us to the greatness we deserve."

"Greatness," the Flamen Quirinalis agreed with a thump of his fist.

"Is this true?" the Flamen Dialis asked.

"She has betrayed us," Valeria said. "She is a harlot. She must be punished."

Livia fought the tremors in her body as Publius's words screamed in her head. *Do you think everyone is blind? Do you think no one sees you consort with my son?* Had she really been so naïve? She must control herself. She must appear relaxed. She did not answer to Valeria, she answered only to the Pontifex Maximus. The man who now looked at her as if he had never seen her before.

He wiped the sweat from his forehead and placed his palms over his eyes. After several seconds he straightened.

"That is all, Valeria. We call for the testimony of Titus Cloelius Gracchus."

Livia did not hear correctly. She could not have heard correctly. But surprise turned to disbelief when her *lictor* entered the room. He did not face her or acknowledge her in any way. He turned immediately to the line of priests and nodded to the Pontifex Maximus.

Blood beat in her ears and drowned out the voices. They could not question him. All that he had seen, all that he had heard . . .

"Has the High Priestess acted in any way unbefitting her role?"

"She has," he said.

*No, Titus,* Livia pleaded, *do not do this.*

"Describe her actions."

"On several occasions she has gone out into the city without the accompaniment of a *lictor*."

The Flamen Quirinalis made notes on a fresh tablet.

"Do you know the reason for these actions?"

Livia held her breath, afraid of what he would say.

"No, I do not."

He lied. Blessed Goddess, he lied. She exhaled. She wanted to throw her arms around him and kiss him.

The Pontifex Maximus continued his questions. "Has the High Priestess committed any other improper actions while she was in your presence?"

"A number of times I have seen her in conference with a man."

"Do you know this man?"

"I do not recall."

The High Priest coughed and wiped his mouth while he stared at her, watching her reaction. She commanded herself to make no movement and hid her hands in the folds of her *stola*.

"Were they alone?" he asked.

"Yes."

"And what were they doing?"

"They were conversing."

"Is there anything else?"

"Not that I recall."

"Tell me, Titus Cloelius," the Flamin Dialis said, "what *do* you recall?"

Titus stared directly at the priest. "That is all."

"Did they hold hands? Did they kiss? How do you know what they were or were not doing if they were alone?"

Titus remained silent.

The priest slammed the arm of his chair. "He withholds information."

"He is a servant of Rome," the Pontifex Maximus said. "He has sworn to tell the truth." He nodded to Titus. "Do you have any more to add to your testimony?"

"My family has served Rome for generations. I follow in the footsteps of my father and his father before him. It has been my pleasure to attend the High Priestess all these years. *This* High Priestess. Rome will not find a more selfless woman than the one you see before you."

Livia's eyes brimmed with tears of relief.

"Thank you, Titus Cloelius," the High Priest said. "You may leave us."

With a quick glance at Livia, Titus departed. Dear Titus. Noble Titus. Within those stern eyes she saw worry, concern, fear. He was more than just a bodyguard. He was a friend, a trusted friend. When she was cleared of this folly she would see him rewarded for his loyalty.

She focused again on the Pontifex Maximus.

"We call the other Vestals to testify," he said. "Patricia, what do you know of these accusations?"

Patricia meekly bowed her head. "I know nothing of these accusations, Pontifex. Livia is a kind and caring woman." She said nothing more.

"Oppia, speak."

Oppia faced the *flamines*, her hands shaking slightly. She glanced at Livia then back at the priests. "Patricia speaks the truth. Livia cares for all of us. She is not . . ." she paused, her eyes raised upward, ". . . ambitious like Valeria. But she is devoted to us." She turned to stare at Valeria. "And to Rome."

The Pontifex Maximus nodded. The Flamen Quirinalis added these bits to his tablet. "We waive the testimony of Floria and move to Antonia."

Sweet, pale Antonia. Her body trembled as if she were the one on trial. Livia did her best to smile at the young girl, to give her strength for this ordeal. And pleaded silently, *Say only what you must.*

"Step forward, girl," the Flamen Dialis commanded.

"Antonia," the High Priest said softly, "what do you say to these accusations?"

"Livia is kind and sweet and caring."

"Yes, yes, we know that," the Flamen Dialis said. "She is the very image of perfection. Is there nothing else? Has she done nothing wrong, nothing worthy of this trial?"

Antonia's eyes brimmed with tears. "Valeria is the one who is wrong. She hates Livia. She hates us all. She cares nothing for any of us. If not for Valeria, Livia could be with Gaius now. They could—"

"Antonia!" Livia cried.

The Flamen Dialis gripped the arms of his chair, his torso forward, muscles straining. A coiled animal ready to pounce. "Go on."

Antonia looked at Livia in agony, tears sliding down her cheeks. "I am sorry, Livia. But she is so mean. Without her you could be happy."

Livia pushed down her feelings, her love for Antonia, her fear for what the girl had said. She would not appear helpless.

"Speak, child," the Flamen Dialis demanded. "What is this about Livia and Gaius? Who is this person?"

Antonia rubbed her fingers together, her little body tense. "The man you call Gaius. They are in love," she whispered.

"Speak up. What did you say?"

Antonia wiped her tears. "They are in love. They are meant to be together. Anyone can tell. It is the most beautiful thing I have ever seen. And when I am older I hope to be in love too." She smiled at Livia with all her delight.

"I saw them kiss," Valeria pronounced. "In the *Atrium Vestae*."

A loud gasp echoed through the room. Livia glared at Valeria, knowing full well her accuser twisted the truth. It was Kaeso she had kissed, not Gaius. But Livia could neither confirm nor deny the claim without harming her own case.

"Blasphemy," the Flamen Dialis said. "Utter blasphemy." He scowled at the High Priest. "I hold you accountable for this."

"Antonia is a child," the Pontifex Maximus said, his face waxen under a sheen of sweat. His chest rose and fell with rapid breaths. "She knows nothing. You cannot believe her . . . her imaginings."

"Imaginings? Is she not a Vestal? Sworn to uphold the sacred vows?"

Silence spread through the chamber like an evil wind. Valeria once again looked pure and modest. The High Priest's color slowly returned but he would not meet Livia's gaze. Before Antonia they were confused; she had a chance. But now . . .

At last the Pontifex Maximus looked her way. "Do you swear your innocence to the goddess Vesta and the priests gathered here?" he asked.

They were afraid of her. She saw it in Valeria's pride, in the cruel gaze of the Flamen Dialis. She saw it in the forced calm of the High Priest. Rome needed continuity. Routine. Not a Vestal who challenged their manhood. And yet once, hundreds of years ago, the Vestals were not bound by these oppressive rules. Somehow she must make these leaders understand their error. She must lead the Vestals and other women towards a better future.

The Flamen Dialis pounded the arm of his chair. "Answer us. Do you swear that you tell the truth?"

What could she say? How could she swear after Antonia's testimony? Visions of the afterlife filled her head. Charon, the hooded ferryman on the River Styx. Cerberus, the monstrous three-headed dog that guarded the gates of the Underworld. The three judges Minos, Rhadamanthos, and Aeacus who would demand an accounting of her life. What would they say of her? Would they admit her to the Elysian Fields to live in splendor, or would they condemn her to agony in the pit of Tartarus?

Her eyes blurred, her chest ached. Her legs quaked from ankle to thigh. She feared she would fall to the floor with her limbs splayed wide like the harlot they thought her to be. *Help me, Vesta. Save me from disgrace.*

She banished the fearful images from her mind and clung to the grace of the Goddess she knew. The Goddess who had protected her from harm these past thirty years. The one who would protect her now.

Livia dug her nails into her thighs to bolster her courage and spoke from her heart, the place where, once before, she had felt the power of the Goddess. "I did not want this position. Yet the former High Priestess trusted me. She was the one who chose me to lead the Vestals. In her wisdom she placed me here to guide these women. To give them strength and courage and wisdom. To teach them compassion. To show them the true path of leadership. She would not have chosen me were I not fit."

The Flamen Dialis roared his question once more. "Do you swear?"

She had one moment to make this right. One lasting impression to leave on these men who ruled Rome. Aphrodite's message whispered in her mind. *Who but you would know how to love a man?*

Livia said the only words she could. "I swear."

Sequestered in her room in the *Atrium Vestae,* Livia waited, waited, waited until it seemed the day had ebbed into night and become day again. She could not leave the room, nor could anyone enter but the priest stationed outside to guard her door. She did not want for food, but she had no appetite. How could she eat when her future lay in the hands of those men?

Several times she had opened the door to learn of the verdict, and each time the priest shook his head and shut her in. The poor man looked as uncomfortable as she. Dear Goddess, why did the laws subject people to such agony? Let them tell her and end her misery.

Through it all she held fast to her beliefs. Love was hers now. Love and passion in sweet array, stunningly entwined and breathtakingly beautiful. Ahead of her beckoned a road of bliss. She would not give that up. It had taken her too long to find it.

A knock sounded and the priest peered into the room. Livia pushed up off the bed and smoothed her *stola*.

"You are called to appear before the Pontifex Maximus."

The verdict. Just moments before she had wanted an answer. Demanded one. Yet her trembling body showed the opposite. She prayed to Vesta. The Goddess would protect her. Vesta would remember Livia's service, her obedience to the laws of Rome. She would be set free to be with Gaius.

Free to live.

She held that image in her head as the priest led her across the brief space between the *Atrium Vestae* and the *Regia*.

*I am free. We are free.*

It did not matter what Antonia had said. The child's pale face came to mind before Livia could banish the picture. She blessed the dear girl and moved on. Up the steps of the *Regia*, down the hall, into the meeting room.

The High Priest waved Livia to a chair and motioned to her escort to leave them. Moments passed while he stared at Livia, his eyes unreadable, his face blank. So still was he that she could not see him breathing.

Fear exploded. If the news were good, he would not wait to tell her. Her heart pounded a painful rhythm, harder and harder, pulsing against the walls of her chest as if it were trying to escape.

"Livia." He said her name quietly, softly, the way he used to when she was just a child.

Was he preparing her for the worst? Or would he apologize for the way she had been treated?

His hands twisted together and she saw the nervous twitch of his little finger. "You have always been my favorite Vestal. Since the days of your nightmares I have come to love you as a daughter. If there were something I could do to change this." He paused and swallowed, the bob of his throat an ugly animal squirming to get out. "Ever since the Battle of Cannae, Rome has wallowed in grief. The people call for sacrifice. Already two Greeks and two Gauls have been buried alive in the Forum Boarium to placate the gods. But it is not enough. It is the heart of Rome they need to sanctify. Forgive me. You have been found guilty."

She was on the floor, her limbs and *stola* a tangled mess. Somewhere a high-pitched whine grew louder and louder until she realized it was her own voice.

*No. Dear Goddess, this cannot be. No.*

He pulled her gently to her feet and helped her onto the chair. He put a cup of water in her hands but she could not drink. She could not even think.

She was guilty.

He knelt before her and held her hands. "The *flamines* wanted you to appear before them but I insisted I would deliver the verdict on my own. You broke your vows, Livia. There is no recourse for a Vestal who breaks her vows. If I had known . . ."

His eyes were dark shards of torment. Nowhere had she seen such sadness. Not even with Kaeso when she had broken their agreement.

"I do not want to say this but I must." He turned his head to avoid her eyes. "Under the laws of Rome, you will be taken to the Campus Sceleratus where you will be left to die in an underground vault." When he kissed the backs of her hands and rested his cheek upon them, an unheard of act for the High Priest, tears dripped onto her skin. "Never before has my profession given me such an unholy task. Rome will not be the same again. Nor will I."

He left her then, sitting alone in the chamber, her hands still around the cup of water she had yet to drink.

# Chapter XLIV

This was where it began, sitting in Pomponia's garden with the sun overhead. Despite the shade of the fig trees, the heat bore down on them, harsh, sweltering, draining the moisture from Justina's body until she felt as dried as the dates on the nearby platter. She rubbed at her sky blue dress and wondered at Pomponia's choice of waxy yellow that turned her skin sallow. So much had happened since that other day in May, and if all went as planned, she would once again regain control of her life.

How long must she wait for the news?

"All of Rome is in an outrage," said her friend. "A Vestal at the heart of the city's misfortune. How the gods must frown upon us." Pomponia picked at her dish of dates with fingernails like spears, stabbing the fruit over and over before she maneuvered it to her mouth.

Loneliness lingered in Justina's house, settled on her shoulders, accompanied her to bed. She could not move for wondering about her husband and how he fared since his Vestal had been accused. But Pomponia played with words as she played with her food. If Justina showed her own insecurity, her friend would pick at her in the same manner.

"Which Vestal?" she asked in pretended innocence. "What do the people say about her? You know you are the most wonderful gossip in the entire city."

"You have not heard?" A long fingernail plopped a date into the cavernous mouth. "How out of touch you are, Justina. You really must get out more. They say," she leaned closer, her breasts poised on the edge of the table, "the High Priestess is a child of Pluto. They say she has a lover."

A lover. A self-serving gloat brushed Justina's lips for a moment, a brief, luscious moment before she let it go. Her plan was unfolding with perfection.

"What will happen to this . . . High Priestess?"

Pomponia leaned back, her head tipped slightly to the right. "Do I hear a note of concern? Are you growing soft?"

"Such ideas you have. When have I ever been soft?"

"Since Eros, I think. How is your Greek god?"

Absent. They had been apart for several weeks. There was no word, no indication that he missed her, wanted her, would even speak to her after their last disaster. So often she woke in the middle of the night, turned to feel his warmth, his arms around her, the weight of his body next to hers, but there was nothing. Too many times she had thrown back the covers in horror, expecting to see those red drops bright against the white linen. Would he ever take her back?

Her hand settled in protective measure on her abdomen, on that part of her that was yet uncertain. Child or illness? She had missed one cycle but that proved nothing. Then she noted her friend's keen eyes staring. Before she could move her hand, Pomponia's palm clamped down.

"What are you hiding from me?" The hand pushed harder, fingers spreading, probing. "Are you pregnant?"

Justina pushed Pomponia's hand away. "What nonsense you speak. How could I be? You know I am unable." She hated that knowing look in Pomponia's eyes. The haughty leer that reminded her so much of . . . Publius. Revulsion shot through her. Was this her friend?

Pomponia smirked. "Gaius may not be virile. But Eros certainly is. He has children all over the city."

"He does not."

"Believe what you will."

She knew Pomponia played with her. Usually the game was entertaining, but Justina had grown tired of insinuation, particularly when it involved her. "Tell me of the High Priestess."

Pomponia yawned and waved at the air. "The High Priestess. How such a lackluster woman was put in charge . . . She has no fortitude. Vomiting at the Fordicidia before all of Rome. How dreadful." Her icy smile showed her true delight. "She deserves her fate. Let another take her place."

Justina had heard nothing since the accusation. "Has her fate been decided?"

Pomponia raised her arm and snapped her fingers, holding the elevated flesh in place until a servant appeared. "We are out of dates. And more wine." Only when the servant disappeared did she lower her arm. "You must come to the theater with me next month during the Ludi Romani. You always enjoy the games. There is a comedy by Livius Andronicus. I am sure it will lift your poor humor."

Justina struggled to stay calm, to keep her hands in her lap and not pummeling Pomponia's face. What had happened to Livia? "A play would be wonderful," she lied. Anything to sound carefree. "But what of the Vestal? Do not leave me hanging."

The servant came with dates and wine and retreated quietly. Pomponia chewed on a mouthful of them then gulped her wine like a noisy drunk. "The Vestal, the Vestal. Is that all you care about? I hear that she and her lover will be executed. Publicly. I plan to go, of course, but only if the weather is kind. My skin will perish in the sun."

Lover. Executed. Justina could not breathe. She felt the rise and fall of her chest but her lungs would not inflate. Air. There was no air. Her mouth opened and nothing came in. Gaius. Executed. No, it could not be. That was not the plan. Rome would not kill an equestrian. A centurion. Something was wrong. She had to fix this. It was Valeria's fault. Valeria must have done something wrong.

*Breathe!* But she simply sat there. Paralyzed. Watching Pomponia's fat arms ripple and her wicked eyes gleam.

"You look miserable, my dear," Pomponia said. "Forget your sorrow. Come to the play. If Gaius truly does not want you, so be it. You have Eros. Or find another man, someone *you* choose this time. You are still pretty enough."

At last Justina breathed in and all her fear and outrage spewed out. "Oh be quiet, Pomponia. You are as tiresome as a yapping lap dog."

Pomponia stared in open-mouthed stupefaction. Then she banged her goblet on the table. Wine spattered the cream cloth and the tray of dates. "Really," she huffed and walked out.

Left alone in the garden, Justina tormented herself over the sticky mess she had made of life. But she would not sit still without action. Someone would pay for this disaster.

Garbed once more in her servant's clothing, Justina pounded on the door to the *Atrium Vestae*. Rage simmered in her body like a pot of water about to boil. Any moment the bubbles would burst and she would not be responsible for the backlash. She had trusted, confided in, told the woman things she had told no one else.

Valeria appeared, her manner calm. Gone was the frenzy of the previous day when they had both conversed with the Pontifex Maximus.

"You knew!" Justina cried.

"What are you referring to?"

"The punishment for a Vestal."

"Of course I knew."

Despite all the planning and scheming, the events that had led to this moment, Livia was still a Vestal. A sister to Valeria. They had spent years in each other's company. But there was no regret in Valeria's eyes, no sorrow.

"I meant to demote her," Justina said, "to sequester her. Not this . . . this execution."

"She is getting what she deserves. She tore apart your marriage, did she not?"

"I did not mean for her to die. And what of my husband?"

"Suddenly you are so protective. What does it matter? You do not love him."

"I cannot have him harmed." Though she had little regard for him, he was still her husband. Her lifeline to society. To the position she had fought for, craved, needed.

"You did not mention that when we concocted this scheme," Valeria said. "Now, please excuse me. I have things to attend to."

Justina gripped the door. "You did not tell me the consequences."

"I assumed you were aware."

"You assumed I would lead my husband to his death? What kind of woman are you?"

"One who needs power. Livia was too kind, unfit for the role of High Priestess. The Goddess has spoken to me. I am the perfect leader."

"You are immoral!"

Valeria pushed against the door. "I believe the words of condemnation came from your mouth, not mine. I must go now."

Justina grabbed the Vestal's *stola*. "Stop! I have to save him."

"I owe no allegiance to you. You are nothing to me. You served your purpose."

She clutched at Valeria's gown and pulled. "You could not have done this without me."

Valeria stumbled. She clawed at Justina's hand and released the material. Her lips curled in a nasty snarl. "You may be right. But it is done now." She slammed the door.

Justina snatched her fingers away just in time. "Valeria," she shouted. "I need your help. Do not turn from me now!"

It took Justina most of the day to locate Eros's house. She had never thought to ask him where he lived. He had always come to her. But now she needed comfort. She wanted someone to caress her, to cradle her, to tell her everything would be alright.

Gaius could not die.

She arrived in the Greek quarter just past the dinner hour. Her dress was stained with perspiration, her feet throbbed from walking. There was no servant to let her into the house, no one to announce her. Crates of furniture and household objects filled the atrium. Chairs were stacked, tables upended. Justina shivered and pressed on.

"Eros," she called down the hall.

There was no answer.

She raised her voice, afraid now. "Eros."

Silence followed her to the *peristylium* where she found him standing by a row of plane trees, staring at the still light evening sky. Broken stubs of plants poked out from the trampled ground beneath his feet. She stood beside him. What did he gaze at? Had he lost his mind? "What are you doing?"

"I wondered if you would come," he said without facing her. "I wondered if the wife of the man about to be executed would deign to visit her lover. And here you are." He turned to her. "What is this you wear? Where are your clothes?"

Clothing did not matter. Her husband was important. "Rome cannot . . ." She could not say execute. The finality of that word gripped her gut with icy fingers. "You have to help me. I must save Gaius."

"Help you?" Eros turned to her. "Help you save the man who threatened my life?"

"What are you talking about?"

"Your precious husband pulled a knife on me after he found us together. He told me he would kill me if he saw me with you again."

Her throat tightened, squeezed, trapped the breath within and held it hostage. Gaius had threatened him? Why had no one told her? At last she gasped and coughed and still he made no move. Why was he acting like this? Had he stopped loving her? Was it all just a game?

She briefly rested a hand on the place where her child might reside. His child. "I thought you loved me."

His laugh echoed in the night, wild and unkind. "Justina. Justina. You are a priceless gem among women. There is no one so self-centered."

"Show me another woman who does not think of herself."

"Why would I care about another woman when I have you?"

"So you do love me."

He pulled her into his arms, kissed her roughly, his mouth demanding, needy. "May the gods help me, I do. There is no other for me."

"Then save my husband."

His hand caressed her arm, soft, grazing touches that ignited her desire. "If I save your husband, what then?"

She smiled to herself. This was what she had come for. "All will be as it has been."

"We will continue as lovers?"

"Of course." She leaned toward him but his grip kept them apart. Perhaps he needed coaxing. She had missed him. More than she wanted to admit. Having him in her bed would bring back a normalcy she had come to expect. "I care for you, Eros. Very much. Of all the people I could have asked for help, I chose you."

"How valiant of you."

"There is no one more important to me." How easy it was to charm, to flatter. As he had seduced her with compliments, so she would do with him.

He grabbed her hard by the wrist. "Rome is falling apart. Are you so oblivious? Nothing will be as it once was. Did you know they sacrificed two Greeks already? One of them might have been me."

A violent tremor shook her body. He was exaggerating. She could not lose both her men. The world would not be that cruel. "You have done nothing to Rome. They would not take you."

"What of the two who died? What crime did they commit?"

She had no answer, no defense against his anger.

He let her go with a weary sigh. "I am leaving Rome, Justina. There is nothing here for me."

"What about me?"

"I once asked you to marry me. Are you ready now?"

She was already married. If Gaius lived, if she divorced him, she would have nothing. Eros had no title, no position, no security to offer her.

"I thought as much," he said. He gazed at her for several moments, her eyes, her mouth, the swell of her breasts. His hands ran down her arms then he pulled her close and kissed her until her body throbbed and her legs felt weak.

No man could make her feel this way and not need her as much as she needed him. She exhaled a sweet breath of victory. He would do as she wished.

"Come with me to Greece," he said. "We will make a home there."

Greece? She could not go to Greece. "Rome is my home."

"Greece is mine." He kissed her forehead, her eyebrows, nuzzled the curve of her cheek. "Athens is a beautiful city. It has everything you could wish for. And we would be together."

She wanted him, but he was asking the impossible. "I cannot go with you. What would people say?"

He cupped her face, his hands gentle, his breath warm. "Do you love me, Justina?"

"I . . . I . . . ." Why was it so hard to say the words? The love was there, nestled in her heart, new, untested. Let her just voice it for once. Let her make the sounds and she would have what she needed.

Eros kissed her once more. "My home there is always open to you." He gazed into her eyes with desire and sadness. Then he walked away.

"Eros. Eros, come back and talk to me."

Footsteps echoed in the hall.

"Eros. We have not finished."

The torches flickered in the silent garden. Justina was alone again. And there was no one to blame but herself.

Mired in defeat, she raised her arms in supplication to the gods. A raven perched in the plane tree to her right and croaked once. Ravens were a sign of victory.

A rush of gladness swelled her throat. Hugging herself, Justina watched the sky glow with the red of the setting sun. The gods had not failed her. Somehow she would find a way to salvage her life.

# Chapter XLV

Gaius sat in the garden of Lucius's house, alone, in the midday quiet. The sunlight drenched him with its heat but he was not uncomfortable. He thought of Livia.

Love did strange things to a man. He had skirted the issue of divorce with Justina, content to see Livia and spend whatever time with her he could. That was enough for him. Had been enough. Love and seduction took place moment to moment. He left his strategy for the battlefield. But Livia's plea for marriage, the quaver in her voice, the importance of it all led him to a new decision. He wanted to satisfy her. He wanted the sweet curve of her lips, the glow of her eyes when she looked at him, not the trembling or fearfulness of yesterday. His fingers curled around the arm of the chair, remembering the heat of her body, her joyful cries when they made love, the desire in him that never seemed to fade. She was everything a woman could be, everything he needed. He would deny her no longer.

Justina, Justina. His fingers tapped on the arm of the chair as he wondered how to approach his wife. What tactic to use, what time of day was best. Would it be when she was with her lover? Or on her own? There was no love lost between them. But she cared for his property, his money, his social standing.

It would be a simple thing to divorce because of adultery. And it would save his position and profit. He could not wed Livia empty-handed. But to cast out his wife and bring her public shame? He might as well sentence her to death.

No, he would talk to her and find a reasonable agreement. Anything for Livia.

When he was completely healed, he would see his wife. Two more days of rest the doctor ordered. Then he would confront Justina and set a plan into action.

The magistrates walked in on Gaius seconds after that decision. Four men in toga *praetexta* surrounded him, plus the Master of the Horse. A position Gaius had once dreamed of. Second only to the dictator in these times of military unrest. "By the power of *imperium* and the laws of the Twelve Tables," the Master of the Horse stated, "we arrest you, Gaius Postumius Albus, for committing *incestum* with the High Priestess Livia Caecilia. Take him away."

*Incestum?* With Livia? How did they know?

Two men grabbed Gaius's arms, lifted him out of the chair, and propelled him forward. He struggled to break free, but his strength had faded. His wound protested the action with searing pain. Rather than reinjure himself, he submitted. They meant to scare him but he would not be another scapegoat for Rome. He had loved a woman, not murdered one. How could that be an offense?

Only a manipulating person would have brought him to this. Justina. His beautiful, resentful wife. No one else would have the nerve to denounce him. She flaunted the laws with an adulterous affair, according to Roman law, whereas he simply loved a single woman. "I am innocent of this supposed crime. Who accuses me?"

"Rome accuses you. The Vestal has been tried and found guilty."

Livia guilty? This had gone too far.

They pushed him onward.

"Stop! You cannot do this. Something is wrong. She cannot be guilty."

The Master of the Horse grabbed Gaius's arm, his grip as strong as eagle's talons. "You are right, centurion. Something *is* wrong. You have betrayed your city. Rome should not have allowed you a command. You are not worthy of her loyalty."

"I betrayed nothing," Gaius shouted as they led him away. "Nothing, I tell you. She is innocent. We are both innocent."

Gaius languished in his empty house. Justina did not torment him with her scathing remarks. Even the servants were absent. Two guards kept watch over him while he awaited trial.

He paced for hours, wearing sores on the soles of his feet from the scraping of his leather sandals. His legs ached, his wound burned. He should be resting but his mind wove weary circles of unanswered questions. Where was Livia? What would happen to her? When could he see her?

When the light faded to darkness, he collapsed on his bed and willed himself to ignore the pain. He was a soldier, used to discomfort. He would manage this as he managed his wife and father. Tomorrow would see him released and free of any charges.

Fatigue pulled him down into a murky blackness. He closed his eyes and slept.

Harsh voices dragged Gaius from rest. He sat up slowly, wincing at the soreness in his chest and back. Heavy gray shrouded the bedroom. The guard placed a lamp on the table near the bed before departing. A tall figure entered, standing in shadow. The stranger remained in the dark, unmoving.

Annoyed, Gaius slowly pushed himself up, his body stiff, protesting. "Who are you? What are you doing in my home?"

"Do you hate me so much that you have yourself arrested to prove your point?"

Only one voice sounded like that. Only one man knew how to irritate him so.

"Father. How kind of you to come. Please, have a chair, some wine." He gestured at the cramped space that contained only the bed and table.

"How gallant of you," his father said. "I see you are in good spirits. Only this is no laughing matter."

"I am not laughing. Are you?" Gaius resumed his seat on the bed. His father could stand or leave, whichever he preferred. He hoped the man would leave.

Publius moved closer. "Why do you continue to disrespect my wishes?"

"Because you have no care for mine."

"All my life I have cared for you."

Gaius leaped to his feet and groaned from the sudden pain. "All your life you have cared for only one person." He noticed now the haggard hollows beneath his father's eyes. The sunken cheeks. Age had become his enemy.

"My son." Publius put his hands on Gaius's shoulders. Gaius pulled away. "My son," Publius repeated.

Anger spoke. "I am not your son." He moved away, away from the man who had scorned him as a child and berated him as an adult. His voice was as weary as his body. "I am not your son."

"You are the only son I have left."

"You should have thought of that when you offered me a ship."

"I was thinking only of you."

Gaius turned on him. "Not of my wife? Or my position in society? I seem to recall she was part of the plan."

"I care little for her. You are my son."

Frustration blurred Gaius's eyes and clenched his hands. "Then why do you never treat me as one?" He watched his father's impassive face, waited for a softening, a glimmer of something tender. Nothing had changed. He exhaled a great sigh of futility.

"You can leave now, Father. There is nothing left to say."

"Would you have me deliver your own death sentence?"

"What are you talking about?"

Silence flickered like the lamplight, elusive, wavering. At last Publius said softly, "They plan to kill you."

Not long ago Jupiter had struck him with a bolt of lightning. Now the god's great hand reached inside Gaius's chest and seized his heart. His vision seemed to fade, then sharpen, then fade again. A tremor shook his legs. His father's mouth moved but Gaius heard no sound.

Somehow he was lying on his back, drained, immobile. If he died, what of Livia? If he died, they could not live together. If he died . . .

The sound returned.

"You must renounce her," Publius said. "Renounce Livia. It is the only way. They have agreed to your life if you do. But there must be no delay. Rome is like a flighty woman. Today she will forgive you. Tomorrow she will be out for blood."

*They have agreed. They have agreed. Who are they to agree?* He could not die, but he could not do as they asked. He would do anything for her, anything but that. Gaius pushed away. "I cannot renounce her. She is my life."

Publius clutched his son's shoulders. "She will *take* your life. Let her go."

"I cannot." Despair welled in his throat, his chest. His wound flared and bit with fresh pain. Tired of fighting, he gently loosened his father's grip. "Have you never loved someone more than yourself? In all your life, Father, has there been no one you would give your life for?"

Publius opened his mouth, then swallowed, then stared at Gaius in wonder. "You ask me that when I am here? There has been but one person since your brother died. You."

They were the right words, but still Gaius did not believe them. And disbelieving, he said nothing. All his conversations with his father ended the same way. At an impasse.

"Let me help you," Publius said. "Let me protect you."

"By sacrificing Livia? You are mad. I will not live without her."

"Bravado is a cold companion when the executioner comes."

With an oath, Gaius pushed himself to a sitting position, gripping the bed hard while his head swam with dizziness. He wished he could understand this man who had sired him, raised him, taught him to be a soldier. But they were as similar as Livia and Justina.

"I have faced death before." He had survived the Battle of Cannae. He would survive this madness.

"Gaius," Publius pleaded, "save yourself. Leave Justina, if you must. Find another wife. Have children. I have always wanted grandchildren."

"I will do all those things with Livia."

"You stubborn fool."

"Just like my father."

The blow rocked Gaius's jaw, hard and bruising. Angry eyes met and glared.

"You will do none of it with her," Publius roared. "She will die tomorrow."

"You lie." He would save her just as he would save himself. Somehow. "Our *judex* will see to my defense."

"He was asked to leave Rome. He will not be defending you."

"Does no one have free will? Why did he not stand up for himself? For me?"

"Wake up. Rome has been wounded. Did you think this was just a friendly visit? The people are calling for blood to appease the gods. Livia has been found guilty. Now they demand you."

Gaius tried to stand, tried to leap at his father and throttle him. But his legs failed him.

Publius kneeled before no one. But he kneeled before his son and clasped his hands. "I beg you. Do as you must, not as you want."

Fear, anger, denial burned from Gaius's stomach to his throat. He swallowed painfully and whispered, "I cannot."

Publius bowed his head, their hands still locked. When he looked up there were tears in his eyes. He kissed his son on both cheeks then stormed from the room.

Gaius stared at the doorway for long moments. Then he put his hands to his cheeks that had not been kissed since he was a child.

# Chapter XLVI

Livia's spirit fled. All that was bright and beautiful in her world turned to bitter gray. A gray that filled her mind and soul and left her weak.

Antonia brought sunny flowers throughout the day, passed along by the priest standing guard outside her room. But even those failed to cheer her. Her mind seemed divided, one part taking care of her bodily requirements while another viewed her surroundings with numbness.

She was guilty. And Gaius would be killed. There was nothing for her. The Vestals were not allowed to speak to her. She could not dine with them or pray with them. Even the sacred flame was off limits.

Numbness shifted into despair. The thought of the underground vault caused a spasm in her chest. Her lungs would not fill with air. Panting beneath her sheets and coverlet, she felt her mind slipping away. Come sunup, she would be a shallow shell of the woman she once was. The woman she had hoped to be.

She clutched at the sheets for safety in this punishing mind storm. But the Goddess had abandoned her.

She was alone.

She tossed for hours, thoughts racing through her head, her body uncomfortable in any position. Memories colored the landscape of her thoughts. Riding on Apollyon across the beach. Valeria's accusations. Her childhood mosaics in the dirt outside her parents' house. Justina's warning. Gaius holding her in his arms and kissing her for the first time. The face of the Flamen Dialis. Running down the hills with Kaeso, hand in hand, until one tripped and they both rolled over and over, screaming with laughter. The Pontifex Maximus delivering the verdict. Making love with Gaius under a star studded sky. Her favorite color blue. Vesta whispering that she had broken her vows. Sextus in the market place and the surprising hug he gave her. The look in his eyes that spoke of hurt, distrust, need.

Finally, she slept. And dreamed.

Two figures appeared before her, mere shadows at first that slowly brightened with an inner glow until the bodies were fully formed. Gaius, her lover, stood on the left. Kaeso, her lifelong friend, stood on the right. Both men looked straight ahead, straight at Livia.

A bodiless voice then spoke. "Here stand your options, Livia. You may have one, but not both. Whichever you select will be the one you are with for all time. You may ask each one question and only one question. Choose wisely."

When the voice stopped, soft music began to play, a melody that hummed and sang and wove with quiet intent, wrapping itself around Livia's arms and legs and body and going deep within. Deep into her soul. There the music spread its joy to all her cells and she felt a knowing, an inner truth that she had longed for all her life. This was her moment. This was her destiny. Here, in front of her, lay her choice, the one she had waited for.

There was no indecision. She knew the question as surely as she knew her name. This was her chance. All she had to do was ask.

"Kaeso," she called, her eyes taking her fill of the man she had known since she was just a child. "How will you love me?"

His dark eyes glimmered and his chest rose with a large inhalation. "I will give you patience and kindness. I will give you care and compassion and all the tenderness you need. Every day I am with you I will look upon you with joy and every night I will thank the gods for their blessing of you in my life. You will want for nothing and you will have everything I can provide. This is how I will love you."

Her mind filled with the beauty of his words and lingered on their sweetness. Here was everything she had wanted. With him she would have the lasting love of her parents. A life without struggle. She smiled at him and nodded and said, "Thank you."

Then she looked at Gaius and asked again. "How will you love me?"

The blue of his eyes deepened and darkened until she felt she was on the sea, riding the crest of the waves into shore. Her heart quickened and her skin tingled. And still she waited for his answer. He reached out his hand to her and, even though they could not touch, she felt the pressure of his fingers, the warmth of his skin, the quiver of her body.

*Tell me,* her mind exclaimed, for she knew she could not ask again. *Tell me!*

As his eyes burned into hers, at last he spoke. "I love you with everything I am."

And she made her choice.

When Livia awoke, the dream remained in her mind, every facet crystal clear. The beauty of the music that had awoken her to her truth, the unseen voice that directed her actions, the two men who were fighting for her love. The choice she had made in her dream sifted through her mind. She weighed it, and judged it, and let it gather momentum. And felt the rightness of it.

It was too late to change her path. But there was hope for at least one person. A thread of hope that someone may benefit from all this wrong.

By the light of an oil lamp she wrote to Kaeso. She prayed that some part of him, however small, still cared for her, and if he still cared, then perhaps that caring would extend to another.

> *Dearest Kaeso,*
>
> *I have missed you so. Your smile, your laugh, the warmth of your eyes. Your tender voice that used to soothe my worries. I long to see you again, to calm the anguish between us, but there is little time left. This letter must suffice.*
>
> *I am not the person I once thought myself to be. My emotions drew me out of a life of obedience and habit, away from the safety of the Vestal sisterhood and into experiences I never dreamed I would have. There is no one to blame but myself for acting on my yearnings, for following the urges set before me. I did not know where they would lead.*
>
> *And yet, if I were given a second chance, I would still sacrifice myself for love.*
>
> *For so long now my heart has ached with the sorrow of your pain. I have forsaken you, my faithful friend, my loyal friend. The one who always knew me*

best. I broke my pledge to you, you who did nothing but shower me with love and patience. You once told me where the heart loves, there must we obey. As you followed your heart, so did I follow mine. But I hurt you in doing so. If I could, I would take from you that hurt, that pain, and relieve you of the burden that has haunted me and will be with me always, even in my death.

I regret that our dream did not come to fruition and provide you with children. You would make a wonderful father. For that reason I ask a favor. I ask for Sextus. Deep in that child's body lies a gentle heart. A heart that worries for others, despite his circumstances. He has known poverty and cruelty most of his days, yet still he cares for people. He came to warn me about Valeria's ambition. He asked nothing in return, only my safety and the safety of the other Vestals. For this kindness, he should be rewarded.

I can give him nothing now. But I pray that you will care for him. Sextus needs a guiding hand. A man of fortitude and wisdom to look up to. Be that for him and my prayers will be answered. I also pray that you will find someone to share your heart. Someone who will love you more than I was able. I beg the gods to give you a kind and caring woman to share your home and your bed. Above all others, you deserve that love.

How I wish this was not the end. How I wish we could live on as dear friends. I will hold that longing close when I journey to the afterlife and always think fondly of you.

*In love and friendship,*
*Livia*

The night sky had shed its first cloak of black when Livia finished her letter. She rolled up the scroll and sealed it with wax. She would give it to the priest at dawn.

Until then she would wait for Apollo to bring glimmers of light to the graying air. And hope that Kaeso would do as she asked.

# Chapter XLVII

Must and decay. These were the smells and tastes from the layers of cloth used to bind Livia's body and block her sight. She was tied against her will, carted off like refuse to lie in a chamber that would soon house her corpse.

Fifteen hundred paces from the Forum Romanum to the Colline Gate and her final destination in the Campus Sceleratus, the Evil Field. Fifteen hundred paces the priests would carry her, a contemptible spectacle.

The litter swayed and tilted, each step in complete silence. Her ears were muffled from the cloths that covered her. She heard no voices. No one singing, talking, whispering. Were the citizens of Rome also silent or shouting oaths about her shame?

For weeks the city had mourned the dead of battle. But did it mourn for her?

This finish, this was not what she envisioned. This was not the way her life should end. She yearned for life even as they carried her to her doom. And every moment she prayed for the strength to face her fate with courage. With calm.

Yet revulsion choked her and she fought to breathe. Fought the gag in her mouth that blocked her airway, the layers above her nose that pressed down.

Fear swept around her, seeped inside, caged her with its bony fingers. Even had she wanted to cry out, her mouth would make no sound. The priests had made certain.

Where was she? It seemed they had just begun. Had they turned onto the Vicus Longus? Had they crossed the Via Tiburtina?

The cloth in her mouth kept her teeth from knocking, but her jaw ached from the tension. Her bones seemed to rattle like dried seeds in a cup. Then she thought of Gaius, again, and pictured his blood, rivers of blood and torn flesh and a man in agony. The husband she could not have. The one she could not save.

Still they carried her.

Goddess, she wanted to see. See her friends one last time. See for herself the love in their eyes.

Love had brought her here.

They must be close now. Close to the Via Salaria and Via Nomentana. The last streets before the gate.

She thought of the letter she had written Kaeso. He had told her of his love, his promise, his devotion. All those years of friendship and caring. Tending her land for her. Biding his time for her.

All that love for her.

Movement stopped. The litter tilted precariously, then righted. Cords were cut, bindings released, the layers of cloth flung aside to help Livia stand. Unsteady from the journey, she wobbled and leaned heavily on the priest's arm. A priest she did not recognize.

None of the priests would meet her gaze. She was unchaste, an abscess to be cut out.

Two of the priests set the steps before the hole that led into the underground chamber. Her lungs refused to breathe. Her legs gave out. She would have fallen but for the hard grasp of the priest's hand on her arm. He yanked her upright, steadied her.

The Pontifex Maximus stretched shaking arms towards heaven and prayed to the gods. "Grant us your favor. Accept this sacrifice and bless Rome once more. Lead us out of the depths of our misery and give us victory." There was no nod or friendly gesture from this man who used to care for her. He could not meet her eyes, could not offer her the slightest comfort.

She stood on the top step, appalled at the gaping hole. Fresh earth mounded on either side. The same earth that harbored the tender vines on her property, that nurtured them and fed them and gave them strength. Her hands longed to plunge into the dirt, to breathe deeply of the rich aroma. She wanted to be in the vineyard, to bask in the green and the sun and the open air.

An assistant stood on either side and took her arms.

There is nothing to fear about death, Horatia had told her. But a spasm of trembling began, so great her legs would not move. She could not walk down those steps. Into that place of death. She could not.

The assistants moved ahead. Though her legs shook, she willed strength into her limbs. A few inches. Then a few more. They must know how difficult her task, how much fortitude it would take to descend all the steps.

One step. Then another. Her body convulsed in pain. Tears blinded her vision. The two men let her go near the bottom. She missed the last step and crashed into the wall of packed earth. She moaned, her shoulder bruised by the impact, her *stola* smeared with dirt. When she turned the men had already reached the top and removed the steps.

Before she could stop herself, she cried, "No! Let me out!"

Shovelfuls of dirt pounded her feet, buried them. She pulled loose and backed up, aghast at the sickening pile, the speed with which the hole filled in. Panic set in, and she scrambled over the dirt and clawed with her hands. "Stop! You cannot do this. Let me out. You cannot leave me here."

She tried to climb the mound to the remembered opening, but the dirt slipped beneath her feet and she sprawled face down, at last breathing in the rich aroma.

A sob burst free. Where was her dignity? She had promised to maintain her self-respect. Instead she resembled Sextus at their first encounter.

A few feet away stood a couch and a table with a lamp to represent the eternal flame, milk for the donkeys at the Vestalia, water used in the daily rituals in the *Atrium Vestae*, a loaf of bread for the substances of grain prepared by the Vestals. Should she eat? Should she drink? When she finished the food, then what? How long would the light last?

Would she take her last breath lying down?

She could not bear to sit so she walked, around the couch, in front of the couch, beside the table, in back of the couch. Her sandals wore a path in the soil, up, back, up, back, up, back, until she realized her pacing used up precious air.

Was anyone thinking about her, worrying about her, praying about her? Would they remember her at all? She sipped the milk, took a bite of bread and wrestled with the fragrant taste, the yeasty aroma, the memories of eating with the Vestals, her friends, her parents.

This was her last meal.

In pity she inhaled the morsel of bread, dry and sharp, and she coughed. Coughed up the last bit of food. Coughed until heat throbbed in her cheeks.

"Vesta, save me!" The prayer was automatic, from a routine so deeply ingrained that the words came without deliberation. But Vesta gave no answer.

It was too late to ask. It was too late to pray. The end was near.

Livia had always imagined death as an easy slipping away in her sleep, one moment breathing life and the next drifting off into another world, to the Fields of Elysium or some other paradise that awaited immortal souls. But not this. She was painfully aware of each fleeting second. The air reeked of her sweat. Her hands and feet were numb. When she tried to move them tiny shocks pricked her skin.

She had prayed all night, the same words over and over. *Dear Vesta. I have been a faithful servant. Please grant me release.* The recital became an automatic litany of emotion until exhaustion forced her body into rest. A small piece of her mind hoped for a miracle, some reason to stay the execution. But when she woke early in the morning, the sky turning from dark to just burned ash, she realized that Vesta could not save her.

The tears she had battled all night ran down her cheeks. Time passed in slow agony. Several times she wiped her face, the only witness to her own defeat.

She hummed a melody from her childhood, the tune her mother sang at night when Livia could not sleep. A small yellow flame, softly burning, cast a single shadow on the table. A tiny flame, unlike the fire of Vesta. The sacred flame that she had profaned.

She was the holy daughter who had broken her vows. Valeria would lead the Vestals now. Valeria would take control and rise to power. And the truth would be buried. Livia's dream for a future of powerful women would die with her.

She lay on the couch, her thoughts flitting like the butterflies in the *peristylium*. Antonia's beautiful curls, a hug from Sextus, Gaius's warmth, her mother's soft hands, Kaeso's kindness. Walking in the Elysian fields. Or perhaps a new life for her soul, a chance to right the wrongs of this one.

The flame died and darkness closed in.

She struggled for breath, her tortured lungs grasping at the little oxygen remaining. Her chest heaved, rising, rising, straining. She was suffocating, suffocating in sticky wetness. Her mind was a haze of gray, then black. Then in the midst of that blackness came a soothing blue. Her favorite blue. The blue of the sea.

Time collapsed until there was nothing but blue and the peace that followed. And from that blue a hand stretched out to Livia. A hand that beckoned with warmth and trust.

# Chapter XLVIII

Drizzle wet the streets of Rome the morning of Gaius's trial. A gray pallor hung in the sky, as if the gods were in mourning. First Livia had been found guilty and now he was to meet his fate at the hands of the *comitia centuriata*, the popular assembly. What had happened to Rome? To the solidarity of the Equites? How dare someone indict him like a common criminal?

Yet someone had dared. Someone had put this into motion. Justina.

Two guards marched him in chains to the platform in the Forum Romanum, where benches were placed for the jury. A sea of citizens surrounded him. Once, his status and clothing commanded respect. Today the mob jeered. He did not understand the crowd's revulsion. Rare was the man without a lover. And he had done nothing to earn his wife's contempt. Justina did not love him any more than he loved her. It was only proper for them to live separate lives. How could she complain when he continued to support her and planned on doing so ad infinitum?

What was she thinking to take this blatant action?

He tried to remember the last time he had spoken to her but the days blurred together. After the battle his entire being had focused on Livia. The woman he loved. There was no one more important to him.

The chains pulled, tugged on his shoulder joints and bowed his back. Strained his chest wound. The manacles chafed, rubbed. Gaius vainly wrestled with them, trying to find relief. Many times he had seen other men in this same situation. Criminals awaiting a verdict. How had he ended up here?

He watched the tribunal take position. The censors settled on their chairs like vultures waiting for the kill. What had they done to Livia? Where was she? Why had he heard nothing?

The remaining magistrates assembled, including an older man who leaned heavily on a wooden staff and slowly took his seat. Gaius once again scanned the tribunal until his eyes rested on the praetor. When the man looked up, Gaius felt an icy cold surround him. The air blew through his flesh as if it had separated from his bones. He barely recognized his father in the pallid face that looked back. For one moment their gaze connected, and Gaius saw nothing in those tired eyes to help him.

*No!* he shouted. *You cannot judge me.* But no words came from his mouth, only panting.

The praetor read the charges. Consorting with the High Priestess. Engaging in lewd and inappropriate behavior. *Incestum.*

The crowd rumbled at the final charge. "Murderer," cried a young voice. A boy darted to the front, his face pinched and red and somehow familiar. With fists raised he shouted, "He killed her. He killed Livia." A slender man grabbed the boy and pulled him away.

Murderer? What did the boy mean? Livia was still alive. She had to be. Nothing made sense without her. "Tell me the High Priestess is safe," he commanded the guards. They made no answer. "Tell me!" he demanded. "Tell me that she lives!"

But they said nothing. And fear howled and bared its fangs.

One by one Gaius's accusers took the stage. The Master of the Horse. A *decurion* from a legion Gaius only vaguely knew. The politician who owned the house where he and Livia had made love. Two senators. The vendor from the marketplace where he had strolled with Livia. Even Livia's *lictor*. Every single one denounced the man on trial.

"Traitor," someone shouted, and the word roared through the crowd. "Kill him. Kill the traitor."

The clouds darkened with impending rain but the drizzle stopped. Gaius seethed against this injustice, furious that the people he knew would turn traitor. He searched the faces below. Where were his friends? Why did no one come forward? "Let me speak," he yelled, but the noise of the crowd masked his voice. "I am innocent," he protested.

No one seemed to hear.

The praetor conferred with the magistrates. Heads nodded. The jury disbanded to collect the popular vote while the guards continued to watch Gaius.

"This is a mistake," he told them. "You cannot condemn a centurion." But the guards paid no heed.

Gaius looked to the sky, to the gods of Olympus gazing down at the spectacle below them. *Save me,* he pleaded. *Let me live my life with the woman I love. That is all I ask.* He kept his gaze above the crowd, above the mutinous glare of angry citizens.

No shelter was given him, no food, only sips of water. For the first time in his life he tasted degradation and recoiled at its bitterness.

Rome had changed these last few weeks. Its confidence had slipped. He felt the people's hurt, their need, their fear. Everyone wanted victory. A respite from the past. But Gaius was not to blame for this misfortune. He did not cause the Carthaginian crusade. Let Rome find another way to gain its footing.

Time passed with agonizing slowness. He thought of the woman he loved, her beauty, her radiance, the way her eyes lit when she was with him. These memories helped him through this misery. She could not be dead. He would master this humiliation and rescue her.

Within the hour the magistrates regrouped. How could they have voted so quickly? Had they decided even before the trial? His father's words sounded in his head, words from the previous day that left him stupefied. *They plan to kill you.*

The praetor stood to address the public, leaning on his staff. "The vote is unanimous," he read, his voice ragged. He coughed several times, ending on a wheeze. When he spoke again his voice was a whisper. "Gaius Postumius Albus is found guilty as charged." The verdict wobbled in his hands, then he staggered and pitched forward onto the ground.

"Father," Gaius cried, straining at his chains. "Someone help him."

A censor kneeled beside the praetor while another magistrate rescued the judgment. "He will be flogged before the citizens of Rome," the clear voice called, "then beheaded. The sentence will be carried out without delay."

Before Gaius could protest, the guards lashed him to a nearby post then ripped his tunic from his back. The cloth fell about his hips. Hard wood ground into his face. Guilty? It was a misunderstanding. Someone was coming to save him. Any second the magistrates would . . .

The scourging rods bit into his flesh. He clamped his lips together to stifle his groan.

Was no one coming?

Again the rods sliced his back. Then another slice. The cuts dripped blood, stung with hot barbs of pain. He moaned as the tips pricked his skin like a multitude of thorns.

When they were done with him his raw wounds screamed in agony. Blood streaked the folds of his tunic. Nausea swirled in his stomach and his legs trembled. The guards pulled him back to the open area and pushed him to his knees. Then the *lictor* drew his sword.

Gaius eyed the blade and swayed. There were still no signs of a savior. His stomach heaved and his vision blurred.

"Gaius," his father cried. "My son."

Sunlight bathed the platform with a glare that made Gaius squint. At last the gods had answered. He would be released. He would be free to find Livia.

The executioner raised his weapon. As the blade flashed in a mighty arc, Gaius yelled one last word. "Livia!"

# Chapter XLIX

Night tormented Justina. She had not wanted the emptiness of her own home, the ill feelings within those walls after her failure with Eros. So she begged forgiveness of her friend and Pomponia took her in. For that Justina was grateful. But the bed bruised her hips. Her body alternated between cold and hot. Her dreams were filled with vile visions. Gaius and Livia standing in front of her with their arms around each other, their mouths wide with laughter. Eros asking her to marry him then disappearing before she could answer. Sextus dressed in noble finery while her own clothing was stained and tattered.

When morning came she burrowed deeper in the sheets and finally found the peace of sleep. Midday had arrived by the time she woke to a silent house. Pomponia had left her alone and hungry with no word of her plans.

Justina scrounged for food and found a crust of bread and a bite of cheese. Where were the sweetmeats of yesterday? Did the woman take care of anything? Disgusted, she slammed the plate on the tile then jumped away from the flying shards. "Rot in Hades, Pomponia. You are no friend of mine."

With that, Justina left the house and wandered. The wet streets and stained clothes from yesterday matched her foul mood. She cared nothing for her solitary state. Her life was in shambles. It mattered little if people talked. But the streets were empty, unusually so.

What could she do to bring things back to order? Gaius was in danger and Livia, that harlot, might have escaped punishment. And Eros . . . She shrugged the debacle away. Think, Justina. There must be something. Yes, she would visit the Pontifex Maximus again. This time without Valeria. She would beg the priest to consult the augurs in those horrible jars. She gagged just imagining them. Yes, anything so repulsive must contain an answer for her.

Her mind made up, she headed for the *Regia*. Dark clouds churned overhead. Why were the gods angry now?

A mass of bodies blocked her way at the Forum Romanum. Hundreds of people huddled together. Children sat atop their father's shoulders. All heads turned toward a platform.

Curious, she pushed her way through. What was happening?

"Let me by," she muttered and thrust her arms between two people. "Let me by."

At last she was close enough to see a man kneeling. His hands were chained, his hair plastered to his head. His tunic hung in folds against his sides. Red streaks spattered the cloth.

Then the nearby *lictor* drew his sword. A thunderclap rent the air in warning. The gods had spoken. This is the way we treat those who transgress. This is the punishment for those who break the law.

What criminal was Rome executing today?

"Justice, justice," the crowd chanted and the noise swelled.

Justina strained to see, craning her neck forward until her shoulders ached. Then recognition flared.

Oh, Juno. Not Gaius. Not her husband.

A great shaft of sun illuminated the platform and the man, gilding him like a living statue. Then the sword came down and Gaius yelled, "Livia!"

Justina sank with a whimper. She barely heard the curses from the people next to her. All she could see behind her closed eyes was the swing of the sword and the gush of blood. Her gut clenched in one awful spasm and her body broke. She rolled to her side and moaned.

Around her people shuffled in all directions, bumping her, kicking her, stepping over her. Someone tried to push her aside. She squeezed her eyes tighter, praying for the end.

A gentle hand touched her shoulder. "Let me help you," a man said.

"Leave me alone," she whispered.

"You are bleeding. You need assistance."

She could not think. She could not talk. All she wanted was surcease. A reprieve from the scene that played in her mind. She shook her head and rolled into a tighter ball and let the world disappear.

At last she opened her eyes. The square was deserted. Sun beat upon her back. Her gown was soaked from the wet ground and dark. Dark with her blood that flowed from within.

Tears slipped down her face to join her wet clothing. Justina lifted her eyes to the heavens. "Take me," she cried. "Take me too."

# Epilogue

*September, 215 BC*
*Taormina, Sicilia*
*One year later*

T he fig tree spread a green arch of leaves against the bright blue sky. Sextus knelt at the base of the trunk and wiped the small stone plaque free of dirt. Today was the anniversary of her death. His fingers traced the letters, Latin first, then Greek. Even after a year in Taormina he still stumbled over the unfamiliar alphabet. But the words rang clearly in his head, words that he repeated every time he visited this site.

> *Livia Caecilia, Vestalis Maxima*
> *Beloved friend and servant of Rome*

She deserved more, much more. But the stone carver had demanded more money than Kaeso could spare. Instead, Sextus let his memories express his feelings. She was the third woman he had loved, besides his mother. The second one he had tried to save. They had both died too young. Maybe he was cursed.

He still remembered the day they met. Livia's soft hands and tender voice. The way she defended him against the fruit merchant's curses. He wished he could have lived with her and protected her instead of spying on her and Justina's husband.

Gaius. Sextus spat in the dirt. The only gratifying moments came at Gaius's trial where Sextus had screamed, "Murderer. He killed her. He killed Livia." Thank the gods Rome had found him guilty. Were it not for that pretend soldier Sextus might still be in Rome.

His hand rested on the thin layer of lapis that decorated the top of the plaque, blue brought specially from the Alban Hills for Livia. Sunlight flickered over his skin. He and Kaeso had made the choice to come to Taormina, but not because of Gaius. It was a lie to think that. There was nothing for them in Rome. Here was their future.

Because of Kaeso, the small vineyard up the hill was slowly coming back to life. Sextus's arms and back were sore from tilling the soil, adding in the necessary nutrients, staking the vines. But their work had been rewarded. The grapes grew fat and sweet and juicy under Kaeso's magic touch. And tomorrow they would begin the harvest.

Studying was another matter. Every night Kaeso taught him Greek and Latin and philosophy. Subjects Sextus had little interest in. But they were important to his teacher so Sextus tried. And struggled.

Kaeso was the most patient man Sextus had ever known. And the kindest. Harsh words did not cross his lips. Sextus wondered at the way the Fates had brought them together. He would have thrown a student like himself into the sea after the first lesson. But Kaeso merely smiled and repeated the words over and over until little bits began to sink in.

Some people could learn through books and reading. But Sextus needed to *do*. To learn through living. Like with the girl from the village. Pelagia. Most of the words she said made no sense. They all ran together in a jumble of foreign sounds. But he knew their meaning, deep in his heart, where her voice sang to him.

He was falling for her. Her dark eyes, the swing of her hair, the smile on her lips when he tried to speak in Greek. He could tell she was laughing by the crinkle of her eyes, but she never said so. She came to see him every day. And lately she held his hand when they walked along the cliff above the beach. He liked their walks. He was looking forward to one later today.

Footsteps approached. Kaeso knelt and placed a tray of figs and cheese and wine at the base of the tree. "I thought I would find you here."

Sextus's stomach growled but he was in no mood to be polite. "I am not hungry."

"It is not for you," Kaeso chuckled. "The food is an offering to the gods in Livia's name."

"She is dead."

Kaeso nodded and said nothing.

Sharp pain stabbed Sextus's chest. "Everyone I love dies on me. Why do they all die?"

"The gods make a plan for us. I think it is to teach us certain things about life."

"What things?"

"Love, understanding, compassion."

Sextus understood he had loved Livia and now she was dead. Anger bubbled up and spewed out. "I hate him," Sextus cried. "It is all his fault." Tears burned his eyes and he faced straight ahead so Kaeso would not see. "How can you not hate him?"

"Gaius is not to blame," Kaeso said quietly. "I believe he loved her."

Sextus rounded on his guardian. The tears did not matter. "She loved you first."

"She made her choice."

"She made the wrong one." He hit the stone in his rage and swore, then brought his throbbing hand to his mouth. "You were supposed to save her."

"The gods gave us all free will, Sextus. I could no more save Livia than I could have saved your mother."

What did that mean? His mother had died long before he knew Kaeso. "You could have fought for her," Sextus argued.

Kaeso sighed, a long breath that left him looking older, weary. "I did."

"I still hate Gaius."

"Then you must ask for forgiveness."

"Why me? He was the one who hurt her."

"But he is gone and you are still living. Hate will destroy you like a slow illness. You would not want that, would you?"

Forgiveness, illness, he had no idea what Kaeso was talking about. His hand still hurt and his head ached from trying to understand.

Kaeso rose. "I must get back to the vineyard. Come when you are ready."

"I miss her," Sextus said. He wiped his eyes with the back of his hand. "I think of her every day and I miss her."

"I know."

Sextus gazed up at this tall man who had cared for him this last year. Kaeso was brown from the summer sun and his hair had grayed. The sadness was in his eyes again. It was often there in the early morning and sometimes late at night. Sextus longed to take the sadness away. He wished they could both be happy again. He wished he could say something that would make a difference.

"Sextus, there is something we must discuss. Livia asked me to carry out a request before she died. I wanted to wait until everything was in order before I said anything. The document from Rome arrived yesterday."

"What document?" Fear grabbed him with hands of iron. He had done something wrong again. No matter how hard he tried, he seemed to mess things up. Last week he had forgotten to put away the mended grape baskets and two of them were ruined in the rain. The week before, he had left out the hoe and spade. Each time Kaeso forgave his errors. But the frown on Kaeso's face told Sextus his luck had run out. Jupiter, why did this always happen to him? "Please," he cried, "let me stay. I promise to work harder. I will get up earlier in the morning. And skip lunch. And dinner. And I . . . I . . . I promise not to see Pelagia." She was the best thing to happen to him in a long while. His breath came in gasps. He felt a little dizzy.

Kaeso squeezed Sextus's shoulder. "You have done nothing wrong. It is a good thing."

"Good?" How could it be good when the man did not smile?

"Yes. Livia and I wanted to adopt you. Since she is gone, it is my decision now. Would you like that?"

"Adopt? What does that mean?"

"It means I will take care of you. For as long as I live."

"But you already take care of me. Why do you need something from Rome?"

"It also means you will have my name. If you agree, from now on you will be Sextus Acilius Severus."

*Sextus Acilius Severus.* Not just one name but three. He had gone from a nobody without a father or family to a somebody with a real name. A Roman name. Just like that Sextus felt older, grown up, the man he had dreamed of.

"What do you say?" Kaeso asked. "Will you be my son?"

He faced Kaeso with a stupid grin that widened with each passing moment until his mouth hurt to smile. Happiness spread through him like a growing flame. Then doubt swept in. He was just a thief from the Subura, the poor part of Rome. He had lived his entire life without a father. Kaeso should have a real son. A boy of good standing. "A father would be nice. But I do not need one." He turned away to hide the emptiness in his chest.

"Sextus?" Kaeso brought him face-to-face. "What is it? Am I not good enough for you?"

"You are perfect. Too perfect. I am the problem." All his lies and deceit rose up before him. Things he had done that he could never change. No father would want a past like that. "I could never be a good enough son."

Kaeso rested his hand on Sextus's arm. A solid touch that stayed. "I do not want any other son. I think we are exactly right for each other. If you will have me."

Sextus threw himself at Kaeso and held on with all his might. The warm glow came back. He felt Livia smiling down on them, a brush of air across his cheek that was her kiss.

He was part of a family after all. At last he was where he belonged.

# Bella Toscana

BY Nanette Littlestone

The contemporary sequel to The Sacred Flame

*Bella Toscana* is a romantic novel about a 50-year-old woman emotionally imprisoned by a traumatic death from her past. Follow Toscana's journey as a stranger awakens a history from ancient Rome that leaves her doubting everything she's believed about love and passion. Told from a blend of current time and past life flashbacks, this moving story shows us that life is much richer when you truly surrender and follow your heart.

# Prologue

I loved him before I knew him.

Some people talk of synchronicity. The rhythm of life. I know of rhythm in the lyricism of words, in music, in the ebb and flow of the ocean, in the monthly cycles of plants and trees. A beautiful orchestration exists in the simplest of nature. But my world operates on logic, practicality, reason. I do not believe in a grand plan. I do not believe in God.

And then he came.

Before him, I had a well-ordered life. Habit and routine carried me through the day, warmth and comfort eased me through the night. There were disappointments. Longings. Not all was perfect. But such is life. If there was no great passion, so be it. Peace is preferable to something wild that soars then fizzles and leaves you with an aching heart. I had a different kind of love—security, respect, admiration, friendship.

379

I was fine. Just fine.

He showed me my lies in a slow creep of warmth that grew and teased and eventually began to burn. The thought of him burrowed deep inside me until I could think of nothing but him.

We were soul mates.

Soul mates. I scoffed at that. But we were linked inextricably, inevitably by some deeper force, some older reckoning that began many years ago.

To this day I don't think he knew what would happen. How do you know what fate has in store for you? They say man has free will to act, to choose, to create whatever he desires. But what of other people's actions, choices, desires? What if those choices conflict with your own? We tried to resist the seemingly magnetic pull. We did our best to act rationally, to behave with honor and dignity. To be selfless. But love is not selfless.

Love is selfish. Love craves attention. Love needs to be heard, to be felt. Love is a natural disaster.

You may think this is nothing new. We all know stories of love. But this story is different. This story spans over two thousand years. This story began in ancient Rome.

So I beg you, for as long as it takes to read this story, to put aside your beliefs. Something took hold of me, pulled me along. Was it fate? Destiny? Divine intervention?

Look to your own heart for the answers.

# Chapter 1

There is no indication that today will be the day my past and present collide. This evening I celebrate my fiftieth birthday with my husband Jackson at my favorite Italian restaurant. The staff extends their blessings for a happy day and the owner takes our order. I splurge tonight on osso buco. The succulent veal melts in my mouth and the risotto Milanese is creamy and tender. The perfect accompaniment. I think of my last trip to Italy, too long ago, to the beautiful Tuscan hills and the family dinners with my grandparents and aunt and uncle I rarely see. Love joined their hearts and hands and the food I ate there whispers sweetly in my memory. Despite the lined faces and shoulders sagging with age, they looked so happy. *A tavola non s'invecchia*, my grandmother pronounced. "At the table with good friends and family you do not become old." I think of her words as the number fifty bobs in my head like a heavy weight. Both my grandparents have died and my aunt and uncle have taken over the villa. Life has marched on all these years, with nothing to show for it. But tonight I feel no older. And I will be visiting Italy at last for the Chocolate Festival in Rome, just a few hours from my mother's home.

The waiter delivers a flourless chocolate cake with vanilla gelato and a candle burning brightly. As Jackson sings "Happy Birthday" my eyes fill with joy—he may not be the world's greatest lover but he's the sweetest man alive—and I blow out the candle. I don't need to wish. I have everything I want. I take a bite of rich, warm chocolate and creamy vanilla and sigh satisfaction. Who needs great sex? Give me chocolate any day. While I revel in that thought, Jackson hands me a black box tied with a shimmery cobalt ribbon. Already my heart is swelling. My favorite color on the outside of the box can only mean something wonderful inside. Wrapped in layers of tissue is a gorgeous purse of the softest leather in many shades of blue. It is extravagant and lovely. I can't stop petting it.

"I hope you like it," he says.

"It's beautiful." And perfect.

"Just like you." His puppy eyes shine and I sense his imaginary tail wagging. He's as pleased for me as if it were *his* birthday. "It comes from a shop near Livorno. I was thinking we could go there on our trip. It's not that far from Rome."

"We won't have time. The festival is three days and I want to visit my aunt and uncle."

The light in his eyes dims. I hate taking away his enthusiasm. "We'll see," I say, knowing that will lift his spirits.

In bed that night I thank him once again for a wonderful evening. Then I turn out the light and snuggle under the covers. His hand seeks out mine and our fingers clasp, warm and steady.

Turning fifty isn't so bad after all.

*He kisses my shoulder in the early morning hours. The cluster of candles by the bed illuminates the smooth muscles of his back that bunch and relax as I stroke his warm skin.*

*Warm breath tickles my ear. "I have waited for this," he says in a husky voice that heats my skin and makes my heart pound. Our bodies move in slow motion.*

*His mouth takes mine in a heady kiss, rich with wine and the passion of his love. Our tongues twine in a duet whose rhythm I recognize, yet have never felt before. He trails kisses down my neck and sups at the line of my collarbone. Who is this man who makes me feel so wanted?*

*Hands caress my limbs, invoking a trail of fire that spreads through me. Every graze of his fingertips makes my body clamor for more. "Love me," he says, "for I love you more than life."*

*"I love you," I respond. My heart feels the exquisite agony of a passion so deep that nothing else matters. I press myself closer to him, skin on skin, hearts beating together. "I will always love you." I thread my fingers through his tawny hair, straining to see his eyes as he moves over me. When we come together I feel myself weep. And when I scream my climax for the first time*

*in my life, he covers my mouth with his to muffle my cries.*

*He holds me close then, cradling my back against his strong chest. One hand palms my breast, the other rests across my hips. I lie in his arms, too weak to think, before sleep claims me once again.*

When I wake at my normal time, Jackson is already dressed and sitting on the bed to say goodbye. My husband with his medium brown hair and slightly receding hairline.

I struggle not to blush and casually turn my head, almost expecting to see a stranger lying next to me. But the other side of the bed is empty. There are no candles. Nothing to hint at an unknown lover.

Jackson gazes at me with those brown eyes that make my heart melt. "I'll be back before you know it."

I'm lonely just thinking about the empty house. "I'll miss you." I grab at his coat lapel and pull myself up to kiss him goodbye. A sweet, comforting kiss followed by a long hug. I love our hugs.

"Don't go," I say and hold him tighter. I always tease him this way with every trip, but this time I mean it. Something has changed.

"I'm missing you already," he whispers as he gently pulls himself from my grip.

"Have a good trip. And don't forget about Rome." I watch him leave the room, hear the wheels of his suitcase click on the hardwood floors, the lumbering raising of the garage door, then silence. I am alone. With a sigh, I climb out of bed. We leave for Rome the day after he returns. Anticipation thrums along my skin. The show is six days away.

While the shower gets hot, I close my eyes and remember the blond-haired man with *his* hands on my body, *his* mouth, *his* breath in my ear. A dream, I tell myself, but it seemed so real. I had felt him, heard his voice, tasted him. When had I ever tasted something in a dream? I could recall every moment of the pleasure he gave me.

I usually tell Jackson my bizarre dreams. It lets us laugh, allows us to share something intimate and quirky. But there was no time this morning. Thank God. Some things even married couples shouldn't share.

I think back to the first time I had sex—old enough to know better yet naïve enough to make the wrong choice. I fell in lust with an egocentric musician I met at a college concert. I have a soft spot for a sweet guitar, and his nimble fingers sealed my doom. Before I knew it we were lying naked on his bed and I was confessing my virginity. My chest tightened from nerves. Not at losing the decorated piece of flesh that most women give up at a much younger age. No, I was worried about the mechanics. I didn't understand the supposed *wonder* of the act. It all seemed rather crude and disgusting. The musician, who lost much of his appeal without his guitar, gave me these words of wisdom. *If you've never tasted lobster, you don't know what you're missing.* I held the vision of succulent white flesh dripping with melted butter in my mind and went ahead.

Sadly, there was nothing amazing about it.

The mirror begins to fog as I stare at my reflection, the still black hair, the slight curve of breast and hip. Once again I wish I were more alluring. Then I turn to the shower. Enough, Toscana. This morning is like every other workday. My wonderful store awaits. A long checklist materializes in my head and imaginary pages roll by, one after the other. The tension starts to build and I try to shrug it off under the water. But as silky soapsuds coat my body, I wonder if the man of my dreams will come to me again.

Butter and chocolate melt on the stove as I beat sugar and eggs into pale yellow ribbons and add vanilla and a touch of coffee for depth. I'm experimenting with a new brownie flavor—apricot with almonds and Amaretto. Sunlight brightens the green granite countertops of my kitchen. My place of inspiration. Where I first began Dolcielo, my business. Baking fills my heart with joy. With food I can give the world my love and the world will love me back.

I remember mixing dough in my mother's sunny yellow bowls, my little hands beating with a wooden spoon until I thought my arms would fall off. My mother would say little words of praise, *"Bene, molto bene,"* as she rolled out the dough on the table and patted it into shape for biscotti.

Tears prick my eyes. I miss my mother. She believed in me. "You will be a great cook someday, *figlia mia,*" she said. And I am. People love sweets and I have something for everyone. Starting my own business felt good, right, a way to get myself out of the house. Jackson was happy to let me spread my wings and we financed the company from my savings, with the understanding that joint funds were available if I needed them. After the initial investment I envisioned great success. If only imagination sold products. Dolcielo, Italian for sweet heaven, is barely getting by. I've dipped into our joint funds more often than I've liked, and after five years of little to no profits, it's time for a hard decision.

The drone of the mixer and swirl of the batter let my mind wander to Italy and the Chocolate Festival, which I hope will open new doors for me. It's a gamble but I have to try. A long breath escapes in a wonder-filled sigh. What extraordinary tastes and textures will I find? What will I choose to bring back? Then the dream fills my mind again. *I have waited for this,* he said, the stranger who loved me. Waited? For how long? Was that our first time together? I shake my head even as I recall the ease and rightness of the union. Whoever I am, I am not a virgin. But who am I?

A scorched smell halts my fantasy. I turn off the mixer and look into the pan. The bottom is coated with thick black streaks of char. Burned chocolate. "Damn it." Ruined food is a sacrilege. I might as well just throw my money out the window.

No more daydreaming.

I set more butter and chocolate to melt. The smell of melted butter warms my heart and the chocolate . . . there is nothing I love more than good dark chocolate. As a child, relatives plied me with platefuls of Italian confections, but despite all those rich Italian desserts, I love brownies. When I proclaimed my fascination with this American delight, my mother blurted, *"Maledizione!"* I was shocked by her swearing for days but it didn't change my taste buds. Good brownies are deep dark miracles of chocolate divinity. And Dolcielo brownies are the best. One of my reviewers said, "If Italians made brownies, they would make these."

I take the saucepan off the stove and stir the chocolate mixture. The new batch of brownies goes into the oven and I set the timer, my foot tapping impatiently as I cross my fingers. I want to take some with me to Italy to give to prospective buyers.

I hope they're good. They better be good.

This time I sit down and face the timer, watching the seconds tick by. No more mind wandering.

# Author's Notes

Thank you for reading *The Sacred Flame.* That means so much! I'd love to hear what you thought. If you have any questions or comments or just want to chat about your favorite characters, please contact me at nanette@wordsofpassion.com.

If you enjoyed this book, would you consider rating it and reviewing it? The best way to help out an author is to write a review. Even a very short one is truly appreciated. To post a review, go to *The Sacred Flame* sales page on Amazon. Many thanks in advance!

## Continue the Adventure

If you enjoyed *The Sacred Flame*, continue the adventure with the contemporary sequel *Bella Toscana*. Visit *nanettelittlestone.com/bella-toscana/* to get your copy now!

## Get the News

To stay in the know about new releases, giveaways, inside scoops, and author events, sign up for my newsletter at *nanettelittlestone.com/newsletter/*. Thanks so much!

# Acknowledgments

I've always loved a good love story, for isn't love what we all yearn for? Quiet love, supportive love, unconditional love, tempestuous love. We all want to be loved and loved well. I've devoured thousands of romance novels, waiting for my own Prince Charming, and I found him, but not everyone is so fortunate. Sadly, real-life love isn't always happily ever after. Sometimes the choices people make lead to irreconcilable differences or tremendous hurt.

*The Sacred Flame* began five years ago. I was meeting with my astrologer, Michelle Gregg, who mentioned the asteroid Vesta then pulled out a book called *Asteroid Goddesses* by Demetra George and Douglas Bloch. The story of Vesta and the Vestal Virgins of Rome was intriguing, but what fascinated me was the sexual nature of the Vestals during the reign of the Roman kings. They weren't virgins at all, but sacred harlots who helped

391

continue the royal lineage. As time passed, the patriarchal society assumed prominence, and King Tarquin the Elder decided to pass a royal decree that prohibited the Vestals from breeding upon pain of death. And thus began their familiar role of chastity and servitude to Rome.

The crux of my novel developed from an article that talked about various punishments for the Vestals. If the sacred fire of Vesta died, the offense was punished by scourging (beating with birch rods). This is what Antonia suffers after Livia's absence. The greater offense occurs with sexual relationships which were considered to be a breach of morality and religion (*incestum*) and an act of treason. For committing *incestum*, a Vestal was buried alive. In this same article is a suggestion that Vestals were used as scapegoats in times of crisis. A major crisis occurred in 216 BC when Hannibal's troops invaded Rome. On August 2nd of that year, Roman troops faced the enemy on the Apulian plain in the Battle of Cannae, the second greatest defeat of Rome and a complete catastrophe. Rome declared a national day of mourning and became so desperate that they ordered multiple sacrifices to appease the gods. Using Hannibal's invasion and ultimate victory as the backdrop for *The Sacred Flame*, I created a story of a Vestal who ultimately becomes a scapegoat for the politics of her time.

There is not much recorded information about the Vestal Virgins of Rome, and much of it seems contradictory. I have tried to abide by historical fact where possible, but I admit to some poetic license to make the story more entertaining. On the subject of the Vestals' hair, numerous articles and statuary suggest that their hair was worn short. The romantic in me rebelled against this and I gave Livia long hair. Just this year (2015) I discovered a video by Janet Stephens that explains the *sex crines*, the six braids described by other researchers, which can only be mastered with long hair.

My sincere apologies for any mistakes. I hope you enjoy the story. If you do, then I am content.

So many people were involved with the transformation of *The Sacred Flame* from rough draft to final version. I am indebted to C.J. Lyons who taught an online Plotting class and walked me through the Goal, Motivation, and Conflict chart until the light bulb literally turned on. Thanks to Margie Lawson who taught her online Deep EDITS class and illustrated word power. Thanks also to the enormous generosity of Professor Alexander W.H. Evers from the John Felice Rome Center (several years ago) who spent hours answering questions about history and gave me a personal tour through the Forum Romanum.

My thanks to Clarissa Yeo for the fabulous book cover design. I am so in awe of her talent. And when she suggested a ruby ring rather than the emerald ring already in the story, I gladly complied.

Where would I be without my writers group? Not all of us are together anymore, so my deepest thanks to Harold Ball, Colleen Walsh Fong, Dwain Herndon, Mary Shipley, Aarti Nayar, and Jana Oliver, who gave me wonderful suggestions and encouraged and supported me along the way. And my gratitude to my beta readers Janet Brooks, Teresa Bueno, Colleen Walsh Fong, Betty Fowler, Carrie Murgittroyd, Aarti Nayar, Jana Oliver, Fran Stewart, and Haley Whitehall who helped ensure the story is the best it can be.

I owe a special thanks to Aarti Nayar. The manuscript was languishing on my computer until we had lunch a few months ago and she told me it was a mistake to let it sit; it deserved to be read. Those simple words made me unearth it and give it life.

And last, but by no means least, I give thanks for my husband. When I told him I wanted to be a writer, he said okay, and he meant it. I'm grateful for his endless patience, support, and belief in me, especially when I have doubts (which is always). I love his crazy jokes, his smile, the warm hugs, the 101 things he does around the house to keep things going, and the fact that he leaves me alone to write (when I need to). He constantly lifts me up and is simply amazing. Thank you, Peter.

# References

Bernstein, Frances, PhD. 2000. *Classical Living: A Month by Month Guide to Ancient Rituals for Heart and Home.* Harper San Francisco.

George, Demetra and Douglas Bloch. 2003. *Asteroid Goddesses: The Mythology, Psychology, and Astrology of the Re-emerging Feminine.* Ibis Press.

Sebesta, Judith Lynn and Larissa Boufante. 2001. *The World of Roman Costume.* The University of Wisconsin Press.

Staples, Ariadne. 1998. *From Good Goddess to Vestal Virgins: Sex and Category in Roman Religion.* Routledge.

Wildfang, Robin Lorsch. 2006. *Rome's Vestal Virgins: A study of Rome's Vestal priestesses in the late Republic and early Empire.* Routledge.

Worsfold, T. Cato. 1997. *History of the Vestal Virgins.* Kessinger Publishing.

# Maps

*Roma.* (G. Droysens Allgemeiner Historishcer Handatlas)

Shepherd, William  R. 1911. *The Growth of Roman Power in Italy.* (The Historical Atlas)

Shepherd, William  R. 1923. *Plan of the Roman Forum and its Vicinity at the Time of the Republic.* (The Historical Atlas)

Shepherd, William  R. 1923-26. *Roman Expansion.* (The Historical Atlas)

# Book Club Questions

1. In 216 BC, the Vestals were required to serve Rome chastely for 30 years. What are your thoughts and impressions of that kind of service?

2. Up to about 600 BC, before the patriarchal society assumed prominence, the Vestals were the princesses of the royal line and procreated freely. Do you feel Livia's desire to restore the Vestals' freedoms was warranted? What would you have done in her situation?

3. Life is a constant series of decisions and choices. When Livia and Gaius meet at the beginning, how do their initial choices affect their future? Did they make the right choices?

4. Citizens of ancient Rome believed in Fate and the power of gods and goddesses to oversee humans' lives. How did the characters in this story play out the hand dealt by Fate? How has Fate played a part in your life?

5. Livia ends her relationship with Kaeso to follow her heart to love and passion with Gaius. How does that affect her? How has following your heart affected you? If you had a chance to relive a past relationship, would you follow the same path?

6. What is the significance of the ruby ring that Gaius gives Livia? How does wearing the ring put Livia in danger? When have you done something similar in your life?

7. Livia models her future relationship with Kaeso and Gaius on her parents' marriage. How unrealistic was that? When in your life have you based your relationships on what someone has or has done?

8. What does the sacred flame represent? When the flame goes out, what repercussions does that create? How could Livia have handled this catastrophe differently?

9. How is Livia's compassion for others a weakness? How is it a strength? When have you had compassion for others and how did that serve you?

10. Why does Justina fight so hard for a husband who doesn't love her? What positive/negative characteristics does she possess? How does she use those to gain advantage?

11. What character arc do you see with Sextus throughout the story? Why does he champion Livia? What more could he have done to save Livia at the end?

12. The main theme of the book is the idea of making sacrifices for love. Do you agree or disagree with the main characters' choices? Where in your life do you make sacrifices?

# About the Author

anette Littlestone's emotional stories take the reader on a journey of the heart. An award-winning novelist and gourmet, Nanette believes in happily ever after. Her pragmatic side realizes that most people don't live fairy tale lives, so her stories explore the struggles we face, the plans that backfire, the heart-wrenching decisions we have to make, plus the joy, the delight, the happiness when we courageously embrace our dreams. It's all about the love, and good food.

You can find her books on nanettelittlestone.com: *F.A.I.T.H.* −

*Finding Answers in the Heart, Vols. I and II, The Sacred Flame, and Bella Toscana.*

When she's not working on her next book, she loves to dream of living by the beach, read (historical fiction, romance, and young adult stories), go for walks, watch romantic movies, cook, and savor dark chocolate. She currently lives in a suburb of Atlanta, Georgia with her husband, her own romantic hero and most avid supporter.

www.nanettelittlestone.com

or email her at

nanette@wordsofpassion.com

Made in the USA
Las Vegas, NV
14 June 2022

50223106R00239